The Wolf Charmer

Jane Senese

A Wings ePress, Inc.
Paranormal Romance Novel

Wings ePress, Inc.

Edited by: Christie Kraemer
Copy Edited by: Jeanne R. Smith
Executive Editor: Jeanne R. Smith
Cover Artist: Erin Roberts

All rights reserved

Wings ePress Books
www.wingsepress.com

Published In the United States Of America

Wings ePress Inc.
3000 N. Rock Road
Newton, KS 67114

Dedication

To the wolves in my life... Squire, Lucky and Lani.

* * *

Prologue

Gold Hill, Nevada, 1885

The moon was full over High Street. The silver orb cast as much light as the streetlamps of better neighbourhoods. Ruth Johns took one look out the front door and judged it was bright enough to send her seventeen-year-old daughter down to the saloon on the corner.

"Get a small bottle of corn liquor... you know the kind your stepdaddy likes." She pressed several tarnished coins into Nell's palm. The girl's gaze darted to the man hunched at the hearthside, trying to read a newspaper by firelight. Her full lips pulled back in a resentful sneer.

"Any reason he can't go hiself?" Nell hollered at Lester's back. He simply lifted the paper higher, blotting her out of his view. But Ruth cuffed her daughter's shoulder, hard enough to make her jump.

"None of your sass, now. He's been working hard all week. He's allowed to put his feet up on a Friday night."

"I ain't! And I been working harder than him!"

"Now, Nell. I got the stew and the boys to tend to."

The oldest boy, a half-naked toddler with skin the color of nutmeg, came running up. He seized Ruth's skirt and pulled until she bent down to pick him up. She groaned at his weight as she settled him on her hip, trying to counterbalance her swollen abdomen. He squirmed and gurgled. A chubby fist beat on his mother's belly.

"Stop it, Monty." She swatted his hand away. "And don't you buy the cheap grog and save a nickel for yourself, Nell. I know your tricks."

Nell looked down at the money in her hand. Her brow knit in embarrassment, though her cheeks were too dark to show a blush. "You know they won't serve coloreds at the Maynard," she murmured.

"Then go down to the Capital. Monty, stop it! Leave the baby be."

"Bad baby," he lisped defiantly, getting in one last jab.

"Yes, bad baby's making Momma very tired," Ruth sighed. She fixed her daughter with a scathing glare. "Now! Less you're fixin' to go hungry tonight!"

Nell stamped out of the house, slamming the door hard behind her. The evening air was crisp, and her work dress was getting threadbare where she'd patched the torn seams. She rubbed her arms briskly to keep warm as she jogged down the dirt lane.

High Street wasn't a proper street to speak of, just a strip of dirt running between the houses wedged against the mountainside. In the bonanza days of the sixties and seventies, perhaps it had been a respectable address. But Gold Hill had been bleeding inhabitants for years; those who remained preferred to settle on the canyon floor where the houses were made of brick and proper timbers, not salvaged scraps of wood and sheet metal. Only the poorest folks clung to the cliffside, alongside the town's lone Negro family.

Nell was seething with fury by the time she reached Main Street. The climb down the steep embankment always felt a walk of shame, and doubly so at night, when all decent folks were already readying for bed. She had been working from early morning until sundown; her knees ached from scrubbing floors and her hands were raw from scouring pots. But because she was only a kitchen drudge, paid only twenty cents a day, she was sent out after dark to run errands, while Lester lounged fireside like a king in his castle.

It wasn't even his castle. Her father had bought the house back when homes were cheap in Gold Canyon, and when he died, he passed the title to her mother. Little wonder Lester had come sniffing around within a month of pulling into town.

Nell had begged her mother to leave off flirting with the barber. At eleven years old, she neither wanted nor needed a new father. They already had two incomes between them; Nell had been pulled from school the day her father died. And she would have gladly continued scrubbing pots for pennies if it meant some measure of independence for the Wallace women.

But Ruth would not be swayed. She wanted a man to take care of her. She wanted new babies in the cradle. And Lester wanted a house, with a proper wife who didn't demean herself working for strangers. But Nell could keep her job and pay her way. Because within a year there was one baby boy in the cradle, then a second the year after that, and even the meager wages of a pot girl came in handy.

That galled her the most. She would gladly run and fetch for Lester if that was all he asked of her. But every pay day she had to hand over all but a dime of her own money, to feed a stepfather she'd never wanted and the sons he couldn't afford. Now they had a third parasite on the way. She had no doubt it would be another boy for Ruth to dote on as she never had her daughter.

There was no level ground in Gold Canyon. For much of the town, Main Street ran down a fifteen-degree grade. Nell's calves were in knots by the time she reached the Capital Hotel. Its saloon was small but always crowded beyond capacity. At nearly twenty years old, it was among the oldest establishments on the hill. Nell could hear the clink of glasses and the raucous laughs from the street.

She dragged her feet as long as she could, cursing her mother for sending her out. Ruth knew Nell hated going to the Capital's saloon. The gazes she had to endure from the clientele were growing more lascivious every month.

And on a Friday night, Wes was sure to be there.

She hadn't spoken to him in nearly five years: not since the day he'd decided he was too white to be seen with the likes of her. But in a small town they still crossed paths often, and the mere sight of him was a stab deep in her belly. He was twenty and sporting a stubbly beard just as ginger as the hair on his head. She told herself it made him look slovenly. She told herself that she ought to find him repugnant, with his pale skin and deep-set eyes.

She wondered what he said about her, over beers with his new friends. Had he told them how she had asked him to marry her, and he had laughed in her six-year-old face? Or was he still too ashamed to even say her name aloud?

Nell stepped into the doorway of the saloon and gazed over the heads of the patrons. The bar was crowded with miners, fresh off their shift at the Yellow Jacket Mine. But to her relief, Wes Benedict was nowhere to be seen.

Nell knew better than to step over the threshold. The Capital wasn't one to quibble over color, but the miners made a restless crowd, and she was in no mood for their catcalls and groping, calloused hands. She waited until she could signal the bartender from the doorway. He nodded curtly and fetched her a bottle. It was not the first time she had come by.

One of the miners, a bearded boy only a few years her elder, whistled as she turned to leave. Nell ignored him. That too, had become something of a routine.

Contemplating the slope uphill, she felt her legs turn to water. There was no way she could hike back up the main road. Instead she cut across the street. In the town's heyday, there had been proper boardwalks and staircases leading up the hillside, but they had long since rotted away, or been pried up for firewood. So Nell clambered over the broken ground between two brick houses, hugging the bottle to her chest. She could switchback up the hill on a relatively smooth path, past one of the many dump sites. Everyone knew it as the woodpile, and on any given morning an Indian woman or an Irish child might be seen rooting for decent firewood.

Nell heard a shrill whistle behind her. She turned to see four shapes gathering on the path below her. "Hey, nigger-girl?" the leader called cheerfully. It was the bearded boy from the saloon. "Where you off to?"

She recognized them all: neglected sons of failed parents, poor, weak and prone to taking out their frustrations on anything weaker they came across. The sort of boys who'd set a dog's tail on fire, just to feel powerful. She had crossed paths with every one of them. But always in daylight. And never all four together.

"Nel-ly," singsonged one of the boys.

"Naughty Nelly," said another.

She turned back uphill. She could see gas lamps burning in the windows of High Street, but between her and safety lay a steep embankment of earth, some twenty feet high. The only way around was a loose gravel path skirting the edge of the woodpile.

"Oh, where she goin' now?"

"Come on, now. We're just playin'!"

"Nel-ly! Oh, be a sport."

She knew better than to answer them. She kept her stride long and her pace measured. She kept her head bowed, her shoulders hunched just a fraction. The trick was to show the merest hint of submission, no more and no less. A shivering Negro was an inviting target, but a proud Negro was a challenge. She had no intention of being either.

"What'ya got there?" the ringleader called. "Hey, how 'bout sharing some of that?"

"Bet she's looking for a good time."

"You lookin' for a good time, Nelly?"

The laughter behind her was turning increasingly ugly. She kept her eyes on the ground, watching their shadows slowly gaining on her own. She was almost level with the houses—one more switchback around a small tailings pile would put her on High Street. Not that she expected much help from her neighbours. Her own home was still thirty yards uphill.

"Where you goin'—hey, we're talking to you!"

"Don't you walk away from us, girl!"

She saw a shadow lunge across the broken ground. Nell hugged the bottle and started to run.

It was a mistake. The ringleader let out a whoop and they gave chase. The boys quickly overtook her. A hand caught her elbow. As she tried to twist away, the bottle slipped from her hands and shattered on the ground.

"Aw, look at the mess you ma—" the ringleader began, before Nell's fist connected with his jaw.

She'd never punched anyone before. It was not nearly as satisfying as she'd hoped... the impact reverberated up her arm, making her cry out. She staggered back, clutching her throbbing hand. The boy rubbed his jaw and stared her down with animal rage.

Nell screamed for help, as loud as she could. The pack closed on her. In seconds she was on her back, and the ringleader was on top of her. He returned her punch with far stronger effect. Her head snapped back and pain like she'd never known before exploded behind her eyes. She barely felt the cold air nipping at her legs as her attacker thrust her skirts up about her legs. When she first heard the growl, she thought it was one of lust.

The growl became a snarl, undeniably bestial. The weight on Nell's chest lifted. Dazed and bleeding, she pushed her dress back down over her knees and scrambled backward, just as a four-legged shape leapt between her and the ringleader.

"Whoa... good dog," the boy laughed nervously, raising his hands. "Good doggy..."

It was no dog, Nell knew at once. And it wasn't the half-tame coyote who liked to beg for scraps at the south of town. It was too large, too savage. Shoulders hunched and hackles raised, it looked like something out of a nightmare.

One boy began to slowly bend his knees. His hand stretched towards a large stone. The creature's mouth opened on a series of bloodthirsty snarls that sprayed the ground with saliva and scattered the boys down the path.

Nell couldn't move. Couldn't breathe. The creature slowly turned. Nell braced herself for the attack.

Don't look an angry dog in the eyes, her mother had always warned her. But she couldn't help but stare. Instead of the burning red gaze of folktales, the wolf's eyes were a watery blue. They looked almost human.

A whimper escaped her and she heard the beast whimper back.

When it ducked its head to sniff her, Nell shrieked. The wolf recoiled, startled. It shook its head once then fled into the shadows of the woodpile. To Nell's dazed eyes, it seemed to have turned to smoke and scattered on the wind.

Nell waited several long minutes before getting to her feet. As she had expected, neither her screams nor the boys' had brought any help.

Her swollen face and bloodied nose bought her no sympathy when she returned to the little shack on High Street. Lester was annoyed by the wasted money, yet took no notice of the muddied state of her skirt. But his indifference bothered Nell less than her mother's sad glare of reproach.

"I thought I could trust you with this," she sighed, before she turned her back to answer Monty's lisping pleas.

The next day, Nell moved out.

One

1897

Frank Maddock's GENUINE Indian Exhibition, read the flyer tacked to the wall of the Capital saloon. Featuring Wonders of the Natural World. Nell flicked at it idly as she waited. The show was still two days away, yet the poster was already fading in the Nevada sun.

Full Color Stereoptical Scenes of America

A Demonstration of Chief Buffalo's Miracle Cream
Live Animals – Cultural Scenes
Natural Curiosities: the JACKALOPE –
Colter's Horned Hare!
Human Museum: Meet WHITE MOON –
the Pale-Faced Squaw!
Witness BLACKFELL – the FAMED Navajo WOLF-CHARMER!
Only 10 cents for Adults and Children Alike

Nell knew well enough that an act so loudly touted as "genuine" was anything but. Still, the big circuses never came closer than Reno, and new entertainments were few and far between.

When Nell had been a child, she'd heard stories about the celebrities who would pass through the Comstock... actors performing Shakespeare at the Opera House, society belles riding the brand-new elevator at the International Hotel. But as the sun dropped behind Mount Davidson, the only folks on the street were a few shiftless youngsters.

The miners would start filing home in another hour, a parade of spent men in faded clothes. Each year the parade shrank a little more. Nell found it hard to pity their lot. At least they had work.

The depression was nearly twenty years old then, and the cause was simple: the Comstock was emptied out. Mount Davidson had seen its hillside shaved away; the original "Gold Hill" was a shallow depression in the canyon walls. Two miles north in Virginia City, the ground underfoot was literally hollowed out: every few months another sinkhole opened up under someone's house. In places, Nell heard, the mine shafts reached some three thousand feet deep, halfway down to sea level.

Still the economy limped along. The men blasted still deeper shafts, certain another lode lay just out of reach. They milled the low-grade ore they had once ignored, to squeeze out the last of the silver dregs. They dreamed of building a cyanide mill, to extract the still-smaller traces of gold from the tons of waste rock. They hoped for better days.

What else could they do? The landscape was too arid for ranching or farming. Four decades of settlement had stripped the forests and decimated the wildlife. Yet the two generations born and raised on the Comstock could not imagine living anywhere else.

Nell could imagine living somewhere else. When she heard stories of San Francisco—its vibrancy and diversity, its bright future—she easily envisioned herself walking its streets. But what she had in imagination, she lacked in hard currency.

She saw her mother coming up the street, shoulders bent under a heavy sack of linens. Nell cursed under her breath and began to turn away, but it was too late. The hunched figure had spotted her.

Ruth Johns was a small woman, thin and prematurely aged. Nell had vague memories of her mother as a delicate beauty with creamy brown skin, but now her face was pinched and hard, skin rough like old leather.

Nell had never been delicate. She'd inherited her father's height, his broad shoulders and large hands.

"Eleanor! I haven't seen you about lately."

She knew better than to trust her mother's smile. She couldn't remember the last time she had seen the woman genuinely happy.

"Well, you're seeing me now."

"Mm, loitering on a street corner."

"I'm waiting for someone."

"At this hour? I raised you better."

You didn't raise me at all, Nell longed to say. Her earliest memories were not of her parents, but of the impoverished white widow who had earned a dollar a week bringing Nell up alongside her own child.

"What do you want, Momma?" Nell asked instead.

"I want you to come home."

"Pft. We both know that ain't gonna happen."

"I just don't understand why you throw your money away on a rented bed when you have a family ready to take care of you."

"I don't need taking care of."

"Nell, I worry about you."

Picked a hell of a time to start. "Why?" Nell fought to keep her voice reasonable. "It's got nothing to do with you."

"You quit your job. You're sleeping on a rented bed. And what will you do when your money runs out? Who's going to take care of you then?"

"Who says I need to be taken care of?"

"Nell, you're almost thirty. No one in their right mind wants to hire an old spinster when there are young'uns looking for work. And with your reputation, what man will take you on?"

Nell heaved a sigh. "I thought we settled this."

"If you'd just talk to Shiloh—"

"No!" Nell stamped her foot in the dirt, startling them both. "No," she repeated, more gently. "I ain't baggage to be 'taken on.' And I ain't your problem to be fixed. We made a deal, remember? I take care of myself now. I don't ask for anything of you, and you don't get anything from me."

"Why do you have to see everything like... business?" Ruth spat out the word with righteous disgust. "You're my daughter. I love you. That isn't something I can just snuff out."

"Aw, you're just not trying hard enough."

Nell felt a cold sort of triumph as she saw her mother flinch. The satisfaction was short-lived; remorse came swiftly on its heels. Nell hunched her shoulders, the brooding posture of a shamed child.

Ruth should have known better than to bring up her lack of work, she thought resentfully. Everyone knew if you stirred a hornet's nest, you were liable to get stung.

"I just want what's best for you," Ruth murmured contritely, wringing her gnarled hands. The laundry lye had left her dry skin laced with scars, and years of hemming plainwork for pennies had shriveled her fingers to claws. Nell clenched her own hands reflexively, feeling the knuckle joints with her thumbs. Was it only her imagination, or were her own fingers somewhat thinner of late?

"Wish you'd trust me to know what's best for me." Nell glanced downhill. A rider was coming up the road, followed closely by a large gray dog. "Look, I gotta go, Momma. I told you, I'm meeting someone."

Ruth followed her daughter's gaze, and her mouth puckered in disapproval. "The deviant."

"Don't you call her that!" Nell snapped hotly.

"I ain't the only one, and you know it. She's a bad influence on you."

She was right, of course, but Nell would never admit it. "At least she's married. Might rub off on me."

"When will I see you again?"

Nell shrugged. "It's a small town."

'Will you at least come to dinner one night? The boys miss you."

Nell doubted it. But she was willing to say anything to end the conversation.

"Fine, fine. I'll come... Sunday, okay? You go on home. Don't stand around with that load on your back all day."

Ruth narrowed her eyes. She clearly didn't trust Nell's sudden obedience, but she was used to taking what she could get. "Sunday," she said firmly. Then she turned and resumed her weary march uphill. Nell watched her go until her chest ached. Only then did she realize she had been holding her breath.

They had not always been so estranged. For much of Nell's adult life, mother and daughter had treated each other with a distant courtesy. It had been easy enough; their busy lives had left little time to brood on mistakes of the past. Every so often, they reconnected over tea and said nothing of consequence. That too was part of the deal; least said, soonest mended. The rest of the time, Nell scarcely thought of her mother, and she assumed Ruth did the same.

Then Nell had found herself out of work for the first time since leaving home, and Ruth decided to take an interest in her wayward daughter once more.

Nell had no one to blame but herself, according to her family. Only a fool walked away from a paying job in the middle of a depression. No matter that she had been treated little better than a dog. No matter she was the last to be praised, but the first accused when something went missing. A colored maid could expect nothing better. Most expected much worse. She had been given food and board and left unmolested. It was sheer selfishness to ask for more.

And she was selfish. She made no apologies for it. She valued herself highly; she had to, for no one else would. The world had no place for women like her.

Nor was it particularly accommodating to the approaching rider. Nell felt a weight lift from her shoulders as she hailed her friend. Only with Charlie Franklin did she feel like something more than an outcast.

"So this is the horse you've been raving about," Nell said.

The paint horse was tall and well proportioned, but his nervous bearing was apparent even to Nell's untrained eye. Nell couldn't blame him. The grinning wolf-dog made just about everyone nervous. When the canine got too close, the horse drew up short of the hitching post, and blew out a loud snort through flared nostrils.

"Garou!" Charlie snapped. "Leave off!"

The dog scurried back obediently, but the horse was slower to settle. When Charlie pulled hard on the reins to correct him, he reared up, causing her to cling to the saddle horn as her hat went flying.

"Damn it, Clem!"

"Well, shoot," Nell laughed. "If you haul on the reins like you're spoiling for a fight, he'll give you one. Even I could have told you that."

Charlie eased her grip on the reins, and the horse slowly relaxed. He even took a step towards the hitching post of his own free will. Charlie grinned sheepishly. "I guess I'm used to wrestling with Connor's horse."

"Reckon that's why he bought you your own."

"He calls it an early birthday present. But you're right... he was getting a bit sick of sharing." Tentatively, she stroked the horse's neck. "There, Clem. You're a good boy."

Nell raised a quizzical eyebrow. "Clem?"

"Short for Clemens. You know: Mark—"

"—Twain," Nell finished for her. Of course. Charlie had every book Sam Clemens had ever written. Nell didn't quite understand the appeal herself. The man tried much too hard to be clever.

Charlie swung down from the horse with a practiced air. The wolf-dog had already retrieved her hat from the lane, and trotted over to her side, tail wagging.

"Aw, thank you, Rou." Charlie pried the hat out of his jaws and shook off the worst of the dust and saliva. It wasn't the dainty sort of felt hat most lady riders fancied, but a big Stetson Boss, already well-worn and creased after a mere four months of use.

Nell had known Charlie would be trouble from the first. The unwanted relation of Nell's former employers, she had shown up in cropped hair and denim trousers, stinking of the big city. No one could have predicted she'd end up wed to the richest man in town. Or that Nell would come to count her as that rarest commodity—a genuine friend.

Unadorned, she was a strangely sexless creature, with her blunt features and her flat chest. All the paint and lace in the world couldn't give her womanly grace. When she got herself up in buckskins and pulled her Stetson down low over her face, she could easily pass for a boy. But this evening she was indulging what passed for her femininity: pairing a tailored woman's jacket and colorful kerchief with her wide-legged riding culottes. Her blonde hair had grown out somewhat since Nell first met her, and she let it hang loose in a shaggy bob about her jawline. Nell had once asked her if she intended to let it grow properly, now that she was a married woman, and Charlie had laughed and said her husband forbade it.

Like sticks to like, Nell reckoned. Connor Franklin was quite the queer thing himself.

"Were you talking to your ma?" Charlie asked, as she tied up the horse. "I would have loved to meet her."

"No, you really wouldn't," Nell said brusquely. When Charlie blinked at her in confusion, Nell was forced to add, "She don't much approve of you."

The younger woman smirked at the thought. "Most mothers don't." She gave the horse a gentle rub on the muzzle. "What do you think? Just signed off on the papers today."

Nell recognized the brand at the horse's left shoulder: a P wearing a jagged crown, over a Lazy M. The Crown Point Livery Stables traded in only the finest mustangs.

"He from the batch they bought back in May?" Nell asked.

Charlie nodded. "At first I had my eye on the other mustang, but as soon as Garou ran over, he was fixing to kick his head in."

"To be fair, lots of folk think about kicking your dog's head in," Nell said wryly.

Garou blinked up at Nell, all puppyish innocence.

"But Clem just sort of shied off, so we knew he was the one," Charlie went on. "Connor says it's probably 'cause Wes broke him himself."

Nell was surprised at the sudden pang in her heart. "Wes is breaking horses again?"

"Why? He wasn't before?"

"Shoot, not in the last ten years. He used to. Got his start working for Grant Weatherbee as a breaker. But he never got the hang of it. Always took too long." She couldn't imagine any horse trained by Wesley Benedict would come out calmer for the experience.

The boy she had once loved had grown into a brooding, nettlesome man. He'd done well for himself: a solid income as a farrier, a partnership in the livery stables, and a fine house he owned outright. Yet he carried himself as if crushed by some unspeakable burden. When he drank to excess, which was too often, he was prone to self-pity and quick to anger. Sober, he shunned the company of others, preferring to take out his ill-defined frustrations on his anvil. Nell often wondered how he could take so little joy in life, so little pride in himself.

It enraged her sometimes, to think about all those advantages squandered on a man who couldn't appreciate them. Mostly it just made her sad. Something was very wrong, if she could find more satisfaction in her life of drudgery than Wes could in his of privilege.

So she tried not to think about it. She tried to not think about him.

Charlie jerked a thumb towards the saloon door. "Come on, what'll you have? I'm buying. You be good, Garou, and guard Clem for me. All right? Sit. Sit!" she repeated with emphasis, when the dog began to sulk.

Nell took what had become their usual table, wedged at the very rear of the saloon. The rock walls kept the corner relatively cool, but the lack of fresh air meant it was always the last to be claimed. Nell caught a dirty look from a man deep in his drink, but she couldn't tell whether it was meant for her or Charlie. Most saloon owners had figured out they could serve unescorted women without the sky falling down, but their patrons still lagged behind the times.

Charlie paid for their drinks—a weak ale for Nell and a bottle of soda for herself—and brought them to the table, along with a big bowl of Saratoga chips. "So how's your ma doing?" she asked. "Still wringing her hands over you?"

"Trying to act like it. Truth is, I don't think she wants me to find work. Just another distraction keeping me from my God-given destiny as Mrs. Shiloh Todd."

"Shiloh? Shoot, you'd think she'd realize that ship has sailed."

"Uh-huh." Nell helped herself to a handful of chips. "Reckon even Shiloh has figured that out. God knows it took him long enough. But... he is the only colored man in Gold Hill I ain't related to." She flashed Charlie a pained smile. "And as Momma loves to remind me: I already let him sample the wares, so who else is gonna wanna buy the goods?

"Of course, if I want to be all pig-headed about it, there are two unattached Negroes up the hill in Virginia who might be tempted, and neither one a day under fifty! Plus a fella down in Dayton who may or may not be spoken for. And it is so sad that I know all o'that."

"Suppose he has to be colored, huh?" Charlie commiserated, before taking a long pull from her bottle. Nell cast a nervous glance around the bar, then lowered her voice to a whisper.

"Of course he has to be colored! What kinda question is that?"

Charlie shrugged. Nell had to remind herself that the urchin had never had a proper upbringing. Running around Frisco's tenements where all sorts of folks mixed around, Charlie was as heedless of the rules that governed race as she was of those concerning their sex. It was at once her most endearing trait and a constant source of frustration.

"Guess it depends how badly your ma wants you married, that's all," Charlie said.

"She wants me to tell her she was right all along. That a woman ain't nothing without a man."

"If that ain't some bassackward ignorance," Charlie sneered.

"Says the gal who met and married her beau all within a week!"

"Two weeks," Charlie corrected. But she smiled rather guiltily all the same. "Never said a man ain't a pleasant thing to have around… long as he knows his place."

"Yours does, and no mistake. Where is he, anyway? After buying you a horse, I figured he'd be keeping you close for some *gratitude*."

Charlie laughed at her suggestive tone. "How much does a horse go for, in gratitude?"

"Damned if I know. Only thing Shiloh ever gave me was a pinwatch, and he thought that was worth giving up the whole shebang."

"Must've been one hell of a watch."

"I wish. Cheap tin. Still lasted longer than Shiloh. But a horse… shoot, y'oughta be on bedrest for a month afterwards."

Charlie clapped a hand over her mouth to keep from laughing. "You shush! You're gonna get us thrown out. Anyway, Connor's already off at work. Took off with the marshal somewhere… some to-do at the Indian camp."

Nell glanced at the open doorway. "Awful early, ain't it?"

"He's started winter hours: four to four every weekday now."

"Still bright out there. He gonna be all right?"

"Should be. I made him take his spectacles."

Nell could never understand why a silver magnate would bother holding down a regular job, let alone the irregular one of a night watch deputy. But what other job could a man like Connor Franklin take, when he didn't dare go out in broad daylight?

It was a weakness in the skin, Charlie had once explained. Some missing protein made him burn like a baby in the sun and laid him low with migraines. Nell didn't believe a word of it. She'd heard the other rumors about the deputy: the strange lethargy when he ventured out on cloudy days, the persistent anemia requiring a diet heavy in red meat. Nell could think of only one explanation, and she suspected half the town would agree with her.

She hoped she was wrong. Despite all his strange notions, Connor Franklin was a good man; she didn't like thinking of him as a diseased monster.

But all the signs pointed to syphilis. What else could it be?

~ * ~

Connor Franklin paced along the neat row of graves, squinting against the brightness of the late afternoon. The disk of the sun had already disappeared behind the mountains, and an angry blue sky was starting to soften with the dusty haze of the long Comstock twilight. Still, the ambient light was enough to make his eyes water behind the tinted glass of his spectacles. He kept his hat pulled down over his brow and did his best to walk in the marshal's shadow. Bill Crawford didn't seem to notice.

The Paiute Indian camp lay some two miles southwest of Gold Hill, on the sloping valley called American Flat. The dome-shaped tents held some dozen households, all connected by blood or marriage, all bearing the peculiar surname Marsh.

In the days before the Silver Rush, they had been a nomadic people, moving with the seasons, keeping one step ahead of the summer droughts and winter storms. Nowadays most of the Marshes preferred to do their hunting at the local grocer's. They traded in herbal remedies and day labor, and a few men even held steady jobs in town. Yet they remained a breed apart from the white settlers. It seemed only fitting that they would remain so in death.

Bill's hand stole to his pocket watch. It was the third time he'd checked it since Connor had come on shift.

"You looking to light out?"

"Ah, the landlady's been on my case. I miss one more family dinner and I'm on jail rations for a week."

"Tsk. Not two months and henpecked already."

"Well now," Bill mumbled into his chest. "The kids like it when we're all together."

He was trying for the old cantankerous growl, once second nature to him. Yet he couldn't entirely smother the note of pride in his voice. Connor had never heard a man so happy to be domesticated.

"Henry still calling you 'Marshal Crawfish'?"

Now Bill beamed. It was no secret he doted on his mistress's young son. "Heck no," he said proudly. "Now I'm Uncle Crawfish!"

"He'll be after you to make his ma an honest woman, you wait and see."

Connor didn't need to look at Bill to see that his face had gone red... he could smell the rush of blood to the skin, and hear the racing heartbeat in the marshal's chest.

Bill cleared his throat loudly. "Well now, much too soon to be fretting about that. There it is," he pointed out the last grave in the row. In place of a mound lay a shallow trench. The earth was freshly turned, exposing the broken layer of clay underneath the topsoil. An old Paiute man stood guard over the damage, thoughtfully puffing on his clay pipe. Connor was not surprised to see him. The Marsh tribe had no chief as such, but it valued its elders, and the gray-haired patriarch was the last of his kind. He'd been a wily youngster when the first miners had staked their claims to the Comstock and changed the Indians' world forever. No other Paiute had weathered the upheaval with quite the finesse and good humor of Captain Marsh.

Bill hailed the old man with a wave. "Brought him like you said."

Connor smiled inwardly at that. "'Evening, Cap'n."

"It is an evening," the Indian agreed. "A damn rotten one."

"That's why I left 'good' out of there." Connor knelt at the graveside and inspected the damage. "So what do we have? Animal?"

Captain Marsh stared into his pipe bowl as he considered it. "Could be. Could be. Your coyote, though, he usually prefers a fresher grave. He also don't tend to use a spade," he added archly, "but these are modern times."

Connor knelt to better examine the site. The old man was right. Whatever had disturbed the grave had left very straight, even lines in the earth, like the scrape of a tool blade.

"Whose grave is it?"

"Fanny Rollins," Bill said. "Ben Marsh's wife."

"Rollins? Like the dairy farmer?" He'd never heard of a white body buried in Paiute soil.

"His sister." Bill made a discreet nod towards the mourners gathered beyond the boundary stones. Several Paiutes—the men in worn work clothes, the women in flounced calico—were all gathered protectively around a lone white man.

"Died back in the diphtheria outbreak," Bill explained. "Her boys work at the dairy now."

Connor nodded thoughtfully. He had only a passing acquaintance with the Rollins family; American Flat was at the limit of his jurisdiction, and he had long since lost his taste for milk. But he'd sometimes see the dairy cart making the rounds just before daybreak. The driver was always a young Indian, the milkman a tow-headed boy who would leap off at each stop to swap empty bottles for full.

"So what are you thinking, Cap'n? Vandals?"

"More like to be grave robbers. Seen enough in my day. The pea-brains hear tales of Indian chiefs buried with golden hoards... and never mind that we bury our folk with less frippery than your Christians." He turned and spat. "Pale-faced eejits! Still... I'd rather they were after Fanny's old locket than anything else of hers."

"What else would they want?" Bill demanded.

What else is left? Connor sifted a handful of soil though his fingers. A small yellow shard emerged from the dirt. Connor held it up to the light. "The bones?"

"Jesus Murphy!" Bill snatched the fragment out of his hand. "Leave the girl a bit of dignity, will you?"

Connor ignored him. Dignity was the purview of the living, not the dead. "Do we know if any bones were taken?" he asked Captain Marsh.

"Couple of pieces were scattered around. We put what we could find aside. The family wants to do a reburial later on. But we ain't about to dig Fanny out and count her ribs."

"Why on earth—" Bill began in a roar. Heads at the boundary stones turned towards him, and he moderated his tone with visible effort. "Why would anyone want old bones?"

Connor shrugged. "Sell 'em? I dunno… aren't they mad for those Egyptian mummies in the right circles? Might be some rich folks fancy collecting Indian bones. And these graves don't have names on them. There'd be no way of knowing this one belonged to a white gal. The man might have just picked the one farthest from the tents. Polish it up nicely, he could pass Fanny's skull off as Sitting Bull's."

"That's a bit of a stretch," Bill said.

"Surely is," Captain Marsh agreed. "But you'd better hope that's all he wants them for."

"What else could it be?"

The captain took a long draw on his pipe. The smoke curled out through the gaps in his teeth as he spoke. "Can't speak to your folk. But there's only one thing my people use human bones for. And that's witchcraft."

Connor stared at him blankly. Bill gave his deputy a wry smile and a pat on the shoulder. "And that's the end of my shift. This one's all yours."

~ * ~

The sun had long set by the time Connor was satisfied with the state of Fanny's grave. He took a few witness statements, none of which offered any promising leads. He helped the men drape a heavy canvas over the grave and secure it with stones to keep scavengers at bay, until a proper reburial could be arranged. He swore Captain Marsh to secrecy regarding his witchcraft theory.

"No call to be riling anyone up just yet. Let me try out a few other angles first." He knew a fence up in Virginia City who was likely to come across anyone dealing in grave goods.

The marshal's office sat in the Gold Hill, just north of the main intersection. Connor smiled when he saw the paint horse tethered outside it. He had hoped his wife would join him at work again. After such a depressing start to the evening, he could use a pleasant diversion.

He was prepared for the sight of her, perched on his desk with an air of casual entitlement. What he did not expect was the mouthwatering smell of warm batter and powdered sugar. It struck his heightened senses like a rush of nicotine.

Charlie was working her way through a bag of bite-sized doughnuts, fresh from the fryer. Her lips and fingers were dusted in sugar, and she had untied her kerchief, baring her long, white throat. The candied aroma filling the air was a perfect complement to her own distinct scent, sweet and heady as only a human's could be. It filled him with a hunger he could feel deep in his bones.

Garou ran to the door, tail wagging and tongue lolling. Connor knelt and caught him about the neck for a friendly wrestle. "No, I didn't bring you anything, so don't bother begging."

"Oh, he doesn't want food, just sympathy," Charlie explained. "I've been neglecting him for my fellow humans again."

"How are you liking Clem so far? I figured you'd be out putting him through his paces."

"I wanted to see you. How was it down at the Flat?"

Connor grimaced. "Grave robbing in the Indian cemetary, if you can believe it."

"Oh, Connor!"

"Naw, it's all right. It used to happen a lot more often. But I'd kinda hoped we were past that in this day and age."

"You think you'll find who did it?"

"Not likely." He sighed as he shed his heavy coat and hat. "Still, I'd rather get called out for old bones than a fresh body. If this is the worst that happens tonight, I'll count my blessings." He flashed her a grateful smile. "But I'm glad you're here."

She returned his smile, but her brow was still knit in concern. "Now I feel guilty. Here I had brought a treat for you—"

"Oh, I could use a pick-me-up, believe me." He raised a quizzical eyebrow. "But you know I haven't been able to eat pastry for the last hundred-odd years."

She was the picture of innocence, save for the wicked light dancing in her eyes. "The doughnuts? Oh no, they're for me. Brought you something else." She idly fingered her jacket collar, brushing a fine trail of sugar across her neck. The motion could not fail to draw his gaze to her pulse point, visibly thrumming just under her skin.

The dull ache in his belly had suddenly become a burning need. The predator inside him was screaming for release. He forgot all about the business at American Flat. Nothing existed outside the room. Nothing mattered except the beautiful creature perched on his desk, and the memory of how her blood tasted on his tongue.

"Did you now?" he drawled.

She gave a tempting roll of her shoulders. "You were so nice, giving me Clem and all... seems the least I could do."

"I'm on duty."

"Well, if you're not interested..." she started to straighten her collar. Connor turned and locked the door.

"You know, I'm thinking I want to give you something else."

"What's that?"

He parted his lips in a slow revenant's smile, baring his sharp canines. Charlie's pulse started to race; it sounded like a drumbeat in his ear. Her eyes darkened with the same feral intensity. Her muscles tensed; she became a prey animal poised for flight.

"A five second head start," Connor breathed.

Charlie launched herself from the edge of the desk with a cry of joy. She ran for the jailhouse door. Her hand was already on the knob when her five seconds expired.

Connor crossed the floor of the office in three running strides. Charlie was barely inside the empty jail when he caught her.

His arm came up around her, staggering her, lifting her off the ground. He swung her around and pinned her to the wall of the closest cell. Her hands braced against his shoulders; her breaths came fast and shallow. When she turned her face away the tendons of her neck strained against her skin.

Connor sank his teeth into her throat, and the rush of scalding blood filling his mouth was almost as sweet as Charlie's moan of pleasure. Her arms wound tight about his shoulders, one hand pressed hard against the back of his head. He hitched her legs up around his hips as he ground her against the iron bars. He drank until he was almost senseless from the taste of her. He drank until he felt her racing heartbeat falter, until she shuddered under his month and cried out her release.

One day, he wouldn't stop. One day, he would drain her dry.

Two

Wes Benedict watched his mother fidget under the attentions of the old doctor. She had submitted gamely enough to having her pulse read and her throat examined. She'd even unbuttoned the collar of her shirtwaist to let Doc Sheppard put the bell of his stethoscope against her breast. But when he suggested she change into a dressing gown so he could examine her more thoroughly, her patience came to an abrupt end.

"Out of the question!" She slapped her hands down on the armrests to propel herself upright. The show of modest indignation did not impress the doctor, however, and only left her fighting for breath. At the sound of the now-familiar wet cough, Wes hastened to pass her a fresh handkerchief.

"Please sit, Mrs. Benedict," the doctor said sternly.

Lucy Benedict was in no shape to refuse him. She sank back into the armchair and bent her head, steadily working the phlegm out of her throat.

Wes felt the weight of the doctor's disapproving gaze. He should have called Sheppard in long ago. But it had been so easy to believe his mother when she insisted it was nothing more than a summer cold.

Lucy Benedict had always been strong, in body and will; circumstances had demanded nothing less. At seventeen, she had left war-torn Tennessee with her infant son and travelled across the country in search of a new home. At twenty-three, she had already turned down five offers of marriage, preferring to work her fingers to the bone rather than entrust her child to another's authority. Wes remembered the nights she had gone without supper so he could have a full plate. He remembered her tending his monthly infirmities without complaint, seldom in need of nursing herself. As recently as spring, she had been glowing with health, her hair dark and glossy, her skin clear and rosy.

What a difference a season could make. Now her face had the sallow cast of sickness, accentuating the lines at her eyes and mouth. Her dark hair had grown brittle as hay. The pleasing plumpness to her flesh was slowly melting away. As she clutched the handkerchief to her bloodless lips, Wes realized she had the hands of an old woman.

She first came down with a runny nose and a burning throat in July. Wes hadn't worried. The summer pollen could waylay the strongest constitution. But the wildflowers bloomed and went to seed, and the hacking cough slowly moved deeper down into Lucy's chest. Still, she had carried on all through August and most of September, brushing off his concerns. She was not a woman who liked to sit idle. Only when the simplest chores left her gasping for breath would she admit that perhaps she needed a little rest.

Now, watching her suffer, Wes prayed it wasn't too late.

At last Lucy's fit passed. She drew a deep breath, then began to fold the cotton square. Sheppard promptly snatched the evidence from her hands to examine the sputum.

"Really now, Doctor," Lucy moaned. She turned her gaze on her son, wide China-blue eyes imploring him to eject the vulgar man from their house.

"Can you tell what's wrong with her, Doc?" Wes asked Sheppard instead.

"Quite conclusively." Sheppard said cheerfully. "You have acute bronchitis, Mrs. Benedict. That is, an inflammation of the upper airways—"

"I know what bronchitis is," Lucy said wearily. "We do carry a medical almanac."

Sheppard was only flustered for a moment. "Well, I wouldn't trust a word of those books. Rubbish, for the most part... glorified advertisements for the worst sort of nostrums."

"Is she going to be all right?" Wes asked.

"If she follows my treatment. Mustard-seed plasters, ipecac as required, up to four times a day. Plenty of hot liquids. I recommend coffee for its stimulant properties. Some coca wine, if she can tolerate it. And most importantly: bed rest. For a month at least."

"A month?" Lucy stammered.

"It's imperative we arrest the disease's progression. That means no physical exertion, no exposure to airborne irritants, and above all, a diaphragm unimpeded by corsetry."

"Really now!"

Sheppard's smile was paternalistic. "Vanity must cede priority to health, Mrs. Benedict."

"It's not a matter of vanity so much as back support!"

"Which you will not require on bed rest," Sheppard pointed out. He turned back to Wes. "You'll need to bring someone in to look after the house while your mother is recuperating. If you like, I have the names of several girls I think would be suitable."

"Impossible," Lucy interjected.

"Ma, please."

"I'm not going to loll about in bed like some slattern while a stranger makes a mess of my house!"

"No, you're going to lie in bed like an invalid, Mrs. Benedict," Sheppard said sternly. "Which is what you are. I will not mince words, ma'am. The natural evolution of this disease, when unchecked, is towards pneumonia. And at your age, that would be a death sentence."

"Jesus, Doc!" Wes exclaimed. "She's only forty-nine!"

"And if you would like her to see fifty, Mr. Benedict, you will heed my warning. I reckon you have two months in which to turn the tide."

Wes frowned. "Why? What happens in two months?"

"Winter," Sheppard said simply, letting the word hang in the air.

Wes saw the doctor out the front door. "Be straight with me, Doc," he said, once they were well out of earshot of the parlor. "Is it really that bad?"

Sheppard looked him up and down, making little effort to conceal his personal distaste. "I thought I had made myself clear."

"I only mean... if you're trying to scare her into taking better care of herself—"

Sheppard folded his arms across his chest and told him straight. "I'm trying to scare *you* into saving her life. For if she continues like this—managing the entire house alone, refusing to properly care for herself—I have no doubt she will be dead by New Year's.

"I know she is a proud woman. And I know you don't want to hear this. But now is the time for you to repay the debt every son owes his mother. Whatever her objections—whatever yours—she must submit to bed rest and daily treatment. Hire a girl to come in, preferably to live in. One with some experience at nursing. As I said, I can give you names if you need." He clapped a hand on Wes's shoulder. "Hang the inconvenience, man. That woman has never hesitated to sacrifice for you. Now it's your turn."

Wes nodded dully. "Thanks, Doc. I... I'll come settle up later."

Sheppard grunted softly and went on his way. It was clear the doctor didn't have an ounce of faith in either Benedict. Why should he? Wes thought glumly.

Wes knew what the townsfolk thought of him. A grown man who still clung to his mother's apron, who had wasted his best years in saloons and whorehouses, and who had earned nothing by the sweat of his own labours. That he had risen to become partner in the livery stables was only because Lucy had campaigned relentlessly on his behalf, to the point of flirting quite shamelessly with the right men, if one believed idle gossip. That the Benedicts' friends knew better was a small comfort. Circumstances dictated solitude; the fewer friends, the better.

Circumstances, that was what Lucy always called it, in hushed tones. She kept the Southern gentility of her girlhood, and she loved her son too much to call it what it truly was. A curse.

A large oval mirror hung in the foyer, by the coat rack. Wes caught sight of his reflection and sighed. He had little to complain about at present, save for the advancing stripes of gray over his ears. A shave, a haircut, and a new suit were all he'd need to mingle with the society set at the Miners' Hall. A few of the local debutantes might even try to catch his eye, he thought with fleeting vanity. They would ask their mothers, "Who was that dapper swell?" and refuse to believe it could ever have been poor pitiable Wes.

Yes, he could fool them for a night, maybe a week. But it wouldn't last. First the nerves would steal whatever clever words he might say. Then would come the jaundice and the jitters. Sleeplessness would rob his wits and drain his strength until he could barely shoe a horse properly. And finally would come the agony, all in the service of one night of madness.

Wes returned to the parlor. His mother was still sitting in her armchair, her gaze distant and unfocused. Doc Sheppard's words returned to him.

That woman has never hesitated to sacrifice for you.

He knelt at her feet. "Ma? How are you holding up?"

She smiled wanly. "Don't you listen to that quack. I'll be just fine."

"You need to take better care of yourself."

She gave a dismissive wave. "I'll look into it. Maybe we can get a girl to come every other day, to help out with the big chores."

"You need more than that."

"I am not taking a month's bed rest. He's being ridiculous." She saw the stubborn set to Wes's face and her voice softened. "Wes...

you know we can't take the risk. To let some stranger in our house, at all hours of day... who knows what she might overhear."

"So we don't get a stranger. We get someone we know. Someone we can trust."

She clucked her tongue. "But who can we trust? What have I always told you?" She reached out a cold hand to brush his hair out of his face. "I promised I'd always look after you. That we never needed anyone else. Wes, honey, we can't afford to need anyone else."

Her eyes were moist. Wes understood her sense of shame. Weakness was a failing Lucy would not allow herself to afford. Sheer determination had sustained her against all odds... against war and poverty and the ravages of the curse itself. But it could not protect her from old age. She knew what had to be done, but she couldn't bear to admit it.

And Wes knew what had to be done, too. He had one last card to play that would trump all her arguments. But it pained him to the core to play it.

That woman has never hesitated to sacrifice for you. Now it's your turn.

"You're right," he said sadly. "We've only ever needed each other. But, Ma... you won't always be here. And when you die, who's going to look after me then?"

He could only think of one person.

~ * ~

Nell staggered out of the Masonic Lodge, her wash bucket in one hand, three tarnished coins clasped tight in the other. Her mother was right; she was getting old. Worse, she was out of practice. Her knees ached after an afternoon on the floor, and she was bent over with a dowager's hump from the stabbing pain in her lower back. Her apron was soaked through with soapy water, and hot spots on the palms of her hands hinted at the blisters to come.

She remembered when she could spend a whole day on her knees, scrubbing floors and cleaning fireplaces. But she had been spoiled the past few years. Housekeeping at the Canyon Hotel, she had supervised the heavy work, but her hands were more often occupied taking inventory or folding linens. Even on laundry days, she had worked from the comfort of a cushioned stool.

Now she was starting again from the bottom, breaking her back for mere pennies. But at least the Freemasons seemed satisfied with her work. If their regular custodian kept to his sickbed a little longer, she might be able to secure a proper arrangement. In time, she might even be able to ask for a dollar a day. Add that to the other odd jobs she was finding, and she might make it through the winter before she'd be reduced to begging for money from Charlie.

The Capital sat just across the street from the Freemasons. Nell was due to meet Charlie for a night at the Indian show in just under two hours, and she needed a wash and a half-decent meal before then.

She went around the back, towards the outbuilding where she lodged. Wes Benedict was waiting for her.

Her guard went up at the sight of him. He'd taken to seeking her out more and more lately, as if trying to revive their old carefree friendship. She wished he wouldn't. They weren't children anymore; she couldn't be seen idling with white men if she wanted to find an honest job.

"Hey, Nell. Got a minute?"

"One," she said cautiously.

"You haven't found work yet, have you? Full-time work, I mean."

Nell shook her head. "Just bits and pieces. Day-to-day."

The grin burst out on his face before he could check it. "Aw, that's perfect. Listen, Nell, you can do me such a big favor! My ma… you know she's still fighting that chest cold. Well, the doctor came 'round today. Says it's gotten worse. Says she needs bed rest and nursing. That we need someone to come stay at the house, keep the place running and help Ma through this."

"Shoot, haven't I been saying as much?"

"You're preaching to the converted. But you know how Ma is. She never wants to admit she needs help. But I thought… you… that is…" he raised his eyebrows hopefully, willing her to take his meaning. When Nell continued to regard him skeptically, he added,

"If I told Ma how hard it is for you to find work, and how much she'd really be helping you out—"

"I don't need your help," Nell cut him off. When he flinched, she forced herself to soften her tone. She knew why he was making the offer. When she'd first walked out on her job at the hotel, she'd been stupid enough to boast about it to Wes. And in one of his rare moods of optimism, Wes had encouraged her rebellion, filling her head with dreams of a better future free for the taking. He had climbed out of poverty, why couldn't she?

But of course there was no better future, and no jobs for a nettlesome Negro who'd deserted her last post without notice. Even Wes had to realize that. And now he was making a belated apology for making yet another promise he couldn't keep.

"I appreciate the offer, Wes. Really, I do. But I ain't quite ready to be a charity case."

"But see, you'd be doing me the favor," he insisted. "Ma will find fault with every nurse and every housekeeper I bring home. But she can't turn you away. You know how fond she is of you. You're practically kin!"

"Hm. Kin that works for money. Sure."

"Please, Nell. I don't know who else to ask."

He sounded genuinely pained. She could feel herself weakening.

"I want to help your ma. I do. She's always been good to me."

"Then what's the problem?"

Where to start? The fact that he expected her to sacrifice her dignity so his mother could keep hers? His utter blindness to the power he would hold over her?

"What if it doesn't work out?" she asked. "What if I can't bear taking orders from you? You said you want someone live-in. But we can't go more than twenty minutes without finding something to scrap over. Wes, we've just started talking again, really talking for the first time in fifteen years. I don't want to ruin that. "

"We won't let that happen. I promise. Please, at least say you'll give it a shot. We can try it for a spell, and if it doesn't work out, then we'll say 'lesson learned' and no hard feelings."

"I don't know. I haven't done much nursing."

"But you know how to run a house."

He knew how to flatter her. She thought about it a moment. After managing a six-room hotel and three quarrelling maids, a small household would be child's play. "Suppose I'd be doing all the cleaning and cooking. You do your laundry in-house?"

"Only the little things. We send the heavy stuff out once a week. And we keep pretty civilized hours. Ma used to keep the house running like clockwork, and she still made it to bed every night at ten. Of course you'd get Sundays off. Or whatever day you'd like."

"Wages?"

He shrugged. "Thirty a month sound good?"

Her mouth opened on a strangled cough of disbelief. "You making me pay you back for room and board outta that?"

"Of course not!"

Nell slowly considered it, eyes narrowed. He was serious. He was either a bigger fool than she ever credited, or he was genuinely desperate.

"A month's a long time," she said at length. "Can we work it by the week?"

"Sure. That's what... about six-fifty a week?"

"And I stay on until your ma's well?"

"Until New Year's at least. But if you're willing, I say we try for as long as we can."

"Then I get Christmas Day off too," she said firmly.

"Sure."

"All right. We'll try it."

Relief washed over him; he was visibly giddy, so much so that Nell almost believed his lie that she was doing him the greater favor. When she offered her hand, he pumped it eagerly.

"You good to start on Monday morning?" he asked. "Say... nine o'clock?"

"Monday at nine," she confirmed.

He was still holding her hand tight inside his sweaty palm. Nell extricated herself with a tight smile. Wes flushed sheepishly, and jammed both hands deep in his pockets.

"You don't know what this means to me, Nell. Honest. I couldn't trust anyone else with this."

Her brow furrowed at the statement. She didn't how much trust was really required to cook and clean house, but then Wes had stopped making sense to her long ago.

She sent him on his way and let herself into her rented room. It was little more than a wooden box, one of five crude additions to the main body of the hotel, rented for twelve dollars a month. In contrast to the homey little rooms inside the hotel proper, her room came with a bed and a small washbasin. Everything else, from her candles to her chamber pot, she had to supply herself.

Sunlight slipped through the many cracks in the walls, painting the narrow confines in swaths of dusty gold. The air stank faintly of urine, despite her best efforts with a scrub brush. Her south-facing wall was a popular spot for the drunkards to relieve themselves in between pints. On blustery nights the winds coming down the mountainside made the cheap shingles of her roof rattle, and come winter she knew she would freeze.

But she wasn't going to be here for the winter. A slow smile broke out on her face. She was trading the cramped hovel for a proper room in the Benedict house. Room and board and enough money to replenish her depleted savings within a season.

Before she knew it, she was back out in the afternoon sun, locking the door behind her. Pride swelled in her chest; she could no longer feel her aches and pains. She wanted to share her good news with someone, anyone. She couldn't wait the two hours for Charlie to arrive. She needed to crow that someone found her invaluable.

The five minutes it took to hike to High Street convinced her Wes was telling the truth. It was common knowledge that under all her Southern gentility, Lucy Benedict had an iron will that bent to no one. She had never tolerated a hired girl for more than a week at a time. The more she thought of it, the more it made perfect sense she would not surrender her authority to anyone other than a trusted acquaintance. And hadn't Nell proved herself an excellent household manager in her years working at the Canyon?

As for the wages, they were ridiculously inflated, but she could easily put that to Wes's inexperience, rather than blatant charity. Besides, he knew his mother best. Perhaps the demands she would make as a patient were deserving of extra compensation.

Nell reached her childhood home and wrapped twice on the door before her mother came to open it. Ruth's eyes narrowed in suspicion. "Nell. We weren't expecting you until Sunday night."

The front door opened directly onto the dining area, where the Johns family was in the process of dismembering a limp-looking meat pie. Lester Johns sat at the head of the table, a little plumper and a little greyer than Nell remembered, flanked by a quartet of boys. Nell couldn't help but notice the eldest two still had a large helping of meat and pastries on their plates, while nine-year-old Abraham was already reduced to nibbling on his crusts. The lion's share always went to the breadwinners.

She fought against the initial stirrings of sympathy. The boys were Lester and Ruth's making; Nell refused to let herself become involved.

Thirteen-year-old Garrison was the first to look up from the table. "Nell! You joinin' us for dinner?"

"I wish you had told me you were coming," Ruth said pointedly. "I would have made more."

"Oh, I ain't staying. Just came by to tell you that you don't have to worry about me anymore, Momma. I got me a new job!"

"That's my girl!" Lester cried, with such genuine pride Nell could forgive him for the possessive. "This calls for a toast. Do we have any of that good malt left?"

"Not for two nights," Ruth said. "You'll have to make do with sweet tea."

"You don't have to," Nell began, but her stepfather wouldn't hear of it.

"Gary, go get another cup. Uly, move over, make some room for your sister."

Ulysses shot Nell a surly look, and made room. She didn't take it personally. At fifteen, he was always scowling. Garrison returned with a chipped earthenware mug brimming with cold tea, and the entire table tapped cups with varying degrees of enthusiasm.

"To Nell," Lester said. "Our career woman."

"To Nell," Garrison chimed, with a broad smile. The older boys grunted. Nell tasted her sweet tea; it was the same watery mixture she remembered from her childhood. Every morning Ruth would boil up a large pot of weak tea to last them the whole day. Even sweetened with a touch of molasses, it was as bitter as the local water, though somewhat less likely to cause dysentery.

"It'll be your turn soon," Lester told Garrison. "This time next year, I expect we'll be toasting your first pay day."

Nell frowned. "You're quitting school, Gary?"

"End of this year." Garrison shrugged indifferently, though his smile diminished.

"Thought you wanted to graduate."

Garrison's gaze flicked towards his father. "Guess I don't see the point anymore," he said dutifully. "Teacher says I already know what I'm gonna need in life. And it's time enough I started pulling my weight. So I'll finish off the seventh grade and call it a day."

Lester nodded approvingly. Then Garrison brightened and jerked his thumb in Fremont's direction. "It's three years better than this one could manage, after all."

Fremont cuffed him on the back of the head, hard enough to make his teeth clack. Lester sighed wearily and passed on a similar smack to his eldest.

"You mind your manners. Both of you. Now then, tell us all about your job, Nell. You get another lodging house to pick you up?"

"Please tell me it's not a saloon," Ruth said anxiously.

"Actually, it's the Benedicts. Mrs. B's still awful sick, and she's finally admitted she needs a housekeeper. Wes told me she wouldn't settle for anyone but me," she added with a proud lift of her chin.

Dead silence greeted her pronouncement.

"I... don't know what to say," Ruth murmured at length.

"You could say you're happy for me."

"It's pretty funny, really!" Garrison piped up. He looked about the table, and saw the stony faces of his parents, the disbelief in his brothers' eyes. "Be-because Mrs. Benedict took care of Nell when she was a kid... and now Nell is sorta paying her back..." his voice petered out to a meek whisper. "What?"

"Nell doesn't owe Mrs. Benedict anything," Ruth said. "She was well-paid to mind your sister."

"Well, now I'm being well-paid to mind her," Nell countered. "And it's live-in, so you don't need to worry about me 'wasting' my money on a lodging house."

"Boys... will you excuse us," Lester said at length. "We'd like to talk to your sister alone."

"Hell with that," said Fremont. "I ain't missing this."

"Now, Monty!"

Fremont reluctantly got to his feet and followed the other boys out. Nell's stomach clenched as she heard the door to the bedroom click closed.

Her mother spoke first. "I don't know what possessed you. Living under his roof? What will people think?"

"It's a bad idea," Lester agreed. "Now I got nothing against the lady. But Wes Benedict is a no-account drunk—"

"So are half the men in this town," Nell pointed out.

"And it stinks something fierce, him waiting until you're desperate before showin' up with this offer."

"Who says I'm desperate? I still got three months of savings. And it's a good offer."

"I'm sure it looks good to you right now," Lester dismissed. "Roof over your head and a couple dollars a month—"

"Try thirty!"

Two blood-filled shadows blossomed on Lester's cheeks. His voice was low and frosty. "Well now... for a price like that, a man might expect more than a clean house and a good meal."

Nell got to her feet. "Thanks for the tea."

"Tell me I'm wrong."

"You're wrong. If Wes wants a whore, he knows where to find 'em."

"He does. Often. I hear he's a regular up at a cathouse on D Street."

Nell turned so they couldn't see the grimace that crossed her face.

"But suppose he can't be bothered to make the trip," Lester went on. "'Specially when he's got a sweet little piece under his own roof. What are you gonna do when he comes a'knocking at your door late at night?"

"He won't! You know Wes. He... he don't see me like that."

She could hear the distress that crept into her voice. So could Lester. He gave a barking laugh of disbelief. "And you still wish he did."

"I don't," she snapped. "Not that it's your business, anyhow."

"You watch your mouth," Lester warned. "I'm the only father you have, girl!"

"Pft. And you see how far that gets you."

"Nell, will you just listen to us?" Ruth pleaded. "He's not a good man. You know that. He'll hurt you. He's done it before."

Nell whirled around. "He was a stupid kid, and so was I. We both know better now."

"But you don't. You're still in love with him, Eleanor."

The words were like a slap in the face, made worse by her mother's defeated tone. "I'm not—" Nell began. Ruth waved her objections away.

"Yes, you are. And you still think you can change him. I remember what a sweet boy he was... I do! But that boy's been dead nigh on twenty years now, and all that's left is a sad, ugly man. Maybe he can still fix himself up. But it won't be a'cause o'you."

You're wrong, Nell wanted to protest. Lester's face was swollen with simmering rage, but it was nothing to Nell compared to her mother's sorrow. When Nell summoned her voice to protest, Ruth held up a gnarled hand.

"But all he's gotta do is whistle, and you'll go running to him. Mark my words, you keep acting like his dog and he'll keep treating you like one."

Nell stared at her mother across the room. At length she spoke, forcing the words through clenched teeth. "Guess I won't be coming by on Sunday after all."

"Guess not," Ruth agreed.

With a muttered oath, Nell wrenched the door open. She left it swinging as she strode out onto the street, head held high. She waited until she was around the corner and out of sight before she gave in to despair.

She leaned against the wall of the abandoned grocery and hugged her sides to keep herself from shivering. She would not cry. She would not give them the satisfaction. This was good news, no matter what they said. This was still a victory for her.

When she regained her composure, she continued down the street towards the Capital. But she found she was no longer looking forward to Charlie's arrival. Step by step, doubt crept into her head. By the time she reached the boarding house, her victory felt hollow.

Lester could rain judgment on her until his throat was sore, and she would just shrug off the blows. Against her mother's sad logic, she had no defense.

What Ruth said was inexcusable. And every word of it was true.

Three

Charlie Franklin checked her appearance one last time in her bedroom mirror. The twill mauve suit she had once considered her Sunday best seemed coarse and ill-fitting after a summer spent in soft buckskins and tailored riding skirts. Glumly, she supposed she would have to invest in some proper dresses if she wanted to attend social events. Though a finer fabric and a smarter cut would do little to mitigate the discomforts of fashion. Already she was getting a headache from the hairpins grating against her skull, holding her man's cap perched at a jaunty angle.

Circumstances dictated the blouse with the highest neckline. The starched collar came up all the way to her chin, chafing the tender bruises on her neck. She wriggled a finger under it to worry an itch.

"The wages of sin," Connor murmured, with a kiss to her cheek.

"Mm." She arched an eyebrow. "No matter how she goes about getting it, seems a girl's always got to pay for her thrill. I've half a mind to take myself off the menu," she added provocatively, watching her husband in the mirror.

"No, you won't," he said, without so much as a blink. Charlie giggled at her reflection.

"No, I really won't."

Revenant venom: their saliva worked as an opiate on most prey animals, numbing them long enough for the revenant to safely feed. In Charlie's case, however, the effect was something closer to Spanish fly. The merest brush of his lips set her skin to tingling, and when he sank his teeth in her veins, she could feel every inch of her body come alive with sensation. If human blood wasn't so addicting to revenants—or so dangerous—she would beg him for a good bite every day, and never mind the scars.

But she couldn't, of course. The more human blood Connor drank, the less human he'd become. Even now, three nights after their love play in the jailhouse, he still felt the effects. By day his sleeps were deeper; by night his heart beat slower. Charlie had seen what human blood could do to a revenant who fed on nothing else. The result was a walking corpse, stinking of death and nearly witless, yet filled with an animal strength that made it stronger and faster than any living man.

Connor would die a second time rather than become such a creature. For a man with eternity ahead of him, that was no idle pledge.

"Ready?" Connor asked, offering her his arm. Charlie took it.

The old stairs creaked ominously as they descended to the ground floor, the perfect complement to the house's decaying interior. Charlie didn't doubt every fixture had been the height of fashion when Connor had first commissioned the house; just as she believed her husband when he said he hardly noticed the threadbare curtains and the peeling wallpaper. When thirty-five years passed in the blink of an eye, who had the time to bother with conventional aesthetics?

Besides, the house's decrepit exterior served as an excellent deterrent to the curious. No travelling salesman or gossipy housewife dared to make the mile-long walk across the barren hillside to the crumbling old manor house. Several cab drivers had made it clear they would not take passengers to what everyone in town called the Crypt. Only the rare schoolboy ever summoned the courage to climb the teetering porch steps and try to peer though the boarded-up windows. And Garou could always be counted on to deal with them.

The wolf-dog was sulking at the door. He could already tell he was not invited on their outing. Charlie could feel the brunt of his disapproval aimed squarely at her. Garou adored her when she was at his beck and call, but the moment she took Connor away from him, she was demoted to interfering female.

She couldn't really blame him. He and Connor had spent the better part of a century together before she came along. No man could live alone and stay sane. Lacking a willing human to become his immortal companion, he had settled for making a canine one.

"You be good," Connor warned Garou. "We'll be back before sunup."

Garou gave an annoyed huff and wandered off into the parlor.

The evening light was still bright enough to make Connor squint as they stepped outside. Charlie felt a stab of pity. It was her blood that caused his discomfort. On his usual regime of rare meat and animal blood, only direct sunlight could hurt him.

Connor had already hitched his horse Washington to their little buggy. Now, ever the gentleman, he helped Charlie up onto the passenger's seat before climbing in himself.

"You sure Nell won't mind my tagging along?" he asked.

"Can't see why. You're only giving us a ride, after all."

"She's afraid of me, you know."

"No! Nell? She thinks mighty highly of you. 'Your man's one of the good ones'... that's what she says to me."

"Maybe so. But she still starts stinking of vinegar if we trade more than a dozen words."

Charlie considered the revelation. "I think Nell's afraid of most men. White men, anyway. Don't take it personally."

"Oh, I don't," Connor said, cheerfully enough. "Most folks are at least a little afraid of me, you know. It's true," he said when she opened her mouth to deny it. "Even if they don't realize it. They can feel, deep down, that I'm not one of them." He flashed his revenant's smile: easy and charming, but showing a bit too much teeth. The smile that never quite reached his eyes. It always sent a shiver down her spine.

He was watching her closely, attentive to her altered breathing, the flutter of her pulse, the minute muscle twitches under her skin. "Even you could tell," he murmured. "But you were never afraid."

"I was... a little," she admitted. "Just not enough to stop me."

This time the smile did reach his eyes. "Thank God for that, honey girl."

Nell met them outside the capital, dressed in a long gray coat, her hair primly tucked under a felt hat. She had wound a red wool shawl about her shoulders in imitation of more fashionable wraps. At the sight of the deputy driving the buggy, her eyes widened a fraction, but her expression remained the model of courtesy.

"Evening, Deputy."

"Nell, I love your shawl," Charlie exclaimed. "Is that new?"

"Hardly." She looked up at the crowded buggy seat. "I'll follow you up on foot, then."

"Don't be silly." Charlie hastened to make room. "We can all fit."

Nell shot a questioning look at Connor, then gamely climbed into the buggy.

"Connor's starting his rounds at the north end of town," Charlie felt compelled to explain. "So he offered to save us the walk."

"I'm mighty grateful," Nell said, though her rigid posture of discomfort belied her words. Pressed up against Charlie's shoulder and hip, Nell held herself stiff as a corpse. Charlie felt her wince with each bump in the road.

The exhibition had set up on the fairgrounds just above the canyon, on the southern limits of Virginia City. By day, the whole span of Gold Hill could be seen from the plateau. By night, the canyon was a winding snake of light, as oil lamps flickered in windows and electricity surged through the sodium lights at the mills. The fairgrounds themselves were brightly lit by open bowls of flame.

An aging carnival barker in a patched duster and top hat collected dimes at the front gate. He looked Nell over suspiciously as Connor paid for the trio.

"This Negress is with you, sir?" he asked.

Connor's mouth set in a thin line. "I just paid for her, didn't I?"

"So you did." The barker summoned an obsequious smile. "You enjoy yourselves, now."

"I'd like to speak to the manager, at his convenience. A business proposition."

"You're looking at him. Frank Maddock, at your service." He doffed his hat, revealing a head of unkempt gray hair. In the firelight, his skin seemed to have the consistency of sweating cheese. "And, uh, what sort of business would you be proposing?"

"Police business."

"Oh." He replaced his hat with a heavy sigh. "Look, I already came to an 'arrangement' with the mayor. I didn't think the police needed a cut too."

"This isn't a shakedown. I just have a few questions to ask you. About your Indian artifacts."

A line was forming behind them: families in their Sunday best, miners in their dusty work clothes. "Can I have a few minutes?" Maddock asked.

"Take your time." Connor motioned Charlie and Nell onward. "You ladies go on ahead."

They left Connor at the gate and followed the other visitors onto the fairgrounds. Charlie looped her arm through Nell's. "Where should we start? I want to see everything, now."

"All right, but don't pout if this ain't what you're expecting. We don't get the fancy shows you're used to in Frisco."

Charlie snorted in derision. "What fancy shows? Only circus I could afford was a tatty little one-ring with a sick elephant and a pair of dwarfs."

They visited each tent in turn, working their way clockwise around the fairgrounds. The first one housed an archaic stereopticon, projecting colored slides of landscapes and vignettes from native life.

The pictures were beautiful, but the crush of bodies in the tent soon blocked the projector and turned the air dense and fetid. Charlie plucked at her collar irritably.

"Y'all right?" Nell asked.

"Aw, something took a bite out of me the other night, is all."

"Pft," Nell dismissed with a wave. "You'll grow a tougher skin after a few summers here. I never notice the bugs anymore."

The second tent held taxidermy specimens, ranging in size from a tiny squirrel with golden fur to a snaggle-toothed grizzly bear. Charlie stared wide-eyed at the horned jackrabbit.

"Is that real?"

Nell tutted. "Lord, you're a greenhorn."

The "live animals" turned out to be the mules and draft horses that hauled the wagons from town to town. They were gentle enough animals, and eagerly took bits of hay from the hands of giggling children. A man in buckskins and feathers mixed pemmican over a small fire. "If he's a bona fide Indian, then I'm President McKinley," Nell quipped, prompting a laugh from Charlie. Still, they paid a penny for a tablet of the rosy mixture and broke it between them, grimacing at the texture.

"So... Wes offered me a job," Nell confessed, as they strolled over towards the next tent. The banner over the door read: *WHITE MOON – Captive of the Comanches.*

"Housekeeping and nursing his ma," she explained. "Six-fifty a week, plus room and board."

"Nell, that's wonderful!"

"Not really. Dunno why I agreed to it."

"Why? You and Wes... you always talk about him like he's family."

"Oh sure, we ran together when we were kids. We also fought like cats and dogs. When we weren't going years without talking to each other. Now... I dunno what we are to each other anymore."

"Friends?"

Nell shook her head. "Friends are equal. And that's something Wes and I'll never be. And now I'm gonna be working for him, too...

taking money from his hand? That just puts him one more notch above me."

"I don't think Wes reckons it like that," Charlie said gently.

"Course he doesn't. He doesn't need to."

"Why did you agree to it, then?"

"I need the work. Besides... sounds like Mrs. B is in a state. I owe it to her."

Charlie smiled at that. Nell might convince herself it was just a matter of duty, but she wore her heart on her sleeve as far as Wes Benedict was concerned.

The interior of the tent was decorated with brightly colored tapestries. A pair of women sat behind a tasseled rope, one spinning wool by hand, the other weaving on a large loom. The weaver was approaching middle age. She boasted copper skin and a hard sort of beauty. The spinner was a girl Charlie's age, with pale skin and paler hair. She kept her head bent over her distaff. Charlie read the signpost mounted behind her.

KIDNAPPED at AGE 8 by COMANCHE braves!
SOLD as a WHITE SLAVE!
REDEEMED 13 Aug 1894 — but left UNABLE to return to CIVILIZED LIFE!
NAVAJO BLANKETS – 10 dollars

"Hello," Charlie said awkwardly, when she and Nell took their turn at the rope. "Looks awful nice, what you're doing. Must take a lot of patience."

White Moon stole a fearful glance up at the visitors. Her eyebrows, Charlie noticed, were a dark brown, though her braided hair was so fair as to be almost colorless.

"She cannot speak," the Indian woman explained gently. "As for the work, you are quite right. One of these blankets takes about three months to complete."

"She can't speak?" Nell interjected. "Why not?"

"She was beaten by her captors for speaking her Mother tongue. They thought it would help her learn the Comanche language. Instead it stole her wits." She laid a hand on the girl's shoulder. "I am called Brightfeather, and I am a sister to White Moon now. I speak for her."

"Are you Comanche?" Charlie asked.

"I am Navajo. Please, examine our textiles at your leisure. And do not forget to stay for our husband the Wolf Charmer. His performance begins at seven o'clock."

"*Our* husband?"

"Of course." Brightfeather's smile was mild. "As I said, we are sisters now."

"Some sisters," Nell muttered, giving Charlie's arm a tug.

Outside, people were beginning to gather in front of the main stage. Roustabouts were setting up long wooden benches, and families were staking claim to the best seats. The women moved towards the back of the crowd, content to stand.

"Well, now!" a familiar voice chimed. "Speaking of human curiosities..."

Nell's arm went rigid as iron about Charlie's. Together they turned to face the speaker.

He would tower over them, even at a polite distance. But he wasn't being polite. He strode up to them until their boot-tips were nearly touching, heedless of the flustered woman trailing on his arm. Nell looked down at the dirt rather than meet the man's flat gaze. Charlie couldn't blame her. The last time Nell had crossed paths with the hatchet-faced deputy, she had spent the day behind bars.

"Good evening, Mrs. Franklin," the deputy said, his voice mild. "I almost didn't recognize you in a dress."

"Garrod. I thought you had crawled back under your rock for the weekend. What brings you 'round?"

"Enjoying the entertainment, same as you. I find Indian culture quite fascinating. All primitive cultures, really. And I see you brought your little friend along." An imitation of a smile played across his face as he looked to Nell. "Well, I'm sure she's very appreciative. Aren't you, girl?"

"Yessir," Nell muttered, still not looking up.

"You're a pig," Charlie sneered.

"Please, Mrs. Franklin. There's no need to be crude."

The woman on Garrod's arm cleared her throat genteely. She looked to be roughly his age, but the forty-odd years sat more harshly on her face. Perhaps it was the fault of her pinched lips, but Charlie could hardly blame her for being peevish, with such an escort.

"Where are my manners?" Garrod remarked. "Dorothy, this is Mrs. Franklin, Gold Hill's resident revolutionary. I believe I have mentioned her several times in the past. As a cautionary tale. My wife, Mrs. Garrod."

"Charmed." Dorothy Garrod began to extend a gloved hand, but her husband checked her with a practiced wave of dismissal.

"My sympathies," Charlie replied. "Come on, Nell. I'm sure we can find a better spot that this."

"You gotta stop sassing him," Nell warned, once they were safely on the other side of the milling audience. "One of these days your mouth's gonna get you in trouble."

"One of these days I'm liable to break his nose."

"See, that's what I'm talking about. Didn't your daddy ever teach you to pick your battles?"

"Not really, no."

"Figures." Nell let out a wistful sigh. "I'd like to live in that world of yours. Don't think I'd last long, though. Look, there's your man."

Connor and the disheveled carnival barker were both making their way towards the stage. Connor spotted the women and left Maddock to join them.

"Any luck?" Charlie asked him.

"Well, if our robber was looking to make a sale, he didn't make one here."

Charlie watched as the barker climbed onto the stage and raced his hands for silence.

"So he says."

"I'm inclined to believe him. Fellow like that can't lie well." He shrugged. "It was a long shot."

"John Garrod's here," Charlie warned.

"Mm, I can smell him from here." Connor remembered their guest a moment too late, but by her neutral expression, Nell seemed to take his words for a figure of speech.

"I'd better light out before he spots me."

"Why? You got a reason to be here—you're on a case."

"*You* know what the sheriff thinks of me playing detective, Charlie-girl." He did a passable imitation of Sheriff Quirk's angry growl, "'You're a deputized citizen, dammit, not a Pinkertons' man!' I don't need the headache tonight. You keep the cart; I'll just walk back to the station when I'm done here."

"I'll come find you later," Charlie said, letting her hand brush his elbow as he turned to go.

"No hurry." Connor tipped his hat to them both. "You ladies enjoy yourselves."

"What was a long shot?" Nell asked, after they lost sight of Connor in the crowd.

"Oh, just tracking some stolen goods."

"Mm. It have something to do with that ruckus at the Indian graveyard?"

So much for keeping a lid on it, Charlie thought. She wasn't too surprised. On the Comstock, gossip spread like a rash. She affected a disinterested shrug. "Couldn't say."

"Uh-huh," Nell replied, her tone one of cynical doubt. But she didn't pursue the matter further. The show was starting.

"For centuries," Maddock cried over the crowd, "the Indian has lived in this unspoiled wilderness, like a red-skinned Adam. And the red man learned to speak to the beasts of this world, and to live with them in harmony. And this land was a paradise. Unspoiled, virginal. Then the white man came!

"He brought guns!" Maddock was working himself up into a lather, whirling his fist overhead. Spittle flew from his mouth. "He brought disease! Like the serpent in the garden, he brought the apple... and with it, the red man's undoing! Now the powers of the Indian are fading—their magic corrupted by the march of progress. But tonight! Tonight you will all bear witness to something extraordinary! Tonight you will witness one of the last remaining miracles of the savage world. A Red Adam! A man from the Garden, who can talk to the beasts of the world—"

"*BE QUIET!*" thundered a voice behind the curtain, making Maddock jump.

The Wolf Charmer stepped out into the light. He was a giant of a man, dwarfing the flustered barker. Charlie reckoned he would top John Garrod by half a head. Long snarls of black hair framed a scowling face. He was naked to the waist, and his copper skin glowed in the lamp light, stretched taut over his heavily muscled frame. It was a formidable sight. Several husbands immediately gathered their wives and children and fled. At Charlie's side, Nell covered a sudden intake of breath with a cough.

"Easy girl," Charlie teased. "He's got two wives already, remember?"

"Oh shush."

"Hold your tongue, little man," the Wolf Charmer growled, and Maddock scurried off the stage to laughter. Then the Indian turned his piercing gaze over the audience, and the laughter died away.

"I am Adam Blackfell. But I never knew your garden! I was born of the Exodus, the Long Walk of the Navajo that saw my people marched from their homeland at gunpoint. For four hundred miles they marched, like your Moses in the desert. But there was no Promised Land, only the squalor of the reservation: starvation and slavery. Is it any wonder my people fought back? Some with weapons. Some with witchcraft."

Witchcraft. Charlie looked in the crowd for Connor, but he had already made his escape.

"The Navajo have always been masters of the Witchery Way. We deal in curses, in plagues. But during the Long Walk, we needed darker magic. It was then that the cruelest witches learned they could steal the skin of the beasts. They could become shapeshifters. Skinwalkers."

Blackfell paced back and forth across the stage. He held the crowd's rapt attention. "The skinwalkers terrorized the white man.

But like all wild beasts, they could not be controlled. They turned on their own people, and they became a scourge on the Navajo. My people survived the Long Walk. We made peace with the white man. But still the skinwalkers stalk in the shadows. And it falls to a chosen few to hunt them down.

"I could bring out a chained wolf and make it beg for a bone. I could play lion tamer for you." He pointed to Maddock, cowering by the stage curtain. "He'd like that. But I am not an actor. I am a hunter. Yes, I know the animal tongues. And I can look within and find the beast that lives in us all. All in the service of one goal: to find and eradicate this plague my people have unleashed on the world.

"You doubt me. I can see it in your eyes. You don't believe in fairy tales." He smiled wolfishly. "Believe this!"

On cue, Maddock pulled back the curtain to the gasps of the crowd.

The taxidermist had been a master at his work; poised in mid-lunge, the creature looked liable to come alive. It stood on its hind legs, easily seven feet tall. Under the thick brown fur, its frame was eerily human, with a narrow pelvis and long torso. Charlie stared at its five-fingered hands, its opposable thumbs tipped with wicked claws.

The massive head was unmistakably lupine. Its skull tapered to a long, tooth-filled muzzle. Yet the glass eyes that stared out from large round sockets were mournful, almost human.

"That is no jackalope," Charlie whispered.

Nell was silent. When Charlie glanced her way, she saw that the blood had drained from Nell's face, leaving her skin the color of ash.

Four

Everyone started murmuring at once. Within moments, the crowd segregated itself into skeptics and believers. The dissenters rocked back on their heels, arms crossed, chins raised. The converted strained forward, trying to get a better look.

"It is real!" Blackfell brushed a hank of hair out of his face to reveal a long white scar cutting across his left brow. "This is the mark the beast left on me. Three years ago, in the Arizona Territory. I tracked the witch for five months, watching his tracks turn from man's to wolf's.

"This is the third skinwalker I have killed, but the first who died in wolf form. When you wound a skinwalker in his beast form, the pain will always force him back to his true shape. But if your aim is true and you can pierce his heart while he wears the beast's skin, he will remain a beast forever in death. Do not think the skinwalker is an easy prey. Many men... red men, white men... have died trying to claim a skinwalker's hide."

"Then how come we've never heard of 'em?" cried a heckler.

"They are a great shame to my people. For we created the skinwalkers, and we cheered them as heroes… until they turned on us. Many fear the wrath of the white man, if he learned what evil we unleashed on him. But I am not afraid." He thumped his chest. "The spirit of the wolf lives inside me, and I am charged with a sacred duty: to hunt down these beasts, in whatever form they take, and cleanse the curse from the earth."

"What forms do they take?" demanded a boy in the front row.

"They prefer the skin of the wolf: the most dangerous of beasts. But they can wear other skins: fox, mountain lion, bear. I have even heard tell of skinwalkers who could wear the feathers of an owl. But always the form is not perfect. See here, how the beast could never be mistaken for a true wolf. The man within can always be seen."

"Didn't I always say it?" a man whispered to his wife. "I knew that were no ordinary coyote I saw."

"Wound a skinwalker as a beast and he will bear the scars as a man!" Blackfell continued. "Find a creature that leaves no footprints in the dust and you'll know it's no ordinary beast! And if you find yourself alone on a road with a dog whose eyes do not glow gold in the dark…" he smiled cruelly, "then you'd better pray you never gave a red man cause to curse you."

"Eyes don't glow…" Nell murmured to herself, reliving her torment at the woodpile.

"Hm?" Charlie turned. "Nell, what is it? You don't look good. You feeling sick?"

Nell couldn't find the words to answer. Her memories of that terrible night long ago were fragmented: she could never quite be sure of the words said, nor the scale of the wolf crouched over her. But she would never forget the beast's eyes.

Several more people had questions, and the Wolf Charmer answered them with the same easy confidence. The doubters were slowly bleeding away, shrinking the crowd to a core of some thirty converts. When the carnival barker judged he had lost a critical density, he skipped down from the stage and waved the guests toward the next entertainment.

"And now, ladies and gentlemen, a demonstration of the healing properties of Chief Great Buffalo's Restorative Cream!"

Faced with the choice, a few of the more timid guests decided to follow Maddock. Blackfell crouched down on the lip of the stage, the better to address those who remained.

"We all carry a beast inside us," he explained. "A totem, a spirit that will guide us. Protect us. By knowing your totem, you learn to better know yourself."

"How?" asked a blushing girl. She could not quite take her eyes off Blackfell's bare torso. "Can you teach us?"

"I can, little sister," Blackfell smiled, promptly a flurry of giggles from the girl, and a glower from the older man chaperoning her. The Wolf Charmer untied a small leather bag from his waistband and set it open on the stage. "For one penny, I can tell you all your animal within."

The mention of further cost spurred three men to leave. The rest began to form a line as men dug in their pockets and women fumbled with their reticules.

"Charlie, you got some change on you?" Nell asked.

"Oh, I'm game if you are. But are you sure you're all right?"

Blackfell took each customer's penny and hand in turn. "Eagle," he pronounced to one man. "Crow," to another. The smitten girl never got her chance; her chaperone yanked her out of the line as soon as he realized she would have to hold the Indian's hand.

"Horse," Blackfell told the man in front of Charlie. "A hardy animal, with the wisdom to know when to submit to the reins and when to run free. You should be very proud. It is a powerful totem."

Charlie stepped up and offered her hand.

"Rooster," Blackfell ruled, with a hint of a smile.

"Rooster?" she repeated in disbelief. "Come on, read it again."

When he would not, Charlie snatched her hand back. "You're telling me everyone else here is getting horses and eagles and I get a chicken?"

"I hear it crowing within you." His lips twitched archly. "It's... quite loud."

Someone nearby snickered. Charlie stalked out of the line, cheeks flaming. When Nell stepped forward, Blackfell must have read the dread in her eyes.

"There's nothing to fear, sister," he said gently, and held out his hand.

Nell paid her penny and placed her palm against his. Blackfell cocked his head and looked at her through narrowed eyes. His dark stare unnerved her. She let her gaze drift up to the mounted monster looming over them. Those eyes were at least glass.

"You've seen one before, haven't you?" Blackfell asked.

Nell started. Reflexively, she made to draw back her hand, but the Wolf Charmer held it fast.

"You have the wolf within you," he murmured.

"What?" Charlie pressed close beside her. "Nell, you saw one of those things? You never told me that!"

"Never told anyone," Nell whispered. It was true; she'd never dared report the wolf attack. Doing so would have required her to explain why she was sprawled in the woodpile after dark. And from the lack of hysteria in the days following that night, her tormentors had obviously decided to hold their tongues as well.

"It didn't look like that one." Nell indicated the mounted specimen. "Not exactly. But it was dark... I couldn't see it that well. I just remember its eyes. Blue eyes."

Behind her, Charlie swore under her breath. Blackfell sprang to his feet and dismissed the remaining spectators.

"I'm sorry, but I must go. The... the spirit is leaving me. Please go enjoy the... uh, buffalo cream. Good night. Go!" he snapped, when the last customers were slow to disperse. "I'm done here!"

He led Nell away from the central yard. The performers' covered wagons were sequestered a short distance from the tents. Five were simple prairie schooners with canvas tops, but the largest was a solid caravan, its wooden sides emblazoned with Frank Maddock's name in bright scrollwork. Blackfell produced a key and unlocked the door.

"We can talk better in here." He helped Nell up the step and into the trailer, but when Charlie tried to follow he moved to block her path.

"Hey, I'm with her," Charlie protested.

"Go find something else to crow about, little rooster. This doesn't concern you."

"Says who?"

"Your pale face."

"She can stay," Nell spoke up. "You can trust her. Please, I'd like her to stay."

Inside the caravan, Blackfell lit a candle and gestured for them to sit. Maddock lived well inside his travelling home; Nell sat in a plush armchair, while Charlie took the leather ottoman. Blackfell knelt on the floor across from them and set the candleholder in the middle of the triangle they formed.

"Tell me everything," he commanded Nell.

"It was… shoot, twelve years ago. I was out fetching some liquor for my stepdaddy."

"Here, in this town?"

"Just down the road in the canyon. And when I was coming home, I… I fell. I was cutting up a back road through the woodpile and I guess I just lost my balance. And when I sat up, it was there. Just… standing over me, all 'What big teeth you have, Grandma.'"

"Oh God," Charlie's hand flew to her mouth. "Is… is that why you've always been afraid of big dogs?"

Nell didn't bother to answer that. Blackfell pressed closer. "What did it look like? You said it was no ordinary wolf."

"I don't know what it was. It wasn't as human-looking as your critter. And it was down on all fours. But it was big and hairy and sorta crouch-backed… and it had really long, pointed ears. Bigger than Garou's. Looked almost like… I don't know, devil horns?" she laughed humourlessly.

"Garou?" Blackfell queried.

"My dog," Charlie spoke up. "He's got a lot of wolf in him."

"You mentioned the eyes."

Nell nodded. "They didn't glow, like you said. And they were blue."

"You could see their color? In the dark?"

"The moon was up," Nell said. "It was pretty bright... reckon it had to be full."

Blackfell nodded thoughtfully. "A witch's magic is always strongest at the full moon."

"The way it looked at me... it was almost like it recognized me."

"It could sense the wolf spirit in you. You said it stood over you. What then?"

"We just... sorta stared at each other. I know you're not supposed to, but I couldn't help it. And it growled a bit and I thought 'This is it.'" But... it turned and ran off. What you said about not leaving tracks... I don't know about that. But the woodpile was just filled with junk, so it should have made a goddawful clatter running away. But it didn't. It just... vanished."

Blackfell studied her face for a long time. Nell found herself growing ever-more uncomfortable. She was used to being mentally undressed by louts and lechers. But this man's eyes were peeling away more than clothes.

"You're holding something back. I can sense it."

"Well, it's all you're getting," Nell hugged her elbows, withdrawing into herself. She bent her head rather than meet his gaze, but it did no good. She could feel him under her skin, probing ever deeper, searching for any chink in her armor.

"How did you really fall?" he asked. Nell's head snapped up in alarm.

"Hey, she told you to leave off!" Charlie protested.

"Someone else was there with you," Blackfell pressed. "Who?"

This time Nell could not look away. She stared at him in helpless silence.

"Tell me," he said, and his gruff voice became warm and comforting.

"The boys." She felt him pull the words out of her, against her will. Her throat ached from trying to hold back the truth. "They were laughing. One grabbed me. He pulled me down. He was going to hurt me."

"Oh Nell," Charlie murmured.

"Then the creature appeared," Blackfell finished for her. "And it drove them away."

Nell nodded.

"And left when its work was finished."

"Finished? I don't—"

"The beast was protecting you," Blackfell explained. "It defended a fellow wolf."

"Fellow wolf?" Charlie asked. "So, you're saying, what? Nell's a skinwalker?"

"One laugh and you're gone," he snapped.

"What are you saying?" Nell demanded. "That I've got some kind of guardian monster?"

Blackfell shook his head. "The skinwalker is an evil thing. If it fled from you, it was because it feared you. It feared your magic. But it has marked you all the same, sister, as another once marked me." He gestured to the scar on his eyebrow. "Your mark runs deeper. It burns... here." He touched Nell's forehead lightly. "Like a beacon. Calling the beast back to you."

"Oh, stop it," Charlie said. "You're just trying to scare us now."

"Why? What would a skinwalker want with me? I never riled up any Navajos. I never even met one of your folk before tonight!"

"The skinwalker will always seek out the wolf charmer. And your beast was not one of my people."

"But you said—"

"Blue eyes," he reminded her. "Your skinwalker is a white man."

~ * ~

Images of fur and fangs filled Nell's dreams that night. She found herself back on the woodpile, screaming in terror as the wolf-man charged towards her. Charlie appeared and leapt between them, but the beast cut her down with a broad swipe of his clawed hand. Then Nell was running, all but flying over the ground, the creature at her heels. She reached the safety of her old house on High Street, only to find her family slaughtered, and Adam Blackfell sitting at the table, eating a bloody steak.

The beast hammered on the door with his massive fists. The banging went on even after she awoke in her narrow cot. Heart pounding, she looked around in confusion. The door groaned against its frame as if it were liable to shatter under the repeated knocks.

"Nell? Nelly, I know you're in there!"

"Oh god," Nell moaned, rolling over. It wasn't a skinwalker; it was worse.

"I heard what you're planning. Are you out of your mind?"

"Go away, Shiloh!" she shouted.

"I ain't gonna let you do it."

She laughed into her pillow. As if he, of all people, could stop her. She raised her head just enough to bark, "You keep hanging around beating on Capital property, they'll send for the marshal to haul you away."

"Good! They can haul both of us away. A stint in jail might teach you to see reason."

"You get me thrown out of here, and I'll just go to Wes that much sooner!"

Blessed silence. She waited as her old flame slowly digested the threat. Finally he turned and stalked off, angrily crunching the gravel underfoot. Nell let out a sigh of relief.

"What do I gotta do to that man to make him leave me alone?" she asked her pillow. Die, like as not. Even then, he would probably pester her gravesite every Sunday, telling her how to run her afterlife, even though he could scarcely plan past his next payday.

Why did I ever put up with him, she wondered. But she knew why. Because he'd been available. Because after vigorously defending her virtue for twenty-five years, she'd decided to give sin a try. She'd wanted to know what it felt like to be courted, to be desired. She'd been a laborer all her life – just for once, she'd wanted to be a woman.

She should have known better. Women were fools. And Shiloh was just like all men – sweet as honey on the surface, but rotten at the core.

Still, she had learned a lot from him: the economics of love, for one – the going rate for a kiss, or a quick grope against the wall. The miserable odds of a woman finding her pleasure when all a man thought about was taking his; the precise ratio of ergot and pennyroyal needed to bring on a bleeding, when sea sponge and lambskin failed. And above all, the need for self-sufficiency.

No one will ever value you more than themselves. You can't afford to think differently.

~ * ~

The walk down to the Benedicts' took her a mere five minutes. With its whitewashed walls and distinctive three-gabled roof of slate-blue shingles, the house stood out among the wooden stables and dull brick dwellings scattered across the shallow terminus of the Gold Canyon. Nell remembered watching the framework go up from the window of the nearby schoolhouse. If someone had told her then that the Benedicts would ever live in such luxury, she would have laughed.

Old Grant Weatherbee had built the house for himself, the same year he'd founded the Crown Point Livery Stables, but as his family grew apace with his business, he'd built a larger – though to Nell's eyes, uglier – brick house set further back from the noise of the road and the smell of the stables. The Benedicts had rented from him for years, until Wes earned enough to buy the deed. Mrs. Weatherbee had just died, and rumour had it Grant let Wes have the house for a steal, on the other understanding that Lucy Benedict would be forever indebted to him. If so, the man learned too late that not all women settled their debts on their backs.

Nell knew there was a certain set of women who would never forgive Mrs. B for breaking Grant Weatherbee's heart. Nell herself preferred to side with those who mocked the old man behind his back for losing a house on speculation. A businessman should have known better.

Nell stopped first at the forge, expecting to find Wes bent over his anvil. But the workshop was deserted, and the forge was still cold. She went around the back of the Benedict house and knocked on the wood frame of the screen door. The door was unlocked, and as the minutes passed without an answer, Nell fought the temptation to let herself in.

Finally Wes appeared, looking bleary-eyed and charmingly disheveled. "Hey, there you are. Sorry for the wait: I was expecting you at the front door. Here, let me get those." He shouldered the door open and took both her bags over her protests. "I'll show you up to your room."

She followed Wes down the narrow hallway, past the kitchen and through the parlor. A quick scan showed the rooms were already feeling Lucy Benedict's absence. Dirty dishes were stacked in the kitchen washbasin, and the parlor stank of wood ash from a poorly swept fireplace.

Nell had never been upstairs before. Above the parlor stairs she found a long hallway filled with light from the large gable windows, and five identical white doors. Wes led her down to the far end of the hall. On the right-hand side, a series of bare wood steps led up to a sixth, unpainted door, and what Nell took to be the attic. She steeled herself for a sweltering garret room, covered in a decade of dust. Instead, Wes opened the last door on the left and showed her into a well-kept bedroom.

It must have been built for one of Grant's children; it had the dimensions and pastel-striped wallpaper of a nursery. The full-sized pine furniture seemed a little too large for the room. And the Benedicts had not scrimped on the amenities. A table-height dresser with vanity mirror shared one narrow wall with a fully-stocked washstand. The bed featured a sturdy frame and a voluminous quilt, made of brightly-colored remnants.

"Hope this'll do," Wes said. "You let me know if you need another chest for your things. I think I've got a footlocker that should fit right under the bed."

Nell stared at him in disbelief. A tart quip was poised on her tongue, but she bit it back at the sight of his hopeful smile, his genuine eagerness to please.

He could really be so sweet when he was sober. It reminded her of the boy he'd been, when they'd both lived in a simpler world.

"Should do just fine," she said.

"Suppose I should give you a little while to get settled."

"Time enough for that later. Figure you ought to show me to my patient first." Then, worried she sounded too brusque, Nell added, "If she's receiving, that is."

"Oh, she'll be glad for the company. Just don't let her hear you call her your patient."

All weekend, Nell couldn't help but wonder if Wes was exaggerating his mother's state, simply to make his offered charity easier to swallow. She was disabused of that notion the moment Wes let her into the master bedroom.

The room reeked of camphor and laudanum. Lucy Benedict lay propped up in bed, cocooned in a heavy wool dressing gown and several blankets. The curtains were drawn tight around the gabled window, but her haggard state was visible even in the gloom. She had lost weight since Nell had last seen her; her round face was tired and lined. The luxuriant dark hair Nell had only ever seen meticulously coiffed hung over her shoulder in a limp braid. Her breathing was a labored rasp through parched lips.

"Nell," Lucy looked up at her, and a flicker of the old light danced in her blue eyes. "Honey, it's so good to see you again."

Nell knelt down at her bedside and took her cool hand. "How are you doing, Mrs. B?"

"Oh, don't you start fussing, now!" She withdrew her hand with a peevish cluck of her tongue. "Everyone acts like I'm at death's door. Oh, but I do appreciate it, your coming in to help Wes out this next month. I hope it won't put you out too much. I should be back on my feet again by November."

Nell glanced at Wes, who shook his head imperceptibly.

"It's that dreadful – Doc Sheppard's fault," Lucy went on, stopping to catch her breath every few words. "But – it seems my son trusts him – more than he trusts his own mother. So I've become a prisoner in my own bedroom."

"Men ain't always the brightest of folk," Nell agreed. "But they mean well, by and large. Sometimes you gotta just humor them."

"Well, if I have to have a jailer," she glared up at her son pointedly. "I'm glad it's you."

"It won't be so bad." Nell insisted. "Think of it as a nice vacation without all that hassle of packing. And don't you worry about the house. I know just how you like everything run. Now, how's about we let some light in here?"

"Doc says—" Wes began.

"Oh, yes please! And could you open the window, dear? I think I'll go mad if I have to spend the next month stinking of camphor."

Nell went to the window, ignoring Wes's protests. Lucy drew in a deep rattling breath of satisfaction as the morning sun hit her face. Next Nell propped the window open, and clean air rushed in with an audible puff.

"But Doc says the dust—"

"When your ma's so desperate for fresh air that the horse manure next door smells good to her, dust is the least of your worries," Nell countered.

Lucy smiled triumphantly at her son. "Thank you, Nell. And maybe you could see your way to liberate my sewing from *certain persons*."

"Sewing?" Nell looked at Wes for guidance. He could only shrug awkwardly.

"Doc said the full rest cure."

"I've got bronchitis, not hysteria!" Lucy exclaimed. "He doesn't even want me reading, Nell—can you believe that?"

"You're supposed to be taking it easy, Ma."

"Then why don't you just dope me with laudanum for the next month straight?"

"It's getting mighty tempting!"

Suddenly, six-fifty a week seemed perfectly reasonable. Nell hastened back to Lucy's bedside, stepping between mother and son. "Hold your fire, now. Wes, your ma is gonna go stir crazy in here if she doesn't have something to help her pass the time. I'll find you your sewing, Mrs. B. But hand-stitching only," she added. "No hunching over the Singer. And I can read to you in the afternoons if you'd like. There's no need to be wrecking your eyes squinting at type."

A quick glance at both Benedicts suggested it was an acceptable compromise. Nell could taste the triumph on her tongue.

"Now, what have you had to eat so far, Mrs. B?"

"Oh, I'll be quite all right until lunchtime—"

"I made her oatmeal but she wouldn't touch it," Wes protested in an injured tone.

"Honestly, Wesley, I know you're trying to help, but it's like eating glue—"

"How's about I make something up?" Nell encouraged. "Toast and some tea with honey? And maybe a little bit of egg. Nothing too heavy, I know," she said, before Wes could protest. "Lots of hot drinks, that's the key. You're looking awful parched."

She knew how to strike the right balance of cajoling and commands. Lucy Benedict nodded gratefully and settled back against the pillows. "Not too much honey, mind..." she murmured, meek as child.

"You're a godsend," Wes whispered, as they tiptoed from the bedroom together. "Honestly, Nell, I don't know what I'd do without you."

Heat filled her chest, a burning knot more heady and thrilling than a sweetheart's kiss could ever inspire. This must be what normal women felt, she imagined, when they won their gold rings at last, or when they held their firstborns in their arms. The ultimate validation: to be utterly indispensable to another human being.

Five

She had no idea how much she meant to him.

Wes Benedict sat at the table, nursing his sandwich, watching Nell clean up in the kitchen out of the corner his eye. It took some getting used to, eating alone while she busied herself with her chores. He had invited her to eat with him, her first day at the house, but she had politely demurred. She was used to taking her meals alone; she claimed it was more professional. As if there weren't nearly thirty years of history between them.

Now she moved about the kitchen with the efficient stride of an army sergeant, stacking dishes to wash and wrapping food to store. She hummed a little bit of ragtime well-loved in the dance halls. *There'll be a hot time in the old town tonight.* The jaunty tune had the effect of turning her movements into a dance.

It was a particular gift she had: no matter the task, she always seemed to carry herself with a silent dignity and a fluid grace. She could make scrubbing tiles seem stately. When she turned to take out the slop bucket, the hem of her skirt snapped like a flag in the wind, revealing a flash of pristine white petticoats.

She'd been his little sister, his childhood sweetheart and personal gadfly; his oldest friend and harshest critic. Now she was his maid. The injustice of it was enough to turn his stomach.

The fault was his. He'd never deny it, though he had spent years trying to convince himself that he'd had no choice. She'd been a child of twelve, yet she looked at him with a woman's eyes. He'd been sixteen and on the brink of manhood. Everyone was beginning to whisper. Worse, with each passing year, his monthly affliction had only grown worse. He didn't know how much longer he could have hidden the truth from her.

So he had pushed her away. Better to cause her a lesser pain, in order to spare her a larger one. At least, that's what he told himself. He'd worked hard, trying to frame his action as some grand sacrifice. But in his heart, he knew better. His whole life he'd taken the easiest path, the coward's way out.

He found himself thinking of the last time he'd fought with Nell. It had been late spring, and she'd been raging at him. For what, he couldn't quite remember – wasting his life, meddling in hers; their screaming matches were always variations on the same theme. But he would never forget the words she'd thrown at him. They still cut deep.

"Man could be a goddamn saint," he'd accused, *"and you'd find something wrong with him."*

"No, he'd just have to be a man. Not some thirty-year-old boy too lazy or too scared to grow up!"

He wanted to be a man. He wanted, at long last, to be worthy of her. But doubt gnawed at him. His whole life, he'd been a monster in hiding. Maybe it was too late to be anything else.

"Not hungry?"

Lost in thought, he hadn't noticed her approach. "Guess not," he said. It was true. What little he had eaten sat like a lump of stone in his gut.

Nell reached down to remove the plate, and her knuckles brushed against the back of his hand. Wes flinched violently at the unexpected touch. He yanked his hand into his lap and made a fist.

"Sorry," Nell murmured. He could hear the edge in her voice, razor sharp.

"My fault. Just... a little jumpy today, I guess."

The muscles of his fingers continued to contract painfully. He clenched his fist until the spasm passed up his arm and disappeared. He knew it was only the beginning. The moon was nearly full.

~ * ~

Something was wrong with Wes. Nell could practically smell it on the air: the stink of cold sweat and fresh guilt. She was no fool; when she'd agreed to the job, she'd known what she was taking on.

The first few days had passed like a dream. After years of keeping a hotel fully swept, laundered and stocked with supplies, keeping one house in order was almost child's play. Even the cooking proved easy enough. Both Benedicts had simple tastes, and Nell's childhood lessons soon came back to her.

As for her tyrannical mistress, Lucy Benedict proved a model patient – so long as Nell kept Wes out of sight. She took her medicine without protest, and kept to her room as ordered. But no amount of persuasion could keep her from spending the afternoons sitting at the open window, knitting needles clicking as she watched the traffic bustling up and down the canyon road. Nell often joined her at the window seat, her mending work in her lap. There were moments, when Lucy's cough was sitting dormant in her chest, that Nell could pretend she was not so much a nursemaid as a hired companion.

She knew the idyll wouldn't last. Still, she wished Wes could have lasted the week before sneaking off to the saloon to pickle his liver. She'd learned to forgive him for his adolescent cruelties: his past bigotry and his utter selfishness. But she would never forgive him for the damage he kept doing to himself.

The worst was she had actually *believed* him, this last time he'd sworn to mend his ways. For years she had grown accustomed to his pattern of penance and relapse. But he had been looking so healthy all summer: bright-eyed and straight-backed, almost boyish again. Nell had allowed herself to hope.

In vain, to judge by the tremors in his hands he was trying so desperately to hide. His last bender must have been a doozy. Most drunks who lived to his age had learned to pace themselves. She hadn't heard him sneak out after she'd gone to bed, but that meant little. His bedroom was on the ground floor, just off the back hallway. He could come and go through the yard behind the house like a thief in the night. Or he could have a case of whiskey hidden under his bed; likely that was why he wouldn't let her into his room to change his linens or empty his pot.

If Wes was jittery at luncheon, he was unbearable at supper. He staggered in from the smithy, looking as wrung-out as a washrag. His face had taken on a jaundiced cast, and dark circles ringed his eyes. He seemed to have aged five years in five hours.

He barely touched his food. The soup was too salty, he said. The bread was too dry. When she opened the window the breeze was too cold, but when she closed it, he was suffocating. When he announced he was going to take the air, Nell was aghast.

"You going drinking?" she challenged.

"God, you're like a dog with a bone over that. Can't a man take a walk in peace?"

She heard the warning in his voice. She knew she ought to hold her tongue. But she found herself chasing him down the hallway, pleading, "Just stay in tonight, will you? You don't look good."

"Too stuffy in here, is all. I just need to clear my head."

"You need to go to bed. You look ready to fall over."

He shot her a murderous look. "I ain't paying you to be *my* nursemaid!"

He might as well have struck her. Her head snapped back under the force of his words. Wes reached for his coat, and underneath the sullen knit of his brow, Nell swore she read a cold satisfaction in his eyes.

She wanted to strike him. She had in the past, more than once. But he wasn't paying her for that either. She had to remember how they stood now.

"No, you ain't," she said stiffly. "But you keep this up, I might ask for a raise."

"You do what you gotta," he said at last, in a childish grumble. His coat hanging askew on his shoulders, he staggered out into the evening, slamming the door behind him for emphasis. Nell fought the urge to yank it open, just for the pleasure of slamming it herself.

Goddamn him! The curse pressed against her clenched teeth, trying to burst free. But she was angrier with herself. She kept letting him hurt her. And she kept being surprised by it.

Bile burned her throat. She was ready to bolt upstairs and pack her bags. She'd rather starve in the gutter than take another cent from Wes Benedict's clammy hand.

Instead she went to Wes's room. She rifled through his chest of drawers; she looked under his mattress; she dug into the pile of dirty laundry at the foot of the bed. She'd hoped for empty bottles or pillboxes; at that moment nothing would have given her greater pleasure than to turn up a brick of opium. But all she found were old socks and a dog-eared men's magazine. She flipped through it idly, hoping for a laugh. But she had heard all the dirty jokes before, and the photographs of fair-skinned, buxom nudes depressed her.

The clock in the parlor began to ring. Time for Mrs. B's mustard plaster, Nell remembered.

Lucy Benedict was sitting up in bed knitting, her empty supper tray at her bedside. "Least someone likes my cooking," Nell remarked as she cleaned up. "And I thought we agreed no fiddly work after dark? You're gonna hurt your eyes, squinting in the lamp light."

"The problem's my chest, not my eyes," Lucy said. But she laid the knitting aside all the same. "Did I hear the door slam a while back?"

The moment called for a pleasing lie, but Nell had no talent for deceit. "Wes... went out," she admitted, as she spread the pungent mustard paste over a folded cloth. "I think he wanted a drink."

The smell of the plaster prompted a phlegmy cough from the patient. "Well, can't begrudge a man a little company on a Saturday night."

The thought nettled her. She tried not to show it. Lucy only meant the company of his fellow drinking men, coming together after a long week's work. But Nell remembered Lester's parting shot about Wes being well-known at the cathouses. She wondered if he had a regular girl, or if he didn't care who was under him, so long as he found relief.

"He should get married," Nell found herself saying. "Reckon it would settle him: a wife and kids."

She didn't believe a word of it. Marriage and breeding had never changed anyone for the better, in her experience. Men would always do as they wanted, and their women and children would endure as best they could. But she knew it was what decent people were supposed to want; a family out of a painted Christmas card, smiling faces gathered around the hearth.

"I don't think Wes is the marrying type, dear. Maybe it's for the best."

Nell motioned for Lucy to unbutton her nightgown. The older woman complied with visible reluctance. Their mutual discomfort had become routine by now. Lucy bared her skin to the breastbone, all the while looking away miserably. Nell hastened to cover the exposed flesh with the plaster, all the while trying not to stare. She had never seen skin so pale: blue-veined and paper-thin. Wherever the plaster touched, a red rash bloomed like a sunburn. The sight put Nell in mind of a skinned chicken.

The fumes made Lucy cough violently. Nell forced an encouraging smile. "Just means it's working," she murmured. "Keep breathing deep now. Gotta dry up all that muck in your lungs."

Lucy clenched her jaw and nodded. When the phlegm started to move, Nell helped her sit up and held the bowl for her while she hawked and spat. When she was done, Nell wiped the spittle from her lips and pretended not to notice the tears welling in her eyes.

"What did you mean about Wes?" Nell asked gently.

For a long moment, the only sound was of Lucy's laboured breathing. "Wes has... a wildness inside him," she said at length.

"Something that can never be settled. He holds it in when he can. But when it gets loose, it scares him. I think… it will scare you, too."

"Does it scare you?"

The question prompted a fleeting smile. "No. Never. But I'm his mother." She patted Nell's hand, and her expression grew solemn once more. "You should be prepared. It's going to get worse, before it gets better."

The gravity in her voice set off a chill down Nell's smile. She forced herself to shrug. "I ain't the fainting type."

"And you'll stand by him, no matter what?" Lucy's gaze was intense, searching. Nell wondered what sins the word "wildness" could cover, and again she fought the urge to shudder.

She wanted to pull her hand free. She wanted to find her courage and say there were some things she could not forgive, not even for six-fifty a week. She wanted to cry *I am not Wes Benedict's dog!* and actually believe it.

Instead she smiled weakly and murmured, "Don't you fret, Mrs. B. I ain't going anywhere."

~ * ~

When she finished putting Lucy to bed, Nell dampened the fires and locked up the house. Then she sat up in the darkness, waiting for Wes to come home.

She gave up around midnight. Loyalty had limits, weighed against a good night's sleep. In the privacy of her bedroom she slowly undressed. Without the weight of her petticoats, her entire center of gravity seemed to shift. She peeled off her corset and drew in a deep breath, feeling her rib cage expand. She stretched her arms over her head, then bent to touch her toes. When the muscles in her back felt hot under her skin, she stood tall and thrust her shoulders back, admiring her straight spine in the vanity mirror. Too many girls expected their steel ribs to do all the work for them, but strip them of their armor and they had the sagging breasts and humped backs of old women.

She washed quickly with icy water, then pulled on her nightgown before she began to shiver. She rubbed palmfuls of cold cream on her skin until it shone the color of burnished walnut. She sat in front of the vanity mirror and began to take down her hair. When she was done, her face was almost lost behind a great cloud of black coils.

Her mother never understood why she bothered. Ruth Johns wore her hair tightly braided and pinned against her scalp, and only took it down for its monthly wash. Hair was only a woman's crowning glory when it was properly subdued.

But Nell treasured her nightly undressing. She loved the sudden feeling of lightness, and the tingling in her scalp as it shrugged off the weight of the pins. She loved her hair's texture: how its curls tightened before her eyes, after a long day shackled in plaits and pomade. Above all, she loved its scale: its wild, unfettered femininity. She only felt truly beautiful with her hair unbound.

Her bed was the most comfortable she had ever known, yet despite the late hour, sleep eluded her. She tensed at every creak in the timbers, wondering which sound would herald Wes's return. At length she drifted into fitful dreams of doors breaking in, and Wes standing over her bed, smelling of whiskey and lust, and some undefinable animal wildness.

She resisted at first, just enough to ease her conscience. Then she surrendered to his superior strength, as he pushed up her skirts and took her so roughly she thought her bones might break.

A distant crash startled her awake. She rolled over on her side, drawing up her legs and hugging her knees, determined to hold onto that flush of heat between her thighs, before shame could curdle it. Of all her dreams, no other felt so good at the time, nor left her feeling so wretched the next day.

She heard the noise again; a clatter of wood and metal. She hadn't dreamed it after all. Taking care to be quiet, Nell climbed out of bed and lit her candle. The little clock read three-thirty.

Nell looked out into the hallway, but the second floor was still. Mrs. Benedict's bedroom door was still closed, and when she put her ear to it, Nell could hear the halting snores of a congested sleeper.

She descended to the ground floor. A single light was flickering in the kitchen. Her heart in her throat, Nell tiptoed across the parlor. If it were a prowler, she could only hope he was a coward. Shading her candle with one hand, she peeked around the wall, then let out a strangled laugh.

"Wes? What are you doing?"

Wes was marooned in a sea of spilled tins and boxes. He'd been trying to peer into the overhead cupboards by the light of a dying oil lamp, but he'd only succeeded in knocking half the dry goods to the floor.

He looked terrible. His skin shone under the oil lamp, clammy with sweat. As Nell drew nearer she saw that he was shivering.

"Where have you been?" She was torn between compassion and rage. She forced him into a chair then knelt to examine him. She was close enough to smell his breath, and it had the sour note of bile. But to her surprise, she couldn't smell any alcohol. When she touched his forehead, it was scalding to the touch.

"You're burning up!" She went straight to the water pump and wet a dishcloth. He flinched when she pressed it to his forehead. "Have you had anything to eat?"

At the mere mention of food, his throat tightened visibly, and he clenched his jaw tight against a wave of nausea. "All right, then." Nell got to her feet and went to light the stove. She filled a saucepan with water and set it to boil. Wes watched as she moved through the mess he had made, collecting supplies.

"What're you doing?"

"Making you some ginger tea." She chopped up the root with a practiced hand.

"Aw, I don't think I can keep anything down."

"You'll keep this down."

The water began to boil. Nell dropped the ginger into the saucepan then clapped a lid over the steam. "There now. Just take down the fire a bit...." She glanced over to see Wes watching her with an amused expression.

"What?"

"Your hair."

Belatedly, she remembered her immodest state, and her skin burned with embarrassment. There was nothing she could do for her nightgown, save for throwing a dishrag over her shoulders. But her hands went to her hair, hastily compressing it into a clumsy bun.

"It's okay," Wes said quickly. "I don't mind if you don't. Honest. It's just: I forgot how...big it gets."

"Yeah," she said archly. "Like big ol'tumbleweed, huh?"

Wes didn't seem to hear the bitterness in her voice. Nor did he remark on her state of undress. Somehow, that only made her feel more uncomfortable. Standing as she was between Wes and the oil lamp, she had no doubt he could make out her silhouette through her nightgown. Nell felt her shoulders hunching, her arms crossing over her breasts. But when she stole a glance at Wes, she saw neither revulsion nor appraisal in his face.

He'd notice a white woman parading around half-naked in front of him, Nell thought peevishly.

But Wes was still transfixed by the puzzle of her hair. "How do you even get it into those two little braids?" he asked.

"*Little?*" Nell raised an eyebrow. "First of all: those braids weigh something like a quarter-pound each. Cut one off and I'd wager you could club someone to death with it."

Wes laughed. "Now there's a sight I'd pay to see. And second?"

"What?"

"You said 'first of all.' And second?"

"And second: hairpins and ties, a quart of good pomade and a half-hour every morning – that's how." She turned her back on him, to stir the simmering tea. "You think on that, the next time you decide you can't even be bothered to trim your whiskers."

He smiled bashfully at that, and rubbed his bristly jaw. "Hey, remember those girls they used to have in the sideshows? The white girls with the big black hair. What did they call those?"

Nell stopped stirring. "Circassian Beauties," she said, her voice clipped.

"Their hair never looked as good as yours."

"'Course not. It wasn't real."

"Didn't... didn't I have a nudie card of one of those Circassian girls? And I gave it to you. Remember?"

Nell kept her back turned, so he couldn't see her face. "Not really."

"Sure, I had a whole pack of dirty cards. Got 'em from Grant. And you said you'd tell on me. You must have been... nine, ten? You made me give you one to shut you up. Remember?"

"Maybe," she remarked idly. "Sounds kinda familiar."

"Wonder what happened to it?"

"Reckon Momma found it and threw it out." She brought him his tea. The cool cloth had revived him somewhat, but he still looked drawn and haggard.

"Don't rush now," she warned. "Just drink it slow."

Wes smiled gratefully. "Thanks."

"You need anything else?"

"Naw... I'll be all right. I just... need a good night's sleep."

"Y'always did have trouble sleeping." A thought occurred to her. "You get these fevers a lot too?"

He nodded. "I take quinine. Helps sometimes. But it always comes back."

"You mean an ague? Like... malaria?" Unconsciously, Nell took a step back. Wes saw the fear in her eyes and gave a helpless shrug.

"Something like that."

Slowly, Nell made the connection: his frequent tremors, his foul temper and slurred speech, the trips to the saloon when he couldn't bear it any longer. "You... don't shake 'cause you drink, do you? You drink 'cause you shake. Wes, why don't you ever say anything? The whole town thinks you're a drunk."

"Better that than diseased."

"Don't talk like that. If you've got agues it's not your fault." She thought of the many times she had shamed and rebuked him over the years, and she felt sick with guilt. Wes only shrugged again.

"I still drink," he admitted. "Not as much as you think... but more than I ought to. Sometimes, it's the only thing that'll work."

"And there's nothing more than you can do? Can Doc Sheppard—"

"No! You can't tell anyone. Please, promise me. Not a word. I don't want anyone to know. I don't need the attention. And I don't need the... pity."

Nell nodded. She knew how sour pity tasted. But Wes was not yet satisfied. "Promise me," he repeated gravely.

"I promise, Wesley," she said, equally solemn. "Not a word."

His face broke out into a broad grin that crinkled the corners of his eyes. "Wesley. Can't remember the last time you called me that."

She looked away, uncomfortable. His smile always had that effect on her. "I dunno, probably the last time you called me Eleanor." Looking for something to do, she bent down to start picking up the spilled tins.

"Aw, just leave 'em," Wes said. "It's my mess. I can clean up in the morning."

"It *is* morning."

"It can wait until sunup. You go back to bed. I'll be fine."

"You sure?"

"Go on. I've kept you up long enough already."

The kindly thing, she knew, would be to protest, and stay with him until he was ready to sleep. But she saw the stubborn set of Wes's shoulders as he breathed in the steam off his tea, and she knew sometimes the kindly thing wasn't wanted.

She picked up her candle and turned to go. Wes called her back.

"Nell? I know tomorrow's supposed to your day off. But... could you maybe take it Monday instead? Just in case I need help... with Ma."

She saw what it cost him to ask. "Sure. You sleep well, now."

Back in her room, she closed the door and set the candle down at her vanity. She kept her duffel bags under the bed, empty but for a small tin strongbox. Nell took out the box and unlocked it. Amid the coins and keepsakes, she found a battered postcard. Its corners had worn down to nubs, and it was creased in the middle, the scar of a rip Nell had painstakingly mended.

Nell studied the faded pornography under the candlelight. The Circassian Beauty stared back at her, a knowing half-smile on her lips.

~ * ~

He had to tell her.

Wes had scarcely slept all night. He'd kept his tea down, and even managed to swallow a few mouthfuls of soda cracker. But the pounding in his head and the ache in his limbs wouldn't grant him a moment's peace. When he finally crawled under the covers just before sunrise, he was lost in a dazed stupor, somewhere between awareness and true sleep.

Nell came in to check on him at one point. He remembered the touch of her hand to his brow: the rough skin of her knuckles, the sweet smell of her pomade still clinging to her fingertips. He'd tried to speak to her—he was certain he had—but she had only made a shushing sound and piled another quilt atop him.

He got to his feet around noon, but the short walk to the kitchen left him exhausted. When Nell caught him trying to brew coffee, she promptly sat him down and made fresh ginger tea instead.

She brought him some dry toast next. His stomach was painfully empty, but his throat closed up with every swallow, and it took him forever to clean his plate. Then Nell put him back to bed, ignoring his protests. "You just sleep all you want. I'll get you in time for supper."

He didn't sleep. He couldn't. But he lay in darkness, rehearsing what he would say to her, when he couldn't delay any longer. He slept in brief snatches, waking each time to a blinding headache and a racing pulse. At teatime he forced himself to get up and walk, to ease the ache in his muscles. He found Nell at the kitchen stove, brooding over a pot of chicken stock. The sky outside was painted in vivid brushstrokes of orange.

"Ah, thought the smell might get you up," Nell began cheerfully. But when she turned to face him, the smile fell from her lips.

He knew he looked a fright. His shirt was untucked and misbuttoned, and he had rolled his sleeves over his elbows. He followed her gaze to his bared forearms, covered in wiry hair and streaked with long white scratch-marks. When he tugged his sleeves down to his wrists, he noticed his knuckles had sprouted coarse brown hairs too. He rubbed his cheek to find the stubble had become a dense beard.

"Nell... there's something you gotta know. No, leave the soup," he said when she turned back to the stove. "This is important."

He took her hands in his, felt her recoil at the heat coming off his skin. He began to lead her towards the parlor. "I been keeping things from you for years. About me... and my family, and my agues."

"Well, shoot, it weren't none of my business," Nell began uncertainly.

"I wanted to tell you. But I was afraid you wouldn't understand."

The edges of her lips began to twitch. Clearly, she wasn't sure whether she ought to smile or not. Her hands turned restless between his palms. She tried to wriggle free, but he held her fast.

"This sickness I got... it's bad. Something worse than agues. It... shoot, it turns me inside out. Changes me." He mustered a pained smile. "I mean, look at me, I'm sprouting fur!"

Nell tutted nervously. "Ain't as bad as all that, surely. Come on, Wes. Let me go light a lamp—"

"I don't want you to be afraid."

This time his words reached her. Her eyes widened; her lips pressed together tightly. "Your ma said I'd be afraid. Wes—why should I ever be afraid of you? Why won't you let me go?"

"Because I need you to listen." But before he could say more, a spasm of pain gripped his abdomen. It forced the breath from his lungs and forced him to his knees. He pulled her down with him. She stumbled to keep from stepping on her skirts.

"Wes! Please—where does it hurt? What do you need?"

"Listen to me—"

"I'm getting the doctor. I don't care what you say—"

His hands squeezed tighter, silencing her. "He can't help me. I'm changing! And in a minute you're gonna want to go running out of this house. But I want you to promise me that you won't. Whatever happens, I want you to promise me: you'll stay here until morning."

Her breath came in shallow gasps. "What's – what's going to happen? What are you going to do?"

"No matter what I look like, I'm still me. You gotta remember that."

The pain in his limbs was no longer the ache of sore muscles, but an agony he could feel in his very bones. He let out a cry from deep in his throat, and it rang like a bestial howl in his ears.

"Please let me go," Nell begged.

"Promise you'll stay!"

"Oh, God, Wes, your arms!"

He followed her gaze down to his forearms. The wiry hairs were standing straight up, and the flesh beneath rippled with tiny tremors. He released her hands; he fumbled with the buttons of his shirt. But his fingers wouldn't obey him. They curled inward with a crunch of breaking bones.

He struggled out of his shirt and suspenders. Nell gave a fearful sob. By the horror in her wide eyes, he knew his transformation was well underway. "Don't be afraid," he tried to say, but his lips could scarcely form the words. His teeth were too large for his mouth. He could feel his jawbone coming unhinged.

He clawed at his waistband, trying to unbutton his jeans. His hands were useless lumps. He looked up at Nell one last time, willing her to meet his eyes.

Don't be afraid.

Then his arms lurched out of their sockets and the bones of his face shattered and reassembled themselves into a long, narrow muzzle. His back arched out, then snapped back into shape with an agonizing whiplash. He bucked and writhed to free himself of the constrictive clothing. With a bestial yowl, he dropped on all fours, and when his head came up again, there was nothing human left in him.

Six

Nell stared in silent terror. She could feel her heart lurch in her throat.

Wes was gone. In his place was a large red wolf, struggling out of his jeans. It teetered on shaky legs and shook its great head repeatedly, whimpering softly.

A small sound escaped Nell's lips, little more than a whistle. The wolf looked up. Long ears went back against the dome of its skull and its lip curled back to reveal a pink tongue and gnashing white teeth. Nell clapped her hand over her mouth to stifle a scream.

It had blue eyes. Wes's eyes.

Oh God...

She was seventeen years old again, back at the woodpile, staring down the maw of a monster. Blackfell had been right all along. The skinwalker had come back for her.

What big eyes you have, Grandma...

Woman and wolf stared at each other, deadlocked in mutual fear. Then a hoarse voice called down from the second floor.

"Wes?"

The wolf's head swung about, and its ears went up. Lucy Benedict staggered into view at the head of the stairs. At the sight of the massive wolf, a smile came to her bloodless lips.

"Come here, Wesley."

"Mrs. B, don't—" Nell began in vain. The wolf took up the stairs at a run. Her skirts still tangled about her heels, Nell could only watch as Lucy knelt and spread her arms wide.

She thought the wolf would bowl her over. But it slowed respectfully at the top step and greeted Lucy with a puppyish whine and a lowered tail. The foaming pink tongue lapped at her jawline eagerly, while Lucy sputtered and giggled.

"Oh, there's my good boy. Yes, I love you, too." She seized either side of the wolf's massive skull and tussled with it as Nell had seen Charlie do with Garou. At length the creature calmed, and Lucy lifted her head to gaze down at Nell.

"Are you all right?"

Nell groped behind her, trying to find the doorknob. At length she grasped it and used it to haul herself to her feet. Her throat worked frantically to produce some sound. A half-dozen different retorts crossed her mind, but she couldn't make her lips work to say them.

"That's Wes," she managed at length, pointing at the wolf.

"Yes, of course it is," Lucy said patiently. She rose on unsteady legs, and the effort left her gasping for breath. "Would you be a dear and help me back to bed?"

Her sense of duty triggered, Nell moved in a daze towards the stairs. She studiously avoided the wolf's questioning gaze as she gave Lucy Benedict her arm.

~ * ~

"Why didn't you tell me?" Nell asked, as she tucked Lucy back under the covers. "I don't mean riddles. All this talk of 'something wild in him'—how the heck was I supposed to know what you really meant?"

The older woman's smile was pitying. "Would you have believed me?"

I'd have called you a raving loon, she admitted inwardly. Then a more frightening thought occurred to her. *Maybe I'm the loon. Maybe I'm already locked away, doped up on morphine and talking to the walls.*

Nell cast a nervous glance at the red wolf lying placidly on the braided rug by the foot of the bed. "Is it really him?" she asked, as if she hadn't seen him change shape before her eyes.

"It's really him," Lucy confirmed.

"Is it—how long is he gonna stay like that?"

"Until the moon sets. Then he'll be human again."

As if in reply, the wolf gave a forlorn whimper and shifted on his side. He scratched his ear with his hind leg, then twisted around to gnaw an itch on his back. Nell wrinkled her nose in disgust.

"Why does he do it?"

"He doesn't have a choice! You saw what he goes through. Do you honestly think he wants this to keep happening?"

"No," Nell murmured, chastened.

"It's like an ague," Lucy continued. "The fever rises and cools; there's nothing for it. All we can do is keep him calm and comfortable. Get through the night, then brace ourselves for the next time."

"The next time?"

"The full moon."

A laugh rose in Nell's throat. She tried to quell it, but it came out as a nervous hiccup. Startled, Wes looked up from the rug. The way his brow knit in confusion struck her as undeniably human, and she covered her mouth against a flurry of hysterical giggles.

Lucy did not seem to see the humor in the situation. "Have a seat, Nell. You look like you need it."

Stumbling backward, Nell dropped down onto the bedside chair. Wes padded over to investigate, tail wagging slowly from side to side. Nell winced and withdrew into herself, her arms crossed and her feet drawn up from the floor.

"Oh, he won't hurt you," Lucy assured her.

"What—what does he want? What do I do?"

"Give him your hand."

"What?"

"Hold out your hand. Let him smell you."

Nell extended a trembling hand. She felt the cold wetness of the wolf's nose bump against her knuckles, followed by a hot stroke of his tongue. Nell yelped and withdrew her hand.

"Wes!" Lucy cried. "Oh, he didn't catch a tooth, did he? He doesn't mean to—"

"No, no." Nell wiped her hand. "He… just gave me a kiss, that's all."

Lucy let out a sigh of relief. "A Southern gentleman. Good to know I raised that boy right."

"Does he know who I am? Does he know who he is?"

"Oh yes. He's still Wes, under all that fur. Just a little wilder."

Wes set his chin against Nell's knee and blinked up at her, human eyes staring out from a lupine face. "Can he understand us?" Nell asked. Part of her expected the wolf to bob his head.

"Somewhat. Maybe not all our words. But he'll get the gist of it. Actually, I think he understands a lot more than he ever lets on. The question is how much he remembers come morning."

"How did he get like this? If it's a sickness, he must have caught it from somewhere." Her thoughts turned to a rabid dog's bite, or some heathen ritual under a harvest moon—Adam Blackfell chanting in a foreign tongue.

"He was born with it."

Nell stared at her in disbelief.

"He was two weeks old at his first full moon. High fever and shakes—I thought I was going to lose him to apoplexy. Then, before I knew it… he became a little wolf pup in my arms. And he's been doing it every month ever since."

"But when we were kids… I—I would have noticed!" Nell insisted. "I was at your house every day!"

Lucy's calm smile was maddening. "But never after dark. Never after the moonrise. He had the fevers then too—really, it's just the first stage in the transformation. Wolf's blood runs hotter than ours. But they weren't as severe. And by the time you were old enough to take notice, well, you were off at school by then. It was no harder to hide from you than from anyone else."

"From... how did you hide it? You lived on High Street—cheek to jowl with everyone!"

"We managed. In summers, I'd smuggle him out of the house before sundown... and no one would notice that we wouldn't come home until the next dawn. Winters were harder." She bent her head in remorse. "Sometimes, I'm ashamed to say, I fed him some meat dipped in laudanum and let him sleep it off. And those times Wes does drink to ease the pain... I suppose I was the one who gave him the idea.

"But it got better when we moved out here. Sneak out of the house on clear nights—there's a series of gullies just south of American Flat where the land folds up and swallows whatever sound you make. And there he can run to his heart's content. He's a bright boy. He knows to stay away from the city lights."

Lucy held out her hand, and Wes moved to his mother's bedside. When she began to scratch behind his long ears, his tail thumped against the bed and he let out a deep whuff of satisfaction.

"I always used to tell him: 'We got each other. We don't need anyone else.'" The sorrow crept back into her tired eyes. "When you're young, you think you'll always be strong."

"I wasn't brought on to take care of you," Nell realized. "I'm here to take care of Wes."

"I can't handle him like I used to. And at my age, it's only going to get harder. He deserves better than having to chain himself in a cellar every month. He deserves someone... who cares for him."

"I don't even like dogs," Nell mumbled. She felt a pain in the palms of her hands and she realized she was clenching her fists.

"Oh, Nell, the times he'd beg me to let him tell you," Lucy went on, as if she hadn't heard her. "We used to fight about it constantly. He wanted so much for you to know. But I forbade it. I told him— we couldn't risk it. I made him—" a cough cut her off, and she plucked a fresh handkerchief from the nightstand. By the time she'd cleared her throat and spat into the kerchief, Nell knew what she was going to say.

"I made him push you away."

Nell felt her face growing hot. "But now you need my help. Now I'm trustworthy."

"You're upset."

"I got a right to be!"

She hadn't raised her voice to Mrs. B since she was a toddler. Wes swung around, shoulders hunching like a whipped puppy. But Lucy was impassive, composed in the face of Nell's anger. Even ailing, she was solid as bedrock.

"You didn't deserve to carry this burden. You don't now. If it were up to me, we never would have brought you on." She glanced down at the wolf. "But it's not up to me anymore. I have to make my peace with that. Did he make the right choice, Nell? Are you glad you know?"

"I ain't 'glad' about any of this!"

Lucy narrowed her eyes. "I'll understand if you don't want to stay on," she said, every word dripping with frosty censure. "I warned Wes it was too much to ask of you."

"Wait! I didn't say I was leaving. Look, I promised Wes I wasn't going anywhere until we got a chance to talk this out properly. And you oughta know I'd never leave you two in the lurch."

She swore Wes understood every word she'd just said. His ears pricked up happily, and he bared his teeth in a lupine grin. Nell recoiled at the sight of his long canines.

"But you can't tell me I'm supposed to be happy my boss is a werewolf! I mean, what do I do? I've never looked after a dog before."

"Just be there for him," Lucy said. "Keep him company. Keep him calm. He's only ever trouble when he gets too excited."

"What's 'trouble?'"

"Oh, he'd never hurt you intentionally."

Nell fought the urge to laugh. *Oh no, the men never mean to hurt you!*

"But it's probably best not to try and play anything too rough just yet."

"Rough?"

"He loves to wrestle. And he'll probably try to get you to play tug-of-war with one of his old rags. But you can pat him. He likes to fetch. Oh, and if you have any soup bones left over he adores them—"

"Oh shoot!" Nell leapt from the chair. "The soup!"

She pushed Wes out of the way and bolted down to the kitchen. She could smell the burning chicken fat from the parlor. Even with a low fire burning, the broth had boiled away, leaving a sticky mass in the bottom of the pot.

Grimacing, Nell heaved the pot off the stovetop. She was waving away the pungent smoke with a rag when Wes reappeared, ears perked and head cocked to one side.

"What big ears you have, Grandma," Nell said bitterly.

She felt like crying.

~ * ~

Midnight saw her sitting on the sofa, in front of a roaring fire. It wasn't quite cold enough to merit one, but she was sick of squinting in the lamplight. If she had to stay up all night minding a wild animal, then she was going to do it in comfort.

Her employer lay on the floor at her feet, gnawing on a beef bone. At rest, his fur lay flat on his back, and he looked smaller, somehow tamer. But Nell wasn't fooled. She had seen how he had bolted down that raw rib roast.

She was seething. She couldn't decide which Benedict to curse the loudest. They had no right to drag her into all this. She had been quite happy thinking Wes a simple lout, looking for courage at the bottom of a bottle. She didn't need to know the truth.

And she didn't need to know that Lucy Benedict thought a Negro girl's heartbreak was a small price to pay for peace of mind.

She wished she could talk to Charlie.

"Can't even do that," she muttered under her breath, shooting daggers at the wolf. "You lot might be able to stab me in the back with a clear conscience, but damned if you'll catch me doing the same to you. Though you'd deserve it."

Wes rose and stretched, first his front legs, then his hind. He panted up at her hopefully, and she stared him down.

"At the very least I'd say you owe me a raise. And don't pull that puppy-dog face at me!"

Wes snapped his jaws and dropped down in a bow. When Nell drew back in alarm, he seized the hem of her skirt between his teeth. She pulled one way, he pulled around, and Nell heard an audible tear.

Her first instinct was outrage, not fear. She swatted him hard across the nose, and Wes released her.

"Bad dog!" Nell snapped, with as much authority as she could muster.

Wes lowered his head and his tail in submission. A low whimper escaped his muzzle, almost achingly contrite.

"Oh, what do you want now? I told you, I don't know how to play with dogs."

Wes made another huffing sound, like a quiet bark, and loped over to the front door.

"Oh no," Nell warned, as he started to claw at the base of the door. "You are not getting outside."

Wes began to scratch at the floorboards, as if he meant to dig his way out. To Nell's horror, his claws were already leaving scuffs in the wood.

"You stop it, Wesley! I mean it!" When he wouldn't heed her, she picked up his discarded shirt and slapped it across his haunches.

It failed to have the intended effect. Wes spun around and grabbed the shirt, pulling with playful growls. Nell gave up and let it fall. As tempting as it was to have him destroy his own clothes, she knew she'd be the one patching them up come morning.

Wes shook the shirt in his jaws like a dead animal, then walked back to the door. He started to lift his leg when Nell's shriek brought him up short.

"Don't you dare!"

Wes froze, leg still in midair.

"I'm drawing a line, now," Nell said sternly. "I do not mop up wolf piddle!"

Wes scratched at the front door again. Nell couldn't believe his cheek.

"Oh, that's your game. Well, you can forget it. You can just hold it in until daybreak."

Wes cocked his head to one side, as if in challenge. With great deliberation, he started to lift his leg again.

"Wait!" Nell looked around frantically. Her gaze settled on Wes's jeans, still lying in a pile on the floorboards. She unbuttoned his suspenders and tested their strength. Satisfied the cloth would hold, she tied the two front straps around the wolf's neck in a crude halter.

"We go out the back door and I don't want any whining from you."

Wes fell into heel obediently. Nell had never seen a creature look so smug.

She cracked the back door open and looked around. Satisfied there was nothing in the back yard but dust and moonlight, she opened the door further. Wes bounded out, dragging her in his wake.

"Gentle, will you?" But Wes hauled on the leash mercilessly. He bent his nose to the ground and started chasing scents. He stopped at the woodpile, the fencepost, even the edge of the smithy, each time marking his territory. Nell wondered how she would ever look him in the eye come morning.

Something caught his attention, and he strained towards the horse corrals. "Oh, no!" Nell dug her heels into the ground. "That's enough now. We're going back inside."

Wes had no intention of moving. Nell hauled on the leash until she thought she would tear her arm out of its socket, but she could not move him even an inch. His ears were pricked high, and his tail stood up like an arrow.

"It's just horse stink, now come on!"

Wes pulled against the lead, lifting Nell off her feet. She could feel her fingers losing purchase. When he pulled again, the straps scraped across her palm, leaving her with a friction burn and an empty fist.

~ * ~

The wolf ran free over the ground. Freed of the annoying weight dragging on his shoulders, he tossed his head, trying to shake off the collar. He ran up to the corral posts, to rub his neck against the wood. But Nell had tied the halter too snugly.

Nell called to him, annoyance in her voice. Wes turned back and offered her another play bow in apology. *Don't worry*, his cheerful huff of breath told her. *I'm not going far.*

She made a lunge for the trailing suspender straps. He darted out of reach.

"Wes, please!" She held out her hand, palm out. To Wes's lupine mind it was an encouraging gesture. He took a step towards her, ducking his head in submission. But when her hand snatched at the leash again, Wes again retreated.

That's the spirit! Wes thought. He chuffed to show his approval, and Nell waved her hands, making shushing sounds.

"Keep it down, will you?"

Wes bowed low then made a feint at her skirts. This was much better than playing with Connor Franklin and his dog. Nell always ran when chased, and was always eager to join the chase herself. He led her all around the corrals. He shimmied under the fence into the corral, and when she clambered after him, he wriggled right back out again. He was teasing her mercilessly, he supposed. But she kept chasing him, as eager as a puppy. And when she looked like she was tiring of the game, he had only to let out a warbling yowl, and she would find new strength to rush at him and flap her arms. He wondered why he had never invited her to join him on full moons before.

Maybe he had—his wolf's brain could never quite recall his human memories. But it seemed to him they had shared a night under the full moon, years before. He had been following the scent of a coyote right towards the old woodpile, and he had heard her screams for help...

She had been afraid of him then. But she wasn't now. He ran up the hill to the railroad tracks then beckoned her with a wagging tail.

"Oh... Wes... can't you just... behave your damn self for once? It would serve you right if I went back inside and locked the door!"

Wes paid her complaints no more mind than the play snarls of a fellow wolf. And sure enough, she hitched up her skirts and climbed after him.

He loped along the tracks, heading south. He decided he'd take her out past American Flat, towards the slot canyons where he could yip and howl to his heart's content, knowing the rocks would swallow the sound.

The wind shifted, and his hackles went up. The scent of the dairy teased his nose. Cow patties and wet hay and fresh cream... and something else—an animal he couldn't immediately identify.

The Rollins dairy. Something's going on there.

Wes quickened his pace, his nose to the rail tracks.

~ * ~

Nell stumbled to keep up with the red wolf. She could barely see the railroad ties; only by taking absurdly deliberate steps could she keep from tripping. Wes took no notice. He was lost in his own world of sounds and smells. Afraid to raise her voice, Nell could only whisper his name imploringly as she dropped further and further behind. Soon she lost sight of him entirely.

"Goddammit it, Wes, where are you?"

She couldn't remember the last time she had felt so helpless. She looked around, trying to get her bearings, but night had obscured all the familiar landmarks. The world was one great featureless shadow.

She glanced back towards the house. What else could she do? The faint reflection of the moonlight off the metal rails was the only guide she had. If she stepped off the track onto the treacherous hillside, she was liable to walk right into a sinkhole. Men had been known to break ankles and worse, even in broad daylight. Yet for all she knew, Wes was already a hundred feet above her, chasing a hare up the canyon wall.

She was starting to shiver. The air was still, but the October nights were bitterly cold at six thousand feet, and here she was in a cotton housedress.

Behind her shone the lights at the Crown Point Mine, beckoning her home. Wes could surely find his way back before daybreak, she reasoned. He knew how to take care of himself. He had been getting loose for at least the last twelve years, and no one had caught him yet.

Who are you trying to kid? If you had it in you to leave him, you'd have left him back at the house.

Nell continued down the tracks. Every few minutes, she called for Wes, as loudly as she dared. She told herself the silence that answered was preferable to a string of loud yips. Above all, he couldn't howl! Not with the air so clear the sound would carry all the way down to Silver City.

The tracks curved to the right, towards the broad gully of American Flat. Nell passed beneath a rocky overhang, and the railway fell into shadow. The wind had scraped away much of the soil underfoot, leaving an uneven surface of dried clay. Her pace slowed to an awkward hobble as she maneuvered over the raised ties.

I'm a wolf charmer, she repeated to herself. *Wolf calls to wolf.*

Adam Blackfell didn't know the half of it.

The silent darkness was oppressive; she found herself singing haltingly under her breath to steel her nerves. "'When you hear dem a bells go ding, ling ling/ All join 'round and sweetly you must sing—'"

Something scurried out of the brush, and she gathered her skirts tightly about her legs in anticipation of a rat… or worse. But the creature disappeared from view, and the only sound to keep her company was the crunch of her shoes on the gravel.

"'And when the verse am through, in the chorus… all join…'Wes, I swear to God I will skin you for this!"

Up ahead, a shout: wordless and angry.

Nell walked faster. Her heart sank when she spotted the tiny lights flickering to life. Another shout, higher in pitch, travelled on the air. The Rollins dairy farm was no more than a quarter mile down the track, and the Paiute camp another mile farther. She didn't want to think what sort of havoc Wes could wreak in his playful mood.

More lights appeared in the windows of the Rollins dairy. A wild shriek echoed off the hillside, followed by the report of a rifle.

Nell started to run.

She came upon Wes at a bend in the track. Her foot caught on something and she went down on all fours, bracing herself on her forearms. When she got back up, the red wolf was back at her side, panting hard. His breath was steaming in the moonlight.

Nell was too furious to feel surprise. "Where have you been?" She seized him by the scruff of the neck before he could bolt again. He looked to be in one piece, but she was afraid she'd find him covered in blood and chicken feathers once she got him back into proper light.

Another distant gunshot made them both flinch. "Come on," Nell seized Wes's halter, and this time he offered no resistance. Woman and wolf turned and started back for the safety of town.

~ * ~

Nell awoke to a sore neck and the smell of coffee. She lifted her head from the arm of the sofa to see Wes standing over her, a steaming cup in hand.

"'Morning," he said sheepishly.

Nell sat up with a start. The last thing she remembered clearly was locking Wes in his bedroom some hours before dawn. She must have dozed off at the fireside waiting for the moon to set.

She was sure she looked a fright. But Wes looked none the worse for wear. He had washed and shaved, and the only marks of his ordeal were the heavy circles under his eyes, and the jaundiced cast to his skin. He smiled awkwardly. "Wild night, huh?"

Nell snatched the cup from his hand. Her brain was in desperate need of a stimulant. The coffee burned her tongue, but she didn't mind. He had made it just the way she liked it, with lots of milk and a touch of sugar.

"What time is it?" she asked, when the caffeine had restored her powers of speech. Her throat was sore, and she blamed the night air.

"About eight-thirty."

"Shoot, gotta check on Mrs. B—"

"She's fine. She's still sleeping too. Reckon we all deserve it."

"Ain't that the truth."

"Well," Wes risked a smile. "As nights went, that wasn't too bad, was it?"

Nell shot him a murderous glare over the top of her mug. Wes rubbed the back of his neck. The grin became a grimace of anticipation.

"That all you got to say?" Nell demanded.

"I... I dunno." He rocked on the balls of his feet, looking guilty. "I thought you did a really good job. And I'm real sorry I couldn't find a better way of telling you. But, well, I know you, Nell. You wouldn't believe it 'til you saw it with your own eyes. Nell? Are you okay with this?"

"What kinda question is that? Am I 'okay'with this? No! I am nowhere near okay!" She didn't care if she lost her job. She didn't care if she damaged their friendship beyond repair. "I always knew you had a lot of nerve. But to come in here, playing the angel, after what you did last night? What you put me through—"

Wes held up his hands to stop her. "Look, I'm sorry if I scared you. Wait, wait, did I hurt you?" He looked her over anxiously for signs of injury. "I know I tore your dress a little—"

"My dress? You think this is about my dress?" But her anger turned to confusion as she read the genuine bewilderment in his eyes. "You really don't remember, do you? You ran off! I took you out back for a piddle, and you yanked the leash right out of my hand and took off."

"Oh." Wes gave a guilty wince. "Yeah. Next time you should really just let me go in the house if y'ain't willing to chase me. But don't feel too bad. Seems I'm always finding new ways to break out." He chuckled at the memory. "I used to lose Ma at least three times a year. Though the leg-lifting trick hasn't worked on her in ages."

"You think this is a joke? Do you have any idea how worried I was?"

"Come on, I was only loose for... what, five minutes? We played a bit of chase... we went for a walk together. Reckon we lost sight of each for a little while, but soon as I noticed you'd fallen behind I came right back. How bad could it be— what?" he asked, as her expression turned more and more incredulous.

"Five minutes? You were gone a good half-hour at least! I chased you all the way to the pass at American Flat. Don't you remember any of that?"

By Wes's stunned face it was clear he did not.

"Was it that long?" He paced back at forth in front of her, lost in thought. She watched him calculate, weighing his own hazy memories against her word. At length he shook his head and sat next to her on the couch.

"God, I'm so sorry, Nell. I thought —I never imagined I was gone that long."

"You wolves can't tell time that well, huh?"

"Oh, it's like being in a dream. You know those dreams you have... where you're flying or dancing underwater or talking to a bear, and you oughta know it can't be real, but it just seems so reasonable? That's me at the full moon. I honestly thought I was only gone for a minute. Please believe me. I never meant to worry you."

She was touched by his sincere repentance. "Well, no harm done, I reckon," she said at length. "Apart from my skirt and that dishrag. It ain't ever touching dishes again after wiping up your dirty muzzle."

"I didn't get into the horse shit again, did I?" he asked, pained.

Nell couldn't help a short laugh. "Good lord—you do that?"

"Sometimes."

"Well, none of that last night. If you had, dunno if I'd still be here. No, just a lot of dirt and spit— looks like you were trying to root out a prairie dog or something. You remember any of that?"

He shook his head. "I remember… shouting… and I think I heard a shot fired." He grimaced with the effort of remembering. "Someone was with me… maybe it was just you. It's all muddled up."

"We're just gonna have to put in a long chain out back for next time," Nell said firmly. "Because I am not letting you slip loose again and I am not letting you mess in the house!"

"Next time?" He brightened. "That mean you're staying?"

"I— I… suppose I'm willing to try," Nell admitted. "Against my better judgment. But now that we can talk about this, I want to draw up some proper rules. Like how I'm supposed to know what you want from all your huffing and yipping. And how much time I get to sleep in the day after."

He grinned. "We got twenty-seven days to iron it all out."

"Wes…" she looked down at her hands. "I want to thank you, for that night at the woodpile. When you got between me and those boys."

Wes didn't answer her straight away. When she stole a glance, she found him lost deep in thought.

"I gotta say," she went on. "I hated you then, and for a lot of years afterwards. Thought you were a real horse's ass, just another stupid spoiled white boy. And now… well, it makes me sad… me thinking that about you when you'd stuck your neck out for me. You saved my life."

Wes started to shake his head. "Naw, they were—"

"They would have killed me. You know me. I would have made it so they had to. What were you even doing running around loose like that?"

"Oh, when I was younger, Ma would take me out into the hills. I listened to her more. She thought she could trust me not to do something stupid. I thought she could. But I started getting wilder. Got away too many times." He smiled. "You never told anyone about the wolf."

"My folks didn't seem to care that I nearly got raped," she sneered. "Didn't figure they'd care about a wolf on the loose."

"The boys never told anyone either. I would have heard." He was grinning at the memory, but his eyes were mournful.

When he spoke again, Nell could hear the tremor of emotion catching at the back of his throat.

"I wasn't proud of much I did, back then. And I always wanted to believe I did some good. But you know, until today, I was never entirely sure I didn't imagine the whole thing."

"You didn't." She touched his bicep gently. She could feel the heat of his skin through his shirt sleeve. "Shoot, are you still running a fever?"

Wes shrugged. "Usually do, for a day or a two afterwards."

"You should go back to bed. Reckon you got even less sleep than I did."

"You'd be right." Wes slowly got to his feet. "But wake me around one, will you? You deserve some time off your feet too."

Nell smiled wryly. "If I let you oversleep, you gonna turn into something else?"

"If I do, it'll be the death of me." He stretched his arms high overhead, then rotated his shoulders with a grimace. "Unh, I feel like I got caught in a stampede."

Someone knocked at the door, an urgent staccato of knuckle raps.

"You expecting someone?" Nell asked.

"Don't think so."

Nell went to answer the door. It was the town marshal, Bill Crawford. Behind him stood a middle-aged white man with pockmarked cheeks. Nell knew the face, but she couldn't immediately place it.

Crawford tipped his hat politely. "Nell. Nice to see you found a place. Benedict," he looked over Nell's shoulder. "You got a minute? Mr. Rollins and I wanted a chat."

Reluctantly, Wes came to the door. There had always been bad blood between him and the marshal, Nell knew—some old schoolyard grudge never entirely mended.

"Now's not the best time, Bill."

"Just wanted to know if you had any disturbance last night 'round quarter to one. Strange noises? Horses fussing?"

Wes frowned; the time meant nothing to him. But Nell felt her blood run cold.

"Won't have any trouble from the horses," Wes said. "I got 'em all in the stable at night these days."

"But you must have heard the gunshots?" Bill pressed. "Ted Bittner said the echo woke him up out of a sound sleep."

"Gunshots?" Wes started as if he'd just remembered. "Gunshots… yeah, reckon I might have. Heard something in the night, now I think of it. You hear it, Nell?"

"Maybe," she said casually. "Couldn't tell you what time, though. Why? What happened, Marshal?"

Bill Crawford was grim. "Afraid we might have a rabid dog running about."

"I know dogs!" Rollins interjected. "That was no dog. It was a wolf as big as a man, and faster than anything natural got a right to be!"

"Attacked the Rollins' farm last night," Crawford explained. "Harassing the cattle. Bit Mr. Rollin's oldest boy."

"Oh my God," Nell looked to Wes. He had gone deathly pale.

"It's Joey, right?" he asked. "From the milk run? How's he doing?"

"'How's he doing?'" Rollin sputtered. "He's a cripple at fourteen, is what he is! That thing damn near tore his leg off at the knee. It'll never mend right."

"He's already running a fever," Crawford said. "And if the dog was rabid…"

"It was no dog! I told you, it's a monster!"

"Well, whatever it was, I aim to put it down," Bill said. "Before it gets anyone else."

Seven

Connor read through the report, his mood darkening at every new line. John Garrod's prose was as tedious as his scent, but he was nothing if not thorough. He had even measured the distance between teethmarks so he could sketch out a diagram of the boy's mangled leg to the proper scale.

"There was a mess of tracks all over the place," Bill explained. "Man, dog, horse—couldn't make heads nor tails of it. The Rollins' yard was full of paw prints. So was the Benedicts'—"

Yeah, I bet it was, Connor thought grimly.

"—but damned if I could trace a proper trail between the two." Bill retrieved a bottle of whiskey from his desk and poured himself a shot.

"Mr. Rollins remains convinced we're dealing with something... diabolical in nature," Garrod spoke up. "I quoted his description verbatim."

"Don't see why you bothered. Half of it's bull. We all know wolves don't stand upright on their back legs."

"Of course not. But the description of the head—and the beast's overall size—seem consistent with the teeth marks. We're looking for a canine no less than sixty inches in length, with exceptionally strong jaws." Garrod's flinty gaze flickered over his fellow deputy. "Where is your mongrel, Franklin?"

"Your shift's over, so why don't you light on out? I'm sure you have a baby to eat or something." Connor flipped the sheet of paper over. Phrases like "dragged the victim across yard" and "severe trauma to calf muscle" leapt off the page. He felt his evening breakfast sour in his stomach. *Goddammit, Wes! How am I supposed to cover this up?*

He could guess what had happened. Wes had come to him two nights past, shivering and exhausted, but still determined to endure the transformation alone. "How can I hide it from Nell if you show up with Garou looking to take me for a walk?" he'd argued. Connor's suggestion of meeting at the Crypt well before sundown had met with a similar dismissal.

"Don't you worry about me. I have a plan, all right? Shoot, Ma and I have been managing this long before you came along. Nell won't find out until we know she's ready. Trust me."

Famous last words, but Connor was not one to meddle in his friends' affairs without good reason. And like a fool he'd left it at that, and spent his weekend in blissful indolence at the Crypt, while God-knows-what was unfolding at Crown Point.

Garrod turned to the marshal. "Sir, are we just going to keep ignoring the fact your deputy marshal keeps a feral wolf-dog? One he lets run loose at all hours."

Connor gave a snort of derision. "That's it, Garrod. Whine to Daddy."

"Any wolf that encroaches on town limits is ruled a dangerous nuisance and must be destroyed," Garrod shot back. "The law is very clear. I don't see why it should be any different for a half-wolf."

Bill looked up skeptically. "Don't you? Are we even talking about the same critter? Shoot, Franklin's wife is a bigger nuisance in my books!"

"And proud of it," Connor remarked.

Garrod failed to see the humor. "I don't doubt it, sir. But if a man cannot control his own wife, what chance has he with a half-wild animal?"

Bill let out a weary sigh. "Where was Garou last night around one, Connor?"

"Begging scraps in my kitchen. It was right around our lunchtime."

"And where is he now?"

"With Charlie."

Bill looked at Garrod pointedly. "Satisfied?"

"Would you be, sir? If that was your son lying mauled within an inch of his life?" A thin smile crossed his lips. "But you're not a father, are you, sir?"

Connor held his breath as he glanced at his superior. But Bill was the model of civility. Only the throbbing vein at his temple betrayed a heart hammering in rage.

"And your shift's over," he said, his voice dangerously soft.

If Garrod had any inkling he had broached the one subject guaranteed to spark violence in Willard Crawford, he didn't show it. "Then I'll say 'good night', sir. Franklin."

He let himself out, closing the door gingerly behind him. Connor counted the seconds in his head. He was impressed: Bill waited a full count of ten before springing to his feet and throwing his empty shot glass against the door.

"Nice thought," Connor remarked. "Slow reflexes."

"It's the thought that counts," Bill growled, as he pushed a shock of hair from his flushed face. Connor waited, listening to Bill's heartbeat gradually quiet, wondering if tonight would be the night the marshal would finally speak of his lost son.

But a silence of twenty years didn't break easily, and Bill simply knocked back another shot of whiskey straight from the bottle. By the time he recapped and stowed it away, he was determined to scrub the moment from his memory.

"He's running right to the sheriff, you know."

"'Course he is." Connor glared at the door. The residual stench of Garrod's carbolic soap lingered like a cloud. "Shoot, he's only on the payroll 'cause Quirk wants a spy."

"And he's right about one thing: folks will be out for blood. Rollins is already talking about setting out traps. And I'm sure every man with a gun will be out on the Flat tonight. Don't reckon any coyote within ten miles will be safe. What?" Bill studied his deputy's face at length and found something disquieting. "What is it?"

"Charlie... she went down to the Benedicts'," Connor admitted. "She wanted to see how Nell's getting on in her new place." *And boy must she be getting an earful*, he thought ruefully.

"Jesus Murphy, Connor! And she's got the dog with her?"

"Well, how were we to know?"

"You gotta get him out of sight. Before Rollins or any of his folk sees him running around loose. Don't look at me like that now! You know these people, Connor! Your dog's life ain't worth spit to them. They'll gun him down in the street, and the law will be on their side."

"The man who lays a hand on my dog is going to lose it!" Connor declared hotly.

Bill's gaze did not waver. "I don't doubt it." He clapped Connor on the shoulder, squeezing hard. "That's why I'm warning you, as a friend. Keep him under lock and key. Save us all a world of hurt."

Retreat was not in his nature. But he understood the wisdom of it. Grudgingly, Connor nodded, and Bill released him with a murmured, "Good man."

Bill was turning back to his desk when another thought occurred to him. "Oh... and see if you can't get him to gnaw on an old soup bone or something. Wouldn't hurt to have a measure of Rou's bite to compare against the teethmarks left in the kid's leg. It'd shut Garrod up awful quick. And tell us just how big a critter we're really dealing with."

"That's—that's a good idea, actually."

"I have had a few in my day," Bill said archly.

~ * ~

The Benedict house was a short walk from the marshal's office. Connor went down on foot. The light had faded enough that he could dispense with his blue-tinted spectacles. Charlie's paint horse was tethered at the stable doors. When Connor knocked on the door, his wife answered promptly.

"You heard, then?" she asked. At his terse nod, she murmured, "Kid gloves, okay? He's already beaten himself up enough for one day."

"Doubt Joey Rollins would agree," Connor muttered.

Garou met him on the way to the parlor. The wolf-dog gave him a whine and an encouraging lick to the hand, but Connor was in no mood. He found Wes sitting by the fire, staring glumly at the crackling flames. Nell hovered behind him, wringing a scrap of her apron between her hands. Connor was hard pressed to tell which one of them looked more guilt-ridden.

"Wondering how long it'd take you to get here," Wes said tonelessly.

"The police report took a while to get through. Miss Wallace." Courtesy required a brisk nod. "You mind giving us a moment?"

From the acrid whiff of terror coming off her skin, he expected her to flee at the first chance. But she held her ground.

"If you're going to arrest someone, Mr. Franklin, it oughta be me. I'm the one who let him out."

The confession surprised him, but only for a moment. At his side, Charlie clucked her tongue in sympathy. She started to advance awkwardly, but Nell fended her off with a wave of the hand.

"I—I had him on a lead. I thought it would be all right. I didn't know how strong he was." She flinched under the deputy's critical stare. "He... got away from me, took off along the railroad."

Connor turned his disbelieving glare on Wes. "You let her watch you? Her first time? Where was your ma during all of this? You promised me she was well enough to manage!"

"Well, I lied, didn't I?"

"Obviously!"

"Keep your voice down!" Wes hissed. "Ma—she... she doesn't know," he confessed miserably. "Not all of it. She's upstairs resting—she's finally sleeping well for the first time in weeks. Please... she'd never forgive herself if she knew."

He was right, of course. And at the thought of Lucy Benedict bearing her son's sins as her own, he felt himself start to weaken. Much to his annoyance.

"You can't keep her in the dark forever, Wes," he said softly. "Odds are Joey Rollins is going to lose his leg, at the very least."

"But Wes didn't hurt that boy!" Nell protested. "He couldn't have. Tell them, Wes. Tell him you don't even remember being near the Rollins farm."

"I honestly don't know. I keep going over it in my head—I can't keep track of all the details when I'm a wolf, you know that, Connor. But I remember the important stuff. And how do you forget tearing up a dairy cow and nearly wrenching a kid's leg off at the knee?"

"You've lost entire nights before," Connor pointed out.

"But why would he do it?" Nell argued. "He's still Wes under all that fur! Maybe he can't reason like a man, but he's not... wild."

Her blind faith was touching. Connor tried to keep his voice gentle. "I'm guessing he hasn't told you about some of our shenanigans. Believe me, he's more than capable of tearing a man apart when he's provoked. And I don't doubt it was self-defense. Just like I don't doubt the Rollins boy was only trying to protect his dairy cows."

"Then where was the blood?" Nell persisted. "He came back covered in dirt and slobber, but when I wiped him off, there wasn't any blood on the rag. Tell me, Deputy: if Wes did all that to Joey Rollins, he couldn't have helped but get all bloodied, right?"

Connor considered it. "Sounds like the bite didn't hit any major blood vessels—if it had, Joey'd be dead by now. But... there would have been some blood, sure." He knew he shouldn't get his hopes up. "Nothing he couldn't have wiped off himself, given time. How long was he out of your sight?"

"Half an hour… maybe less. Probably less. But between the gunshots and him coming back to me, it couldn't have been more than a minute," she added confidently.

Mortals made poor liars, as a rule. Usually their blood gave them away, rushing loudly through their veins, filling their cheeks with heat. Or their throats constricted, distorting their voice to immortal ears. He could find none of the signs in Nell. She was utterly convinced of Wes's innocence.

He hoped she was right.

He turned to Charlie. "I need you to take Rou back to the Crypt."

"Why?"

"Because the last thing folks around here want to see is a wolf-dog running around at twilight. He stays up at home until we can put all this to rest."

"Nell?" Charlie asked. "Are you going to be—"

"Stop fussing, will you? I ain't a child."

Charlie slapped her thigh with a whistle and Garou trotted to her side, tongue lolling in oblivious joy. *He wouldn't go so eagerly if he knew he was headed for house arrest,* Connor thought sadly.

"I'm so sorry for all of this," Wes said.

"Sorries won't help much now," Connor said.

"What can I do?"

"You can stay put. But I'll need Miss Wallace to show me—the best you can recall, now—just where you both got to last night. Do you think you can do that?"

Her expression was doubtful, but Nell nodded.

"I can help—" Wes began to rise, and Connor held up his hand to stop him.

"I don't need your muscle, and your memory's next to useless. Right now the best thing you can do is give yourself an alibi. Stay here and look after your ma," he added, more gently.

Wes accepted the assignment with fairly good grace, all things considered. But to judge by her scent, Nell's courage was rapidly deserting her. Still, she wasn't one to shirk her duty. She obediently donned her long woolen shawl and felt hat, and checked the oil level in the barn lantern. Connor offered her an encouraging smile, which she did not return.

The evening sky had turned dull violet by the time Nell led him past the corrals to the train tracks. The moon hung well above the canyon walls, but Nell still turned the lantern's flame as high as it would go. They walked in silence along the railroad, Nell watching her feet, taking two mincing steps for each of Connor's easy strides.

"Thank you," she finally said, "for not asking me if I'm square with all this."

"Seemed plain enough. Dunno if you know this," he added after a moment's thought, "but I'm fairly sure you're the first person Wes has told of his own free will."

"Wasn't quite a matter of telling exactly." A few more steps in silence, then: "How did you find out?"

"The smell." The words were out of his mouth before he remembered Nell didn't know everything. He glanced across and found her frowning in confusion. "Garou—he's happy to ignore Wes most days," he explained. "Then I noticed he got real friendly right before the full moon. Took me a while to put the pieces together and little longer to get up the nerve to stop by the Benedict house at the right time. Mrs. B had him locked in his bedroom, but Rou sniffed him out, and the two of them were yowling at each other like a pair of puppies through the door." He chuckled at the memory, and the ease in its telling. Lying was a matter of course to him; it was such a pleasant novelty to speak the truth. Or the better part of it, anyway. In reality, it had taken him a matter of days, not months, to ferret out Wes's secret. By the time the shakes set in, the man's scent was indistinguishable from a wolf's.

"And you weren't afraid, sir?"

Connor shrugged. "Like you said, he's still Wes. And I got experience handling wolves."

"I mean… the idea of it."

"Oh. Well, I've always had a healthy respect for the inconceivable. You can call me Connor, you know. If you'd like."

"I'll… keep that in mind."

They had left the homes of Crown Point well behind them. The railroad turned out of the canyon into American Flat. The last gloaming of sunset still clung to the western horizon, and set against it Connor could make out a faint curl of wood smoke.

"There's the Rollins'dairy."

Nell squinted in the twilight. "Where?"

He pointed out the dark wisp rising in the distance. Nell stared a moment longer before she gave up with a shake of her head. "No wonder sunlight hurts your eyes—they must be sharp as an owl's!"

"Was this about where you found Wes?"

She looked around the hillside. "I'm not sure. I thought it was further on."

They walked a little farther, until Nell could clearly see the lights twinkling in the farmhouse windows. She stopped, bit her lip, and turned the lantern about to better inspect the curves of the hillside. "No… no, this is too far. I think. I'm sorry. I don't know how much help I'll be."

"You said Wes was back within a minute of the gunshots?"

The whites of her eyes shone in the lantern light. "Is it too far to run? Can we prove he didn't have time?" Hope made her voice leap in pitch. Connor wished he could let her keep her illusions.

"A minute's a long time for a wolf in full sprint," he admitted.

"What will we do? About Wes? If we can't prove he didn't do it."

"What can we do? Can't exactly lock a man for lycanthropy."

"You could try." Her gaze was faintly accusing. Connor met it with a reassuring smile.

"Suppose I could. But I won't. Besides, I reckon his conscience will be punishment enough."

"And mine."

She wasn't a woman to be coddled. Connor could see why Charlie admired her. "I'm 'fraid so."

Nell lowered the lantern, casting her face in shadow. "Thank you all the same."

"Wes is lucky to have a friend like you; I hope he knows that—"

The attack came without warning: a sledgehammer to the chest, as the stench of unwashed hair and human sweat filled the back of his throat. His legs went out from under him; he fell spread-eagle on the ground. His head struck the iron rail, and stars exploded behind his eyes. Nell's scream was almost drowned out by the hungry snarls of the creature crouched atop him.

Instinct took over. One hand went to his revolver, the other to brace on the beast's hairy chest. But he had landed square on his holster, pinning the Colt against his hip. And the creature was easily his equal in strength. It was all he could do to hold off the snapping, slobbering jaws. Hot flecks of foamy saliva spattered over his face. Pain seared his shoulder as the beast dug five long claws into his flesh.

Then a ball of light struck the creature with the sharp crackle of splintering glass, and the creature bounded off with a shriek. Connor swatted the glowing embers out of his face and rolled onto his stomach. He drew his Colt and fired off into the twilight, fanning the hammer until he'd emptied the cylinder. But when the smoke cleared from his last shot he could still make out the silhouette of the beast. It fled south, its gait bounding and erratic.

He started to push himself up on his knees, and the movement provoked a fresh wave of pain in his shoulder. His cry brought Nell to his side.

"Mr. Franklin! You're hurt!" Her arm came around his ribs and she hauled him to his feet in one fluid motion, as she might a brimming pot of water. She was panting hard; her breath carried the spice of adrenaline.

"Only my pride—hsst, maybe a little more." His shirt hung in tatters at his shoulder; he felt his body's meagre heat leaking into the night air. Grabbing a fistful of material, he pressed it hard against the wound to stanch the bleeding. "Reckon I owe you for the lantern. That was some quick thinking."

He scanned the southern landscape, searching for the slightest movement. Whatever it was had disappeared into the shadows of the rocks and sagebrush. Yet Connor couldn't quite shake the feeling of being watched.

"What the hell was that?"

"It's a skinwalker," Nell whispered. "Like at the Indian show."

"Come on," Connor said. "Let's get you back home. I don't like being out here." He liked the pins and needles in his hand even less. The claws must have nicked a nerve. He'd be useless at reloading his gun until it healed.

Nell offered no protest as he hustled her back along the tracks. She moved as if in a daze. Periodically, a laugh threatened to erupt, and each time she forced it down with a raw catch in her throat. "He was right. That goddamn Wolf Charmer was bona fide after all!"

"Like I said, healthy respect for the inconceivable."

"We gotta track him down," Nell said firmly. "The Wolf Charmer. He'll know what to do. You can't kill this thing with ordinary bullets. I remember that much."

Connor gave a snort of derision. "Give me five minutes and a length of chain to hold it still, I'll figure out a way."

She cast a critical eye over his makeshift dressing. "That's gonna need stitching up proper."

"Naw, it's fine," Connor said, grateful for the darkness. "It looks worse than it is." He felt sure the gashes were already closing over. His wounds healed cleanly and quickly, since he'd come back from his first death. Worse indignities had always faded within the hour, sooner if he had fresh blood to speed them along. He would be well on the mend by the time they reached the Benedict house. The sharp twinge of pain he continued to feel with each step was simply his bloodied skin sticking to his shirt.

~ * ~

He was wrong. Safely behind closed doors, he washed his wound by electric light. Underneath the clotted blood his skin was flayed open, exposing the tendons. A steady trickle of dark ichor continued to seep out, thick as molasses, and from deep inside the wound came the stench of death.

Eight

The Wolf Charmer wasn't easy to track down. Between them, Bill and Connor sent several dozen telegrams to their various counterparts in neighbouring towns, until they finally caught Frank Maddock's show preparing to perform over in Truckee Meadows. By the time Maddock agreed to part with his headline act, the moon had waned to a crescent, and old Doc Sheppard had given up hope of saving Joey Rollins' leg.

Connor's shoulder demanded its own attention, but circumstances dictated a different sort of doctor. The evening the Wolf Charmer was due to arrive by train from Reno, the two Franklins walked up Ravine Road to visit Captain Marsh.

The old Paiute had already set up his winter tent, a sturdy dome of woven branches and canvas tarpaulins, in the shadow of a tailings pile. The low door forced them to bend at the waist to enter, but inside the tent was large enough to sleep some three or four men comfortably. The embers in the fire pit gave off a welcome heat.

Connor grimaced at the stiffness in his shoulder as Charlie slowly helped him out of his shirt. He was used to pain, sharp yet fleeting, invigorating in its way. He'd welcome a good agony, knowing it would soon fade, rather than endure another night of this chronic unrelenting ache.

"I think it's looking a little better," Charlie lied, as she peeled back the last of the dressing. The dark blood on the gauze belied her words. Across the glowing hearth, Captain Marsh took out his clay pipe and started to pack the bowl with a mossy substance. His face folded into a pensive scowl at the sight of the wound.

The ragged seam ran from Connor's collarbone to the top of his left bicep. Doc Sheppard had stitched the wounds closed the night of the attack, yet the catgut showed little sign of absorption. Which was just as well, Connor thought, as the flesh showed no sign of healing. Between the sutures, the skin gaped, raw and wet. With the pressure of the dressing gone, thick blood began to bead once more in the crevices of his flesh. The bleeding wouldn't stop. Connor had to drink an extra pint of pig's blood every night just to keep his strength up.

"Looks fresh," Captain Marsh observed. "And you got this—"

"Night after Joey was bit."

The captain let out a thoughtful whistle through the gap in his teeth. "At least it's not festering. You came away luckier than Joey."

"There's… something," Connor insisted. "I can feel it. Like…a knot. Like I got a ball of lead inside me." He could feel it shifting with every movement of his arm. He could smell it seeping up through the sutures—the sickly scent of putrefaction.

"Like I'm rotting inside," he finished bleakly.

"Don't say that!" Charlie snapped. Captain Marsh only chuckled.

"Oh, I wouldn't worry my pretty head about that, if I were you. Death's something your fella's got a knack for cheating." His dark eyes twinkled with mirth as Charlie's mouth formed an O of surprise. He lit his pipe and took a long draw. Fragrant smoke filled the tent. "Why the tales I could tell you… 'course they're all from the days when he was pretending to be his own daddy."

"You got it backwards, Cap'n. Now I'm pretending to be my own son."

Charlie looked at her husband sharply. "You didn't tell me Captain Marsh knew—"

"He doesn't. He suspects." He turned his wry smile on the captain. "But then you've always been an awful suspicious sort."

Captain Marsh laughed. "Well, you made it easy for me, didn't you? Forty years since you first passed through these hills, and you haven't aged a day. Now you might have the other old timers fooled, but it'll take more than shaving off your beard and slapping 'Junior' on your name to fool Cap'n Marsh!" He turned to Charlie. "All I know is that's some awful powerful medicine your husband's got. That little scratch won't be killing him anytime soon."

"But it won't heal by itself either, will it?" Connor asked.

"I was afraid of this when I saw Fanny's grave all dug up. This witch is using curse magic. Stronger stuff than I've ever seen. Only one way to lift it."

"Ask the critter nicely?" Connor quipped.

"I was thinking more of putting a bullet between his eyes. But if you want to be a gentleman about it, you're welcome to try. In the meantime..." he passed Connor his pipe. "Try a little kinnikinnick. It'll help with the pain."

"Kinik-kinik?" Charlie stumbled over the word.

"My own recipe," he said proudly. "Best medicine in the west. Premium Kentucky tobacco, powdered willow bark, a dash of sage..."

Connor drew on the pipe, and promptly began to cough. "And enough hemp to choke a horse," he finished, his voice scratchy from the smoke.

"*Mari huana*, old man. That's what we young'uns are calling it now." He winked at Charlie. "It'll be bigger than opium. You wait and see."

"I wouldn't hold your breath," Connor rasped. The perfumed smoke was a decided improvement on the smell of decay. Hesitantly, he took another draw. This time the smoke slid down his throat smoothly. The scent of herbs tickled his sinuses pleasantly. "It's not bad though."

"This Wolf Charmer fella you got coming… you think he'll be able to flush our witch out?" Marsh asked. "After I've had my boys searching the mountains for near two weeks now with nothing to show for it?"

"He says he's hunted skinwalkers before. And we know the critter's still stalking around the Flat."

"That we do. I saw the tracks myself. Came within twenty yards of my nephew's tent, then— pff—disappeared like the thing grew wings."

"Do you think he did?" Charlie asked. "I mean… Blackfell said they could take other forms."

"Damned if I know," Marsh grunted. "But last night Jim Crook and Li'l Tom laced a pig with strychnine and left it out on the old game trail. The damn thing turned up back on their doorstep this morning."

"It's playing with us," Connor murmured.

"You're gonna need something special if you're going to bring this critter down."

"Got something in mind?"

The old man's eyes twinkled. "These are trade secrets, you know." He turned to his bedroll and rummaged through his belongings until he uncovered a small leather pouch.

"The night I saw Fanny's grave dug up, I told my boys to arm themselves," he explained as he stirred the ashes at the edge of the hearth. "Burning sage'll slow a witch down, but there's only one thing that'll kill him."

Connor watched him sift a handful of white powder into the pouch. "Wood ash? I ain't planning on making soap, Cap'n."

"I should hope not. Skinwalker doesn't care if a man's clean or not. But a pinch of white ash…" Captain Marsh tied off the bag and tossed it across the hearth. Connor caught it out of the air with his good hand.

"Keep that on you, and dip your bullets in it before loading your gun." At Connor and Charlie's skeptical expressions, he flashed them a crooked grin. "It's the damnedest things that work some times. Fella I learned it from said it's some kinda countering curse. A witch needs to burn, so you infect it with what you mean to make of it— ashes. Might be so. Might be the critter just can't heal cleanly if the wounds gets dirty. Don't much care about the 'why's m'self. Just the results."

"You know it works?" Connor asked.

Old Marsh cackled. "What, you think this ol' town was quiet all those years you weren't around to raise hell? You missed some great monkeyshines, old man. I'll have to tell you one day."

~ * ~

The evening train came in from Reno well after dark. Charlie pointed out Adam Blackfell and his wives as they disembarked. Connor had imagined them in their flamboyant buckskins and beads; instead they were all soberly dressed in travelling clothes. White Moon's shockingly fair hair was concealed by a fur-trimmed bonnet, and only Brightfeather's strong cheekbones and copper complexion set her apart from the other prim matrons disembarking. But there was no mistaking the Wolf Charmer himself. He towered over every other man on the platform, his clothes one size too snug for convention, to better accent his powerful physique. He wore his long hair oiled and unbound, and his duster flared at his hip rakishly, revealing a Bowie knife strapped to his thigh. At Connor's side, Bill Crawford took one long look at the man and flushed to the tips of his ears.

"Jesus Murphy!"

"Makes quite the impression, doesn't he?" Connor remarked.

"Tell me again why we've deputized a circus performer?"

Connor ignored him; he had no stomach to reenact the argument all over again. "Mr. Blackfell," he hailed with a wave. Blackfell turned, and an amused smile crossed his lips as his gaze fell on Charlie.

"We meet again, little rooster," he called across the platform.

"Rooster?" Connor glanced at his wife. Charlie's reply was a grimace and a roll of the eyes.

"My spirit animal," she muttered, her voice dripping with scorn. "Apparently."

Connor chuckled. When Charlie's scowl only deepened, he couldn't resist running his hand up the back of her head, raising the fluffy cowlick just behind her crown.

"I can see it."

Charlie swatted his hand down in annoyance.

"Will you two behave for once?" Bill growled. "Mr. Blackfell," he stepped forward, hand extended, eager to assert his authority. "Marshal Crawford. Welcome to Gold Hill. Welcome back, I should say. We're really hoping you can help us with our little wolf problem."

Blackfell responded with a handshake hard enough to make the stoic marshal flinch. "It's my sacred duty," he said solemnly. Bill waited hopefully for him to say more, before deciding the Indian was not one for small talk.

A short man in a shabby coat came huffing and puffing behind the trio, weighed down by several suitcases and one battered trunk he was dragging by its handle. Connor felt his nose wrinkling in distaste. He remembered well that particular smell of cheap cologne and incipient tuberculosis.

"Mr. Maddock. We thought you'd be staying with the show in Reno."

"There—ugh—is no show without the Wolf Charmer." The carnival barker let the many bags tumble to the platform with a grateful sigh. "I have this man under a three-year contract and I don't intend to lose him." He straightened, dusted off his jacket, and turned an appreciative eye over White Moon. "And since he took my two leading ladies with him—"

"My wives go where I go."

"Yeah, we hear that a lot around here," Bill muttered.

"I let the rest of the crew go—roustabouts are a dime a dozen—and put the assets in storage." He turned to Bill, and his watery eyes went straight to his silver badge. "Ah, you're the man in charge then. I assume you accept my terms? All meals and lodgings paid for, one article in the local paper now, another once Blackfell kills the beast, and I take possession of the creature's hide, yes?"

"Don't meddle, Frank," Blackfell growled.

"Listen to him!" Maddock tittered, his tone that of an indulgent parent. "Now, I'm sure Adam here is chomping at the bit to go hunting, but I for one would like a hot meal and a good smoke."

"Deputy Franklin, Mrs. Franklin." Bill pointed them out in turn. "You'll be staying with Mrs. Franklin's family while you're here. They have a mighty fine hotel just up the road."

And a hankering for any scandal that'll rent rooms, Connor thought. He and Charlie had only to mention—and slightly magnify—the Wolf Charmer's fame to secure Blackfell room and board for next to nothing.

"Looks like you'll be needing two rooms," Charlie remarked. "But I'm sure that won't be a problem this time of year. You might want to decide now which one of you is going to be Mrs. Blackfell on the register, though. I'm fairly sure Aunt Katy don't cotton to bigamy."

"Or miscegenation, for that matter," Bill muttered.

"Quite right." Brightfeather turned to her companion. "It's safest if the redskins stick together. You can be Mrs. Maddock for the next while."

The carnival barker leered at White Moon. "Mm, I like the sound of that." He started to reach for her elbow, and the girl swatted his hand away. Charlie had said she was dumbstruck, yet the voice that tore out of her throat was loud and shrill.

"Paws off, Frankie! Y'ain't paying me enough for that!"

"Moon, please. I'm a gentleman born and raised." To prove it, he tipped his hat at Charlie. "We're in your hands, Mrs. Franklin. Now, which one of you ladies is going to help me with the bags?"

Neither Mrs. Blackfell offered assistance, and after a moment Charlie stepped up to heft the closest suitcase. "Much obliged," Maddock said, as he struggled to rebalance the remaining luggage.

"So... 'captive of the Comanches,'" Charlie remarked to White Moon. "That a load of bull too?"

"Folks call it 'acting!'" the girl sneered. She jerked a thumb in Maddock's direction. "It was his idea!"

"Hmm, well let's keep acting, Moon," Maddock said. "Else these good folks might start hankering for a refund. Shall we, Mrs. Franklin?"

Charlie lead the unlikely trio towards the street. Blackfell did not turn to bid them goodbye. "You said the skinwalker attacked a boy. Has it only been the one so far?"

Connor nodded. "The only human. We've had some livestock lost, but opinion's a bit divided on just what killed them."

"I need to see the family right away."

"You sure you don't want to settle in first?" Bill asked. "No one would blame you for starting fresh in the morning."

"Skinwalkers don't attack randomly. The sooner I can speak to the family, the sooner I'll know what the witch wants."

~ * ~

Blackfell took one look at young Joseph Rollins and curled his lip back in disgust. "*Yee naaldlooshii*," he growled. "There's no doubt. This is the Witchery Way."

"Hush," Connor said sharply.

The boy stirred in his sickbed; slowly he opened his bloodshot eyes to regard the Indian standing over him. "Jimmy?" he asked weakly.

"No, Joey," Wyatt Rollins spoke up. "This here is Mr. Blackfell. He's come to help heal you."

Fever slurred the boy's voice. "He gonna cut off my leg? It hurts somethin' awful."

"Joey... your leg's already gone."

Joey Rollins struggled to prop himself up on his elbows. Connor knelt down and lifted the covers, as gently as he could. The sawbones had taken off the limb cleanly at the knee. Cauterized with a hot iron and wrapped in daily plasters, the incision was healing well enough. But the persistent fever suggested a slow poison in the blood, gradually sapping away what little strength Joey had.

"What did you see of the beast?" Blackfell asked.

"Just… a shape… dark fur…" the boy said. "Pa, could I have some more water?"

Wyatt Rollins hastened to fill a glass then helped the boy to sit up and drink. "He's always thirsty," the father explained. "Drinks and drinks and never seems to piss anything back out. Heh. But Doc Sheppard said it's a good sign. Can't be rabies if he's drinking so much, can it? It's a good sign." He said it as if he almost believed it.

A loud snort was Blackfell's opinion of the good doctor's advice. Connor shot him a hard look, but said nothing. The sodden bed linens spoke for themselves. Joey Rollins was sweating the water out faster than he could drink it. And if dehydration didn't kill him, kidney failure would.

"Where's Ma?" Joey asked next.

"Oh, she's worn herself out looking after you, the poor gal," Connor said sympathetically. "Ain't your pa a good man, filling her shoes like he does?"

"You just rest, Joey," Wyatt Rollins said. "Try to get some more sleep."

"How is Mrs. Rollins?" Connor asked in a whisper, after they had closed the door on the sickroom. The dairy farmer shook his head.

"Can't understand the woman. Just locks herself upstairs, nursing the little one. 'Gracie needs me,' she says. Joey needs her. But she acts like he's already dead. She acts like she's already in mourning." He looked at Blackfell urgently. "Doc Sheppard said it was just a fever from all the germs in that wolf's mouth. 'Bacterial infestation,' he calls it. And Joey is getting better—"

Blackfell shook his head. "This is no natural illness. The creature that bit him was a skinwalker, a man changed into a beast by means of powerful magic. Your son lies under a curse, conceived by moonlight. And by moonlight the fever will rise and fall in his blood. He appears to improve now, but as the moon waxes, he will burn again. No water will quench his thirst, and no sleep will restore him."

"But you can heal him!"

"I am sorry. I cannot cure your boy myself. This curse was cast by a powerful witch, and only death can lift it."

"My boy's death? And what do you mean by 'curse?' Who'd want to hurt Joey? We don't even know any medicine man. Unless you count ol'Captain Marsh!"

"I wouldn't count what he smokes as 'medicine,'" Connor remarked.

"Ask anyone in town," Rollins went on. "My family has lived alongside the Paiutes here since the eighteen-sixties, and I have been nothing but respectful. Most of my workers are Paiutes, and I got no quarrel with a'one of them—shoot, I got more quarrels with my own race!"

"A skinwalker need not be one of the People... only taught by one."

"So it could be anyone? Is that what you're saying? Any one of my neighbours could be dressing up in wolfskins and laying curses."

Blackfell shook his head. "The ritual is complex. It requires particular songs, particular tools; the skin of a beast killed by the full moon; a fire fed with the proper herbs; a poultice of rattlesnake venom and white ash and ground human bone."

"Human bones?" Rollins looked at Connor in horror. "You don't think..."

"What is it?" Blackfell demanded. "What happened?"

"My sister Frances... some whoreson desecrated her grave. Not a month ago. Oh God! Human bones— my Fanny?" The man's pockmarked face turned crimson with rage. "He dug up Fanny's bones for some heathen poison?! Why?" He advanced on the Wolf Charmer, his fist drawing back of its own volition. "Damn you, you tell me why!"

"Easy, now." Connor caught the arm before Rollins could swing it. "He's going to tell you. Now calm down... think of the rest of your family. Reckon they've heard enough screaming in this house the last while. Blackfell, you better start talking. Did your man Maddock tell you I asked him about that looted grave?"

"Maddock? Do you think I listen to a word he says? Wait... he did mention Indian bones. The police were asking, he said."

"She was buried in the Indian cemetery," Connor explained. "Wed to one of the locals."

"Really? Happily?"

Wyatt Rollins raised his chin defiantly. "Show me the man who says they weren't. I told you, my family has always gotten on with the Paiutes. Shoot, Joey's been playing with his Marsh cousins since he was a tyke."

Blackfell clapped his hands together. "And you asked for provocation. Don't you see?" he prompted at the men's puzzled faces. "The skinwalkers were born of the red man's rage at the white man. What greater insult to a witch consumed by hate than to think of both living in peace?"

"You don't have to look so proud of yourself," Connor drawled. He was starting to see what Charlie disliked in the man. "That doesn't get us any closer to finding the man."

"Finding him is my job," Blackfell dismissed. "You need to keep the boy safe. The skinwalker could return any day. Someone's burning sage; that's good. You'll need small fires burning throughout the night, all around the house. Do you have any Mexican hysopp? Never mind. I'll have my wife bring you some tomorrow. Burn it at the boy's bedside—the smoke will help drive down the fever."

"And you?" Connor asked.

"Tomorrow I start my hunt."

~ * ~

Blackfell outlined his plan as Connor walked him back to town. "I'll need a good map of the area, showing all the ravines, mineshafts, anywhere a man could hide."

A man could hide in the shadows just off the road, Connor thought. But for the watchfires burning in each front yard, the darkness of the mountain valley was absolute. Connor saw that it weighed on Blackfell. Each time they left an island of light, the man's pace quickened, and he kept his eyes fixed on the reflective pebbles scattered across the road. Only once they were safely within the glow of the next house did he feel safe to resume his inspection of the hillside.

Connor didn't know what to make of him. He looked like a normal man, albeit an exceptionally fit one. He smelled like a human should, of saddle oil and old leather and warm sand. Although, so did Wes, twenty-five days a month.

What is he? Experience told him most men who claimed to have knowledge of the supernatural were frauds. Half were dangerous frauds. But every now and then in his hundred-odd years, he had come up against someone who truly shared his world.

Some had become friends. Others, uncertain allies. Most, he ended up killing.

"We've already searched just about every square inch of these hills," Connor said. "But if you want to try, you're welcome to it."

"I will fast tonight, and pray. Tomorrow I'll start behind the Rollins house, and work out from there. I'll spend the mornings at the hunt, the day at rest. The nights I'll spend at the house. It's only a matter of time. The skinwalker will return."

"Awful convenient for all of us this fella decided to strike right around when your lot came to town."

"Convenience had nothing to do it. Why do you think I signed up with Maddock? His Indian show takes me through every small town in the West. Past every wretched reservation, every old battleground. This land has seen too much blood. There isn't a corner of the West that doesn't hold a wronged witch, plotting his revenge. And this isn't the first skinwalker to pass through here."

"No?"

"Your wife—when we met at the fair, there was another woman with her. A Negress. She told me of a creature she'd seen years ago. An unnatural wolf with blue eyes."

A cold dread started to gnaw at his belly. "You're talking about Nell Wallace," he said slowly.

"Has she seen the beast that attacked the Rollins boy?"

"I—now, how the hell did you—" he caught himself before he could say more. Blackfell gave a brief grunt of satisfaction. Connor had the disquieting feeling of being played for a fool.

"So she did. I'm not surprised. She has a wolf's spirit. It's her totem," he explained to Connor's skeptical frown. "A strong one. Any skinwalker who wears a wolf skin will be drawn to her."

"I thought you said the skinwalker was targeting the Rollins family."

"He is. But the angry wolf eats its own kind. That woman has strong magic. She must be warned."

He contemplated making excuses. Nell was out of town. Nell was sick. Nell was a known liar with bad eyesight. But with his luck, she would see them hiking up the road and come running out of the Benedict house and tell him God-knows-what.

"Nell works for a family just up ahead. It's still early. We'll drop by and see if she's in." He only prayed her blue-eyed employer wasn't.

American Flat Road led into the Crown Point Ravine and under the ninety-foot-tall railway trestle. By the time they emerged from under its shadow, they were back within the electrical glow of the town proper. The evening shift change had come and gone, and they met few people on the streets as Connor led the way to the Benedict house. To Connor's horror, Wes answered the door.

"'Evening, Franklin. Is this him, then? Wes Benedict." He held out his hand gamely, and before Connor could warn him, Blackfell subjected it to the same crushing grip he had Bill's.

"Adam Blackfell."

Connor braced himself for some terrifying recognition on Blackfell's part. But he released Wes's hand without comment, and a quick scan of his face and throat revealed a neutral expression and a steady pulse.

"Mr. Blackfell would like to talk to Nell, if it's not too late," Connor explained.

"She's up reading to Ma. Hang on, I'll go get her." Wes was halfway to the parlor before he remembered his manners. "Oh, come on in. Won't be long."

Nell was still rolling down her sleeves when she met them in the entryway. Her hands smelled of camphor, and she wiped them hastily on her apron when she saw Blackfell.

"Wolf Charmer! You came."

"I go where I am needed, sister. I hear you've seen the creature. Was it anything like the one you described to me back at the fair?"

Her gaze flitted to Connor, and her eyes widened. "Oh—oh, no! No sir!" she said emphatically. "That wolf was... well, it was a big dog. This thing... it was just like your stuffed critter—like a big hairy man with a wolf's head. It tore up that boy out at the Rollins farm, and it was fixing to do the same to Mr. Franklin."

"You must be on guard, sister. You escaped the first skinwalker because your totem was stronger than his. But this one is much more powerful. And it has come for you once already."

"Me?" Nell laughed nervously. "Naw, he was going after Mr. Franklin."

Blackfell smiled patiently, almost pityingly. "I'm sure it looked that way. But you have the spirit of the wolf. And you've been marked by one skinwalker already. Guard yourself, sister. Stay away from the Rollins farm. Stay inside on nights when the moon is at its darkest and its brightest. And leave nothing of yours lying about outside where the witch could find it!"

Nell nodded, even as she took a step away from him.

"All right, that's enough," Connor said. "Now you're just scaring the lady."

He touched Blackfell's shoulder, gently enough he thought, but the Indian jumped in alarm. He spun around, catching the offending hand in his viselike grip.

"What do you know of these things? You're a blind man stumbling in the dark—" he drew up suddenly, scowling, as Connor smiled tightly and squeezed.

He needed to use only a fraction of his strength. He fully expected Blackfell to break away long before he applied enough force to break bones. But instead the Wolf Charmer merely loosened his grip, and deftly flipped Connor's hand over, so he was cradling it. His free hand came down atop Connor's palm, and he closed his eyes in concentration.

Blackfell let out a hiss of alarm. He sprang back, eyes wild, heart pounding.

"What are you?" He turned to Nell for guidance. "What is he?"

"What?" Connor and Nell blurted, nearly in unison.

"You have no totem! No animal spirit—no soul!" Blackfell's terror was palpable. "I don't know what you are, but you're not human!"

Nine

The day before Halloween, two hunters marched up the road from Devil's Gate, dragging a great mass of black fur behind them. The child they asked for directions to the marshal's office promptly set off running, screaming the alarm.

"They's got it! They's got the skinwalker!"

Within minutes, Main Street was filled with the curious and the indolent, jostling about the hunters and their carcass. By the time the victory march passed the Crown Point Livery Stables, Wes could hear the commotion from the back of the forge.

"You need a break anyway," Wes told the piebald gelding, as he set down a half-cleaned and swollen hoof. The horse winced and tugged at its tether, trying vainly to free itself. Wes clucked his tongue in sympathy.

"See what happens when you don't let someone near your feet? You think about that while I'm gone."

He hiked up the road to join the growing crowd at the marshal's office. The hunters, Californians by the looks of their coats, had lashed the black carcass against the hitching post. One man held open the great jaws for the crowd, while the other bartered loudly with the marshal and his deputy. Wes worked his way to the front of the mob for a better view.

"Freak of nature, just like they said. Heard that Injun was promised five hundred bucks and the front page of the paper. We want the same!"

Bill Crawford looked over the beast skeptically. "That's a bear."

Someone in the crowd laughed. The Californian flushed under his moustache.

"'Course it's a bear! Whaja think we're dealing with?"

The black bear had been a prime specimen once, Wes could tell. But old age had winnowed all the meat off its bones. Without an ounce of fat, its proportions were rangy, almost unnatural. Its skull was laced with scars, both fresh and old. Its muzzle was infected and swollen, lending its face a canine air. The hunters had sat the bear up against the post, legs splayed in the dirt, almost comically. When one man let the great head go, it lolled like a drunkard's, tongue protruding from between slack jaws.

"Look at these claws," the hunter insisted. "Look at the teeth! That's a maneater, all right."

"By the look of him, this wretch hasn't been eating anything in ages. Where did you find him? Rooting in the junk pile?"

"Shot it down on the plains south of Devil's Gate. See, way I figure," he went on authoritatively, "this ol' fella was sniffing around the dairy, looking for something to eat. Boy corners him, bear bites boy. Bear can't bite hard, on account all these sores. But all this here muck gets in the wound. Bite turns rotten, boy gets sick. Injun shows up and spins a few yarns—there's your skinwalker."

"That's quite the yarn you're spinning."

"We getting our reward, or ain't we?"

"There is no reward. Least nothing we're offering," Bill said. "You want money, go drag that thing off to the Rollins house and try your luck there."

Wes watched as John Garrod drew Bill aside and murmured something in his ear. Bill reacted with predictable irritation. "No! We ain't a trapper's office."

Someone in the crowd called out, "Hey, I'll give you ten bucks for the hide. I could use a new coat."

"How much you want for the claws?" someone else asked.

Garrod continued to argue with the marshal in hushed tones. Wes caught the word "procedure" before the chatter of the crowd became too loud. People continued to bid on the bear, some in jest, some in earnest. Small children gathered their courage to run up and poke the beast.

Finally Bill threw up his hands. "All right, let's have some order here. This ain't an auction. Move along, all of you. We've got this in hand. Gentlemen, you want a feature in the paper? Then you'd best run up to their office yourselves and let them know. Well, get along, now!" he snapped, when the two hunters stared at him blankly. "Just up the road. Tell them to send down their photographer, if he's working today."

Bill started to untie the bear from the post. "Hey, that's ours until we get paid!" the hunter with the big mustache protested.

"Not anymore. I'm arresting this bear."

That got a laugh out of the crowd.

"On what charge?" the hunter demanded.

"Vagrancy."

A few more laughs, but fainter this time. The audience sensed the show was over. One by one, the spectators began to drift away, even as the hunters made no move to abandon their trophy. Bill got the last of the ropes off and tried to drag the bear up onto the sidewalk. "Unh... could use a hand, Garrod! You're the one who wants to process this thing."

Reluctantly, Garrod bent down and helped Bill lift. Even skin and bones, the bear was too heavy for them. Bill scanned the bystanders who lingered in the road. "Mac! Benedict! C'mere, make yourselves useful."

Phil McCafferty, a freckled boy of nineteen, stepped up eagerly. Wes hesitated. "I got a horse to see to—"

"And yet here you are, standing around gawping at this circus! Five minutes, you goldbricker. Now get over here and grab this leg."

Wes obeyed. With a man to each limb, they heaved the bear off the dirt and carried it around behind the jailhouse. At the back of the yard, a wooden shanty nestled against the canyon wall. Young Mac slowed his pace at the sight of the death house. "We ain't going in there, are we?"

"Doubt we could get him through the door, let alone on the table," Bill said. "No, might as well examine him right here. Lie him down nice and straight, now," he cautioned, as they eased the bear to the dirt. "Deputy Garrod wants to measure this thing properly, don't you?"

Garrod looked affronted. It seemed to Wes to be the only emotion he showed willingly. "We'd be derelict in our duty if we didn't, sir."

"Course we would. Well, let's get this over with before he starts to stink. Phew. Mac, you wanna run into the office for me? Top middle drawer of my desk, there's a tape measure. Grab a pencil and my pad of paper while you're at it." He straightened and brushed himself off. "This show's all yours, Garrod. Try to keep it under five pages this time, will you?"

"And where will you be? If someone asks. Sir."

"Rounds."

Wes tried to slip away behind Bill, but Garrod called him back.

"Benedict. Help me measure this beast."

This time Wes knew better than to argue. Jack Morrison made the mistake of backtalking the deputy once, and he'd been charged with disorderly conduct. When the bartender at the Maynard House refused to give Garrod any more coffee on credit, the deputy suddenly noticed all the underage drinkers in the saloon. And when Nell had refused to be suitably cowed by his icy stare...

It still made his blood boil to think of it. To hear Nell tell the tale, she simply cooled her heels in a cell, after which Connor Franklin sorted it all out. But Wes had gotten the full story soon enough.

If he were a real man, he would have done something about it. He would have found some way to strike back, to repay Garrod for the pain and humiliation he had dealt. He would have devoted his days to ruining the man utterly, or failing that, he would have cornered him in some dark alley and taught him something about fear.

But he took the coward's way, as he did in everything, and kept his mouth shut.

Mac returned with the measuring tape, and Wes held one end to the bear's scarred nose, as Garrod ran the tape all the way to its bony rump. "Eighty-one inches," Garrod pronounced, and Mac whistled appreciatively.

"No wonder they all thought it was some wild man," he murmured. "Stand him up on his hind legs in bad light..."

"You don't seriously think this is our skinwalker?" Wes challenged. "Rollins and Franklin talk about it running faster than a horse in full gallop. This old thing looks so crippled up, I doubt he could outrun your grandmother."

"We'll know soon enough." Garrod measured the skull next, then a paw. "Hold his jaws open, Benedict." When Wes did so, Garrod stretched the tape from one stubby canine to the other. "I have measurements of Joseph Rollins's bite. We can compare the two." He read the tape and tutted in disappointment.

"Not it?" Mac asked.

"Not unless our skinwalker has grown considerably in the last two weeks." Garrod let the bear's head fall to the ground. "I'll take the beast's jaw, just to be prudent. We can examine the teeth more closely once it's properly defleshed."

"C'mon, deputy, you don't really believe it's some Indian werewolf running around, do you?" Mac asked eagerly. "That Blackfell fella—he's full of it, right?"

Garrod gave a non-committal bob of the head. "The bite pattern suggests some kind of dog. Still, the concept of the werewolf is common across many cultures. And twenty years ago, the common redskin was as savage as any wild beast. Perhaps we're looking for some sort of missing link." He looked at Wes. "Like the Negro and the ape."

Wes felt his fists clenching. "Wouldn't know about that," he said blandly. He dug his nails into the flesh of his palms until the urge to break Garrod's even white teeth passed.

"I hear you took on the Brennans' girl," Garrod continued casually, as he probed the sores on the bear's snout with his pencil.

"She hasn't been the 'Brennans' girl' since the summer." *Her name is Nell, you ignorant prick! Eleanor Wallace! You wrote it down in your precious logbook—have you forgotten it already?*

"Either way, she's your girl now."

Beside him, Mac stifled a laugh. "This ain't the olden days," Wes heard himself protest. "I don't own her." But in his mind, the words kept repeating. Your girl, your girl, yours.

"I'm sure she's a competent maid," Garrod said dismissively. "They usually are. Though I wouldn't trust her to look after *my* mother."

You had a mother? Wes wanted to quip. *Say it, you coward, and wipe that prissy little smirk off his face.*

"She's a thief, you know. That's why the Brennans threw her out."

And is that why you denied her water and left her to sweat in a hotbox in the middle of summer? Say it, coward! "Those charges were dropped," Wes said slowly, suddenly very aware of Garrod's open notebook, and Mac hanging on every word. "And she quit the Brennans of her own free will."

"I'm only warning you as I would any citizen. Your mother is very well-respected in this town, I gather. I would be mindful of that, if I were you. A man is judged by the company he keeps."

"My mother and I have known Nell since she was a baby. Anyone who wants to judge us for that has done it long ago."

"Mm. Well, I'd never tell an honest man how to run his household."

"Funny, I thought you were doing just that."

"Not at all. I'm merely assuring myself that your household is indeed… honest."

"What's the supposed to mean?" Wes demanded, even as he felt himself sliding into the trap. *She's your girl now…*

Garrod leaned over the bear and lowered his voice to a whisper. "Miscegenation is a crime in this state."

Wes found his courage at last, and laughed in his face.

It was loud and long, the sort of full-bellied roar that invited everyone to join in, whether they got the joke or not. As Garrod stared at him blankly, poor young Mac gave into temptation and added his own uncertain chuckle.

At that moment, Garrod's mask slipped. All the little muscles in his face fell slack at once, and for the barest moment, Wes saw the man's true character. It was only a heartbeat, but the expression was unmistakable, and very, very ugly.

It was too late for a retreat. Wes got to his feet, making a great show of dusting off his leather apron. "That's a good one. You know, you're all right, Garrod." He made a little motion with his hand, as if to clap the deputy on the back. Garrod drew back in barely contained disgust.

"See you around." Without waiting for a reply, Wes turned for home, still chuckling. He all but swaggered down the hill, head held high. He couldn't remember the last time he had felt so proud. When the adrenaline started to wane and his cheer with it, he had only to summon a memory of Garrod's shocked face and the laughter brimmed up again.

His sense of triumph lasted until he was back at his workshop, tending to the gelding's sore hoof. The words thrown at him started to creep back to the forefront of his mind, and with them the shame and frustration.

She's your girl now…. Miscegenation… a man is judged by the company he keeps… She's your girl, your girl, yours…

But she wasn't. And she could never be. His rage built up behind his teeth until he couldn't bear it anymore, and he opened his mouth on a wordless cry.

The horse shied in alarm, wrenching its hoof out of Wes's hand with a force that stripped the skin from his palm. In retaliation, Wes hurled the hoof knife against the nearest wall with a curse. The loud crash made the gelding buck and shriek.

'Yeah? You like that?" Wes shot back. "How about this?" He plucked up the long-handled pincers and threw them against the cold firepit. Next went the hammer, and the rasp. By the time the clatter of tools and the horse's enraged screams brought Grant Weatherbee limping in from the stables, the forge was turned upside down.

"Wesley!" the old liveryman boomed. "What the hell is wrong with you?"

Slumped against the forge when his strength had given out, Wes could only heave a broken sigh. "Horse kicked at me," he muttered, wiping at this red eyes. "Sorry."

~ * ~

The wind was up; the windowpane rattled in its frame as Nell heaved the bucket of steaming water off the stove. Clouds the color of lead cut briskly across the sky. Twilight was falling in midafternoon.

Nell carried the bucket through the pantry to the heavy curtain that separated the kitchen from the bathroom. "Looks like a zephyr coming," she announced. "You ready for more water?"

A sloshing sound behind the curtain was her answer. Nell pulled the cloth aside just enough to expose the lip of the hip bath, and gently emptied the bucket. Lucy Benedict let out a muffled moan of sheer delight.

"Not too hot?"

"Oh, Nell, it's heavenly. Thank you. You're sure Wes won't be back for a while?"

"Better not. It's only three." She sat with her back to the curtain and listened to the sound of water lapping against the metal tub. "Only another five minutes, now. You ain't catching a chill on my watch."

The dainty splashes increased in frequency as Lucy began to scrub. "It is just so comforting to have a proper soak. If it were up to Doc Sheppard, I'd be having nothing but sponge baths until summer. Honestly, everyone knows hot water is the best thing for a chest cold."

"Don't you be doing your hair, too!" Nell warned, when the sounds of bathing grew too vigorous. "We'll never get that all dry before Wes gets in."

The water quieted a little. Then: "Tell me some gossip."

"Gossip?"

A flushed face peeked out from the other side of the curtain. "I know you saw Charlie last night. And she always has such good stories. Oh, go on, Nell," she urged, with an impish smile. "I've been terribly out of touch this last month."

"Well, mostly we talked about the Wolf Charmer. He's staying up with Miz Katy. His keeper Maddock drinks like a fish, Charlie says. Already run up a tab as long as my arm. And... uh, he's got these two wives—Mr. Blackfell, that is. Indian thing, I reckon. And this one's supposed to be dumb as a post, but I heard from Charlie she can swear like a sailor... and in a Texas drawl, no less!"

Lucy giggled behind the curtain.

"Oh, and they're still having a social tomorrow night like always at the Miners' Hall. Marshal Crawford wanted to cancel it on account of the skinwalker, but the mayor wouldn't have it." *And Connor Franklin isn't human.*

She wouldn't say that last part aloud, not even to Charlie. Especially not to Charlie. She told herself she was afraid her friend would mock her, if she repeated something so patently ridiculous. But in truth, she was more afraid Charlie wouldn't laugh at all.

Connor Franklin hadn't been laughing when Blackfell accused him of having no soul. Neither had Wes, when he arrived on the scene moments later, drawn by the raised voices. Together they'd ejected the Indian, then Franklin himself had stolen out into the night without a word. The simple exchange of wary glances between men had been conversation enough.

She could have asked Wes then, in those tension-filled moments before he turned to climb the stairs back to his mother. But her courage had failed her, and in the days that followed she had yet to find it again.

Silence was the safest course. A colored girl-child was raised not to remark on so many things. And since the terror of the full moon, and the horror of the night that followed, she had studiously avoided the topic of men and monsters.

Charlie had tried to coax the words out of her, the night before. "You can talk to me about all of this, you know. If you're worried about Wes... or dealing with it..."

Like you deal with a man who can't come out in daylight? Nell had nearly snapped. *Like you deal with everything, flashing that horsey smile of yours at all the wrong times?* But she'd bitten her tongue and kept her friendship.

"Reckon I just need time to sort it all out," she'd muttered instead. "Reckon... I still don't know what to say."

But she did. She whispered it into her pillow every night before bed, an inventory of regrets. *Why didn't they tell me all this years ago? I wanted to know then. I was stupid enough to think I could be brave.* She knew better now.

Lucy's five minutes were up. Nell pulled back the curtain and held open the thick towel. Lucy's legs were unsteady after the long soak. Water splashed over the side of the tub as Nell helped her climb out and dry off. The awkwardness of Nell's first week of work was gone; now patient and nurse moved together in a brisk sort of dance. Within moments, Lucy was warmly bundled in layers of flannel and a quilted wrapper.

"Now, you just take a seat..." Nell guided her through the kitchen, into the dining room. "And I'll brew you a fresh pot of tea."

"This must be what it's like at one of those fancy hotels," Lucy said dreamily. "No, Nell, leave the tea a moment. Come sit with me." She patted the tabletop beside her with a motherly smile. "I haven't apologized properly for keeping everything from you."

"You don't need to—"

"Yes, I do. I've kept you at arm's length all these years, and worse, I made Wes do the same. Now I can dress it up all I like, but the simple fact is, I didn't trust you." Her expression turned pained. "And I'm so sorry for it."

"You had no reason to trust me," Nell said awkwardly. "And I can't blame a mother, looking out for her son. Can't blame anyone... not wanting to talk about it."

"I used to be a more trusting person, you know. About Wes. About everything. Well, I suppose that's how we ended up all the way out West. Never really meant to, you know. I kept hoping... someone would understand. Someone would help us. A young mother and a little boy – and he became such a little wolf, how much harm could he be?"

She sighed ruefully. "A mother's blindness, I suppose. Well, I learned the hard way. There was no place for us in Tennessee, or Arkansas, or the Territories. By the time we got out here, I'd learned we could only depend on each other."

Once again, Nell noticed Wes's father was absent from her story. "Mrs. B... can I ask you a question? You tell me if I'm overstepping now—"

"I don't think there's much left to overstep on, honey. Ask away."

"Wes's daddy."

"Ah." Lucy looked down at her left hand and twisted the tarnished ring around her finger.

"I know you said he died in the war, when Wes was still a baby. But you never really talk about him. And what you were saying about trusting the wrong folk... Did Mr. B run out on you? Because of what Wes is?"

"There was no Mr. B; Benedict's my maiden name. And for all I know, Wes's daddy is alive and well."

"Oh." The revelation sunk in by degrees. Her shock must have shown on her face, despite her best efforts, because Lucy laughed lightly and smacked her arm.

"You young 'uns. Always think your generation invented fornication."

Nell felt her face flood with heat, hearing such a bold word on such respectable lips. "Does Wes know?" But even as she asked, she knew. Mother and son kept no secrets.

"He didn't... for a long time," Lucy admitted. "He had enough burdens to carry. It was a kind lie, a necessary one, for a little boy missing a man in his life. But when he was older, I told him the truth of it. Maybe I shouldn't have. But I figured he deserved to know what sort of man his daddy was."

"Who was he?"

"Man I worked for. Cattle farmer. Wife had just had her sixth baby—all boys, can you imagine?" Her expression was faultless in its gentility, but Nell heard the bitterness creeping into her voice. "I was brought on to help out after the last one. Suppose we had different ideas of what 'helping out' meant."

"You... didn't get a choice in Wes's making, did you?"

"No. But I chose to love him all the same." Her voice caught in her throat, and she blinked at the intrusion of viscous tears. "Seems I was the only one who did. His daddy wouldn't admit to a thing, and my parents... oh, they were Christian enough to keep a bastard grandson, you understand. Just not a werewolf."

Her few words left Nell hungry for details, the hows and whens of the long path that brought mother and son to Nevada. But instead she said simply, "I can't imagine how you managed."

"Some days, I can't believe it myself. No wonder I feel so old. But we managed." She covered Nell's hand with her own. "Still, I'm so grateful to have you now. Oh, I know Deputy Franklin is a good man, and I'm grateful for all the times he's brought his dog around to play. But that man has never stayed in a town for more than five years at a stretch. And we're not his problem. We're not family." Her voice started to shake again. "I used to worry so much... what would happen to Wes when I'm gone..."

"Don't you say that, now. You got long years ahead of you."

"That's kind of you to say."

"It ain't kindness; it's basic arithmetic!"

I'm too tired to argue with you, her smile said. "At any rate... I'm so glad you're family now."

Family... Nell weighed the word on her tongue. So many meanings wrapped in three syllables.

"'Course she's family," a voice announced from the entryway, startling them both. "Ain't I been saying that for years?" Wes came in and took the chair opposite his mother. He looked from one woman to the other with a boyish inquisitiveness. "What are we talking about? And why aren't you in bed, Ma?"

"It's high time she got a bit of exercise," Nell said firmly. "And she'll be joining us downstairs for supper too, from now on. No, Wes, I don't want to hear what the doctor has to say. No one ever got pneumonia from walking up and down stairs."

"Yes'm," Wes said promptly. An impish light danced in his eyes as he added, "But you said 'us' so you'd better be setting a place for yourself too. 'Cause I'm getting mighty sick of you thinking you're too good to share a table with the likes of me."

His smile was teasing, but she heard the firmness of his voice behind it. Nell didn't know whether to feel offended or contrite. When she looked to Lucy for guidance, the older woman clucked her tongue and said, "You did say 'us.' He's got you there."

Nell lowered her voice to a whisper. "Thought we were supposed to be ganging up on him?"

"I'm afraid the Benedicts are sticking together on this one, honey. Wes, what happened to your hand? You look like you've been brawling!"

Wes laughed bashfully as he held up the crudely-bandaged hand. "I was, with Clark. He's going to the glue factory if he keeps it up."

Lucy clucked her tongue. "I don't know why Grant puts up with that horse."

Nell took advantage of the distraction and returned to the kitchen. The fire in the stove was still going strong; she might as well start on the soup stock. Her thoughts chased each other in circles as she worked. She was torn between laughter and tears.

You're family, all right, but only on their terms.

Then: *That's not fair. They're only trying to be kind.*

But there are rules to this world! I follow them, why can't they?

With the soup pot filled and heating over the stove grate, Nell set to emptying the hip tub. The wind gusted in the backyard. She had to lean hard against the pine door to hold it open as she emptied the water onto the dirt.

A flicker of motion caught her eye. A neat bundle of something gray floated across the ground by the fence. A piece of windblown sage? A cat—or something larger? In the failing light it was impossible to tell solids from shadows.

When she returned with the second pail of water, the wind caught her as she tipped it out, and she nearly dropped it. Water spattered over her shoes, and she cursed under her breath. She thought she heard an answering sound, like a horse's snort. She looked to the corrals, but the horses were already stabled. "Hello?" she called. The dark gray lump at the fence was motionless ... although it seemed larger—or closer.

The wind howled, and the shape rushed at her. For a moment she stared dumbfounded, until the shape grew to the size of a large dog, hunchbacked and dark-haired. The wind died down, but the creature kept coming, and she heard the telltale slap-slap of feet on hard earth. A snuffling growl rose in the creature's throat, until Nell's own scream drowned it out.

Her cry brought Wes running. He reached her mere moments after the creature drew up at the stoop, threw its fur cape back, and became a child.

"Scared you!" the boy crowed, waving his arms inside the voluminous sleeves of a grown man's buffalo-skin coat. "Scared you! Scared the black off you!"

"Nell—what?" Wes's arm came around her waist effortlessly, drawing her against him. He was breathing hard, spoiling for a fight. Then he saw the laughing boy, and his face turned scarlet with rage.

"Bobby Bittner, I'll tan your hide!"

The boy danced back out of reach. "It's Halloween, Mist' Ben'dict!"

"Not until tomorrow. You get out of my yard right now, or I'll drag you back to your daddy and show him what you did with his good coat!"

That threat clearly carried more weight. Bobby hitched up his coat and hightailed it from the yard. Only then did Wes seem to become aware he was still holding Nell fast.

"Are you all right?"

His breath was hot on her cheek. He bore the bulk of her weight against his ribs; she couldn't help but hold onto his shoulder for balance. If she turned her face slightly, they would be nose to nose. A giddy flutter seized her belly; she felt like a young girl falling in love all over again.

"Fine… he just startled me."

Slowly, hesitantly, Wes released her. Nell let her hand fall into the curve of his arm, but she made no move to remove it completely. Their faces remained mere inches apart. This was the point in all her fantasies when his restraint would give way and he would finally— finally—kiss her. She would resist at first, as any good woman would, but he would not be denied. He would cajole and caress away all her arguments, then carry her off to bed. Or he'd crush her against the wall and have her right there, and damn the consequences.

He didn't kiss her. Nor did he step back. His eyes were searching hers. Nell wondered why she never dreamed of taking the initiative. Surely there was room in her imagination for a world in which she moved first, rising up only a little on her toes, taking his scruffy face in her hands and parting his lips with her tongue.

"Wes? Nell?" Lucy Benedict's reached them, distant and reedy. "What is it?"

Wes turned away. "Nothing, Ma!" he hollered down the corridor. "Everything's fine."

Nell clucked her tongue as she bent down to retrieve the wash bucket. *Yep, everything's fine*, she thought miserably. *And I'm family*. Praise seldom came more bitter than that.

The bucket lay in the mud where Nell had dropped it. When she tugged, it came free with a wet, smacking sound. She beat it against the side of the house until the worst of the mud fell off. She looked up at the horse corrals one last time as she reached for the door.

A figure stood on the rise, tall and man-like, but for its narrow head and pointed ears.

"Get!" Nell shouted, waving the bucket. "He told you—it ain't Halloween yet!"

The silhouette stood its ground. The only motion was the gentle rise and fall of its shoulders, and the curl of its long fingers, slowly clenching and unclenching.

"Wes..." Nell fumbled for the handle on the door.

The skinwalker cocked its head. One claw-tipped hand extended, reaching for her.

Nell shrieked, and slammed the door.

Ten

"And I'll take five pounds of sugar, too," Nell said, as she lined up the tins of coffee and canned vegetables along the counter. The grocer paused in his count of the cans to flash her an impish smile.

"And would that be white or brown sugar?"

"White."

She thought she heard a genteel titter behind her, from one of the housewives awaiting her turn at the cash register. "You heard her, Gus," the grocer hollered down to his son, standing by the bulk bins. "The girl likes the white sugar!"

The dainty titter became a full-throated guffaw. Nell clenched her teeth and fought the urge to look over her shoulder. The grocer turned back to her, innocent as a child. "That'll be two dollars and twenty-five. Next, please."

Gus took his time bagging her sugar. Nell waited by the shelves of soaps and hair tonics. She looked over the labels, the delicate colors and feminine script. Perhaps she would indulge herself next time, and buy one of the fancier-looking bars for an extra nickel. She could certainly afford to now. *Soap is soap is soap*, her mother used to say, as she commanded her daughter to wash with the scraps of harsh lye. But Nell wondered what it would be like for her hands to smell like flowers at the end of the day.

A pasty-faced matron stepped up to examine the bundles of candles, as her younger companion chattered at her elbow. "Did you hear? That dirty old Indian's tent burned down last night. Up at the old Franklin Mine."

"Fell asleep at his fire pit, did he?" the older matron clucked her tongue. "Good – maybe someone will finally do something about him. I'm sick of him selling that nasty tobacco of his to all our boys. Rolly's always coming home stinking of it."

"Well, I heard it was some boys that set fire to the tent, don't you know."

"Pft. Probably the same lot that soaped up all the windows on Halloween."

"Was he hurt?" Nell interjected. Both women turned to stare at her, their faces stamped with an incredulous horror.

"Beg pardon?" the older one finally said, frostily.

"Captain Marsh—was he hurt?"

"Well, how should I know?" the younger woman tittered nervously. "Come along, Sarah dear." She looped her arm through her companion's and drew her away. Just then the grocer's son arrived with her sugar. Nell squeezed it into the basket on top of the canned goods and headed for home.

She had overloaded the basket; the wicker handles dug into the crease of her elbow, and she had to alternate arms every dozen steps. Three blocks shy of home, she heard a familiar voice call "Nelly!"

Nell walked faster. But weighted down with groceries, she had no chance of outpacing him. The lanky black man drew up alongside her, teeth bared in an ingratiating smile.

"Help you with that?"

"No thanks."

"Can we talk?"

"Not on your life."

Shiloh stepped around her, blocking her path. Nell sighed and altered course, skirting a wide path off the boardwalk and down the middle of the road.

"Nelly, come on."

She ignored him, picking her way around a mound of fresh horse droppings.

"I know you're his fancy maid!"

Nell stopped. Slowly she turned around. Perched above her on the grade, he towered over her, a smug, gangly giant. His lips curled so easily into a sneer; she wondered why she had ever thought him handsome.

"I'm his maid. Ain't nothing fancy about it."

"That's not what Hack Bittner says. He heard from his li'l brother you two were feeling each other up out in the yard, in broad daylight."

"Then his li'l brother's a liar!" But even as she protested, she remembered the grinning boy in the buffalo-skin coat, and Wes's arm tight about her waist, and she felt her cheeks burning.

"Jesus, Shy! Last time we fought, you were accusing me of sleeping with Fat Joe Brennan."

He flinched at the memory. "Well, this is different, ain't it? It's him, ain't it?" His voice was foaming with bitterness. "He threatened to break my legs, you know, back in June, if I didn't stay away from you."

If he expected shock from her, she was determined not to show it. "I'd rather he break your jaw," Nell hissed, matching spite for spite. "It would shut you up for a while."

He did not try to stop her when she turned away again. But he could not resist one last parting shot. "Where are you gonna go when he turns you out? 'Cause he will, you know."

Nell shifted her basket so she could raise her middle finger high enough for him to see. Shiloh spat curses into the dirt, but his voice grew fainter with each step downhill. She found herself smiling at the thought of Wes threatening to break bones for her sake. There seemed to be no end to the surprises from him lately.

Two Cornish washerwomen crested the hump in the road, their backs bent under their load of linens. They saw Nell coming and changed trajectory, risking the dusty road rather than cross her path. Nell paid them no mind until she heard one stage-whisper to the other, "That's the one. The farrier's whore."

Nell's head whipped around. The women continued uphill, heads together, tongues wagging too faintly for her to hear. But now she saw the others scattered along Main Street: the man unloading his cart outside the Capital Hotel, the mother and child idling by a shop display, the pair of vagrants sitting on the edge of the boardwalk, playing dice. All of them stared at her, and by their faces they had overheard all they needed. Nell's heart sank. Her first helpless, morbid thought was: Wes couldn't possibly break enough jaws to silence them all.

~ * ~

Connor found the old Indian perched on a rock next to the remnants of his tent. "So you heard, old man!" Marsh hailed with a cynical cackle. "Can you believe it? Goddamn kids these days got no respect!"

All his salvaged possessions fit inside one bedroll. The tent itself was a loss; one side had burned down to ashes, leaving a skeletal half-dome of scorched branches and tattered canvas. Connor sifted through the debris at the base of the ash pile, and found broken glass and bent metal. When he sniffed the largest glass shard, he could smell the remnants of kerosene.

"Breaking glass and Apache war whoops—that's what a man's gotta wake up to at God-knows-when in the morning!" Marsh's voice was raw as gravel, and he panted for breath. He struggled with a second match, but the pipe only smoldered. At length, Connor took pipe and matchbox away from him.

"More smoke's the last thing you need," he warned, as he cleared the pipe's airway.

"We can't all live forever."

Connor got the pipe to light and took a long draw as his fee before passing it back. "So what did Bill say?"

"Paugh! Says I was damned lucky it wasn't worse. Like it's my fault! Wants to herd me back to the camp. City can't go taking responsibility for stray Indians, don't you know."

"He's got a point. There's safety in numbers. And I don't just mean from drunk kids slinging hurricane lamps." Connor slowly turned around, scanning the walls of the ravine. Outlined by the last pink rays of the sunset, the ridgeline was a black maw, poised to snap closed over their heads.

"If nothing else, there's a frost coming tonight. And you've got a bad cough. You need a roof over your head."

Marsh spread his arms wide, to encompass the great bowl of the sky. "Biggest roof there is," he said cheerfully.

"I'm not letting you set up camp in November with nothing but a tinderbox and an old blanket."

"Let me?" The captain's good humor evaporated. "And who said you get any say what I do in my own home."

"Cap'n," Connor said patiently, "your home burned down."

"This is my home!" He stamped his foot on the red earth. "The rocks and the brush and the sky overhead. My kin were hunting and roaming and fending for themselves long before your kin sailed outta England!"

And dealing with witches, too. Connor thought. *But how many of them ever lived past sixty?* He shook his head sadly. "Hate to do this to you, kiddo, but I'm going to have to take you in."

"I ain't going back to Jenny—"

"Don't need to. You got a warm bed waiting for you in the lockup. Let's get your things, now."

Captain Marsh blinked. "What—the jail?" a hopeful note crept into his voice.

"That's right. Charlie'll have the stove all fired up by now. Bet she'll even fry you up some cornbread if you share some of that kinnikinnick with her."

"She's a sweet girl, your Charlie."

"Reckon she's fond of you, too. I know she'd love to hear one of your stories about the old days."

The deal was clearly sounding sweeter by the moment. Still, the captain made a show of reluctance. "That jackass Garrod on duty?"

"Not until noon tomorrow. And unless Morrison starts getting drunk on Mondays, you'll have the back room all to yourself."

The old man tried to swallow his smile. "Well… if you're insisting. Reckon a night or two wouldn't hurt."

A night or two of free room and board, and we might never get you out, Connor thought wryly. Captain Marsh knew a good graft when he saw one.

They walked down the hill together at an easy pace, and Connor could see the toll the previous night's excitement had taken on the captain. He walked stiffly, favoring one leg and pausing for breath every few dozen steps.

"If you see that vaudeville Indian, you make sure to tell him it weren't no skinwalker that burned down my tent, will you?" he wheezed. "Ain't about to become a victim in one of his ghost stories."

"You don't think much of him either, do you?"

"Pft. Half o'what comes out of his mouth is straight bull. Hell, I'd bet money he's not even Navajo." He squinted conspiratorially. "Looks kinda Mexican, if you ask me."

Connor tsked. "Got a problem with Mexicans now, Cap'n?"

"Got a problem with frauds. Got a problem with swindlers playacting at being red men. Selling his useless medicine bundles, reading people's palms, singing critters to sleep—he's every cheap 'Injun' carny act come to life! Caught him telling an old Creole werewolf story the other day, and passing it off as his own."

"Sure seems better playing to the crowds than actually hunting, don't he?"

"He's dangerous, is what he is!"

"I'm inclined to agree with you." Yet in Connor's mind, the danger was not to be found in Blackfell's showmanship, but in his perception.

You're not human; the accusation still haunted him.

To judge by the lack of gossip, Blackfell had yet to share his discovery with the rest of the town. But he had yet to speak a word to Connor that wasn't grudging, and his pulse raced whenever he caught sight of the deputy. All it would take was one word in the right ear, and the skinwalker would become the least of Connor's problems.

"I told him those medicine bundles were useless," Marsh complained. "Not three days ago I warned him. 'Look, fella,' I said, 'I don't care where you say you learned your tricks, but you're only hurting these folks with all this. Real red men don't talk about this sorta witchcraft with anyone who pays to hear! That sorta foolishness just brings the witch closer to you. Now I'm the first to say it: I dunno about this Witchery Way, and I don't wanna know. Ain't my tribe, ain't my fight. But seeing as how you're muddling up half a dozen different ghost stories, I'm guessing you don't know the first thing about it either!'"

"Uh-huh. Here, watch your step."

"Well, he just laughed in my face. No respect for his elders. No respect for real witchcraft, for that matter! I told him so. Told him I'd see him run out of town! Are you listening, old man?"

He was. All at once, the captain had his complete attention.

"When did all this happen?"

"Couple days ago. Before the weekend. Why?"

"You... you go on ahead to the jail. Charlie can brew you up some coffee. Tell her to hold down the fort for another hour or two. There's someone I need to see."

He started back up the road before the captain could object. He told himself he was leaping to conclusions, looking for an easy fix to his own problems. He had no business confronting any man without proof, and certainly not a man who could destroy the life he'd made in Gold Hill. But he thought of Captain Marsh's laboring breathing, his pathetic bedroll, and his rising anger drowned out all the arguments for restraint.

He ascended Ravine Road at an easy pace, mindful of the scattering of households that still called the ravine home. As the last of the buildings fell behind him, he gradually lengthened his stride and increased his pace, until he was effortlessly bounding up the near-vertical grade. To his surprise, he found himself smiling; he seldom indulged in properly exerting himself, unless it was a matter of life and death. He had forgotten how good it felt to run at full bore, for no other reason than to raise his pulse and make his leg muscles ache.

The climb might have taken a human a half-hour with a rope and pickax. Connor scaled it in under a minute. Suddenly he stood on the saddle ridge, some seven thousand feet above sea level. He wasn't even winded. His heartbeat was a slow, steady thrum in his ears.

Above the shadow of the canyon, the light was still golden. To the southeast, one could see for nearly a hundred miles. For a moment Connor simply stared, struck by the severe beauty of the land.

From a ridgeline sloping southwest, he could survey the expanse of scrub and winding gullies leading down to American Flat. The settlers' houses looked like children's toys from his vantage point, and the domed tents of the Paiute camp all but disappeared into the rolling landscape.

A solitary campfire burned a quarter-mile upwind of the Rollins dairy. When Connor squinted, he could make out a man squatting over the fire pit, warming his hands over the flames.

Connor sprinted down the steep ridgeline. Where the last weekend's windstorm had blasted away the loose soil and bared the rocks, he leapt from foothold to foothold without breaking stride. When he reached the rolling Flat, he drew a deep breath and smelled charred wood.

The campfire was out by the time he found it, half-hidden in the folds of the hillside. Dirt choked the center of the fire pit, hissing from the heat. Connor crouched down and sifted through the cooler dregs at the outer limits of the fire pit. Freshly-charred kindling sat atop a thick layer of white ash; the site had been tended over many nights. A foul smell of herbs and charcoal scratched at his throat.

He thought he smelled a human on the air, though it was hard to be certain. The sooty smell of the campfire made a clever mask.

When he looked down at the sandy topsoil, he only saw his own footprints.

Where'd that slippery bastard get to?

He searched all around the fire pit next, gradually expanding his circular pacing until he had covered the entire hollow, some fifty yards in length, and perhaps half that in width. From the southern lip of the basin, he had a clear view of the Rollins dairy. On the north side, several large stones lay clustered together in a crude pyramid. Connor stared at them a long moment, trying to decide if the shape looked natural or not. An animal had been digging at an old burrow at the base of the rocks. Furrow marks streaked the dirt.

Connor crouched down in front of the burrow. It was long-abandoned, too heavily eroded and excavated to be of any use to its original inhabitant. The dirt smelled of dried blood and dog dander. He reached into the burrow, feeling around for the bottom.

Nothing. He reached deeper, until the earth swallowed his arm to the elbow. His fingertips brushed something soft and furry. He flexed his fingers, trying to get a grip.

Two pinpricks stung the web of skin between his thumb and forefinger. Connor yanked his hand out with a yelp. The rattlesnake followed, already drawing its head back for another strike.

"Son of a bitch!" Connor sprang to his feet, narrowly missing a bite to his ankle. He danced back, clutching his bleeding hand. The massive rattler coiled itself at the entrance to the burrow. Its rapidly vibrating tail raised an unholy racket.

"All right, all right! I don't want your dinner!" Connor snapped. "Hope you choke on it."

Laughter greeted his pronouncement. Connor turned to see Adam Blackfell standing by the fire pit. But for the naked Bowie knife in his hand, he had the look of a man on an afternoon stroll.

"Did he get you?" Blackfell asked. "Those rattlers are deadly, you know. To humans."

"Don't worry 'bout me," Connor said confidently. The pain had lost its sharpness. Gradually, he eased the pressure on his hand. The twin punctures had already faded to bruised dimples. At least the rest of him was healing properly. For now.

"You watching the Rollinses? Funny place for it."

Blackfell frowned. "You think so?"

"Oh, your sightlines are good, but the breeze is behind you. Suppose the critter decides to come from the west. You don't think he'll smell you?"

Blackfell gestured to the smothered fire with a tight smile. "A smoke mask. Old Indian trick. You might have heard of it."

"Is that what it is?" Connor nudged the ashes with the tip of his boot, exposing the old char underneath. "Thought you might be trying to make white ash. I hear it's supposed to be good against skinwalkers."

Blackfell's face darkened. "You've been talking to the old man."

"So have you. Hear he didn't take kindly to your little shows up at the hotel. Says a real holy man wouldn't be so eager to sell all his people's secrets to the highest bidder."

"You hear a lot of things."

"Did you tell some boys to burn down Cap'n Marsh's tent?"

Blackfell threw his head back and laughed. "What do you take me for?"

"A showman. A good one, mind. And maybe you are a Navajo holy man too. Maybe. But for all you've been running your mouth about your mission, you're a lot better at lining your pockets. You've been here over a week now, on my dollar, and all you've done is get people more riled up."

"People have cause to be afraid."

"Before you arrived, folks were coming to the marshal and me every few days, saying they saw something running around out here. Now we're getting five reports a night! Coyotes sniffing at garbage pits, folks running errands at sundown—shoot, one call last night turned out to be a loose horse! You got folks jumping at shadows and spitting at every Indian they see. Now I hear Captain Marsh calls you out, and two nights later his tent gets torched. Makes a man wonder."

"A man? Is that what you are?"

"I'm gonna start asking questions, starting at the hotel. And if I hear you mentioned Cap'n Marsh to your... followers—"

"White men don't need a reason to attack red ones," Blackfell said, a little too quickly. He had a good poker face, but Connor could smell the unease on his breath.

"Still, I'm betting you gave them one anyway, with all your talk about curses and medicine men. And I aim to find out."

"Why do you care what happened to these people? Why do you pretend to be one of them?" He took a step towards Connor, gesturing with his naked blade. "I know what you really are."

All right, Connor thought. *I'm game. Let's both show our hands.*

"Then tell me. What am I, that can spook a big fella like you?"

"You're the evil I've vowed to destroy," Blackfell pronounced. "A skinwalker by another name. Oh, I don't think you're the one who hurt that boy—you're worse. The witch I'm hunting is a man dressed in wolf skin. You're a monster dressed up in human skin."

The back of his neck prickled with unease. Still, Connor kept an easy smile on his face. "Keep running your mouth like that. I'd like to see you get laughed out of town."

"Don't think so. See, I've asked around about you. Heard how you're never seen in daytime, how you drift in and out of towns every few years, how you're supposed to be the son of some rich miner who just... disappeared. Half the town already thinks you're a criminal... or a monster."

"Better the devil you know."

"But who knows you, Franklin? Who really knows? I wonder... if I were to skin you, what would I find under there?" He tapped Connor's wounded shoulder with the flat of his knife, unleashing a fresh bolt of pain.

Suddenly Connor was behind him, and Blackfell's knife-arm was twisted back and around, so that his knuckles dug into his shoulder blades. Connor squeezed Blackfell's wrist until he dropped the knife. The voice that hissed out between Connor's teeth was low and vicious, almost inhuman.

"Don't ever touch me again!"

The threat failed to have the desired effect. Though straining with discomfort, Blackfell chuckled humorlessly. "Now what man can move that fast?"

Connor's free hand went to Blackfell's neck. It would only take a moment's work. The human spine was woefully vulnerable.

"What do you want from me, Blackfell?"

His voice swelled with bravado even then. "I just want a reason to kill you."

Connor released him. Blackfell retreated out of reach. His eyes darted to the discarded knife. Connor kicked it across the dirt towards him.

"Well, you're honest, fella. I'll give you that much."

Blackfell slowly bent to retrieve his blade. His eyes never left Connor's face. He seemed amazed at the turn of events. Connor could read the crude calculation in his gaze—gauging distance, weighing the chance of survival. He was a creature caught between fight and flight.

"I'm only going to say this once," Connor warned. "This is my town, and these are my people. I protect what's mine. You understand me? So you think long and hard about whether you wanna get between me and them."

They were at a stalemate. It seemed they passed an eternity staring at each other, locked in mutual mistrust. Finally Blackfell sheathed his dagger. The tension began to leave his frame as he judged the crisis had passed. "I have a house to stake out," he said haughtily.

"Think I'll stick around for a while."

He expected Blackfell to protest. Instead the man merely gave a grunt as he retrieved his pack and rifle. He cleared a patch of dirt at the southern mouth of the hollow, then lay down on his belly. "Don't fidget and stay where I can see you," he ordered as Connor crouched down beside him. "I don't trust you behind me."

You took the words right out of my mouth.

They waited. The light faded and the shadows rose up from the ground. His stomach pressed to the cold ground, Connor felt the warmth seeping out of him. Before long he was hungry again. His shoulder continued to throb where Blackfell had poked it; he wondered how the man had known to hurt him. He was trying not to favor his right arm; to everyone but Charlie and Captain Marsh he insisted the wound was healing cleanly. Had Blackfell heard the story of his wound from Doc Sheppard or Nell Wallace? Or perhaps it had been an honest accident, if honesty could be applied someone like the Wolf Charmer.

"Supposing the skinwalker's moved on?" Connor asked in a whisper.

"He won't. He'll return to complete the curse."

"Why bother? If you're right, the fever will kill Joey given enough time. Why take the risk to finish the job himself?"

"Because he wants to show us he can."

Blackfell got up long enough to stir the fire pit. Once he'd kicked off the cover of dirt and fed in some fresh kindling, the flames awoke with a vengeance. Something on the hillside stirred at the sudden light and the crackle of burning wood. Blackfell raised his rifle and took aim.

"Rabbit," Connor said.

"How can you..." Blackfell's voice trailed off, and he sullenly shouldered his rifle.

"Not human, remember. You're not very good at this, are you?"

Blackfell grunted and lay fresh sage over the fire. He fed the fire in silence until a breeze coming down the mountain propelled the smoke southward. Then he kicked fresh dirt over the fire to dampen it and crouched back down beside Connor.

The darkness was nearly complete. Houses boarded up for the night, candles burning behind shuttered windows, American Flat was a sea of flickering lights. The Rollins farmhouse was the closest; a new light appeared at the rear of the house, bobbing and weaving uncertainly. Blackfell tensed.

"And that's a hurricane lamp," Connor drawled.

"Mr. Blackfell?" Wyatt Rollins's disembodied voice echoed feebly in the night. "Are you out there? Is Mr. Franklin with you?"

"Damn fool," Blackfell growled. "What's he shouting? Hey, what—"

Connor stood up and cupped his hands to his mouth. "How do, Rollins!"

Rollins couldn't hear any better than Blackfell. Sometimes Connor wondered how mortals coped with their handicaps. "Mr. Franklin? Is that you? Your missus is on the telephone!"

Connor smiled down at the uncomprehending Blackfell. "Duty calls. Looks like you'll be getting rid of me after all."

~ * ~

Charlie was pouring Captain Marsh a cup of coffee when the telephone rang. "It's the dog I don't understand," Marsh was saying. "A man comes home after thirty-odd years, hasn't aged a day. So he says: 'Naw, that was my daddy—take after him, don't I?'I can see people falling for that. Oh, no thanks," he held up his hand to ward off the sugar. "Gotta look after what teeth I got left."

Charlie smiled and instead tipped the spoonful into her own mug.

"But the dog! The exact same dog, with the exact same name, and no one notices!"

"Thirty years is a long time in a place like this. Really, how many people would remember Connor... or Garou?"

"Not many," he admitted. "And most are even older than me. Heh, I thought I'd try out ol' Colt McCafferty. I asked, 'Didn't Franklin's daddy have a dog following him everywhere too?' You know what he said? 'Oh aye, but his was a lot smaller!'" He laughed heartily at the memory. "'Course Colt's been half-blind for years."

At the jarring tocsin of the telephone, Charlie grimaced. She got to her feet, muttering, "Can you believe some folks keep these things in their houses?"

"Kids today," Captain Marsh bobbed his head in sympathy. "Hey, where is that dog, anyway? I remember your old man used to bring him on rounds all the time."

"We're keeping him at the house," Charlie called back as she reached for the receiver. "Too many folks looking around for wolves to shoot these days. Hello, Gold Hill Marshal's office—"

The shrill voice that assaulted her ears was almost worse than the phone's brassy rang. "Marshal? Deputy Franklin? Who's there? I need an officer of the law!"

"Aunt Katy?"

"Charlotte? What in heaven's name are you doing on the line? Where is the deputy? You fetch him right now!"

Charlie flashed a grin at Captain Marsh. "Oh, he's out on rounds right now, Aunt Katy," she said brightly. "I'm manning the desk. But I can take a message for him if you'd like."

"You mind your cheek, young lady. And you tell him—no! No, you come up here right now and deal with this mess. I won't have them in my establishment one moment longer."

"Won't have who? Aunt Katy, slow down."

"Don't 'Aunt Katy' me! Did you know about their shenanigans? Bet you thought it was funny, sending me this, this *smut* to keep under my roof like decent folk. No more, you hear me! Now you get up here or my next call will be to the county sheriff!"

She hung up with a violent clap of metal on metal. Charlie sighed and replaced the earpiece.

"Trouble?" the captain asked.

"Ain't it always? Did Connor say where he was going?"

"Think he was looking for that Blackfell. Down by the Rollins dairy, I reckon?"

Charlie checked the roster pinned to the wall next to the telephone box. "Thank God. They've got a phone too." She picked up the receiver and began to crank the handle. "Be damned if I'm gonna deal with Aunt Katy on my own."

~ * ~

By the time Charlie reached the Canyon Hotel, her aunt had hauled the offending parties into the Brennans' parlor. Charlie hadn't been inside it since her wedding to Connor five months past. She'd been all ajitter in silk and lace then; she took no small pleasure in returning wearing work boots and black wool trousers.

Blackfell's wives sulked at opposite ends of the room, bedraggled and resentful. Brightfeather's dress was ripped at the shoulder, baring her chemise, and White Moon's elegant pompadour was a rat's nest of snarls and loose hair. Frank Maddock seemed intent on hiding behind the settee, though Charlie couldn't tell whether in terror of his performers or the proprietress. Katy Brennan stood in the center of the room, huffing like a steam engine.

"Charlotte, there you are! I want these degenerates on the road, and I want their bills settled."

"Calm down, Aunt Katy. What happened?"

"What happened? Bigamy, that's what happened. Prostitution. Not to mention brawling like street urchins. Swearing and scratching and throwing things, the three of 'em. Broke a perfectly good washbasin and pitcher. The whole hotel could hear them."

"Um… in point of fact," Maddock piped up, "the fight was strictly between the ladies."

"In point of fact?" Katy mimed in disgust. "And what about the fact your heathen redskin is keeping a harem like some… some *Mormon*? I won't have it under my roof—don't you dare laugh, Charlotte!"

Charlie pressed her lips together, but the aborted laugh whistled out her nose.

"You knew, didn't you? Oh, you and your deputy probably had a good laugh at our expense. Well, I want the lot of them out of my hotel. And I want what's owed to me. Near thirty dollars they've cost me so far in bed and board."

"I want what's owed me!" White Moon piped up. "I want to report a crime."

Maddock rolled his eyes heavenward. "Moon, now's not the time. She's a little dim at times, Mrs. Franklin."

"He's been holding back my pay for near two weeks now! I gotta right to wages."

"We haven't been working, Moon!"

"Haven't I? I've been biting my tongue and shuffling around playing 'Captive of the Comanches' for ten days straight! I can't go out shopping; I can't go anywhere without you or Julie trailing me. And never mind Adam calling me all hours o' the night, whenever he's got an itch to scratch!"

Katy let out a wordless cry of horror. Maddock looked down and plucked at the collar of his shirt as if it held some fascinating appeal. "Well... that's really something to take up with him, isn't it?" he mumbled at length.

"I'm taking it up with you. I want my wages, or I'm leaving."

"You can't leave," Brightfeather said sharply.

"Why? Because you're too good to put up your own legs? Oh, poor, poor Julie. Well, you can find another whore to do your dirty work. I quit."

"You can't quit, Moon," Maddock said wearily. "You're under contract."

"Your contract ain't worth spit." She turned back to Charlie. "I want my wages. If he won't pay me, it's theft, right?"

"I... can't really answer that. I think it's something you'd need a court to decide. "

"A whore taking her pander to court?" Katy scoffed. "Not even in Nevada!"

Again the ill-timed laugh lodged in Charlie's throat, but she swallowed it with a grimace. "Look, why don't we just calm down and wait for the deputy to get here?"

They passed a tense ten minutes in the parlor, waiting for reinforcements. When Connor arrived with Blackfell in tow, White Moon turned as pale as her hair. She tried to bolt for the door, but Blackfell stopped her. Trapped between his arms, she began to tremble. Her head barely reached his shoulder.

"Explain yourself," he growled.

"Let me go."

"Moon, what is this?"

"Stop calling me that! I'm sick of playacting. I'm sick of hiding in that room with that smelly old man. I'm sick of keeping my mouth shut. And—and I'm sick of being your whore because Julie can't be bothered to be your wife!"

Blackfell sighed through clenched teeth. "You're making a spectacle of yourself."

"Let me go." When he held her firmly by the elbows, she began to pummel his broad chest with her fists. "Let me go! You can't hold me!"

"She's right," Connor spoke up. "You got no right."

"She's my wife."

"Not by Nevada law. Turn her loose now."

Reluctantly, Blackfell released her. White Moon skipped out of reach, breathless and grinning. "You heard him. Y'all got no rights over me. Keep my wages. Ain't nothing I can't earn back in a night. But I'm taking all my things, and if anyone else raises a hand to stop me, I'll cry assault."

"You leave now, you'll never get another dime from us," Brightfeather vowed.

"That's the great thing about being a whore, Julie. There's plenty of buyers."

"Moon, don't go," Blackfell murmured, his voice uncommonly gentle. "Wait until morning."

"She'll leave now and so will the rest of you," Katy insisted.

"It is aw-awful dark outside now," Maddock remarked. "And there's a dangerous animal on the loose. Surely we can come to some sort of compromise... Christian charity—"

"Now!" Katy commanded, while White Moon turned back from the door with an hysterical laugh.

"Jesus, Frankie, let it go. You know as well as I do, there is no skinwalker!"

A dropped pin would have sounded like a gong in the awkward silence that followed. Charlie's gaze darted from one face to the next. Katy's chin had retreated into her jowels in a recoil of skepticism. Maddock looked furtive, guilty, while Blackfell looked oddly pained. But Brightfeather's face was a bronze mask, utterly unreadable.

When Connor spoke, his voice came out rough as sandpaper. "What do you mean 'there's no skinwalker'?"

"Adam and Julie have been doing it for years. They join a traveling show, put on their Wolf Charmer act in every town—sooner or later someone gets mauled by a dog while they're in the neighbourhood. Then it's all running around in wolfskins and scaring folks by night, and bilking them out of their money by day. Why do you think everyone keeps seeing a creature since we came to town, but no one else has been bit?"

"A swindle, oh I knew it!" Katy cried with relish. Maddock became absorbed in the threads of his collar again. Blackfell ground his teeth. Brightfeather alone seemed unfazed by the accusation.

"If you leave now, you're on your own. We won't be able to protect you."

White Moon's answer was a derisive laugh and a slammed door.

"Well, good riddance to her, and now it's off with the rest of you," Katy Brennan declared. "I assume you'll be able to settle their bill, Deputy."

"I'll need to get some money from the safe. Charlie, mind looking after things here?" he raised an eyebrow meaningfully.

She was already exhausted after a mere quarter-hour of her aunt, but Charlie nodded. She understood her real assignment; it was amazing the things folk might blurt out when there was only a woman to overhear them. Even a woman in pants.

"I'll take care of this, Aunt Katy," she said. To the brooding trio of outcasts, she remarked. "Come on, I'll help you pack up. I used to work here, you know."

She led them out of the parlor, down the back hallway to the hotel stairs. Maddock went willingly enough. He hunched his shoulders like someone used to defeat. Blackfell and Brightfeather followed in proud, defiant silence.

"I do worry about Emmy... I mean Moon," Maddock fretted. "I wonder, Mrs. Franklin, if your husband could keep an eye out for her. Oh, I know she's... resourceful enough. But she's so young. And not the brightest of girls."

"She won't be safe on her own," Blackfell agreed tersely. "She has no idea what's out there—"

"She'll be back," Brightfeather said. "Once she calms down and realizes we're still the best deal she has."

~ * ~

With Charlie's help, the Wolf Charmer and his entourage were packed and on the road within the hour. Connor grudgingly settled the bill, then sent Charlie back to the marshal's office while he escorted the trio in search of less discriminating establishments. The clock struck midnight before he returned, looking weary and chilled to the bone. By then Captain Marsh had retired to sleep in his favorite jail cell, and Charlie was on her second cup of coffee of the night.

"Well… I got them set up at the Capital. Cost me an extra dollar for the week, because of course someone got wind of the scene they'd made at your aunt's place. Dunno if we need telephones in this town; the grapevine sure seems fast enough for my taste." Connor hung up his hat and coat. "And I told them this is the end of the money. Blackfell's got 'til the full moon to give me results. After that, he can fund his own damn hunt. Aw, hell."

The shoulder of his shirt was stained with three dark spots, each the size of a thumbprint. Charlie's heart ached at the sight of it. "Oh, Connor. Here, let me help."

She brought him a wet handkerchief and a fresh handful of boiled rags. Together they unbuttoned his shirt enough to bare his shoulder. The folded cotton Charlie had helped tie on seven hours earlier was saturated with black blood and stuck to his skin.

"Then I managed to make my rounds of the mills," Connor continued, while Charlie unwound the bandage holding the dressing in place. "And wouldn't you know it, some idiot has set traps by the Kentuck Mill's fence. On public land. Oh, just rip it off, Charlie-girl!"

Charlie did as instructed. Connor's only reaction as the clotted dressing came away was a long whistle of air between his teeth. "Well… that wakes you up better than coffee."

"Poor possum." Charlie daubed at the jagged wound with the wet kerchief. "Augh, it looks like one of the stitches broke."

"Yeah, I'm blaming Blackfell for that."

"You're looking awful gray."

"I'm feeling it. We got anything good to eat?"

"Nothing much you'll like, I'm afraid. Chipped beef and some suspect-looking pig's feet Bill left in the icebox. Other than that, it's all bread and canned beans." She cast a glance at the jailhouse door. "And we're all out of ... you-know-what."

"Oh, don't worry 'bout the captain. He's fast asleep; I can hear him snoring from here. I guess it's coffee and pig's feet." He made a face. "I tell you, I have never been so tempted to just slip over to the McCaffertys and steal a chicken."

"Maybe we should keep some at the Crypt," Charlie said brightly. "You know, for emergencies. Okay, let's get your arm up."

He propped his arm on her shoulder awkwardly; hunger make his muscles stiff, she knew. She dressed the wound and bound it up with a practiced hand. Connor grimaced.

"Suppose we never find the thing that did this?" he asked. "Suppose you'll be stuck playing nursemaid to me for the rest of forever?"

"I'll divorce you," Charlie said, matter-of-fact. When Connor started, she swatted his bicep. "You dummy. I make you pig's blood cocktails every night! Do you really think this is gonna put me off?"

He let his arm down around her waist, pulling her close. "You're one in a million, Charlie-girl."

Her hand came to rest on his chest, and he quickly covered it with his own. His skin was uncomfortably cold against hers, but she made no move to pull away. She let him lean against her, drawing the warmth from her flesh. When he let his eyes slide closed and pressed his forehead to hers, she felt him shudder with hunger. She shifted her head to one side, offering him her neck. His head was dipping inexorably towards her throat when he checked himself.

"Charlie... I can't."

"Of course you can."

To her surprise, he drew back. She could see the effort it required. "You're losing too much blood," she insisted. "You have to feed."

"I know. And that's why it can't be on you."

She stared at him in confusion, and no small amount of disappointment. "I don't understand. You've done it before when you're hurt."

He nodded. "Because I knew it would help me heal. But you can't heal this, Charlie. All you can do is... fill me up for a night."

She smiled hopefully. "That's something, isn't it?"

"That's food," he said sharply. "And I swore I'd never use you like that."

Her face must have fallen at his blunt pronouncement, because he softened almost at once. "Oh, honey-girl, c'mere." He drew her back into his arms and held her snug against him...gently, yet with a possessive determination.

"You're my wife, not my dinner. Dessert, maybe," he added with a twinkle of mischief in his tired eyes. "You're the most important person in my life," he continued earnestly. "But if I start thinking I can just take a bite out of you every time it hurts, then you're nothing but... prey. And I'm no better than a hungry dog. Besides, when I do take a bite out of you... well, I never want to be so hungry I can't appreciate you properly."

He dropped a quick kiss on the bridge of her nose. "Now, go brew me up some coffee, woman."

She poked him in the stomach playfully, then she turned for the kitchen. Connor let her get almost out of arm's reach before he caught her hand and pulled her back.

"Hey. I love you. Have I said that tonight?"

Charlie smiled back. "Can't say I recall."

"Well, now I did."

"Say it again." She rose on tiptoes and touched her nose to his.

"I love you," Connor murmured against her lips. "I love you, I love you, I love you," the words ran together into a nonsensical hum as Charlie kissed him.

Outside, the tethered horses whinnied in alarm. A heavy thump resounded just beyond the door. Connor turned, positioning himself between Charlie and the noise.

"What—" Charlie began.

Connor opened the door. Charlie let out a gasp.

White Moon was back, though not quite in the same condition as when she left. The girl lay sprawled across the doorstep, her belly torn open, her blood steaming in the night air. Crouched over her was the skinwalker.

Eleven

Everything happened at once. The smell of fresh blood struck Connor like a slap to the face. His head spun and his knees buckled. Charlie cried out. Revenant and skinwalker lunged for the door at the same time. Somehow, even cold-blooded and half-numbed with hunger, Connor reached it first.

He slammed it hard, a split-second before the full weight of the skinwalker collided with the aging wood. A shriek went up as the door shook on its hinges. Connor hastened to brace his body against it as the skinwalker charged the door again and again.

His gun belt hung on the wall peg next to his hat and coat, just out of reach. But his loaded Winchester lay propped against the desk. "Charlie!" he shouted, gesturing towards it.

She didn't need to be told twice. Charlie reached the desk in two bounds and threw him the rifle. He stepped back from the door, reaching out. His fingers closed around the stock as the skinwalker burst inside.

He swung the rifle about, racked it, and fired. A flash of

"

gunpowder blinded him momentarily. When he could see again, the skinwalker was gone.

The sounds of fighting had roused Captain Marsh. He limped out of the jailhouse murmuring, "Where's the fire—" only to let out a horrified yelp at the sight of the corpse lying just outside the door.

"Deal with her!" Connor ordered without looking back. He leapt over the body, into the street.

The horses were screaming in terror. Connor turned to find the skinwalker bounding onto the hitching post. He raised his rifle but he could not get a clear shot. Not with his Washington bucking and thrashing, and Charlie's Clem rearing as high as his tether would allow, forelegs pawing the air desperately. Perched between the two panicking animals, the skinwalker turned its long face towards Connor. He swore he saw something like a smile cross its distorted muzzle.

Then a report sounded, and the creature pitched forward with a cry. Connor smelled copper mingling with the gun smoke. Charlie's enraged bellow echoed in the street.

"Get the hell away from my horse!" She had the Colt already cocked for a second round.

The skinwalker took off down the street at a four-footed sprint. Both Franklins fired, but the bullets pocked the dirt harmlessly in the creature's wake.

Charlie jammed the revolver through her belt and ran to the hitching post. She soon had both horses by the halters as she tried to calm them. One look at Washington's abject terror and Connor knew he'd make better time on foot.

He spotted the skinwalker again at the derelict Yellow Jacket Mine, fifty yards downhill. The creature scaled the fence and disappeared inside the yard, only to reappear a moment later, a dark blot climbing up the headframe. By then the shouts and gunfire had roused the night owls from the saloon at the Capital Hotel. Some dozen drunks and their keepers spilled out onto the street, all jabbering and staring vainly in the streetlamp's faint glow.

"Get back inside!" Connor shouted, but no one listened. The bartender pointed at the fencing and hollered "There!" and the blind gawkers all surged for the fence.

"Goddamn it, stay back!" Connor fired a warning into the air. The crowd staggered to a halt, but the damage was done. When Connor looked back at the headframe, the creature was gone.

He jogged around the perimeter of the mine's fencing. Behind the Capital, he nearly collided with Blackfell. The Indian staggered out half-dressed: boots unlaced, nightshirt hanging down over his jeans. But his eyes were bright and focused. He held his Bowie knife at the ready.

"I heard gunshots!"

"He's this way."

Connor took the lead, and Blackfell followed without demur. They skirted the edge of the mine until they reached the train tracks, then followed the rail down towards the Crown Point Trestle. Just shy of the plunging ravine, a little supply line led off the tracks. Connor heard shrieking and breaking wood coming from the string of cabins that lined the road.

"Here!" He turned off the tracks. Blackfell staggered to keep up. No streetlamps lit their way. No poles of telephone wires stood out against the star-filled sky. From his uneven footfalls, Blackfell was running blind, but Connor could see fine. Three houses up, something was raising hell.

The skinwalker had found a chicken coop. When it heard Connor's approach, its head snapped up. Connor could see the gore and feathers staining its muzzle. Connor dropped to one knee and raised his rifle. The skinwalker opened its jaws and yowled, a bone-chilling union of a wolf's howl and a banshee's scream.

Connor fired, catching the skinwalker square in the chest. The beast buckled under the impact, but only for a moment. Then it scrambled to its feet and ran on.

Blackfell caught up to him. "Bullets won't work!"

"What will work?"

"Me."

They chased the skinwalker back towards the light of the main road. Next to the abandoned hoisting works of the Yellow Jacket, an immense tailings pile of waste rock sat sixty feet high. The creature tried to beeline right over the top of it. But it lost its footing on the loose gravel halfway up, and tumbled onto the street. A half-dozen of the fittest barflies from the saloon had followed the noise too. Connor and Blackfell emerged from the shadows of the tailings pile to see one particularly foolhardy man lumber towards the dazed beast.

"I'll be gol-derned..."

"Get back— do you want to die?!" Connor shouted, just as the skinwalker raised its head and snarled. The man tripped over his own feet in his haste to retreat.

The skinwalker rose on shaky hind legs. It took a step towards the fallen man.

"*Yee naaldlooshii!*" Blackfell boomed. "Stop! I command you!"

The skinwalker froze in mid-stride.

Blackfell advanced on the beast, slowly but confidently. "I am a Wolf Charmer," he said. "Your magic is strong, but mine is stronger. You will obey me!"

The skinwalker let out a pained shriek as it dropped down on four legs.

Then Blackfell began a deep baritone chant, in what Connor could only assume was the man's native tongue. He sang out long strings of high-toned vowels and humming consonants. He stamped out a beat with each slow, heavy footfall, as he continued to bear down on the skinwalker.

The song's effect on the beast was immediate. It thrashed and pawed at the ground. It shook its head and whimpered like a frightened puppy. Foam frothed between its grinding teeth. Connor glanced at the bystanders and found them utterly spellbound.

"You will obey!" Blackfell repeated, his voice softer now, almost soothing. Connor saw why. He led with his left shoulder as he approached the beast. In his right hand, he held his knife at the ready.

He resumed his song. He was only a few paces from the beast, and steadily closing. When the skinwalker moaned and bent its head, Blackfell raised his blade.

The skinwalker shifted its weight to its hind legs; Connor heard the telltale scratch from its claws, saw the muscles bunching beneath the thick gray fur. Blackfell noticed none of it. His entire being was focused on the creature's quivering neck. The skinwalker's head came up as Blackfell's arm started to come down in a languid, deliberate swing. Connor saw in an instant that the creature would strike first.

He racked his Winchester and fired a shot at the skinwalker's skull. Blackfell's cry of surprise was almost as loud as the rifle's report.

The beast dropped like a stone and the drunks behind him let out a whoop. But the cheer died on their lips. The skinwalker had barely struck the ground when it simply scrabbled around and took off again. This time it scaled the rock pile without incident, and disappeared over the summit. In the seconds it took for the skinwalker to escape, Blackfell had stood pinned to the spot, his face blank with shock.

"It's heading back for the ravine!" Connor turned back for the side road.

Blackfell rounded on Connor, stabbing his knifepoint in the air for emphasis. "You betrayed me! You let it escape!"

Connor let out an incredulous laugh. "I just saved your life, friend. You might try being grateful."

"I would have killed it!"

"It would have torn your throat out."

"I had it subdued. I could have ended it tonight!"

"Bullshit!"

Blackfell turned to the onlookers. "Did you see? Did you see what good the white man's gun does against a skinwalker?"

"You gonna stand around flapping your jaw or you gonna help me track it?"

"You can't track it!" Blackfell spat. "It's gone. We've lost our chance. You cost us our best chance!"

Suddenly Connor was too tired to argue. The crisis passed, his hunger returned full-force. His hands began to cramp around the stock of his rifle, a precursor to the crippling numbness that accompanied too deep a drop in body temperature.

"Brightfeather," Blackfell murmured. "I— I have to get back to my wife. The beast will know my scent now. It might go for her."

"Blackfell... wait. There's... something's happened."

"What?" Blackfell squinted; he couldn't see Connor's face well enough to read it. But he heard the faint catch in the revenant's voice, and he knew that once.

"Who?" he demanded. "Who did it kill?"

Connor led Blackfell back up to the marshal's office. He showed him the body, dragged inside and discreetly covered by a jailhouse blanket. He remained at a respectful distance as Blackfell fell to his knees in the doorway and began to sob. When the Indian's wails of grief became too sharply pitched for his aching ears, Connor paced over to the hitching post, where Charlie continued to soothe the horses. Washington had begun to settle, but Clem still snorted and pawed at the dirt.

The motion drew Connor's eyes down. A swath of drying blood showed where the skinwalker had fallen. Connor stared at it for a long moment, uncomprehending. When he took a pinch of the blood-spattered dirt and sniffed it, the smell was undoubtedly human.

I shot that thing clear in the head and barely slowed it down. But a glancing shot to its shoulder had made it bleed. It made no sense, until he remembered Charlie had fired his revolver... and the bullets he had dusted with Captain Marsh's white ash.

~ * ~

Nell awoke to the sound of gunshots. She sprang out of bed and ran downstairs, nearly tripping on the hem of her nightgown.

Wes beat her to the front door. With one hand he motioned her to stay back, as he checked the street outside. Nell went to the parlor window instead. Several shapes huddled together under the sodium lights, near the Crown Point tailings pile. Waving hands cast long, dancing shadows.

"Another brawl at the Capital?" she asked, even as she knew better.

"No. It's something else." Wes bolted the door. "Draw the curtains. And get back from the window."

"What did you see?" she tried to whisper, but her voice sounded loud as a roar to her ears.

"I didn't... see anything."

"Wes?" As she drew to his side, she realized he was still dressed in wool and denim. "Wes—haven't you gone to bed yet? What time is it?"

"Can't sleep. I've been sitting up."

She touched his forehead without thinking. His skin was cool, unpleasantly damp. "Is it the fever? It's too soon."

"It's just nerves." He caught her hand in his. "Everything starts up sooner when I'm rattled."

"The skinwalker? He's outside, isn't he?"

"I don't know. But I'm... all jittery." She felt a shiver run down his arm, and he squeezed her hand tightly to dispel it. "Cornered. Like I want to run. Or fight. Or... something!" She could not see his face in the dark. But his voice caught in his throat, almost like a sob, and his grip on her fingers tightened until it hurt. "I-I'm a-angry and afraid and I ache all over," Wes stammered. "And there's something out there. Something the wolf wants to fight."

"Wes... my hand."

He released her with a weak moan. "Sorry, sorry." The door thudded as he threw himself back against it, and slowly slid to the floor. Nell could just make out his posture, elbows on knees, head in hands.

"I hate this!" he hissed, between rapid, shaky breaths. "My heart is racing. I want to jump out of my skin. I want to-o-o-o..." his voice came out in a thin whine, an aborted howl that prickled the fine hairs on Nell's skin.

"Why would anyone choose to do this, Nell? I think of that skinwalker going around changing shapes like changing clothes. And I got this thing eating away at me from the inside out."

"Shush. Don't talk like that."

"I mean it. Sometimes, I think I can almost feel it... this... canker growing in me every month. If I thought it could do a lick o'good, I'd go right to that Wolf Charmer and tell him to carve me open and pull it out."

She sat down next to him. "What can I do, Wes? Tell me what I can do."

"Just stay with me," he pleaded. "Talk to me."

She didn't know what to say. Absurdly, a lullaby Lucy used to sing her came into her head. But she couldn't picture herself singing a grown man a sleep, any more than she could see herself holding Wes in her arms, cradling him against the worst of the pain.

Oh, but she wanted to...

She clasped his hand tightly. She let him squeeze her fingers in time with each spasm of pain. She stayed with him until the panic attack passed, until his muscles could no longer hold themselves tensed for battle, until the angry wolf inside him fell silent. When the fit passed, Wes slumped against her, utterly exhausted. Nell helped him to his feet and walked him back to his room, relishing every moment she could touch him without shame, and hating herself for it.

Her stomach curdled with despair. They had won a reprieve for the night. But the full moon was still four days away.

She had thought it would be easier, knowing what was to come. It wasn't. She tried to imagine going through this agony every month without fail, watching him suffer, knowing there was no hope for relief. She wondered how long she could bear to do it.

You think I'm so brave, Wes. But I'm not. I'm not nearly as brave as you need to me to be.

~ * ~

Come morning everyone was talking about the skinwalker attack. Without ready coin for a room, White Moon had taken refuge in one of the less reputable grog shops at the southern limits of town, trading favors for whiskey. The creature had taken her as she'd stumbled outside to relieve herself.

The coroner released her body swiftly enough. Fatal mauling by unknown animal was the official verdict. A crowd turned out at the cemetery to see her off. Nell finished her work early so she could pay her respects.

The weather suited the mood; fog clouds hugged the mountainside, and a cold drizzle fell over the scores of curious spectators. Nell hovered at the edge of the crowd, straining to hear Maddock's brief eulogy over the rustle of clothing and the pit-pat of rain on umbrellas. The barker had washed his hair for the occasion, and his threadbare suit looked freshly pressed. At his side, Blackfell stood bareheaded, hands clasped in stoic misery. His eyes never left the yawning grave and the simple pine box laid deep within. In contrast, Brightfeather held her head high, staring out at the crowd defiantly. She had improvised a mourning veil out of some black net pinned to her hat, though her posture was anything but grieving. Nell supposed of the three of them, she had the least reason to grieve. So much for sisters.

Maddock gave the signal, and the waiting workmen dug in with their shovels. There was to be no filing by the gravesite, no flowers or handfuls of dirt thrown on the coffin. But people stepped forward to offer their condolences all the same. Nell's keen eye soon sorted them into classes: the pious old men who always wept when a pretty girl died; the self-righteous matrons who loved to bear witness to other peoples' tragedies; and above all the swelling ranks of spellbound admirers, new converts to the cult of the Wolf Charmer.

Word of his hypnotic powers had spread all over the Comstock; his showdown with the skinwalker grew ever more astounding with each retelling. Not that it required much embellishment when seven separate eyewitnesses reported seeing a seven-foot tall wolfman whimpering in terror at the Indian's war song, even jaded Marshal Crawford had to take notice.

In a rare show of unity, the marshal and his deputies stood together at a discreet distance from the crowd, Bill Crawford looking vaguely disgusted with the entire proceedings, while John Garrod watched with avid interest. She couldn't read Connor Franklin's face, hidden as it was behind tinted spectacles and the shadow of his Stetson. He'd even turned up his coat's collar to shield his jaw, as though the watery gray light was just too intense to bear. Charlie hung on his arm tightly, almost as if she was helping to bear him up, as if he might collapse at any moment. To Nell's eyes, he'd never looked more alien.

As the crowd dispersed, Bill Crawford stepped forward. Nell slowly skirted the edge of the gravesite so she could listen in.

"This needs to end," the marshal said bluntly. "Now, unless you got any better ideas, I'm calling for a posse, and we'll flush this creature out any way we can. I'll torch the hillside if I have to."

"There is a way," Blackfell said. "The boy, Joseph Rollins. The skinwalker attacked him on one full moon. He'll return to complete the curse on the next."

"So what? We stake out the Rollins house? I thought you and the folks down on the Flat were already doing that."

"We were. Making medicine fires and holding regular watches. And we've kept the creature back. I say we stop... and let the skinwalker come to finish the boy."

"Are you out of your mind?"

"The plan has some merit, sir," Garrod spoke up. "We all know the full moon has a maddening effect on beasts and the lesser orders of men."

Nell fought off a shudder at his words. Beasts and the lesser orders of men... which one was Wes?

"We could set traps along a likely path to the farmhouse, conceal a hunting party in the brush—"

"No," Blackfell said. "No traps. No guns. Just me and the beast. When he reaches the back door to the Rollins house, he'll find it unlocked. And when he opens it, he'll find me inside, waiting for him. I will finish the chant I began last night. I will bind the creature to my will. Then I will kill it."

Bill moaned and rubbed the bridge of his nose.

"Circumstances dictate a certain respect for your... claims," Garrod said. "But I reserve a greater respect for bullets."

"Agreed," Bill ruled. "No more half measures. You had your chance, Wolf Charmer. This is my show now." He turned to address the remaining spectators. "All right. Spread the word: any man who can prove himself with a rifle and wants to help, report to the marshal's office tomorrow at noon! That thing's due back in three days and I mean to be ready for it!"

"I don't want him anywhere near the Rollins farm," Blackfell pronounced. He stabbed the air with a finger, and everyone within earshot turned to look at Connor Franklin.

"White Moon's death is on your hands!" Blackfell accused. "I would have kept her safe. But you let her go out alone into the night. And you let the beast that killed her get away!"

"All right, that's enough now," Bill warned. Blackfell wasn't listening. He turned to the milling spectators.

"Those of you who were there—you saw, you know! He drew his rifle and fired at the pair of us, when I was a heartbeat away from ending that witch! And for what? Pride? Glory? He couldn't stand the idea of a red man doing what he couldn't? Or maybe he wanted the creature to escape." He smiled cruelly. "They're practically kin, after all. Monsters who walk among men."

"Enough!" Bill ordered, his voice carrying. But Connor registered the charge without expression. Something about the tilt of his head made Nell grateful she couldn't see his eyes through the tinted glasses. His composure struck her as infinitely more unsettling than any of Blackfell's accusation.

"Come on, Charles," Connor said deliberately. "Let's get some breakfast."

Charlie glared at the Indian with undiluted rage. Then her gaze fell on Nell, and her expression turned anguished. *Don't*, she mouthed, as she turned away.

"What did you mean by that?" Garrod asked Blackfell curiously.

"He didn't mean anything," Bill said. "He's grieving, ain't you, Blackfell? Grief makes a man all confounded. Still, a man might want to think long and hard before opening his mouth next time. Come on, Garrod."

"He has a point about Franklin, sir," Garrod muttered, as he fell into step behind Bill.

"I ain't in the mood!"

The workmen continued to fill the grave, their rhythm unbroken. A stray clod of dirt fell from one's shovel slapping the side of the Nell's skirt. "Watch it!" the offending workman snapped as Nell retreated.

"Sister," Blackfell turned towards her, his gruff voice suffused with warmth. "It's good to see you again. Even now."

"I... I'm sorry," Nell mumbled. "About White Moon."

"Emmy," Blackfell corrected. "Emmy Cassman."

"I keep thinking, if I hadn't told Mr. Franklin to send for you..."

"No. You bear no guilt for this. Don't even think it." He offered her his arm. "Walk with me."

"I... I really shouldn't." Not with White Moon's body's scarcely cold. Not with half the town gossips watching them. But Nell found herself putting her hand on his damp sleeve and letting him guide her away from the gravesite. She gazed up at his dark eyes in the hopes of finding some answers. Of claiming some of his steadiness for herself. Lately, she felt fragile enough to shatter in a strong wind.

"You don't mean it... about Mr. Franklin being in cahoots with the skinwalker?" she asked. "I mean, the thing attacked him! I had to throw a lantern at it to get it off him."

"You admire him. The deputy?" He made it sound like an accusation.

Nell felt her shoulders hunching. "He's a good man."

"He's not a man. I know his wife is your friend, sister. If you care for her, you'll get her away from him."

"Pft. Fat chance of that happening."

"If she stays with him, it'll kill her. And she knows it." At her silence, he added, "I think you know it, too."

She pulled her hand from his elbow. "I don't know that. I don't know what he is."

"He's death. His heart beats and his blood flows, but there's no life inside him. He's rotting away under his skin. He stinks of the grave."

Nell turned away. "I don't believe you." But her voice held no conviction.

His voice was a tempting whisper. She could feel his breath against her ear. "Why do you think he hides by day?" he pressed. "He'd rot in the sunlight. You'd all smell him for what he is, then."

He kept speaking of smells. She wanted to say only animals lived by their noses; that people knew better. But she thought of Wes, driven into a frenzy by the fleeting scent of the skinwalker. The animal in him was starting to wake. Did that mean his scent was starting to change?

"You're wrong to trust in him," Blackfell continued.

"Whatever he is, he's been good to this town. Good to Charlie. And that's good enough for me."

"It's not up to you."

His calm certainty was growing more infuriating by the minute. "Oh, for heaven's sake! I know you're on a 'holy mission', Blackfell, but can't you admit there might be some nice monsters in this world?"

His answer was short, unequivocal. "No. There can only be what is meant to be, and what is not. What is clean and what is foul."

"So if you met someone... say a skinwalker who turned into a wolf for no other reason than... because he was born that way."

"Such a thing cannot exist. Skinwalking is an act of purposeful evil."

"But say it could exist! Say... he had no more choice in trading skins than...than we have in being stuck in one. Say he did nothing worse with his wolf skin than howling at the moon. Would you call that evil?"

"I would call it sad," Blackfell said. "But I would still kill the beast, if I had the chance."

She looked up at the Wolf Charmer as if for the first time. He met her searching stare with the stony conviction she had always found so hypnotic. Only now it chilled her. What once read as righteousness had become the flat, hard gaze of a bigot.

"I have to go," she said.

He swiftly overtook her as she made for the cemetery gates. "Maddock is returning to Reno on the first train tomorrow. I'm sending Brightfeather back with him. She'll fight me, I know. But it's not safe for her anymore. It's not safe for you, either."

"So you've said."

"Have you any family out of town? Any friends who could shelter you? The beast will come back for you."

"I'll be fine. I'm always home before dark."

"Home? With this man you work for?"

She bristled at his tone. "The family I work for. Yes."

Her affront seemed to amuse him. "Now there's a sight you don't see often."

"What's that?"

"A wolf who works for sheep."

"Go back to your wife, Blackfell. You mind your own business, and leave me to mine."

He blinked, confounded by her sudden frostiness. "Sister, wait."

"Stop calling me that. I ain't no kin of yours."

"It will come for you!" Blackfell vowed. "It has already tried once."

Fragments of thoughts slowly came together in her head. Animal smells. The wolf running off into the night. The skinwalker standing in the back yard, watching, waiting. Her red wool shawl, covered in wolf hairs.

Blackfell was right. It would come back. But not for her.

~ * ~

"It's Wes," she exclaimed as she burst into the marshal's office. "The skinwalker's been after Wes all along!"

The two Franklins stood frozen at her sudden appearance, Charlie's expression one of surprise, Connor's one of guilt. He held a Mason jar of some dark liquid in his hand. Carefully, he set it down on the desk, but not before Nell saw the contents slosh red against the glass.

"What do you mean, 'he's been after Wes?'" Connor asked slowly, as he moved to block her view of the jar.

"The first night he showed up, it was the full moon. Wes caught his scent, took off right after him. I know that's why he ran away. And when the skinwalker attacked us, my shawl had Wes's smell all over it. Blackfell keeps saying the skinwalker sees any other wolf as a rival—he's talking about totems, but I think it's simpler. That thing's gotten Wes's scent twice now. I know I saw something skulking around in the yard last week. And last night..."

"Yes?"

"That skinwalker was a block uphill from us. And Wes knew it. He was acting like a caged animal. He said the wolf in him wanted out. If he could sense the skinwalker, it stands to reason the skinwalker could sense him."

"Did you tell any of this to Blackfell?" Charlie asked. Nell heard the knife edge in her voice.

"'Course not! I ain't stupid. Blackfell would call a posse down on him quick as a wink, if he knew. He'd think Wes was the skinwalker."

"Then Blackfell doesn't know? About Wes."

"Naw," Connor said. "But it was a close thing. When they shook hands that first night he showed up, I thought it was all over."

"It was near the new moon," Nell said. "Mr. Franklin, you said Wes only smells wolf-like when he's close to changing."

"That's right."

"Like... when the fever starts up?"

"Reckon so. I've never made a study of it."

"Nell, what are you getting at?" Charlie asked.

She stared at them, dumbfounded. Why couldn't they see it? "The smell! Wes is walking around smelling of wolf. The house, the yards, the stables—come Tuesday night, that whole strip of Crown Point is gonna stink of it."

"Aw, hell, she's right," Connor murmured.

"But the skinwalker isn't a real wolf," Charlie said. "He knows what he's doing when he's wearing his wolf skin." She glanced at her husband. "Doesn't he?"

"Does he? We only have Blackfell's word on that, and his word ain't worth a Continental. Anyway... if I thought there was a big wolf that only seemed to show up in town around the full moon, I'd be damned curious too."

"If we know he's coming for Wes, we got a chance to catch him."

Connor's mouth curved in a smile. "We?"

Nell felt herself flush. "Well, you."

"Not me. Bill wants everyone at American Flat, watching the Rollins farm. I'd have a hell of a time convincing him I got something better to do at Crown Point. And the last thing we want is more folks nosing around your place."

Connor glanced over at his wife with a knowing smile. "You got an idea, Charlie-girl?"

"Oh... I think I can come up with something."

Twelve

The Rollins farm was a hive of activity. Sharpshooters took up positions inside the dairy, their rifle barrels peeping out through hastily carved slits. Paiute boys strewed hay over well-trodden paths to conceal the glint of metal jaws lying open. The three Rollins' milk wagons sat tightly parked in a line next to the dairy, forming a crude barricade. Twenty paces south, a parallel blockade of farm machinery composed the second half of a makeshift drive line, designed to funnel the skinwalker directly into the snipers' line of sight.

As Bill Crawford had promised, it was without question his show. He stood proud as a ringleader in the center of the yard, as Blackfell protested his every order.

"This won't work. Just because the witch takes the shape of a beast doesn't mean he's as stupid as one. And you think he won't hear all this fussing?" He waved his hand towards the trio of Paiute youths, loudly comparing the merits of the 1873 Winchester over the heavier Model 1882. "How do we know the skinwalker isn't already among us?"

"You got an excuse for everything, don't you?" Connor remarked. "Bill, we got men in the dairy and in the hayloft. I'll cover the roof. That critter sets foot anywhere inside the yard, someone'll have a clear shot."

"Good. Blackfell, you wanna make yourself useful? Go sit up in the hayloft with Garrod. You'll have a front row seat on the action. And you can sing the thing to sleep after we've emptied a few dozen rounds into it."

Blackfell's answer was a deepening of the scowl that had become his customary expression. But he obeyed and hiked towards the southern perimeter. Connor watched how the Paiute boys hastened out of his way, in a mixture of reverence and mistrust.

"You sure that's a good idea, sticking him with Garrod?" Connor asked.

"Ah, Garrod's taken a shine to him. I know—weird."

"Damned suspicious, more like."

"No harm in it." Bill said jovially. "Our Garrod's finally found someone who hates you as much as he does, that's all. But he'll keep Blackfell in line, if that's what you're worried about. You know Garrod. It's gotta be by the book."

"There's a book for this?"

"We'll have to write one someday." Bill raised his hand to shade his eyes from the sunset glow. "Look, Connor, just between us... things might go better for you if you give that Indian a wider berth from now on."

"What's that supposed to mean?"

"You know... riling him up all the time. People are wondering just what you have against him. And... just what he has against you. Hey, I know he's full of it. I know you ain't diseased or cursed or what-have-you. But you know there are folks who've never entirely warmed to you. The sort who want a reason not to trust you. And Blackfell's giving them that. Shoot!" He glanced at the horizon just in time to see the last arc of the solar disk drop behind the hills.

"There it goes. We're gonna start losing the light. I gotta do a perimeter check."

"I'll come with you."

"No. You get in the house. I want you up at the window before the moon comes up." He started for the dairy, then checked himself. "And Connor, mind what I said." He dropped his voice to a murmur. "I ain't asking you to go into hiding. Just... steer clear o' him when you can, will you? Before Garrod tells the sheriff I got a hobgoblin on the payroll."

"Would it make a difference if you did?" Connor asked. He meant the words to sound playful, but they came out bitter as wormwood. He waited a beat too long before he stole a glance at Bill's face.

Bill's mouth worked without sound. Twice his tongue touched his lip in an attempt at a witty retort. Then he simply shook his head and walked away.

Connor watched him go, then turned his gaze east, struck by the sight on the horizon. The full moon was just beginning its climb, and the dust of the Comstock sunset had stained it red as blood.

~ * ~

"Wes?" Nell addressed the closed bedroom door and the scratching sounds on the other side. "You still with me?"

A low moan, pained but undeniably human, was her answer.

"That you tearing up the floorboards?"

He laughed weakly. "No, that's Garou."

In response to his name, the wolf-dog whimpered. The door shuddered as a weight fell against it. If Nell had to guess, she would say Garou had just thrown his entire body across Wes's knees. Wes groaned softly. "Easy, Rou."

"God, he's a bigger suck-up with you than with Charlie."

"Yeah... he—unh—he thinks I'm his boss." His voice was hoarse. "Head of wolf pack, you know. He's always like this once the fever sets in. Big lout ignores me the rest of the month."

"You've got a pack," Nell murmured fondly. "Hey why don't you get a mess of dogs yourself? Then you'd always have company." But she understood why the moment the words leapt her lips. Making a family out of a pack of dogs, knowing you'd join them on their level once a month—the idea struck her as both touching and heartbreakingly sad.

"Naw... they're not all pushovers like Garou. I might actually have to—ugh, Rou!—work to keep their respect. Gotta tell you, I dunno what good this lout will be in a fight... yeah, I'm talkin"bout you, kiss-ass!"

"You gonna be all right for a minute? I want to go check on your ma."

The only answer came in the form of another sharp thud and a wet sputter. Nell imagined Garou was trying his best to lick Wes's beard off him. She smiled at the thought. Must be a briar patch by now. When she'd seen Wes last at lunchtime, he'd already started to look rather wooly.

She double-checked every window on the ground floor, making sure the shutters were secured both inside and out. At Charlie's insistence, she'd sprinkled wood ash from the stove all around the house, though she wondered what good it could possibly do against a skinwalker. Still, she reasoned there was no harm in being thorough.

Wes had done the same. Before he'd lost all dexterity, he had fastened a length of chain around one leg of his bed, and fixed a strong leather collar to the other end. Nell had balked at the idea of chaining him all night, but both Benedicts had insisted on it, and Charlie had agreed.

"You gotta tie him down before he gets wind of anything. I can call off Garou if I have to. But Wes? Trust me, I've seen him in a fight, and once he starts, there's no getting between him and whatever he wants to kill."

Nell believed her. She remembered how Wes had dug furrows in the floorboard when he was driven by nothing more than a full bladder.

She climbed the stairs to check on her patient. Inside the sickroom she found Lucy out of bed and helping Charlie brace a battered shotgun against her shoulder.

"It's lighter than Connor's Winchester."

"He favors an older model," Lucy explained. "But remember, he gets fifteen rounds in his rifle. You've only got five. And you'll get a good spread out of each shot, but they won't have the power of a bullet."

"How's the recoil?" Charlie asked. "Connor's kicks like a mule. First time I shot it I had a bruise for a week."

"This is a bit gentler. But you need to be ready, all the same. It can pull to the left if you don't have a tight grip. And I'd really appreciate it if you didn't shoot our stables full of stray buckshot."

"Mrs. B!" Nell exclaimed.

Lucy turned, knotting her dressing gown snugly over her nightclothes. "What?" she said, in answer to Nell's horrified stare. "I'm warm as toast. See? I'm wrapped all up snug. How is Wes?"

"Any minute now. Is that Wes's shotgun?"

Charlie weighed it in her hands. "It should do. I'll be over in the guest room, Mrs. B. When the skinwalker comes, he'll come from the west. But I can't promise I won't come barging in here. You might be more comfortable down in the parlor."

"Yes, why don't I take you downstairs?" Nell beseeched. "I can make the sofa up right by the fire."

"Another werewolf is stalking my boy and you want to sit me by the fire? I don't think so. Besides, Charlie's never handled the shotgun before. She might need help reloading."

"You—?"

Lucy laughed. "Who do you think taught Wes to shoot?"

Nell left the room shaking her head. Just when she thought she knew the worst about the family. *Well, if they expect me to turn into a gunslinger they got another think coming.*

When Nell returned to Wes's bedroom, the cries of pain had been replaced by eager whimpers. She knocked on the door, prompting a cheerful bark from Garou.

"Wes? You decent?"

She heard claws scratching on wood. She opened the door on a pair of wolves, one gray, one red, crouched on a pile of clothes. Wes's brow was knit over his blue eyes, and he licked his chops nervously. But at the sight of Nell, his ears perked up, and his tail began to wag. Nell held out her hand as Lucy had taught her to do, and he swiped his hot tongue over her knuckles in greeting.

"Guess not," she remarked with a wry smile.

Garou huffed eagerly. Later, Nell would decide he was egging Wes on.

Before she could stop him, the red wolf reared up on his hind legs and planted his front paws firmly against her, one on either hip. Nell let out a squeak of surprise as Wes tipped his muzzle up to lick her chin.

Despite herself, Nell laughed. "Oh, what, you want to dance?" she seized his massive paws and tried to pry them loose as she'd seen Charlie do countless times when Garou got too friendly. A few hops back and forth as if they were at a fandango usually embarrassed the wolf-dog into good behavior. But Wes just clung to her waist, refusing to be budged. When she stepped back, he hopped with her, holding her prisoner.

"You start humping my leg and we're gonna have real trouble," Nell warned sternly, wagging a finger at him. "Oh, all right." She bent her head and let him give her another slobbery kiss across her chin.

Wes dropped down to the floor, satisfied. Nell knelt at his eyelevel as she fastened the collar around his neck. "Does this mean I'm your boss?"

She buckled the collar in place and took hold of his furry cheeks as she'd seen his mother do. "Just my luck," she muttered bitterly. "You only want to kiss me when you're a dog." She wrestled his head back and forth until he huffed and sneezed with pleasure.

~ * ~

By six o'clock, the moon had shed its red mantle. By seven, the sky was painted black and silver. The skinwalker came at eight.

Connor sat at the window of Joey Rollins's sickroom, keeping time by the boy's shallow breathing, and his father's murmured prayers. As Blackfell had predicted, the boy's fever had worsened as the moon waxed. Now he lay drenched in cold sweat, shivering despite the blankets piled around him and the hot stones tucked in at his foot.

Connor spotted the skinwalker slinking through the brush a hundred yards west of the dairy. It crept on all fours, then reared up to sniff the air, its stance less like a man's than a circus bear's. The scattered clouds focused the moonlight in thin shafts of silver. The creature ambled right into one, so it cast a clear shadow on the ground. Connor did not bother to take aim. Not yet.

The skinwalker let out a long, ululating howl. Again Connor felt the tightening in his shoulder, as if something under his skin were reacting to the sound. In his bed, Joey Rollins tossed and moaned.

The skinwalker dropped back on all fours. It bounded over to one of the milk wagons. It climbed onto the driver's seat and put its nose to the wood. Then it turned its head to study the locked dairy. Connor's heart sank. *He knows we're here. Of course he does. All the cow stink in the world won't hide the sweat of a half dozen terrified, panting humans.*

The skinwalker ignored the tempting path between the makeshift barricades. It howled again, and again young Joey cried out. The boy's back arched and his head tipped back against the pillow. Hands feebly pawed at his throat. His stump bucked under the blankets. When Wyatt Rollins tried to hold him down, the thrashing only intensified, until the boy was caught in the grip of a full-blown seizure.

"Get over here and help me, damn you!" Wyatt hissed. Connor ignored him. Gently, he squared the butt of his rifle against his uninjured shoulder. *Come on, shaggy. Just a little closer.*

The skinwalker sprung onto the dairy's tin roof. Its every step struck up ungodly racket of groans and shrieks from claws on metal. To their credit, the men hiding inside the dairy did not betray themselves. They held their fire as they were ordered, even as the creature paced back and forth in provocation.

The men in the barn's hayloft were cut from weaker cloth. Someone panicked; a rifle fired. Then everyone started shooting.

The skinwalker took off into the night. Connor cursed and launched himself out of the second-story window. He dropped to the ground just as Bill's voice boomed over the yard, "Stop shooting! Hold your fire, goddammit!"

Every man uncovered his lantern and struck his match at once. The tiny sparks of light were as bright as flash powder flares to Connor's eyes. He caught sight of the beast tearing for the road and he turned to give chase.

He heard the whistle of air at his right ear and twisted his head out of the way a split-second before the bullet would have caught him. The shot nicked the tip of his ear, and pocked the ground in front of him. Connor whipped his head around, looking for its source. He saw only the dark hulk of the barn, and the thin mist of gun smoke glowing in the moonlight.

Bill came running out of the dairy. "I said 'Hold!' What pea-brained eejit can't speak English?"

"It's heading into town," Connor said.

"All right, we regroup and saddle up—hey—hey, get back here, Connor. Connor!"

Whatever else Bill had to say was drowned out by the wind in his ears. Connor sprinted up the road into town, quite indifferent whether anyone remarked on his speed. Even pushed to his very limit, he doubted he could make up the distance before the skinwalker reached the Benedict house. But he had to try.

The air was cold and still. There was no way Charlie could have failed to hear the gunshots. That gave her a minute's warning, and another minute before he could hope to reach her.

~ * ~

Nell heard the gunshots as a distant rumble, not unlike summer thunder. Garou looked up from where he had been dozing, more curious than anxious. But Wes flattened his ears to his skull and began to growl. Nell checked that the collar around his neck was still buckled tight. He was shivering; she could feel the tiny tremors under his skin, steadily raising the hairs on his back. His lips pulled back from long teeth that shone in the gaslight. Satisfied at his bonds, Nell backed up slowly and smoothly so as not to trigger his hunter's instinct. Her own heart was pounding in agitation, yet now that the moment had come, she found she was afraid for Wes, rather than of him.

"Charlie?" she hollered down the hallway. "Something's got Wes spooked."

The words scarcely left her lips before Wes surged against the chain, pulling it so hard the heavy oak bed actually skipped an inch across the floor. Wes had once told her wolves didn't bark, but he was barking then, deep full-throat barks, interspersed with snarls that sprayed spittle at his feet.

Garou joined in, barreling past Nell to direct his barks at the back door. Nell hesitated in the doorway, torn between running upstairs and staying to guard Wes. The wolf tugged on the chain with all his strength. His claws struggled for purchase on the floor, gouging toeholds where they could. The timbers of the bedstead groaned as he succeeded in dragging it another inch towards the door. From the agonized sounds of struggle, Nell was certain he would choke himself.

"Wes, stop it—please!" She didn't dare approach him in such a mood, but she crouched down as she spoke in a soothing tone. "Look, Charlie's got the watch overhead, and that thing ain't gonna try to break into a locked house. We just gotta sit tight until Connor Franklin get here. We just gotta wait—"

Then she heard the blast of shotgun from the second-floor window, followed by a high-pitched scream.

~ * ~

Charlie racked the shotgun for a second shot. Lucy was right—the gun jerked sharply to the left at the pull of the trigger. She fired again, but the bundle of fur and limbs was already out of sight.

But she'd hit it; the scream told her so. The shell had exploded at the creature's feet, and in the sudden burst of light, Charlie had seen the cloud of scattershot and ashes envelop the skinwalker.

The aim had never been to kill, only to wound. Only to weaken. They meant to take the skinwalker alive.

The wolves were going wild downstairs. Charlie ran into the hall. She made for Mrs. Benedict's room, but a shrill voice stopped her in her tracks.

"—God—Charlie! It's trying to come in!"

Charlie bolted down the stairs. "Garou!" she shouted. "Garou, to me!"

~ * ~

The skinwalker hit the door again and again, throwing all its weight into each charge. The hinges held, as did the heavy wooden bar. But the door itself was beginning to splinter under the repeated pummelings. The wolf strained against his chain, succeeding in dragging the heavy bedstead a little closer to the hallway, freeing a little more slack in the chain.

Somewhere under his territorial rage, Wes wondered why Nell didn't unchain him. Surely she understood he was only trying to protect her. He yipped and whined between snarls, begging her to release him.

The skinwalker was almost inside. A long, hairy finger hooked its way between two slats of old wood and began to pry them apart. Garou sprang at the finger and it withdrew, but only for a moment.

Wes heard Charlie shouting, but he couldn't make out the words.

He lunged at the door again, and again the collar dug deep into his throat, cutting off his air. He fell back with a whimper, struggling for breath.

Nell stood within reach of the door, paralyzed with terror.

He'd never be able to shield her, bound as he was.

But he could still save her.

He turned the full force of his aggression on her. *Go!* he barked. *Get away! Get Ma and run—it's me it wants!* He charged at her, snarling and slavering, spittle flying. He peeled back his lips and snapped his teeth at her shadow, willing her to understand, to flee.

Nell looked at Wes, then at the door. The skinwalker found a weak spot in the splintering door and punched its whole hand through the door.

Nell took off down the hallway.

Throwing all his weight into his shoulders, Wes clawed his way forward. The collar dug deep into the meat of his throat; the pain and lack of air made him see stars. But he could just reach the hallway's edge.

If the thing in wolf skins killed Garou—and it would, surely; no dog as submissive as Garou could hold its own against that monster—then he would sink his teeth into whatever he could catch, and hold on as long as he could. Chained, he wouldn't last long. But it might buy Nell enough time to escape.

Over the dueling growls and barks of Garou and the skinwalker, the sound of a human in full sprint, hard shoes clapping on the floorboards.

Nell was back.

~ * ~

Nell raced for the kitchen. The smoldering fire in the stove was her only guide. She tripped and staggered in the gloom. At the doorway to the kitchen, her toe caught on an uneven floorboard and she nearly fell. But she caught the edge of the doorframe and hauled herself inside.

The stove's grate hung open. Nell seized the first knife she could find, a long-handled carving knife, and plunged it deep into the glowing embers, and the ash bed underneath. Knife in one hand, hitched-up skirts in the other, she ran back towards the sounds of battle.

Wes had nearly made it out of the bedroom. The skinwalker had nearly made it through the door. The gray-furred finger was back at the break in the door, joined by a second, then a third. The entire hand forced its way through and clawed fruitlessly at the air, trying to swat at Garou's snapping jaws. Nell heard Charlie call her name, but there was no time to explain. Nell ran up to the rattling door and shoved Garou out of the way. She jammed the knife through the crack and thrust it home as hard as she could.

She felt the impact ride up her arm, steel sinking into flesh. The skinwalker shrieked, and yanked its hand back from the door. The knife handle leapt up, catching Nell on the chin. She staggered back, colliding with Charlie.

"Get back." Charlie raised the shotgun towards the break in the door.

"No!" Nell shoved her arm down. "Wait! Wait, listen!"

Charlie listened. So did Wes. The wolf was no longer straining against his leash. The assault on the door had stopped. The skinwalker was gone.

The carving knife was still wedged between the broken slats. Nell pulled it free. She took it into the bedroom, to hold up against the gas lamp. The blade was coated in blood.

"I'll be damned..." Nell murmured.

Garou was sniffing the droplets of blood at the back door. Charlie set to work dismantling the locks and bars. "Garou, hunt!" she commanded as she threw the door open. The wolf-dog leapt out into the night with an eager snarl. Charlie slammed the door behind him and hefted the bar back into place. Panting hard, she leaned back against the wall. To Nell's astonishment, she was grinning.

"You enjoying yourself?" Nell snapped.

But Charlie didn't hear the note of disgust in her voice. Or if she did, she was too giddy to care. "They'll get him," she breathed. "Connor and Rou. All they gotta do is follow the blood trail. Goddamn, what a night!"

~ * ~

Connor heard the barking, the shotgun, and the screams that followed. He broke out of the ravine to the smell of gunpowder and fresh blood. Wounded, the skinwalker couldn't run at full bore. Connor read its broken gait from the erratic, deformed footprints: a hobbling jog as it clutched a pierced forepaw to its chest, trailing blood drops across the ground. Canine paw prints tracked parallel to the skinwalker's. Garou was on the chase.

Connor followed the prints by moonlight. The scent of seared flesh and fresh blood drew him like a lodestone. The werewolf could outrun them on four legs, but not on three.

"Garou? You out there?"

A cacophony of shrieks and growls was his answer. Connor turned towards the livery stable.

Garou had the skinwalker cornered on the edge of Grant Weatherbee's yard, up against a stack of winter's firewood. The furry creature thrashed on the ground, mewling and kicking, as Garou held it in place as he might a disobedient puppy, jaws fastened over the back of the skinwalker's neck. At the sight of Connor, the creature let loose a snarl.

Connor calmly drew his Colt. "Don't even think about it. Rou, ease up, now. Just a bit."

Rou slowly relaxed his jaw. The skinwalker started to get to its knees. Connor approached carefully, keeping the barrel of his revolver leveled at its head.

"You know what I got in here, don't you, shaggy? Don't need any fancy songs this time. Just cold steel and white ash. Now, I ain't about to shoot a man in cold blood. A werewolf... well, that's another story." He thumbed the cocked hammer meaningfully. "So if I were you, I'd take off that costume."

The skinwalker's long snout wrinkled. The creature's eyes rolled back in its head. Its hairy, uninjured hand came up. Garou growled and tightened his grip on the beast.

"Off, Rou!" Connor commanded. "This one's not going to give us any more trouble. Are you?"

Garou stepped back, allowing the skinwalker to sit back on its heels. The skinwalker seized its upper jaw, just behind its nose. It pulled its jaw upwards and backwards, until Connor heard bone snapping, until its whole form seemed to shiver in the moonlight, until the great beast's muzzle became a simple cap of wolf skin, and the werewolf became a woman draped in furs.

"Well, I'll be." Connor slowly lowered his gun. "Aren't you supposed to be in Reno?"

Brightfeather hissed a curse at him in her native tongue.

Connor seized her by the scruff of the neck and hauled her towards the Ravine Road. She kicked and cursed, but in human form her strength was no match for his. He dropped her under the light of the closest streetlamp and stepped back to study her.

"Rou, guard."

Garou paced in a tight circle around the woman as she struggled to right herself. Her legs were covered in scratches; the right side of her face was scarred by buckshot. She tugged on her wolf skin with her uninjured hand, desperately trying to cover herself.

It was little more than a long cloak, strategically fastened at her shoulders, waist and thighs. A smaller apron of fur and leather hung over her hips, and furred gauntlets covered her forearms. Her headdress was the most ornate piece of her costume, a large cowl made from several wolves' heads stitched together and stiffened into a long muzzle that shaded her face.

"How do we break the curse?" Connor demanded. "How do we heal skinwalkers wounds?"

Her pained face broke out into a cruel grin. "Does your shoulder still hurt?"

"Do I have to kill you? Blackfell sure thinks so."

She cackled. "Blackfell! Everything he knows he learned from me."

The road was unnaturally quiet for the hour. For once the residents and the millworkers had followed orders and stayed inside. Both revenant and skinwalker could hear the distant scuffle of horseshoes on gravel, and the rattle of wheels amplified in the confines of the ravine.

"You have to let me go," Brightfeather said.

"Do I?"

"What are you going to do—throw me in a jail cell? Charge me with witchcraft? I'd like to see one of your fancy lawyers say that with a straight face." Wincing, she rocked herself back onto her heels. She indicated her bruised skin and limp furs. "You think any of your witnesses will say this is the beast you're looking for? The best you'll be able to prove is criminal mischief. Indecency. Oh, it's very indecent to an Indian these days. Your lawmen will lock me up and forget about me. Maybe I'll escape. Maybe I'll starve to death. But the Rollins boy will die long before I do.

"Or you could turn me over to the Rollins man. And his tame Indians. And they'll see me lynched by daybreak. You want that on your conscience? Bet you don't—I know you don't. You're a good devil, aren't you? So let me go. You won't see me again. You have my word as a woman of the People. And we don't give our word lightly." She smiled. "You can tell Blackfell what you like. Either way, he'll never find me."

"And the curse?"

"I'll lift it. Right now, if you like. Once I have your word."

Connor hesitated. The sound of horse and cart drew nearer. Brightfeather glanced towards the gaping ravine nervously. She readied herself to flee, and Connor advanced on her, barrel aimed between her eyes.

"No. No, you're not getting away that easily. Not when I got so many questions for you and your man."

"My creature," Brightfeather corrected. "He'll just feed you the lies I taught him. And he'll believe them—why would he know better?"

"Franklin!" Bill called from the back of the dairy cart.

"Here!" Connor shouted back. "Hold your fire! I got her."

"Her?"

"You heard me! And don't you dare shoot my dog!"

Again Brightfeather tried to rise on the balls of her feet. Connor shoved her down onto her stomach. Wyatt Rollins drew up the panting horses, and the dairy cart fishtailed to a stop in the middle of the street. Bill was the first out of the buggy. Blackfell and Garrod scrambled out behind him.

"Rou, get behind me." Connor paced around his captive, giving the men a clear view. When Bill saw the woman struggling to her knees, his jaw dropped.

"Brightfeather..." Blackfell breathed. His horror sounded genuine, even to Connor's cynical ears. "No! Oh, no, no, no..."

"That is not what we were stalking!" Bill accused.

"It's the costume," Connor said. "She pulls down the hood and it changes her."

"Show me."

Brightfeather reached for the wolf's muzzle. "No!" Blackfell and Connor cried in tandem. Connor pressed his Colt hard against her temple until she let her hand fall. In the tense silence that followed, Blackfell's whisper cut the air like a knife.

"Kill her."

"What?" Bill stammered.

"Do it now. She'll change. She'll change and she'll run. She has to die."

Brightfeather snarled at him. "You goddamned turncoat!"

"We aren't killing anyone—" Bill began.

A shot sounded, and Brightfeather dropped like a sack of stones. Garou skittered back, whining. Connor looked up in horror at the smoking revolver pointed squarely at his chest.

John Garrod reholstered the pistol with a grim nod. Bill rounded on him.

"What in God's name do you think you're doing?"

"Putting down a mad dog."

"She was an unarmed woman!"

Garrod seemed genuinely bewildered by his anger. "She was only a squaw."

Blackfell approached Brightfeather's prone form. He knelt and rolled her over onto her back. Lovingly, he brushed her dark hair to cover the bullet wound to her temple. "I'm sorry," he whispered.

Wyatt Rollins dismounted and joined the other men crowding around Brightfeather's corpse. He took a long look at the broken body, then cursed and spat hard on the ground. "All's well that ends well," he muttered. "I'm going back to my boy."

"Connor... run and fetch Doc Sheppard, will you?" Bill said at length. "Let's get this gal over to the death house. And find him a jail cell," he pointed at Blackfell. "I got a lot o' questions to ask him, and I reckon I'll have more by morning."

"Sir?" Garrod hesitated. "On what charge are we holding him?"

"Suspicion of conspiracy. That was his wife running around in wolf skins. Don't tell me he didn't know something about it."

"I didn't..." Blackfell protested weakly. "I didn't know... anything."

Garrod pulled him to his feet, not ungently, and led him away. Blackfell offered no protest. He seemed a broken man.

"Don't suppose you're gonna tell me how you managed to wrestle that girl out of her wolf skins," Bill remarked. "Or how you caught up with her so fast. I swear you knew the critter was going to run for town."

"With half the able-bodied men on watch at the Flat, the other half hiding in their beds? I'd run to town."

"Well, next time you go running off, just give me a rough idea where you're headed!"

"Sorry 'bout that," Connor replied in a distracted voice. He watched Garrod leading Blackfell away. "But seeing as one of them had just tried to kill me back on the Flat," he touched the nick to his ear, mildly disappointed to feel fresh scar tissue in place of wet blood. "I wasn't too keen on dragging my feet."

Bill made a face. "Jesus Murphy! So you got a bullet graze? Everyone was shooting at anything that moved back there—it's a miracle we didn't have more folks getting hit. I know Blackfell's a shifty fella, but you can't think he meant to hit you, not with all those witnesses. Shoot, have you even seen him fire a gun?"

No, come to think of it. But Garrod had handled his piece just fine when he'd silenced Brightfeather forever.

~ * ~

The night had dragged on forever. First, the men carried off the body. Then they surveyed the grounds, rattling stable doors and kicking at the dirt. Hurricane lamps lit up the back yards as they looked for clues up and down the row of houses. Each time Nell dared to open a shutter and peer outside, another light winked back at her. Wes paced at her feet, rattling his chain, whining plaintively. The waiting for peace proved far longer and more dismaying than the waiting for battle.

Nell braced herself for the knock at the door that never came. Around midnight, the last of the scouts gave up the hunt. By then the frost lay thick on the ground. It twinkled in the moonlight and crunched under Charlie's boots, as she finally surrendered her vigil.

"I'm off to the marshal's office. Everything looks quiet. If you don't hear from me, then no news is good news."

Nell watched her go from the parlor window, marvelling at her fearless gait, the cheerful spring in her step. This was just another night to her; a job well done.

"Well," Nell said, as she unshackled Wes at last. "We didn't do half badly ourselves. Oh, Wes, look at you!"

His struggles against the leather collar had rubbed his throat raw. Hair came away in patches, exposing reddened skin. Nell found some lard in the kitchen to rub on his wounds, and flicked him on the nose every time he contorted himself in an attempt to lick it off.

She looked in on Lucy one last time, and fed her a little laudanum now that the crisis had passed. She built up the fire in the parlor and huddled under a crocheted throw until she could blame her lightheadedness on the heat. Twice she thought to brew herself something to drink; twice she lacked the initiative to get up. It was made easier by the large wolf asleep at her knee, snuffling contentedly. She combed her fingers through his thick coat in an idle rhythm.

As she had a month prior, she fell into a deep sleep sometime in the early hours of morning. But this time there were no nightmares of teeth and claws. This time she slept like the dead.

The next sensation she registered was a dull ache in her tailbone, and a chill on her brow. Her skin prickled with stale perspiration under her cotton dress. The room was cold; the fire had gone out sometime in the night. A dull gray light teased between her eyelids. It was sometime just before dawn.

Gradually, she became aware something had changed. She was still sitting on the floor, half-propped against the sofa, her head lolled against the cushions. Wes's head was still a comforting weight on her thigh. But her fingers no longer twined through long fur. Her hand rested on something soft and smooth, and very warm.

Blinking away the sleep, she lifted her head from its awkward rest. She gazed down at Wes, her drowsy brain trying to process the image of a naked man fast asleep with his head in her lap.

The first thought she could articulate was, *God, he's so... pink!*

He hadn't moved all night; he still lay on his side, legs drawn up, one arm thrown carelessly over her knee. She could see a red crescent on the side of his neck where the collar had chafed him. She could read the collar- and cuff-lines of his workshirts, the tanned skin of his face and forearms giving way to a redhead's natural pallor. She marvelled at the contrast between her dark, calloused fingers and his smooth, freckled shoulder.

With languid curiosity, she let her gaze rake over him. She made note of the little mole on his ribcage, the ginger down on his belly. She craned her neck just slightly to peer over the curve of his hip, all the while thinking, *Oohh, I'm going to hell for this.*

Her inspection was not as covert as she'd hoped. Wes began to stir. Nell froze. Some still-sleeping part of her brain told her if she only held still long enough, he wouldn't wake. So she held still, eyes open and fixed on his face, hand still cradling his shoulder protectively. She held still even as his own eyes slowly blinked awake, and he gazed up at her in a dreamy fog.

His face looked so young, as if sleep had somehow erased over ten years of cares and creases. If she looked past the gray peppering his scruffy beard, she could believe he was a boy again, and she a young girl.

"Nell..." His voice was a husky murmur. He gazed up at her with an almost child-like fascination. He blinked repeatedly, as if he didn't trust his eyes. Those cornflower blue eyes...

He propped himself up on one arm, one knee. He tipped his head back to better regard her. She bent her head down to meet his.

"Nell," he whispered again. Something twisted in her insides; she could watch his mouth form her name all day long.

Her hand moved from his shoulder to cup his jaw. The brush of his stubble against her palm sent a frisson through her skin. She inhaled sharply at the sensation, and Wes's mouth moved up to cover hers.

"I always want to kiss you..." he murmured against her lips.

The words revived her like a splash of cold water. Nell pulled away at the first touch of his mouth. Wes took a moment longer, before the abrupt rejection brought him back to his senses.

"Oh. Oh, shoot, shoot, I—uh, sorry," he muttered, hastily rearranging his limbs in an attempt at modesty. Nell looked away, cheeks burning, and groped for the blanket she'd left on the sofa. Her fist closed on crocheted wool, and she thrust the blanket towards Wes without looking.

He mumbled his thanks as he got to his feet. She kept her eyes averted until he had left the room. Her heart was a hammer, battering her apart from the inside out. She whistled in breath after breath through clenched teeth.

You only want to kiss me when you're a dog, she'd told him, thinking him insensible.

Hot, bitter tears welled in her throat. She wanted to bite her fingers to keep from screaming. She couldn't decide whether she was deliriously happy or in utter despair. He'd always wanted to kiss her.

Thirteen

The day dawned like any other. Nell lit the kitchen fire and heated up fresh water. She emptied the chamber pots in the outhouse. On her way back across the yard, she ground the blood spatters into the dirt with her heel.

Jimmy Marsh came around at six to exchange the empty milk bottles for full ones. "Did you hear they killed the skinwalker?" he asked by way of greeting. "Turns out it was Blackfell's gal. Hey now!" he warned when a startled Nell nearly dropped the milk bottle.

"Blackfell's wife? But she left town."

"Well, she came back." The Paiute youth grinned. "And our man Garrod put a bullet in her."

Of course he did. 'Our man Garrod.' Nell shuddered at the phrase.

"What happened to the Wolf Charmer?"

"Blackfell? If there's justice they'll string him up too," he smirked. "And if they don't, we will!"

Breakfast was oatmeal and coffee; she brought a tray up to Lucy while Wes ate his in the kitchen. They studiously avoided each other's gazes. Nell began to hope. Perhaps they could dismiss it all as a shared dream. But the oatmeal sat heavy on her stomach. She drank cold ginger tea instead of coffee, hoping to settle her nerves.

Wes held his peace until she was elbow-deep in soapy water, scrubbing out the morning pots. "Uh, look, Nell." He rubbed the back of his neck nervously. "We... uh... we need to talk about what happened... this morning."

"No need," Nell said brusquely, without looking up from the sink. "We were both half asleep. Can't rightly say what happened there, to be honest, excepting we almost bumped heads."

"Oh." Her firmness surprised him. She could see it out of the corner of her eye; the sudden stiffness of his shoulder.

"It's all right, Wes," she insisted. "Just forget about it."

He started to turn away, then caught himself. "No. No, it's not all right. I'm sick of pretending—sick of all the lies we tell each other!"

He took her by the shoulders and spun her around. He held her at arm's length, as her hands dripped gray water all over the floor. He didn't need to hold her; his gaze alone pinned her to the spot.

"We both know what happened, Nell. I was going to kiss you."

"You weren't thinking clearly is all."

"I was. I only wish I'd done it years ago."

"Don't say that."

"Why not? You already know the worst about me. Why shouldn't you know the rest? Why shouldn't you hear that I love you? That I've always loved you!"

Denials came out in broken fragments. "Sure, we're—we're family, ain't we? Said so yourself. Always been. 'Course you love me. You're like my brother."

"Oh God, Nell, of all the things I want to be to you; I do not want to be your brother!"

Her throat tightened at the picture his words painted. She knew she should stop him before worse was said. But she forced her voice out; she had to hear it all.

"What... what do you want to be to me?"

"I want to be your lover," he cried. "Your husband , the father of your children! I—I'd settle for being the dog at your feet, if it meant you'd love me back! But not your brother. Never that."

"You never said…" she whispered helplessly. "I never thought—"

"I tried to stay away. I pushed you away—and not just because of the full moon. I know it's a bad idea. But Nell, I just can't keep doing it anymore. I can't keep pretending. I'm too tired." He laughed bitterly. A hand gestured to his weary face. "I mean, look at me! Do I look thirty-three to you? I've been going gray since I was twenty. I was growing crow's-feet when other boys were trying to grow beards!"

"It's not… that bad," Nell protested.

"Every month takes it out of me. Some days I don't know how long I can keep it up. My joints ache every winter. The fevers are getting worse. I'll be an invalid by fifty. If my heart can even hold out that long."

"Don't say that!"

"You know, deep down, I always figured I'd die long before Ma. It was… comforting, really. She was always so worried about what would happen to me if she was gone. And it was easier to push you away when I thought I was running out of time. Those years… when I wasn't boy, but I wasn't a man—God, those were the worst. It was tearing me apart, every month, and every month it was harder to put myself back together. Honestly, Nell, I never thought I'd make it this far!

"But here we are. Ma's wasting away and I'm still holding up. Maybe I got another four years in me; maybe I got another forty. I don't know. But however many days I got left, I want to spend them with you."

She almost broke right there. She almost gave in to the ache in her heart and the blood rushing in her ears. It would be so easy to pitch forward, to let herself fall into his arms. But she couldn't. One of them had to be strong.

"I wanted to hear you say that for a long time," she murmured. "And if you had told me all that ten years ago… when I was still young and stupid… I might've been of a mind to listen."

"But not now?"

"I know better now," she said firmly. "We both oughta know better."

"You're saying you don't love me."

"Love doesn't matter!" She cracked the wet dishrag angrily against the side of the sink. "Damn it, Wes, you know what kind of a world we live in!"

"The world's changing."

"Not fast enough. Not for us."

"What are you afraid of?"

"What am I afraid of? I don't know... getting hauled outta my bed and whipped in the middle of the night? Watching my house burning down around me? Don't look at me like that, Wes. These things happen! How about watching you lose half your customers? Grant Weatherbee forcing you out of the business? Because it was one thing when you're only rumored to be cavortin' with a colored girl, but another if you're actually setting up house with her!"

He continued to stare at her blankly. Sometimes his ignorance staggered her.

"How 'bout these kids you're talking about?" she went on, her voice rising steadily. "You thought 'bout how they'd turn out? Bastard mulatto werewolves?"

"We... don't know they'd be werewolves."

She fought the urge to ball her fists. Suddenly she was so angry she wanted to strike him. "Why didn't you say something before? I worshipped you, Wes! I needed you like I needed air! And when you ran me off and called me those names—"

"I'm so sorry. You don't know how sorry I am, what I'd do to go back and undo it all."

"No. Because it was the right thing to do. Because it taught me how to live without you. And I worked so hard... to get to a place where I didn't need you. You can't come back now and tell me that was all for nothing."

He bowed his head, ashamed. "You're right. I got no right springing this on you now. You've got your own life, and I keep trying to pull you back into mine. Maybe… you can live without me. God knows I can't live without you."

Her anger burned out; all she was left with was sorrow. "Oh Wes, what do you want with me? I got nothing to offer you. I'm a bitter old maid with no name, no money, and a face most folk want to spit at. You deserve… you deserve some plump little blonde skinwalker with a fat bank account."

"Can you find me one?" Wes challenged. "If you do, bring her 'round. And I can tell you both to your faces that I'll never want anyone but you." He seized her soap-covered hand and and pressed her palm to his prickly cheek. "It's you, you, you," he breathed against her skin. "It's only ever been you."

Gingerly, she slid her hand free of his.

"Tell me it's not too late," he begged.

She wanted to find the words for him. She wished she could see a happy ending.

"I'm sorry…" she murmured as she turned away.

"I screwed up, didn't I? We were doing just fine pretending, weren't we? If I'd only kept my mouth shut, things could have stayed how they were."

Nell stared at the half-finished dishes piled in the sink. No. She was the one who should have known better.

Fifteen years ago, he had cut her loose for her own good. Now it was her turn to return the favor.

"You're going to leave," he said in dull monotone.

"How can I stay?"

She glanced back at him. He had turned his face away to the window; he didn't want her to see him cry. But she could see his tears in the dusty window's reflection. They filled his red-rimmed eyes.

He swallowed tightly, regained control. His voice sounded tight as old catgut, but it held. "Don't go just yet. Not until you get another job. Until you have somewhere safe to stay. You… don't have to keep working here. You don't even have to see me if you don't want to."

"I ain't a charity case."

"I know you're not. But let me do this for you. Please."

She heard the catch in his throat, and again she fought the temptation to run to him.

He loves me. He wants me. He's always wanted me.

They could make it work, if only for a year or two. A year of delirious happiness— wasn't that more than most folk ever got? And when it all fell apart—as it surely would, as it always did—she would have the memory to keep her going through the long years still to face. Better bittersweet memories than the aching regret for what might have been.

If it would only ruin her own life, she'd take her chance without a second thought. She had little enough to lose. But Wes had a booming business and a sick mother, to say nothing of his own ills, and his crippling innocence.

"I'll stay until the New Year. Like I promised."

He turned back to her. Grief and hope were written across his face in equal measures. When he reached for her, she stepped back, out of reach.

It's better this way, she wanted to say. She felt her eyes burning as she stared at him beseechingly. Willing him to understand. *You'll only hate me for a little while. You'll get over it. Just like I did.*

She had to get out of the house. She had to find someone who'd tell her she was doing the right thing.

~ * ~

Garou's thunderous barks woke Charlie out of a sound sleep. She groaned and shifted in bed, feeling very cold and very trapped. The sheets crackled with frost as she moved her legs underneath them. The chilly weight holding her in place turned out to be Connor's bare arm, cast over her hip in casual possessiveness. Charlie pushed him off, and he rolled back onto his back. The sun was up and despite the heavy curtains, enough light stole in that Charlie could see her breath misting the air. But Connor slept on, naked to the waist, utterly oblivious to both cold and barking dog. The open wound on his shoulder looked perhaps a little better than it had when she'd unbound it before bed. The snaking tendrils of rot hadn't advanced any further into his flesh. She wished she knew how long it would take to heal completely, now that the skinwalker's magic had died with her.

Brightfeather... it was Brightfeather. Fresh from sleep, the absurdity of it all struck her anew.

Charlie staggered to her feet, wincing at the cold floor. Groggily, she located her slippers and dressing gown. When she staggered out onto the second-floor landing, the light streaming in from the front hall windows burned her tired eyes.

Garou continued to bark and lunge at the door. His massive paws swatted at the doorknob as if to open it. But his barks weren't angry; she could tell by his pricked ears and his wagging tail that he was aching to greet the visitor.

"All right, all right," Charlie groaned as she fumbled to close her gown over her long underwear. "Let's see who's got your britches in a knot."

She opened the door to find Nell shivering on her doorstep.

Her friend's appearance so stunned her, she forgot to keep Garou back. The wolf-dog easily slithered between mistress and doorframe, and was soon eagerly sniffing Nell's coat for traces of Wes's wolf scent.

"Nell?" Charlie stammered. "What's wrong?" Because something had to be very wrong for her to make the long hike out to the Crypt in the middle of day. Charlie stared hard at Nell's face and took note of the subtle traces of trauma: the swollen skin under her eyes, the purplish sheen to the tip of her nose.

"Shoot, I woke you, didn't I?" Nell said. "I'm sorry."

"That doesn't matter. Is Wes all right?" Charlie spoke the first fear that came into her mind.

"Right enough. Can I come in? I..." her voice quivered, "I really need to talk to someone."

Charlie had never seen her so shaken, so vulnerable. Of the few constants in Gold Hill, one was Nell's stubborn self-control. In rare lapses, she might appear angry or impatient. Never frightened, never despairing. "Of course." Charlie seized Garou by the scruff of the neck and hauled him out of Nell's path. But Nell no longer showed any unease around the wolf-dog, Charlie noticed. She stepped around him as casually as if she had grown up in a kennel.

Charlie led Nell through the parlor. Nell looked around slowly, noting the faded wallpaper, the chipped lacquer on the oak furniture, the sofa's worn velvet pile. "So this is your place," she said, distractedly. "Looks like old money, all right."

"Here." Charlie took her to the kitchen table, and sat her down while she lit the fire in the stove. Ash clogged the pan; the flames were slow to catch on the kindling.

"Could use a cleaning-out," Nell remarked.

"You never know when you might run into another skinwalker." Charlie pushed in balls of crumpled newsprint. The fire took and a sickly smell of burning ink wafted out of the stove. "Hey, did you hear who it was? The skinwalker?"

"Blackfell's wife. Milkman told me."

"Why do you figure she did it? Graft? I know that's what Bill reckons. Sure was a sweet deal for her and Blackfell if they were in on it together. But I dunno. Blackfell sure seemed intent on killing that thing. And Connor says he's hardly said a word since they hauled him off to jail."

"He's in jail?"

"Well sure. Bill's not taking any chances." She chuckled. "It's kinda funny to think of Blackfell really having no idea—guess he ain't that good of a wolf charmer after all. What you think, Nell? Nell!" When she looked up, her friend's face was twisted into a knot of misery. Fresh tears ran down her cheeks, even as she struggled to hold them in.

Charlie slammed the stove grate shut and rushed to her side. When she tried to bend and hug her friend, Nell rebuffed her with an outstretched hand. "I'm fine. I'm fine," she insisted. "I ain't—oh, Charlie, quit it, I mean it—"

But Charlie wouldn't be dissuaded. Her arms came around Nell's broad shoulders and held her fast until she stopped resisting.

With a sob, Nell let her head fall onto the quilted lapel of Charlie's dressing gown. She wept long and loud, her entire body wracked with tremors. Drawn by the sound, Garou padded into the kitchen, head bent and tail curled between his legs. He set his long muzzle on Charlie's knee and whimpered in sympathy. The sight prompted a bitter laugh from Nell. She pulled away from Charlie as sharply as she'd surrendered, and fished in her coat pocket for a handkerchief.

"Aw hell… I'm such a mess," she muttered, as she blew her nose and wiped her face.

"Don't fret about it."

"I hope I didn't wake up your man."

"Nothing wakes him up when he's out for the day."

"Shouldn't have come. Should've known you'd be sleeping."

"Nell, enough! This is what folk do for each other. Now tell me what's happened."

She twisted the sodden handkerchief between her hands. "Wes said he's in love with me."

Charlie waited patiently for the rest. When nothing else came, she could feel her brow furrowing. Nell saw her expression and blurted out, "What, you knew?"

"Nell. The horses know."

"Well I didn't," she protested.

Charlie gazed at her steadily, one eyebrow raised.

"I mean… I thought… he'd joke about it sometimes. About us. But we used to do that all the time when we were kids. Shoot, when I was five I asked him to marry me! Kids do that. And I figured… well, everyone wonders 'bout what could've been. Even when they should know better."

Charlie clucked her tongue. She was too sleepy for tact. "Nell. He adores you. It's written all over his face, plain as day. He lights up whenever he hears your name. And you love him too. Don't you dare deny it! Not to me."

But Nell seemed beyond denials. She looked down at her handkerchief and nodded meekly.

"So what's the problem? What you doing up here when you two oughta be getting frisky as bunnies?"

"Oh, shut up, Charlie! This isn't a joke. We can't be together; you gotta see that!"

"Why?" Charlie asked, gentler now. "Because he's a werewolf? Or because he's white?"

Nell laughed bitterly. "I don't know. Either. Both. He tells me he doesn't know how long he's got before the changes kill him. I don't know if I could stay to watch that. I know I could never have a kid I thought might go through that. It just ain't right. Besides... it'd never be lawful. Wes and me. Any kids we'd have—any life we'd make."

"Lots of things aren't lawful. That doesn't mean they're wrong."

"Think that matters to folks like Garrod? Or whoever burned down Captain Marsh's shack? Or those boys who figured any colored girl was fair game?"

"But does it matter to you?" Charlie pressed.

"I don't know," she admitted. "Wes... he doesn't understand! Neither of you do. You think because you see past color that's all what matters. You're as bad as all those dead white men my brothers are named after. 'All men are created equal'—it ain't that easy, Charlie! Not when you've spent your whole life being afraid. Not when you've been raised up knowing it's that fear that's keeping you alive!"

"How did you leave it with Wes?"

"Badly."

"Do you need a place to stay?"

"Might come to that."

Charlie touched her hand. "Is there any chance for you two?"

"I don't know. I want there to be. But if we tried... and it ended badly, I don't think I could take it. I'd rather never know."

"Really? You'd rather this? It's tearing you apart. Anyone can see it."

"I couldn't take it..." she repeated dully.

"What?"

"If he decided I wasn't... wasn't worth the trouble."

"Oh, Nell."

"A good man doesn't just throw his whole life away for someone like me," she insisted. "He does and he'll regret it. And he'll hate me. And I'd never forgive myself."

"And will you forgive yourself if you let him get away? How many chances for happiness do any of us get in this world?"

But Nell wasn't listening. She nodded to herself, composed once more, resolved. "It's better this way."

"You want my advice?"

"No."

"Tough. 'Cause you go waking me out of a sound sleep, you can bet you're gonna hear it."

"I should run away with Wes tonight?" Nell asked archly.

"No, that's for you to say." The time had come for blunt honesty. It was the only kind she knew. "If you can't be happy with him because of what he is… well, that's your call. My da couldn't be happy with having a daughter. Everyone has his limits."

"Charlie—"

"But if you're sure there's no hope for you two, then you gotta go. And I don't mean just over here. Get out of Gold Hill. Go to Carson City—shoot, go to California. We can give you the money. Start a new life away from Wes Benedict."

Nell flinched as if slapped. "You want me to leave? You?"

"I want you two to stop torturing each other. Because as long as you two are in the same town, you're just gonna keep doing the same old dance. It's exhausting just hearing about it! I can't imagine living it."

Nell studied the scrap of cotton in her hands, contemplating a future without Wes Benedict. Charlie saw how her mouth tightened in a grimace of pain.

"I don't know…" Nell admitted. "I don't know what to do. God… I always know what I'm supposed to do."

"Then don't do anything yet. Think about it. Carefully. Stop chasing your tail in circles and really think." She hesitated, at a loss for better advice. When faced with the rare decision she couldn't make on impulse, Charlie turned to her trusty ledger and tallied the consequences, one against the other. Somehow she doubted Nell would appreciate the suggestion.

"You're right. I don't know what it's like to be colored. I can try to imagine, but I know it won't come close. But... I do know something about being in love with the wrong sort of man. And about being terrified to take that first step, to say 'I understand what I'm risking and I'm ready for it.'"

Nell studied her carefully. "About Connor... Blackfell said—"

"Don't you mind what Blackfell said. I trust Connor. That's all that matters."

"How?" Nell asked. "How do you do it? How do you just... give yourself up like that? How do you take that first step when you got no idea what you're walking into?"

Suddenly Charlie did understand. For all her jaded cynicism and her knowing innuendoes, Nell was green as a schoolgirl when it came to matters of the heart. Charlie summoned a patient smile.

"In the end, you just gotta close your eyes and jump. But then I've always been good at doing that."

~ * ~

Charlie insisted on making Nell coffee. She said it would warm up her blood. All it did was send her stomach roiling. Nell was never so glad to see a fully-functioning water closet.

She didn't escape from the Crypt until noon, but she was in no great hurry to return to the Benedict house. Just the thought of being under the same roof as Wes set her heart convulsing wildly against her windpipe. She wrung her hands and struggled to control her breathing.

Despite the bite in the air, she found reasons to linger on Main Street, looking in shop windows. She bought a hot chocolate and biscuit at the drugstore; the man was glad to take her dime, so long as she drank it out back. Long after she drained her mug, she stared deep into the dregs of chocolate powder, hoping to divine her future.

Finally, the cold spurred her to action where conviction could not. Time to get back. Time to find some work for her hands. Time to lose herself in some mindless monotony of scrubbing or sweeping, until the quarrelsome voices in her head fell silent, at least for a few hours.

She returned to the gabled house to find the kitchen scarcely warmer than the street. The fire in the stove had gone out; the counters were spotless where she had wiped them down hours before. Nell busied herself building the fire back up and set the kettle on to boil.

A peek inside the sickroom confirmed her fears. The little woodstove was still burning, but only just. Wes hadn't been up to see his mother since she'd left him at mid-morning. The sun had long since swung over to the western sky; Nell watched her breath hang like a cloud in the air.

Lucy Benedict lay propped up in bed, her wan face to one side, nose pressed into the pillows. A teakettle's whistle accompanied each shallow breath. The pillow was damp under her mouth. She stirred as Nell gently shifted her onto her back.

"What... what time is it?"

"Nearly time for afternoon tea. I've already got the water heating up."

"W-Wes said you were taking the whole day off."

"Did Wes fix you something to eat?"

Lucy shook her head sleepily. "I'm still bilious from the oatmeal."

"I don't like the sound of that rattle in your chest."

"Rattling's good. Means things are shaking loose."

"You didn't take your ipecac, did you?"

"Oh, Nell. I'm getting better. Even you can see that."

No, you were, Nell corrected silently. *Steady, gentle exercise, warm air and good food had been slowly putting the color back in her cheeks. And the minute I turn my back, you're back to skipping your medicine and doing as you please, and your no-account son is letting you.*

"Where's Wes?" She didn't bother trying to keep the scorn out of her voice. "Why ain't he been by to check on you?"

"Oh, pish. I'm quite contented here. A little lackadaisical today, I admit. But after last night's excitement, I do think I'm entitled. You look like you'd benefit from a little sloth too, if I do say so myself."

You got no idea. Nell turned to the woodstove. Kindling in hand, she took her frustrations out on the smoldering fire. The charred remnants of the morning's fuel collapsed under Nell's remorseless bludgeoning, until the ash nearly choked the last of the flames. But the fresh kindling caught fire, and Nell tossed it in along with a handful of rotted wood chips.

"Everything is all right, dear, isn't it?" Lucy asked when Nell remained mute and kneeling by the stove, long after the fire had rekindled. "Did Wes frighten you again last night?"

Nell stood and brushed the soot off her apron. "Nothing like that. All's right as rain."

"You are... still happy here, aren't you?"

"Surely." But her voice didn't sound very sure to her ears. "Why do you ask?"

"Oh, nothing, dear. You just look a little down, that's all."

Nell made herself smile, a nervous flash of teeth like a frightened squirrel. "Maybe I am, a little. But it's got nothing to do with being here. Don't you worry."

Lucy returned the smile, patient and loving, and Nell could tell she didn't believe a word of it.

~ * ~

Nell sought Wes out at his workshop. She imagined she'd find him over his anvil, beating out his pain on some poor horseshoe. But the forge was cold, the open barn deserted. She tried the corrals next, and the stables, reeking of fresh manure that steamed in the air with special ferocity. She found the youngest Weatherbee boy mucking out a stall, but when she asked after Wes, he shrugged good-naturedly and shook his head.

"Ain't seen him since midday. You tried the forge? Oh. Well..." an incriminating blush stole over his pockmarked face. "He's probably... running errands."

She turned away without a response. She knew what sort of "errands" the boy was thinking of—and God help her, he was probably right.

She went back inside. She had no wish to hunt for Wes in every one-bit saloon on the Hill.

~ * ~

By his third shot, he managed to swallow the sour lump of shame that had lodged in his throat. By the sixth, the constriction in his chest became a pleasant warmth. Outside the stone walls, he could dimly hear the wind whistling, but inside the narrow saloon, he felt snug as a grizzly bear settling down for winter. He tried to say as much to the bartender, who gamely refilled his glass in exchange for another dime. But when the words came out garbled with drink, Wes reckoned it was time to switch to beer.

He had the bar pretty much to himself. Most decent folk had better things to do than get drunk in the midafternoon, and their fastidious new deputy had scared most of the indecent ones off Main Street. Wes had tipped his hat to a pair of toothless relics as he'd entered, but the men had disappeared sometime between shots, and the few customers who'd wandered in since knew enough to give the farrier his space.

From time to time, a rational thought crept in through the liquor, warning him to go home. But he kept recalling Nell's face as she'd left him: jaw set, mouth compressed. Her eyes had been wet with tears. But it hadn't made her stare any less adamant.

He couldn't face her sober. He didn't dare face her drunk. The paradox was too much for his addled mind to properly unravel. So he ordered another stout.

"Boy, when you fall off the wagon, you fall hard," the bartender said, in mingled admiration and pity. "Women troubles?"

The look Wes shot him ended any further attempts at conversation.

He tried to lose himself in his glass. But it was no good. She kept creeping back into his thoughts. He imagined what she would say to him when he finally hauled himself home. He took a grim amusement in trying to script her outrage. If anger were the only passion he could excite in her, he'd devote his life to goading her into a fury. Just to see her cheeks fill with blood; just to see her eyes flash with that spark she worked so hard to keep hidden.

In his more lucid moments, panic gripped him. Would she even be there when he returned home? The mere thought was enough to convince him to drink until the world went dark.

"Not you, boy!" the bartender howled. Wes started so violently, he nearly fell off his stool. The world pitched sharply as he caught hold of the bar for safety.

"I told ya before—no credit for no-accounts!"

"I got money," the man brayed in protest.

Keeping one hand braced on the bar, Wes slowly turned his head towards the light. The wolf had gone back to sleep for another month, but he still felt his hackles rising. His lip pulled back in a snarl as his eyes slowly focused on the figure standing in the doorway.

"And I got new glassware I don't want broken," the bartender said firmly. "Now get! You hear me, boy?"

Shiloh Todd didn't answer. He stared back at Wes with equally murderous intent. Then he turned and fled from the threshold as suddenly as he'd appeared. The bartender tutted in distaste.

"That boy'll come to a bad end," he pronounced.

Wes blinked at him, bleary-eyed.

"Ain't no excuse for it, you know. Look at them Johns folks, now. Model Negroes, the lot of them."

"Whassa supposed t'mean?" Wes asked darkly.

"Nothing," the man looked vaguely offended. "Just what I said." He glanced at Wes's half-empty glass meaningfully. "You look about done for now."

Wes drained the last of his beer in one swig. "Nope. Gimme another."

"Don't you be giving me trouble, now," he warned. But he refilled the glass all the same. Wes drank it down greedily. He needed to feel numb. It was safer for everyone involved.

Shiloh... she'd be better off with Shiloh. Everyone thought so. Even his own mother had clucked her tongue and shaken her head sadly when she'd heard Nell had broken it off with her old flame.

They seemed so well suited, she'd said, even though she'd known nothing about Shiloh. She didn't need to. It didn't matter that Shiloh was an overgrown child, as careless with his temper as he was with his money. It didn't matter that he was five years Nell's junior, yet treated her with a careless paternalism that set Wes's teeth on edge. None of it mattered. In the two years Nell had tried to endure him, Shiloh had been nothing more than a millstone around her neck. But he was the proper race.

Hell, he's the proper species, Wes thought with a bitter laugh. With Shiloh, the moon would never need be more than a pretty light in the sky. Nell would never need manage her fears by the calendar, and spend each twenty-eighth night praying her man would safely endure another change. When she lied to her neighbours, it would be over trivial things... the mundane little falsehoods that kept civilized folk rubbing along together. When her child fell ill, she could send for a doctor without fear.

Children... why had he been stupid enough to mention children? Why had he been stupid enough to even dream of them? He wouldn't wish his curse on a brute like Garrod, let alone his own flesh and blood. The slimmest chance of siring a werewolf outweighed all his selfish longings for a pack of little Benedicts crowding around the dinner table.

In his idle fantasies there were always five of them: three girls and two boys, rambunctious as puppies, all with tawny skin and fleecy black hair.

Nell didn't want children. He didn't know all the details of her brutal break from Shiloh, but he knew a big belly had been the sticking point. Where Shiloh had seen a chance to mend his ways and become a husband and father, Nell had seen a trap closing around her. She'd run, like any hunted creature.

Her greatest fear was losing her freedom. Wes knew that. Yet he had turned around and sprung his own trap on her. He'd brought her under his roof, forced his secrets on her, and bound her to silence. It was a marvel she hadn't bolted after the first night. He should have been grateful enough for that. He should have been content.

But she loves me! he argued with himself, feeling childish. He was too jaded to think love was enough. And he wasn't nearly drunk enough to forget all her admissions had been made in the past tense.

He might have sat at the bar well into the evening, had his bladder not compelled him to settle his bill. Numbed though he was, the cold still took him by surprise as he stepped outside. It almost felt like snow, despite the clear sky.

He staggered behind the Capital, and relieved himself against the stone wall. He fumbled to button up his jeans afterwards. With one pain gone, he was aware of another. It had to be close to suppertime, and he'd had nothing but liquor since breakfast. He'd better pick up something at the chop house, if he knew what was best for him. Even if Nell hadn't packed up and left, she'd be in no mood to cook him a meal. But maybe, maybe if he showed up with supper in hand, she might forgive him for dealing his liver another blow. She might even smile, just a little. And one more smile from her might be enough to get him through another day.

He secured the last button on his fly and stepped back from the wall. He heard the crunch of footsteps on gravel behind him. His mouth opened on a flippant greeting: *All yours, fellas,* an instant before the burlap bag fell over his head, sealing him in darkness.

Fourteen

Sitting in his jail cell, Adam Blackfell gave every indication of being a broken man. Still, Connor was resolved to trust him just as far as he would an angry rattler.

Shoulders hunched, eyes hollow, the prisoner barely stirred at Connor's approach. The tin plate heaped with congealed oatmeal sat forgotten at his feet. The jail was unheated, but the heavy blankets Blackfell had been issued remained neatly folded at the foot of his cot.

Connor waited, studying the man. He tried to ignore the itch at his shoulder, the product of a bandage wrapped a little too tightly. At length Blackfell lifted his gaze from the floor. His dark eyes blinked once, his brow furrowed.

"What do you want?"

Connor lifted the sheaf of papers. "I've been reading over your statement, Mr. Blackfell. Or should I call you Mr. Christian? That is your real name, isn't it? Course you've been lying to us for so long, I dunno why I should expect the truth out of you now."

He'd hoped for a reaction, but Blackfell barely acknowledged the jab. "I don't know my real name," he said dully. "They called me Adam Christian at the mission—they named us all 'Christian'—all the half-breed bastards and orphans. Thought it made a good joke." He made a half-hearted gesture towards the papers. "It's all in there."

"So it is. You do love to run your mouth, even now. And to John Garrod of all people. I'm surprised you're still so friendly with him, considering what he thinks of your kind. But he did your dirty work for you, didn't he? Put Brightfeather down before she could say anything too incriminating."

"I loved her."

"Reckon you had reason to." Connor flipped through the papers. "You say you met her in Sante Fe when you were eighteen. She was still going by 'Julie Wilson' then. Made a living by weaving blankets and telling fortunes... and turning a couple other tricks when business was slow. Quite a change from the girls you knew in the mission house, I reckon."

Blackfell's gaze hardened. "The day I turned eighteen, the mission turned me out. I had nothing but the clothes on my back and a Bible I couldn't even trade for bread! I lasted three days before I was stealing my food. I'd have been swinging on a rope within the year if she hadn't found me."

"So you owe her a lot, then. Including lying for her? Playing the hunter while she played the Big Bad Wolf? It was a good graft you had, if you didn't mind the body count."

"It wasn't like that."

"No... she just taught you all about Navajo witchcraft out of the goodness of her heart."

"I knew nothing of the People. She taught me our language, our stories. She remembered how it had been, before the Long Walk... or, she said she did. She said we had a duty to our traditions. She said her father hunted skinwalkers. Why wouldn't I believe her?"

"And that stuffed skinwalker I heard you were showing at the Indian show? I'm guessing that was just some wolf skins and a good taxidermist."

He nodded. "Brightfeather... she said we needed a draw, something people could see, touch. They'd never understand otherwise."

"And all the skinwalkers you said you killed?"

Blackfell was silent.

"How was this going to play out, then? Would you have run off into the mountains and shown up with the costume a few days later—say you skinned it off the witch? Or were you going to find some convenient body to dress up? What's one more murder at this point?"

"I didn't know."

"Why not Maddock? You know, no one's heard from him since he and Brightfeather caught that train to Reno. We put in a wire to Carson City. I'm betting we're going to find his body stuffed under a boxcar."

"I didn't know! I thought they were going back to Reno. It was my idea to send her away. I didn't... I didn't want her to end up like White Moon."

"Seems Moon knew what was what. And I'm guessing that's why you were so dead set on keeping her from running. You knew Brightfeather would hunt her down. Shoot, she'd probably been itching to for years."

"It wasn't like that. She found Moon for me!"

"So she takes you in, cleans you up, turns you into a performing holy man, and even fixes you up with a fancy gal o' your very own." He whistled. "Now there's a love story."

"I did love her. Until..."

"Until you told Garrod to kill her?"

"She was a skinwalker. She had to be destroyed."

"Did she? Who taught you that?"

"She did." A strangled laugh, half a sob, escaped his throat. "Everything I know... about skinwalkers... about my people... I learned it all from her." His hands came up to cover his face. "What... what if it was all lies?" He looked up at Connor helplessly. "What do I have now? What do I have left?"

The appearance of desolation was so convincing, Connor almost pitied him. Almost.

"The Rollins boy's fever broke in the night," Connor told him. "I looked on him before coming here. Seems like he's fixing to pull through."

Blackfell nodded. "The curse died with her. The boy's body will heal itself. In time. What's going to happen to me?"

"Reckon that's up to Bill and the county sheriff. Dunno if we have the proof to make 'attempted murder' stick. But I'm still of a mind to charge you for fraud and conspiracy."

That got his heart pumping faster. "I am guilty of nothing but stupidity," Blackfell insisted.

"I'll drink to that. Eat up," Connor nodded towards the plate of oatmeal. "You're going to be in here for a while longer."

"How's your shoulder?" Blackfell asked, as Connor began to turn away.

Connor froze. The itch had become a multitude of icy needles under the bandage.

"I don't deserve to stay locked up in here," Blackfell continued. "And skinwalker or not, I imagine a lot of folks wouldn't think Brightfeather deserved to be shot like a dog in the street."

When Connor slowly turned back, Blackfell was smiling, his expression almost beatific in its smugness. "If you do bring me to a judge... I might have to start talking about that."

~ * ~

"God knows I'll be glad to see the back of him." Connor tossed the papers back onto the marshal's desk. Garrod did not look up. He continued to hum softly to himself as he glanced between a logbook at his right hand and a battered almanac at his left. "Oh Susanna" again. His musical repertoire was as obnoxiously consistent as the rest of him.

"He's threatening to blackmail us now—goddamn it, Garrod, why did you have to shoot that gal in front of witnesses? I thought the whole point of the sheriff sticking you here was to make us respectable!"

"Calm down, Franklin. It's an idle threat. The Indian knows as well as I do whose word the judge will accept. Mr. Rollins will not contradict me, and I imagine you and Marshal Crawford both value your employment enough not to cry over split milk." He squinted at the logbook's text. "You should think about modernizing the office. Get your wife a typewriter and you could put her to work transcribing these notes into something halfway legible."

"I got enough work to keep Charlie busy, don't you worry."

"She's not here tonight. I'm surprised."

"Relieved, you mean. She's taking the night off—she didn't sleep well today. Why am I even telling you this? What are doing, anyway?"

"Checking dates."

"For what?"

"It occurred to me, when Blackfell said the skinwalker's curse is linked to the moon: the full moon is a well-known influence on the natural world. Tides. Madness. Female ills. Then I thought of some of the more outlandish log entries I've encountered during my tenure here in Gold Hill: strange animals; unexplained occurrences. I've been checking the dates against full moons for the last five years. The results are striking."

"You don't say."

"Of the past sixty-three nights of full moons, forty-nine of them feature reports of something out of the ordinary. Usually no more than a mention of a howling coyote or noises in the abandoned mines."

"You call that out of the ordinary?"

"Ten nights, however," Garrod went on, undeterred, "involve substantive reports of a wild animal spotted around the Crown Point Ravine. The reports vary. Sometimes it is a dog-like creature—"

"Your howling coyote."

"Sometimes it is something more man-shaped. I even have one, dated from four years back, that describes what Marshal Crawford laconically refers to as 'another banshee.' Now, obviously I share the marshal's skepticism. And I understand the population here has always been rather uneducated... prone to superstition. But I can't help wonder if there might be some common explanation for these events."

"You're not paid to wonder, Garrod. Actually," he paused to check the clock, "you stopped being paid an hour ago."

Garrod folded down a corner of the logbook's page and gathered up his notes. "I'll file Blackfell's statement alongside the autopsy report."

"Autopsy? Did the sheriff call for that?"

"I did," Garrod said blandly. "As the officer on duty, I was well within my prerogative, and Doctor Sheppard was quite obliging. Have you ever witnessed a full cadaver dissection? It's fascinating."

Connor was aghast. "Why, man? We know what she died of!"

"I was curious to see if her physiology differed noticeably from an ordinary human's. Granted, I'm hardly an expert on Indian anatomy, but Dr. Sheppard assured me he has examined enough in his day."

"And?"

"Nothing conclusive. Bones substantially stronger than the doctor expected in a woman approaching middle age. A slightly enlarged heart. The doctor also mentioned a swollen... adrenal gland, I believe. I would have to check the notes again." He stood. "I do believe you, Franklin. I think she did... change, in some way. Some form of self-hypnosis, perhaps. I've read some fascinating articles on the phenomenon of 'animal magnetism.' But without firm evidence I'm afraid we'll have to write this off as just another common madwoman. It's a pity you didn't kill her while she was in her bestial trance. We could have learned so much more."

Connor shook his head. "You're an ignorant son-of-a-bitch, Garrod. So why is it your curiosity scares me so much?"

The counterfeit smile tugged at the corners of his mouth. "Haven't a notion. Goodnight, Franklin."

Connor waited until Garrod was out the door and retreating up the street, still humming the same minstrel song. When Connor couldn't make out the footsteps on gravel any longer, he went into the kitchen and struggled out of his shirt. He unwrapped his bandage, groaning with relief when the damned itching finally stopped. Underneath the folded pad, the wound looked as ugly as ever. The smell of dry mold tickled his nose. When he probed at the raw flesh, he found it as yielding as rotten fruit. His fingers came away bloody. Blackfell was wrong. The curse didn't die with the skinwalker.

He didn't bother attempting to replace the bandage. He'd had enough of cotton dressings. If he bled into his shirt again, so be it. He could always afford new ones.

He thrust the wrappings into the stove, and washed his hands under the water pump. But he swore he could still smell the mold clinging to his skin. Bill kept a little scrub brush under the sink. Connor made a fist and scoured his fingernails until he made his cuticles bleed. The sight was so startling, he dropped the brush like a hot coal.

Without thinking, Connor lifted his chafed fingertips to his mouth. His blood tasted wrong: stale and chalky. He flung his hand away in disgust.

"Goddamn it!"

Later, he couldn't have said how long he stood there, forcing himself not to breathe, staring at the pink-tipped bristles of the scrub brush, wondering how long it would be before everyone could smell the decay spreading under his skin. He might have stayed there all night, had Phil McCafferty not come barging in the door to the office.

"Mr. Franklin! You gotta come quick! There's a big fight out behind the Capital."

"Give me a minute, Mac."

"No, sir! You gotta come now! He's fixing to kill him!"

Connor looked up sharply. "Who's fixing to kill who, now?"

~ * ~

Wes didn't have a chance to cry out before the first blow came: a fist to the kidneys. His legs buckled; he staggered forward, and strong arms came around, lacing under his elbows, forcing his hands behind his back. His captor forced his back straight, so he could take the second punch square in the belly. Wes felt his gorge rise. He tipped his head forward, desperate for air. The bag was loose over his head, but pulled down to cover his mouth. When he vomited, the burlap trapped the froth against his mouth and nose. He heard distant laughter. Then the blows came again. And again. The stomach, the ribs, a glancing blow to his ear when he jerked his head and the fist missed his jaw. Soon his entire body was on fire. He couldn't breathe. The burning smell of bile was choking him.

"Goddamn grayback!" The taunts came between blows. Wes tried to focus on the voice in front of him. "Hey? How you like that, you redneck peckerwood?" The punches came less frequently. His attacker was losing steam. The unfamiliar voice was ragged, equal parts rage and fatigue.

"You like taking from coloreds? Take this!"

Another punch aimed at the head. This one connected with his brow and sent him reeling. He sagged back against the man holding him.

"That's for my sister!" his attacker crowed, breathless.

"Jesus!" hissed his captor, against Wes's burlap-covered ear. The arms holding Wes in place loosened, just slightly. "Will you shut up?"

Wes knew that voice. He'd heard it not an hour earlier.

His head came up. He slammed the back of his skull hard into Shiloh's nose. The arms loosened further, and Wes got a hand free. He groped for the fly of Shiloh's jeans and seized a handful of flesh. He twisted, hard, and Shiloh howled in agony.

Wes broke free. He yanked the fetid bag off his head and drew in deep mouthfuls of clean, cold air. Shiloh was on his knees, moaning like a sick calf. The skinny boy who'd been handing out the beating only moments before backed away, eyes wide with terror.

"You... you had that coming!" Fremont Johns insisted. His hands came up, palms out in self-defense. Dainty hands, fingers slender as a girl's. When Wes advanced on him, Fremont raised a half-hearted fist. His knuckles were split and bloodied.

Without his backup, he was only a frightened child. Wes let him throw the first punch. He ducked under it easily and brought his fist square into Fremont's jaw. The force of it threw the boy against the stone wall.

Shiloh struggled to get to his feet. Blood streamed from his broken nose. Wes towered over him, fists clenched at his sides, waiting. When Shiloh couldn't rise fast enough, Wes seized a fistful of hair and pulled him up, then dropped him with a punch that sent his teeth rattling.

But Shiloh showed none of Fremont's fear. His eyes shone with malice as he bared his bloodstained gums.

"I had her first," he wheezed. "You remember that. I broke her in for you."

In that instant, Wes felt stone-cold sober. The many disparate pains fused into a solid wall of fire. All the day's turmoil, all the conflicting shades of grief and anger, all boiled down to a single imperative. His world shrank to a pinpoint of red.

He heard a scream, raw and bestial. He felt the tremors thudding up his arms with each blow. With each fresh burst of pain in his hands he only struck out harder. Each increasingly feeble attempt of defense only enraged him further. When something beat at his shoulders and tugged at his arms, he lashed out blindly, a wounded beast.

The next thing he knew, he was back on his feet, being hauled away from a cowering lump of battered flesh. It had taken four men to do it. He looked from one bruised face to the next, trying to understand why they were all staring at him so strangely.

~ * ~

Somehow, Nell knew who would be at the door the moment she heard the bell ring. She'd half-feared it would take the deputy to bring Wes home. But she was unprepared for the sight that greeted her on the doorstep. She covered her mouth to stifle a cry.

Wes was limp as a rag doll in Connor Franklin's grasp, one arm thrown over the deputy's shoulder, the other hanging limp and bloodied at his side. His legs sagged; he could barely stand without help.

"Oh, Wes! Mr. Franklin, what happened to him?"

The handsome lines of his face were lost under a blanket of swollen flesh. His left brow was split open, as was his lip. One eye was all but swollen shut. He shivered in the cold... the result, Nell saw immediately, of what looked like a bucketful of water thrown over his head. If the intention had been to clean him up, though, it hadn't been successful. His whiskery chin was caked in dried blood and dried vomit.

He didn't seem to have a clue where he was; Connor Franklin had to walk him up over the stoop like a puppet. The deputy laughed goodnaturedly at his predicament.

"Aw, this is nothing. You should see the other fellas."

She held out her arms. Wes was too heavy to support by herself, so she settled for bracing him against the doorframe. The reek rising off his shirt was nearly enough to make her retch.

"What other fellas? Who did this?"

Connor's smile disappeared. "Shiloh. With a little help from your brother, I'm afraid."

Nell's eyes bulged. She didn't need to be told which brother. "Monty? Monty did this?"

"Jumped... me," Wes managed to slur.

"Oh, I don't doubt Shiloh was the ringleader. By the time I got there, Fremont was blubbering on the ground, nursing a sore jaw and acting like he was dying."

"I'm going to kill them," Nell vowed.

"Yeah... you really don't need to. Wes gave as good as he got. Come on, let me help you get him to bed."

Wes recovered his voice enough to mumble vague apologies as they laid him down, filthy clothes and all. Connor rolled Wes onto his side, while Nell fished out the chamber pot from its hiding place and set it down near the head of bed.

"Nell...." Wes tried to follow her with his one good eye. "Don't go."

"Just to heat up some water," Nell insisted gently. "I'll be right back."

"Is... Shiloh okay?"

"He'll be right enough," Connor said.

"I didn't mean to—" he began, but Connor cut him off. His face was gentle, but his voice was firm as he said, "Yeah, Wes. I reckon you did."

Nell walked Connor back to the front door. "Where are they?" she demanded. "Are they in jail? Tell me you're locking them up for this!"

"Well, once Wes sobers up, he's welcome to press charges. But I'm just hoping the three of them got it out of their systems. You know Wes damn near broke Pa Carlton's nose too, when they were trying to pull him off Shy. I don't know what started this mess, but it's a miracle no one was killed."

Shame burned her throat. Any half-wit could guess at the cause. *God, the whole town's gonna know!* She'd never be able to hold her head up in public again.

"Any rate, I'm off to unload Fremont on your stepfather," Connor went on conversationally. "Reckon he'll put the fear of God in the kid more than a stint in jail will. I'll see Doc Sheppard comes around tomorrow to check on Wes."

"I'm so sorry, Deputy. This is all my fault."

"Can't see how. You're not to blame if your menfolk decide to act like jackasses."

Your menfolk... She heard no judgment in the phrase, merely a statement of fact. As if this was just any other family squabble that had come to blows.

~ * ~

When she wanted to, Lucy Benedict had the ears of a cat. Before Nell could even see to heating the water, she was down the stairs and at her son's bedside. Nell tried not to think about the implications that held for their morning's fight. She knew Wes and his mother had no secrets, yet the thought that Lucy had overheard even half of their morning fight was utterly mortifying.

Had it only been that morning? It seemed a lifetime ago since Wes had nuzzled her hand and whispered that she was the only woman he'd ever wanted.

Now she had a better understanding of the grief she'd heard in Lucy's voice, when she had spoken of forcing her son to avoid Nell for so many years. She'd known all along. And even she had known their heartache was the lesser of two evils.

But she said she was wrong about that, didn't she? She said she should have trusted me.

Trust. Charlie could blithely throw the word around; the worst betrayal she'd ever faced was her father's reluctant acknowledgement of her inferior sex. Nell found it hard to sympathize, when her own multitude of faults had been beaten into her from birth.

Lucy insisted on being the one to wash her son. Nell was glad to let her. She doubted she could look on Wes's battered face without bursting into tears. Or ease him out of his dirty clothes and bathe his bruised skin without feeling somehow tainted.

Lucy surely hated her now. What mother wouldn't loathe the cause of all her son's misery? Yet when Lucy emerged from the bedroom, cradling a basin of bloodstained water against her hip, she patted Nell's shoulder gently.

"It looks worse than it is. But the swelling's already starting to peak, I think." She summoned a bittersweet smile. "One good thing about being a werewolf. You heal lickety-split."

Nell sent her back up to her own bed, promising to make some fresh tea and toast. Then she crept into the bedroom and knelt at Wes's bedside. The room was blessedly dark, and she could hardly see the swollen wreck of his face. He was soundly unconsciousness, lost in what she prayed was a dreamless stupor. But every now and then he twitched like sleeping dog, and he let out a pained whimper.

"I told you, you deserved better than this," she breathed.

Charlie was right. They could not go back to the way things were. And they could not continue to torture each other. One way or another, it had to end.

Fifteen

Nell timed her visit to High Street carefully. By nine o'clock, she reckoned the younger boys would be safely at school. But Lester never opened his barbershop until the genteel hour of nine-thirty, and Nell knew he would not allow Fremont out of the house with his face looking like hamburger steak.

She swung open the front door without knocking; as she'd predicted, no one had thought to lock it in between mid-morning departures. She caught Lester still seated at the table, nursing his coffee and reading the morning paper. His wife squatted in front of the wash bucket, scrubbing out the oatmeal pot, while his eldest son stood in the corner farthest from the stove, hands slung in his pockets, face turned to the wall.

"Nell!" Mother and stepfather cried out at once in surprise. Nell ignored them. She stalked over to Fremont and swung him around, then cracked her hand across his swollen cheek.

"You idiot! Are you trying to ruin my life? Are you trying to ruin yours?"

"You leave my boy alone!" Ruth hollered. Fremont closed his eyes and cowered in anticipation of a second blow that never came. Lester's hand closed firmly around Nell's elbow before she could bring her arm down again.

"You coward," Nell flung at Fremont. "Can't even take your medicine like a man!"

"That's enough of that," Lester commanded sternly. "He's had his medicine already."

He drew her away from her brother, almost gently. Nell was struck by the strength in the little man. Drawn up to her full height, she had to look down to meet his eyes, yet he could move her as effortlessly as a child trailing a kite on a string. When she struggled to free herself, she only succeeded in wrenching her elbow.

"Have you lost your mind?" Ruth exclaimed. "Didn't that brute of yours do enough to poor Monty?"

"Poor Monty? Your 'poor Monty' beat up a white man. In any other state they'd be stringin' him from the nearest tree for this!"

"Of course that's how Benedict's telling it," Ruth sniffed.

"Someone needed to stand up to him!" Fremont protested. "Goddamned grayback thinks he can do as he pleases with our women."

"Grayback?" Nell repeated, incredulous. On a different day, she might have laughed. "He wasn't even born until the war was good as over! And where do you get off, calling me one of 'your' women?"

"His father fought for the South, didn't he?" Fremont shot back. "Fought so his folk could go on slaving our folk! Now he's set you up as his whore—feeling you up in public —and you're so panting hot for him you don't care what fools he's making of us!"

"You snivelling little pissant. I should have drowned you when you were a baby!"

"I said that's enough!" Lester barked. "Both of you. Fremont, get back in the corner. Your sister's right—you oughta be gol-derned grateful you were born in the great state of Nevada, where colored boys are allowed to be just as pig-stupid as white ones!"

Fremont slunk back to the corner. Satisfied bloodshed had been averted, Lester released Nell. She rubbed her sore arm. She watched the stiff way Fremont walked, and she wondered what measure of his strength Lester had loosed on the boy.

"You said you'd be gentle," Ruth reproved. "He's only a child."

"I was a man at his age. Nell was making her own way at his age."

"And we saw how that turned out." She pinned a withering look on Nell. "'Least Monty spares a thought for his kin."

"It was Shiloh's idea," Fremont mumbled a protest to the wall.

Lester heard him. "I'm aware o'that. That's the only reason you're still up and walking. And I swear to Heaven, if you so much as say 'how-do' to Shiloh Todd again, I will beat your fool head in!"

"And how is beating up my boss thinking about me?" Nell demanded.

Ruth clucked her tongue. "Not you. The rest of us. Or didn't you think how it would make us look?"

"My life's got nothing to do with you."

Ruth clucked her tongue. "You've made that clear enough. But folk'll judge us all the same. 'Least now they know we don't approve o'this nastiness. 'Least it's clear there are some folk in Gold Hill still got their dignity."

"Dignity? There ain't anything dignified 'bout any o'this!"

"I brought you up better than this. To think o'someone besides yourself for once. Now look at you. You turn up your nose at me 'cause I work for love and family, and you'll only work for cash. You act like it's better to be a whore than a wife. You'd rather poison your womb than become the mother the Lord meant you to be."

"Don't," Nell warned. "Don't you dare bring that up!"

"And now you side with that drunken fancy-man of yours over your own blood! For what—for thirty bucks a month? Or for sheer lust? Are you really sunk so low you're proud to be his nigger-gal?"

"I'm not—" Nell began to protest. But she knew they wouldn't believe her. She didn't think she believed it herself. She might not be Wes's mistress, but everyone in the room knew she wanted to be.

"You used to talk about being a free woman, beholden to nobody. Oh, you'd trade your virtue for a pin watch, but you'd turn up your nose at an honest marriage. Just another kind of slavery, you used to say. When you know darn well your stepdaddy lived under slavery! When he grew up watching white men doing whatever they pleased with colored gals!"

"Ruth," Lester warned, his voice tight in his throat. "Don't."

"His sisters. His mother. Nothing but so much meat to their masters. Used up and thrown away. You ever thought how that shames your stepdaddy? You ever think what he feels, knowing you want to be used like that?"

Nell stole a glance at Lester. He stood brooding, bearded chin tucked to his throat, eyes downcast in a pose that had always struck her as cowardly until today. The tendons of his neck stood out against his skin; she realized he was clenching his jaw.

"Fremont," Lester barked into his shirt collar. "Go open the shop."

In the corner, Fremont hesitated. "You said I's to stay here—"

"I changed my mind. Now get. I want the stove burning and the porch swept 'fore I get there. Now, boy!"

Fremont leapt at his father's menacing tone. Lester waited until the boy was out the door before he slowly raised his head and fixed his wife with a stony gaze that sent a shiver down Nell's spine.

"You know what's shames me, Ruth? When my wife who was born free, to freeborn parents, thinks she's got a right to pontificate on slavery. Cause you got no idea, woman! And you got no place bringing my ma and sisters into this. They don't need none o'your pity."

"I didn't mean—"

"What shames me? That we did so badly by our only girl—that she grew up thinking so little o'herself—that she gave up her virtue to a numbskull like Shiloh Todd! Don't you give me that 'he's a good boy' bull. He's nothing but a pretty face and an empty head. Couldn't offer Nell spit."

"He offered her a ring," Ruth protested.

"Well, what a goddamn prize! He offers the girl a ring after he knocks her up! Did he have a house to go with it? Did he have a steady job? Did he have a mind to stop wasting his money at cards? You really want your girl wed to an overgrown child who couldn't even support her? 'Course Nell cut her losses. I'm just sorry it took her so long to get 'round to it."

Nell stared at her stepfather. She had never heard him speak up for her so fiercely before.

"You really want her foolin' around with Benedict?" Ruth shot back miserably.

"No, I don't." Lester turned his cold gaze on Nell. "Frankly, it turns my stomach. But I reckon that's our fault too. We didn't do right by you, Nell. Your momma's too proud to say it, but I will. With Monty coming right after the wedding, then Uly right on his heels... well, reckon we were too worn out to offer you much. We were both just grateful you could handle yourself. But we should've done better. I should've been a better father to you."

His confession left her too stunned to speak, at first. She looked down at her hands, knit her calloused fingers together. "I didn't want you to," she murmured, abashed. "I didn't ask for anything from you."

Lester let out a sharp laugh. "I remember! But I should have given something. Maybe if your momma and I had showed you how much you meant to us... well, you might want better for yourself now."

She shook her head in protest. "I do. I want the best I can get! It's everyone else what thinks too little o'me. You and Momma taught me I'd get nothing waiting for folks to give it to me. Whatever I want, I gotta go get myself."

"You want Benedict?" Lester challenged. "What do you want from him? A good time? Your thirty dollars at the end o'the month? You been pining over that pasty-faced lout as long as I've known you. Don't tell me a little tomfoolery's enough for you."

"I'm not stupid. I know he can't marry me."

"Nope, he can't. But he can provide for you. He can stand on Main Street and shout 'This here's my woman, and I'm gonna stand by her whatever y'all think.' Oh, don't look at me like that. Look, girl, we'd all rather you meet a nice colored boy. But they're pretty thin on the ground out here. So pick a white man if you gotta. Shoot, pick whatever color you fancy."

"You can't mean that, Lester," Ruth protested.

Lester ignored her. "But pick a man, not a boy," he told Nell. "A good man. A man who'll do right by you, no matter what. Who's gonna give without ever asking what he's getting back. 'Cause that's what you deserve, Eleanor. Don't you dare settle for less!"

Nell swallowed, as if to better digest such unexpected words. "Thank you, Lester. That's... that's mighty sweet."

"Shoulda said it long ago," he said gruffly.

Nell glanced over at her mother. In the wake of her husband's anger, Ruth seemed to have shrunk into herself. She didn't dare contradict him, yet her eyes still burned with resentment. "I can't stop you," she whispered. "I never could. But I'll be darned if I'll be seen to approve of it."

Her familiar air of martyrdom struck Nell as perversely comforting. She felt a laugh bubbling up in her throat. Yet when she spoke, it turned into a sob. "When did you ever approve of me, Momma?"

"When did you ever need me to? When did you ever need anything from me?"

Oh, Momma, you have no idea, Nell longed to say. But she saw the fire draining out of her mother's eyes. In its place was a flat, weary sorrow. At that moment, Nell understood Ruth's constant belligerence, her resentment of her daughter's freedom. To Ruth, dependence was another word for love.

Nell turned for the door. What more could be said, when they had stopped speaking the same language years ago?

She half-expected one of them to call her back. Neither did. She let the door close behind her and drew her shawl up over head to ward off the chill.

The north wind was gusting. The houses funneled it into a gale down the narrow street. The hem of her coat flapped about her skirts. She had to bend her head and lean into the wind to make any progress. She burrowed her chin into her collar. With her reflected breath warming her face, she weighed her family's words.

Ruth had thrown all of Nell's own fears in her face. She'd named her daughter a whore and a traitor, just another colored girl to be used up and thrown away. Yet Lester's verdict was what haunted her. She thought too little of herself, he said. It was a sobering thought, when she had always thought he'd rated her as nothing but a workhorse.

The walk back to the Benedict house took her past the marshal's office and jail. Some two dozen people milled by the front door, waiting expectantly, oblivious to the cold.

Most of the faces were strange to her; white men in smart tweed suits, and Indians in layers of old wool. Old Captain Marsh sat on the edge of the boardwalk, smoking his pipe. Nell scanned the crowd until she picked out Phil McCafferty hovering on the fringes. He seemed the safest bet; he was a decent-hearted boy, and she didn't hold it against him that his older brother had been one of her tormentors that night at the woodpile. And like all the young men who lived off odd jobs and parental indulgence, he knew every snatch of gossip in town.

"What's the word?" she asked Mac.

The boy favored her with a careless grin. "It's the Wolf Charmer. Sheriff's in there right now. Trying to figure out what to do with him."

She nodded discreetly towards the unfamiliar faces. "And them?"

"Half the Marsh clan. Also a few tourists from up the Hill. Followed the sheriff. I think one o'them's a newspaper man."

"Dunno why they bother," she whispered. "He's yesterday's news."

Mac laughed. "Then you ain't been reading the papers. He's all over page one." He lowered his voice to a whisper. "I hear the other Injuns all want him strung up. Reckon Mr. Rollins agrees with 'em."

She supposed she ought to pity the Wolf Charmer. Misled by his vision and betrayed by the woman he trusted, he'd lost everything. Yet when she remembered he would have surely killed Wes if given the chance, she felt her heart harden.

One thought led to another, until she found herself studying the faces in the crowd. Who among them would be willing to let a werewolf walk free in their town?

She winced to think of how she lectured Wes, with her self-righteous litany of fear. As if she owned a monopoly on the emotion. Of course Wes understood. He'd been living in fear since the day he was old enough to understand what he was. He courted death every day, simply by existing. And he did it with a smile and an easy-going manner, and only let those closest to him see his pain.

Pick a good man, Lester had told her. She couldn't think of a man braver and nobler than Wesley Benedict. And she couldn't imagine going a day without him.

"Hey, where are you going?" Mac asked, as she turned abruptly. "Don't you wanna see what happens?"

"I gotta get home," she said.

Home. The word tasted sweet on her lips. She hadn't dared to attach it to any one place since she'd fled her mother's house at sixteen.

The crush of people blocked the street. She had to pick her way around on the frost-slick boardwalks. Her worn shoes gave her no traction. But she slipped and struggled onward, driven by a sudden need to see Wes again. The fog of crippling indecision would lift at the sight of him, she was certain. Everything would finally make sense, and she could give him the answer they both wanted.

The door to the marshal's office opened. Out of the corner of her eye, she saw Bill Crawford step onto the porch to address the crowd.

"All right, everyone. He ain't going anywhere today. Now the court of Storey County is looking into pressing charges—"

"He brought the witch here!" someone shouted.

"—and until then I'm gonna have order here!" Bill shouted back. "Now clear out, 'less you want a stint in the hoosegow alongside him!"

His threats did little to quiet the Paiutes. Nell didn't linger to listen further. She kept her eyes on the blue-gabled house, just visible beyond the massive tailing piles.

~ * ~

She expected to find Wes where she'd left him, still sleeping off his pain under his buffalo robes. But his bed was already made and his chamber pot scrubbed clean. Her search took her first to the kitchen, then to his workshop.

She found him tending to a huge draft horse. The gray beast towered over him, easily able to rest its chin on his head. Yet Wes had only to touch a foreleg and the horse lifted its hoof with surprising grace. Wes tucked the hoof between the panels of his leather apron, and set to work removing an old horseshoe. Nell watched in silence from the door as he clipped off the nail ends, then eased off the shoe as gently as one might help a child out of slippers.

I want to be the father of your children. Her breath caught in her throat at the memory of his words, the rough whisper in which he'd said them.

She waited until he had set the horse's hoof back down before she spoke.

"How're you feeling?"

He started at the sound of her voice. He straightened and met her gaze across the workshop floor. Lucy was right; he did heal fast. The worst of the swelling had abated in the night, but in its place was a patchwork of bruises in every shade. He could open his left eye enough to reveal the broken blood vessels staining it crimson.

"Old," he said. "Brawling's a young man's game."

"You shouldn't be working again." She motioned to his swollen hands. Wes raised one, examined the split skin over the knuckles with vague curiosity, as if he'd forgotten what had happened.

"I'll be fine. John Henry needs the shoeing. His owner let it go too long as is."

"John Henry?"

"Yeah. You know, 'the steel-driving man.' 'Cause he's so—"

"Big. I get it." She couldn't resist a wry smile. "Shouldn't he be black, then?"

"Well, I didn't name him."

"Naw. You name your horses 'Blondie' and 'Paint' and 'Socks.'"

"Well, when I get a new batch of horses, you can name them. See if you do any better."

His sharpness startled her. She looked down at her shoes, torn between contrition and resentment. "Didn't mean nothing by it," she muttered sullenly.

"Forget it." He walked over to his workbench, selected a curved knife. "Where were you? I got up and you were gone."

"Just running some errands."

"Found another job yet?"

His tone had turned outright hostile. Nell felt herself panicking. This wasn't going at all as she'd hoped. "Ain't starting looking yet," she said, trying to sound light. "Reckon I promised I'd stay on 'til after Christmas." *Look at me, Wes!* she screamed inside her head. *Tell me you want me to stay!*

Wes returned to the horse, and set to paring down the hoof. The silence grated on Nell until she was ready to tear her hair. Or his. She let out an irritated hiss of breath. The horse snorted in reply and tossed its head.

"Look, I'll be busy a while with this," Wes said brusquely. "Why don't you go check on Ma?"

There was no mistaking the air of curt dismissal in his voice. Nell stared at him, utterly at a loss. "Wes... are you angry with me?"

"No. It's not that."

"Do... do you want to talk?"

He sighed. He straightened, and set the horse's hoof down again. The face he showed her was bleak. "Best not. Seems every time I open my mouth, I make things worse."

"I... I'd like to listen," she stammered. "I mean... really listen." *Tell me you love me. Tell me you'd shout it from the middle of Main Street. Tell me you still think we got a chance.*

"I got nothing more to say, really."

Nell felt herself nodding. Soft sounds of protests filled her mouth, but she could not part her lips to let them out. She found herself stepping back out the door, driven back by the force of Wes's despair.

He turned away before she did.

Anyone could be watching her, she knew, as she crossed the side yard to the house. She kept her shoulders back and her pace measured. Not until she was safely back inside the house did she let herself weep.

She'd cursed Wes for waiting so long to speak. But now she was the one who'd waited too long, and she'd lost her chance.

Sixteen

"Cut him loose," was Bill Crawford's verdict as he hung up the telephone.

"You're kidding me," Connor stammered. "We can't even hang some kind of misdemeanor on him? Bill, I know he's hiding something! He knew more than he was letting on."

Charlie looked from husband to marshal. Bill looked just as disappointed with the ruling, but she recognized the set of his jaw that said he was in no mood to fight it. She could sympathize. Sheriff Quirk was not a bear to go poking.

Sitting behind the marshal's desk as if he owned it, John Garrod appeared completely unaffected by the order. By his concentration on the map in front of him, he might not have even been listening... except that Garrod was always listening.

"The court doesn't want to push it," Bill said glumly. "And the sheriff doesn't like all them Paiutes loitering outside. Can't say I do either. Most folk you can reason down. But not the Marsh tribe."

"Can you blame them?" Charlie asked. "Brightfeather terrorized them for the better part of a month."

"Well, they got their justice, didn't they?"

Charlie glanced Garrod's way. He kept his head bent over his map, seemingly oblivious, but she could swear she saw the ghost of a smile tug at the corners of his mouth.

"Sheriff figures the longer we keep Blackfell, the worse the mood's gonna get," Bill continued. "So we turn him loose."

"What about those wires we sent to Sante Fe? 'Adam Christian' might have some outstanding warrants. We oughta give that another day or two."

"Connor, I tried. Our orders are to turn him out at Devil's Gate. Let him be Lyon County's problem. And if one of the Marshes gets a mind to follow him," Bill smiled grimly, "well, that'll be Lyon County's problem too, won't it?"

"Yeah, that sounds like Quirk's thinking," Connor muttered. "So he goes tomorrow?"

"No," Bill said. "Tonight. You do it. Do it quietly."

"Like a thief in the night," Charlie quipped. Bill shot her a sour glare.

"Just like that. Sooner he's across the county line, the better. You don't have to like it. Just get it done."

Bill turned for the coat stand. "You coming, Garrod? I wanna get home before the Hill freezes solid."

Garrod looked up. "Oh, I thought I'd put in another hour or two, sir."

"On your werewolf project? You're getting as bad as Connor, you know."

Garrod's gaze was withering. "Hardly, sir. This is a strictly rational investigation. I am following all the procedures of scientific inquiry."

"Yeah, I don't know what that means," Bill said with a dismissive wave. "You have your fun, college boy. Just remember, you're on shift again at dawn."

"One might think the people of Gold Hill deserved a more educated man as chief of police," Garrod murmured to himself, in the silence following Bill's departure.

"The people of Gold Hill voted him in," Connor pointed out sharply.

"Only because they lacked a suitable alternative."

"What's that, now?"

"Oh, don't mind me, Franklin. Merely thinking aloud."

"I bet you were. Well, if you're going to be hanging around, you might as well make yourself useful. Bust out Blackfell's things from the lock-up."

"That's evidence."

"If Jimmy Quirk says there's no crime, then there can't be evidence, can there? C'mon. Like Bill said, let's get this over with."

Garrod started to protest, but Connor turned his back on him. "Charlie." He held out his hands, and she stepped up to take them. His skin was ice cold, despite the full breakfast he had eaten not an hour ago.

"Could you make up a fresh pot of coffee? I'm gonna need some to see this through."

She stepped closer to him, lowered her voice. "Special coffee?"

"Oh, I think so, don't you?"

"Sure thing." She touched his cheek fondly, and he drew in a sharp breath at the warmth of her fingers.

"Is a little public decency too much to ask?" Garrod piped up. Connor bared his canines in the beginnings of a snarl. Charlie tapped the tip of his nose chidingly.

Behave, she mouthed.

"You keep baiting a dog you're gonna get bit," he whispered in her ear.

She giggled. "You talking about me or Garrod?"

"Haven't decided yet." He kissed her cheek and turned for the jailhouse.

"I hope it's me," she called after him. He stopped at the door to the jail and wagged a finger at her.

"You behave, now."

She winked at him. But her smile soured as she felt Garrod's eyes on her.

"I'm rather afraid to ask," he remarked.

"Then don't. Don't you have a wild goose to chase anyhow?"

Garrod slowly stood. He walked up to her until his head loomed over hers, uncomfortably close. "One day, Mrs. Franklin, you'll find yourself without a man to protect you."

His voice was chilling, his delivery almost conversational. Charlie reined in the urge to spit in his face. *Behave, behave,* she told herself as she turned on her heel, swinging her hips to ensure the heavy leather of her riding culottes slapped his shins.

She went into the kitchen and set some water to boil. She could hear Garrod fiddling about in the main office: opening the safe, spilling the contents of Blackfell's meagre duffel bag on the floor. He would probably catalogue every item once more just to be thorough, and break half of them along the way. Charlie ignored the noise. Once she started to grind the coffee she could hardly hear him anymore.

When the coffee was almost ready, she stepped outside to secure the final ingredient, hidden deep inside Connor's saddlebags. The air was crisp and still. She could hear the notes from the piano at the Maynard Hotel floating on the air: a ragtime tune. The horses looked stoic and miserable under their blankets. Their combined breath hung in a great cloud on the air.

Clem acknowledged her with a hopeful snort. But Washington didn't even lift his head as she dug through the saddlebag for the Mason jar of fresh pig's blood. He knew the routine.

"Thanks, Wash," Charlie said, as she tucked the over-blanket back up to cover the base of his neck. Washington replied with a derisive puff of air.

A spark of light twinkled in her peripheral vision. Charlie looked across the street. Captain Marsh sat outside the Capital Saloon, smoking his pipe, watching the marshal's office.

"Don't worry, Cap'n," Charlie called. "He's outta here tonight."

She tucked the jar inside her coat to hide it from Garrod and headed back in. As she swung the door open, she caught Garrod at the coat stand, his hand on Connor's gun belt and its holstered Colt.

"What are you doing?" she asked.

Garrod plucked the gun belt off the stand, the better to retrieve his own coat on the adjacent hook. "The Indian's belongings are all accounted for." He indicated a bulging duffel bag sitting on the desk. "As for myself, I have no desire to watch you and your husband continue to fondle each other."

"Such language, Mr. Garrod," she drawled, her words dripping sarcasm.

His coat donned, Garrod gathered his many papers into one thick sheaf. "Those better not be official files," Charlie warned. "You know they stay in the office."

He didn't bother to answer her. Research in hand, he made for the door, keeping his gaze fixed on a point just above Charlie's head. She had hop to the side to avoid being run down.

"Asshole," Charlie hissed in his wake, just loud enough for him to hear.

~ * ~

"You're getting out of here," Connor announced as he unlocked the cell. Blackfell stared at him in confusion. When Connor swung the door open wide, the Wolf Charmer's gaze wandered to the empty space in front of him.

"I'm free?" he murmured hoarsely.

"Sure are—now get the hell outta my town."

He hustled the dazed Blackfell to his feet. He jogged him into the main office, and thrust the heavy duffel bag into his arms. "Here's all your stuff. Garrod packed it all up for you. Ain't that swell of him?"

Blackfell closed his eyes and inclined his head, as if giving thanks to a higher power. "I knew I was not meant to wither in captivity. Now my work can continue."

"Thought you were giving up wolf-charming. Since you can't trust a word you were taught and all."

"Brightfeather misled me in many things. But there was truth behind the lies."

Charlie entered, bearing a steaming mug of coffee. Connor drained it in three long gulps. Caffeine and sugar and fresh blood warmed his stomach. He could feel his own sluggish blood stirring in response.

"Skinwalkers are real. Brightfeather proved as much. There must be others like her. I must find them. I must atone for my folly."

Connor clucked his tongue. "Christ. Back to the same old song."

"I have—"

"A sacred duty. I know. Long as it keeps you out of Storey County, I'm happy. Come on, now. Let's go." He glanced back at Charlie. "You hold down the fort, honey. This shouldn't take long."

He strapped on his gun belt, frowning at the scent of carbolic soap. He had to remember to hang his things next to Bill's coat... the marshal's mammalian musk was far easier on the sinuses than Garrod's reek of antiseptics.

Washington lifted his head from the hitching post and nickered a sleepy greeting as Connor untied his reins and removed the winter blanket from his back. "That's right, Wash. We're going for a walk." Connor climbed atop the horse and turned him south. Blackfell hung back on the boardwalk. He wore only a duster over his shirt, but he seemed unaffected by the cold. He clutched the duffel to his breast like a mother cradling her child.

"County line's that way," Connor pointed downhill. Blackfell reluctantly slung his duffel over one shoulder.

"After you," Connor said gamely.

"I said I'd never let you get behind me again."

"You don't have a choice, friend. Walk."

Blackfell started downhill. Connor followed. They'd only passed a half dozen storefronts when he realized they were being followed. Connor cast a glance over his shoulder; old Captain Marsh kept pace from a safe distance.

A leisurely mile south of town, Devil's Gate straddled the county line. The pair of rocky bastions rose some four hundred feet above the narrow gully. Connor could remember when the pass had hosted a miniature town, with saloons and stables, and a toll booth that was a frequent target for bandits. Now only a few rotten shanties remained, casting long shadows in the moonlight.

Connor reined Wash to a halt in the middle of the pass. "Here we are." He pointed to a weathered sign that read: *Lyon County.* Blackfell squinted at the sign, but Connor imagined his eyes weren't equal to the challenge.

"You can see Silver City from here." Connor indicated the lights winking down in the valley. "Reckon you can rent a good room for a dollar a night. And a bedroll under a table for a quarter."

"Brightfeather was not the only skinwalker to curse your town. Deputy Garrod told me of the reports. A large dog only ever spotted around the full moon. Strange howls echoing down the ravines on clear nights."

"It's called the wind."

"You have a wolf walking in your midst," Blackfell continued. "But...you know that, don't you? You know who I mean."

"Not a clue. Get along, now."

"How else did you know to follow Brightfeather to the Benedict house?"

The ache in his shoulder intensified; it was as if Blackfell had stuck a ghostly finger into the wound and twisted. "I didn't," Connor said warily. "I caught her just outside the Freemasons' cemetery. You were there."

Blackfell smile's made his skin crawl. "If you say so. We both know the truth."

Connor gritted his teeth. His hand reached for his revolver of its own accord.

"I confess she had me fooled for a long time. Seems my lot to be deceived by two-faced females."

Connor blinked at him in confusion. "Nell... you think Nell is a skinwalker?" When Blackfell's smug expression didn't waver, Connor let out a laugh. "Well, friend, you just made my night."

"You think it's funny. Of course you do. All that big talk about being a shepherd to your flock, but you're happy to let a wolf steal a few now and then. After all, sheep are meant to be eaten."

"Fella, no one got mauled by wolves until you and your gal rolled into town."

"There are many ways to kill, aren't there? Less honest than a wolf bite. Wonder how long your little rooster-girl will last, before you drain the last of her soul?"

Connor drew his Colt and lined up the sights between Blackfell's eyes. Blackfell smiled tightly. "I'll be moving on, then."

"You're damn right you will. And if I ever see you this side of Devil's Gate again, I will hurt you."

"I'm sure you'll try," Blackfell replied. He turned towards Silver City and raised a hand in farewell. "Take care of that arm, now," he called over his shoulder cheerfully. "And keep an eye on that colored witch. One day she's gonna stop fearing you. And an angry wolf eats its own kind."

He walked tall and proud, all but strutting down the road. Of course he did. Once again, he had gotten the last word. Connor kept his gun trained on Blackfell's back. Each time a hump in the uneven road hid the man's silhouette, Connor stood in the stirrups until he could see him again. He needed to see the man reach the lights of Silver City. He didn't want to return to work until he was certain Blackfell was out of their lives.

Captain Marsh drew up alongside Connor and Washington, thoughtfully puffing his pipe. "'The angry wolf eats its own kind'—pshaw! Wolves are pack animals, don't Vaudeville know that much at least?"

Connor stretched his sore shoulder, trying to ease the sudden ache. The motion drew Marsh's attention.

"How'd he know about your arm anyway?"

"Saw I was favoring it." Connor grimaced. "Shoot… or Brightfeather crowed about it."

"You don't think he was her dupe, do you?"

"Not really, no."

"Still not healing?"

"Nope."

"Hm." Marsh dug deep into a pocket to retrieve some more kinnikinnick. Connor squinted at the southern horizon. Blackfell had yet to reappear.

"Funny thing, that the curse didn't lift when the gal died," the captain remarked.

"Might be that rule don't apply to my kind," Connor said distractedly. He was still waiting for Blackfell to emerge from the shadows.

He could see the valley clearly under the gibbous moon; he could count every rooftop in Silver City. But he couldn't see Blackfell anymore.

The man could have stopped to relieve himself. He could be resting just below a rise, plotting his next move. Or he could be tracking west, planning to double-back up one of the gullies.

"Might be." Marsh bit down hard on his pipe. "Or else... she wasn't the one who cursed you."

Connor slowly turned his head Marsh's way.

The angry wolf eats its own kind, Blackfell liked to say.

But the skinwalker wasn't a true wolf—not like Wes became. The beast was always in Wes's blood, even when it slept. And when it woke, it overtook him completely. The skinwalker was always a crude imitation, a human in disguise.

A costume, Connor corrected mentally.

Costumes could be shared.

"Goddamn Vaudeville," he muttered as he understood at last.

Captain Marsh flashed a triumphant smile. "Ain't that what I been saying?"

~ * ~

Charlie made herself a weak cup of coffee with the last of the grounds. She paced around the office, re-reading the old wanted posters pinned to the wall. When the familiar surroundings no longer interested her, she opened a desk drawer to retrieve a battered novel. She barely made it through three pages of *The Innocents Abroad* before she sighed and closed it. She needed to light more lamps if she wanted to avoid a headache, and Bill had already been complaining about their oil bill. *You know, your man used to go a whole shift on a single candle*, he'd grumbled.

"Should have brought Joan of Arc," she murmured to herself. But she was reading the latest Mark Twain to Connor, and he had strictly forbidden her to read ahead without him. He had been so proud to present her with the one Twain she didn't already have – she hadn't the heart to tell she'd already read most of it serialized in *Harper's Bazaar*.

She decided to call Nell. She hadn't spoken to her since the morning at the Crypt, and though instinct told her to give Nell some space, she was starved for news.

Charlie got the good operator—the old spinster with the slight lisp—far more efficient than the breathy girl who always took a good three minutes to connect a call. Presently Charlie heard the click on the other end of the line, and the low drawl of Nell's voice answering "Benedict house, can I help ya?"

"Nell, it's Charlie!" she piped up.

A long pause, and the faintest hiss on the line. "Uh-hmm," came the soft reply.

"You there? Nell? I'm up at the marshal's office and Connor's gone out."

"Yes, I can hear you," Nell said shortly, and Charlie winced. She was probably hollering like her Aunt Katy. Brassy and loud, and full of false cheer.

"What can we help you with?" Nell asked.

"Well, I just wanted to talk is all."

"Charlie, I'm working. I've got supper cooking right now."

"Right. Sorry." The Benedict receiver would come clapping down on the hook at any moment. Charlie gritted her teeth and forged again. "How's Wes? Connor told me about the whole… fight."

"Ambush," Nell corrected.

"How is he doing?"

"Two bruised ribs. Right pinkie might be broken. Not sure. But he's healing."

"Guess it's good it happened now. I mean, when the moon is getting smaller. He'd be having a worse time of it if it was going the other way—"

"Charlie! Not on the phone!"

"Right, right. Sorry! But how is he? And how are you?"

Another long silence. "Not on the phone," Nell muttered.

"Have you… thought about it?"

"Not now I said!" Nell snapped. Charlie heard the telltale curdling of her voice.

"I'm coming over," she said,

"No! No, please no, Charlie. You'll only make things worse."

"Why? What happened? Nell Wallace, you tell me right now or I swear I will march down there and find out for myself."

Only the soft hiss of electricity. Then Charlie thought she heard a faint mewl against the mouthpiece. "Nell?"

"I said…he won't look at me," Nell repeated, barely audible. Her voice caught again. "Charlie, he hardly says a word to me. And he asked me when I was planning to leave. He can't wait to get me out the door!"

It took all her self-control not to laugh. Charlie tipped her head back to let out a long sigh. "I don't think he wants you out the door."

"You haven't seen him. He's different."

"Have you tried talking to him?"

"I told you. He won't talk to me."

"I said you talk to him."

"I can't," Nell whispered fiercely. "I don't know what to say."

"You could say you love him, you eejit! The poor fellow's already laid all his cards on the table. He's waiting for you to show or fold!"

Silence; but at least Nell didn't hang up. Charlie let her eyes roam about her surroundings as she waited for Nell to find her voice. She glanced towards the large evidence safe. Garrod had left the door hanging slightly ajar. With a frown, Charlie stretched out an arm out to close it, but she couldn't reach.

"I… I have to go, Charlie," Nell murmured. "I…I'll talk to you later, okay?"

Charlie tried her leg next, and found it equally inadequate. She walked to the very end of the telephone cord's tether and aimed a kick at the edge of the door, hoping to catch it on the toe of her boot.

She did, but only barely. Instead of closing, the door rocked on its hinges, swinging open to reveal a gaping black maw.

"Charlie? You still there?"

"Uh... yeah. Yeah, I'm here." She stared at the empty safe. "Look, Nell, I've told you what I'd do. But you gotta decide what works for you. You, uh... you get back to work. Just remember, whenever you wanna talk, I'm here."

"Thanks. I mean it. I... good night, Charlie."

Charlie hung up before Nell did. She fetched the oil lamp from the desk to confirm her fears. The evidence locker was completely bare. Blackfell's effects were gone... and so was Brightfeather's wolf skin costume.

"Goddammit, Garrod! When he said all the evidence, he didn't mean that!"

She supposed it could be an honest mistake. Then she turned around and caught sight of the coat stand. She remembered Garrod's hands on Connor's gun belt.

"Oh, God!"

She bolted out the door, forgetting her own coat in her haste to scramble astride her horse.

~ * ~

Blackfell hummed a high-pitched melody to himself as he donned the wolf skins. Brightfeather had been naked under the furs, but her widower seemed to be in more of rush. He laced the gauntlets about his wrists and arranged the long apron over his torso. The skins that had cloaked Brightfeather completely seemed absurdly undersized on his broader frame, like a too-small shirt. But the lupine headdress fit him perfectly. Sitting on the crown of his head, it gave him the silhouette of man in the midst of being consumed by a beast.

The hum became a song, eerily familiar to the chants he had used in his role as Wolf Charmer. His right foot stamped a rhythm as he turned in a slow circle, first clockwise, then counter. He raised his hands to the night sky as if in prayer and his song became a wolf's howl.

At Connor's side, Captain Marsh cursed under his breath.

Connor decided they had seen enough. He rose from his crouch on the grassy knoll. Marsh followed, his old joints creaking.

Blackfell stopped in mid-dance at the sight of them.

"'The angry wolf eats its own kind,'" Connor quoted back at him. "But as the cap'n just pointed out to me, wolves are pack animals. They gotta be, to survive. Your lone wolf is usually sick, or lame, or just too cantankerous to get along with anyone. And he usually doesn't last the winter. Kinda like the lone skinwalker, right?"

"But a pair of skinwalkers, now there's a clever magic trick," Captain Marsh added. "You ever let your gal take a turn at being the Wolf Charmer too? Naw, I bet you kept that part all you to yourself. You're better at playing to the crowds."

Blackfell let out a sharp laugh. "'The Wolf Charmer.' You know where we got the phrase? This French engraving Brightfeather turned up in the Santa Fe library."

"Why ain't I surprised?" Connor drawled.

"White man's magic," Blackfell went on smugly. "What good is that against the Witchery Way?" His expression soured. "But you didn't use white man's magic to bring down Brightfeather, did you? You used the tricks of a toothless old traitor!" He stabbed a finger at Marsh. "You dare to mock me for speaking lightly of witchcraft, but you share the secrets of curse magic with a walking corpse and a nigger werewolf!"

Marsh scowled. "Werewolf? He talkin' about—"

"Never mind," Connor cut him off.

"You robbed me of my mate, the three of you."

"You were the one who told Garrod to blow her brains out," Connor protested.

"No. She was already dead when you forced her to unmask. But I'll deal with Garrod too, don't worry." He reached for the snout of his headdress.

Connor had the gun drawn before Blackfell's fingers touched the stiffened wolf skin.

When he squeezed the trigger, the cylinder clicked empty.

Connor cocked the hammer and tried the next chamber. Another ominous click. On the third try the realization dawned on him. Someone had emptied the entire barrel.

Blackfell's laughter echoed in the basin. Then he pulled the headdress down over his face.

The wolfs head enveloped him, became part of him. The apron grew, wrapped around his legs. His limbs lengthened and joints shifted position with the sound of tearing cloth and snapping bones. His boots split as his feet deformed. Muscles coiled and flexed as he sprang at Connor and Marsh in mid-transformation.

The skinwalker raced up the hillside on all fours. Connor tried one last futile squeeze of the trigger before he threw the useless Colt at the attacking creature. Blackfell easily dodged the projectile. He reached the pair in three great bounds. Connor shoved Captain Marsh out of the way, throwing himself down over the man as a shield. Blackfell's great claws raked the edge of his coat as he narrowly missed them both.

Connor got to his feet and stood in front of Marsh as Blackfell came around for another charge.

"All right," Connor breathed. "I got your number now." He balled a fist and locked eyes with the snarling skinwalker. "Come on!"

Blackfell charged. Connor struck out with his right arm. His knuckles caught the skinwalker square in the jaw. Some two hundred pounds of fur, bone and muscle came crashing to a halt against the revenant's fist.

Stunned, hemorrhaging, the skinwalker fell on his back. He could do little more than whimper as Connor calmly advanced on him.

Connor took the beast's snout in one hand and the shattered jawbone in the other. He pried the creature's mouth open as far as it could go, then further still. Flesh tore, bones snapped, and the wolf head came off the crippled man as easily as skin off a rabbit.

"Son of a bitch!" Captain Marsh exclaimed in disbelief.

"Y'all right, Cap'n?"

The old Paiute slowly rose, dusting off his legs. "I need a smoke."

"'Y'aw!" Blackfell cried, spitting out blood and shattered teeth. He clutched at his ruined face with both hands. "'Oo 'oke 'y 'aw!"

"Next one breaks your neck." Connor lifted him to his feet by his cloak. "Now, you gonna play nice and take this curse off?" He pinched the side of Blackfell's neck. "Or am I gonna take this skin off, too?"

Blackfell cried out, a hollow wail that sounded almost like "soft."

"What's that? You'll have to speak up."

"'S off! 'S off!"

"Yeah well, you'll forgive me if I don't take it on faith."

He stripped Blackfell of the headdress, which he passed to Captain Marsh. Together, they marched their prisoner back to Devil's Gate. Washington was waiting for him patiently, and Connor found a pair of handcuffs in his saddlebags.

Charlie came riding up as he was in the process of securing his moaning prisoner.

"Connor!" She reined Clem to an abrupt halt. "Captain Marsh?"

"How do?" Marsh cackled, raising his hand to tip an imaginary hat.

"Are you all right?" Charlie blurted

"Had a hell of an adventure," Marsh grinned. "Your husband knows how to keep me feeling young."

~ * ~

Back inside the marshal's station, Connor took a cursory look at Blackfell's shattered jaw, and bound it up with a handkerchief knotted under his chin.

"We'll be hanging onto your wolf's head." Connor explained. "But you can keep the rest of your furs. You'll need them." He smiled at the sorry state of Blackfell's clothes. Underneath the wolf skins, his crisp shirt and calfskin trousers were reduced to rags.

"Thanks for tearing up my coat, by the by. It'll make some mighty fine evidence." He locked Blackfell back in the last cell on the right. "The sheriff's men will be here in the morning," he said. "Looks like you finally gave us a reason to charge you."

"Mo's'er!" Blackfell spat.

Connor smiled easily. "That I am. You best keep that in mind before you go spinning wild yarns about Nell Wallace." He leaned his elbows on the bars of the door and lowered his voice. "Oh, and if my shoulder still hurts at sunrise, I will be back. And next time I won't pull my punches."

Blackfell's eyes widened and he clutched his chin protectively. Satisfied, Connor turned for the door. He had gotten in the last word at last.

"Garrod set you up," Charlie told him in the relative privacy of the kitchen.

"Mm. That's twice in one week he's tried to kill me." He chuckled. "I must really be getting to him."

"Aren't you gonna do something about him?"

"He keeps this up, I might have to," he said absently, as he unbuttoned his shirt to examine his wound.

A grin broke out across his face. His skin smelled clean and healthy. The tendrils of rot were in full retreat, and fresh scar tissue covered the shrinking wound. The curse had lifted.

Seventeen

The full story of Adam Blackfell's downfall came out in snatches of gossip over the next two days. From the Paiute milkman, Nell learned Blackfell had enjoyed less than a half-hour of freedom before Connor Franklin caught him running around in wolf skins just south of American Flat. A customer coming to board his horse mentioned seeing a cohort of uniformed policemen descending the Hill from Virginia City. At sundown, Charlie stopped by to confirm the Wolf Charmer had been moved to more secure quarters at the county courthouse.

He wouldn't stay long. The police in Sante Fe finally answered Connor's telegram; Blackfell wasn't wanted for any outstanding offenses in their county. But neighbouring San Miguel County had an eight-year-old warrant out for a certain Adam Indian, alias Adam Christian, for assault, theft and grand larceny. The description matched Blackfell perfectly, right down to the scar over his left eyebrow.

Even if he managed to find a lawyer slick enough to talk him free of the noose, the Wolf Charmer would never trouble Storey County again. And with his credibility irrevocably shattered, Charlie assured Nell no one would listen should Blackfell decide to accuse anyone in town of lycanthropy.

Nell still couldn't quite believe it. Blackfell had mistaken her for a werewolf? She could accept he had smelled Wes's fur on her shawl, but for him to make the leap that she could ever be something so rare and preternatural boggled her mind.

"He always said you had powerful magic, didn't he?" Charlie had remarked when Nell expressed her skepticism.

"I thought he was just playing me," Nell protested. "We both know I'm nothing like Wes or…" Or your man, she wanted to say, but instead she said, "Or like the skinwalkers. I'm just an ordinary gal."

Charlie laughed as if she'd told the best joke in ages.

"Oh Nell," she'd said, once she recovered her composure. "Ordinary folk don't stick around when they find out their sweetheart's a werewolf."

She didn't correct Charlie on her choice of words. She was just grateful the girl didn't pursue the matter.

Life at the Benedict house continued in what had become the new routine. Lucy gradually spent more and more time out of bed. She even began to sleep through the night without the help of laudanum, though Nell continued to dose her with ipecac over her protests.

Wes continued to be the ideal employer: considerate, impeccably polite and resolutely distant. He only spoke of domestic matters, and his smiles remained modest and closed-mouthed.

Nell continued to agonize over what to say to him. But even if she'd had the words, she never found a chance to say them; he only seemed to approach her when his mother was within earshot. When he summoned Nell to his writing desk late on Friday night, she thought she might finally have her chance. But before she could decide how to start, he handed her the envelope with her week's pay and a shopping list for the next day. The hollow formality was so shocking, she lost all her resolve.

That night she lay awake in misery, tortured by longing. When she could no longer bear to stare at the ceiling another minute, she lit a candle and got up to look through her box of keepsakes. She lingered longest on the card of the Circassian Beauty, caressing its worn corners.

By morning she knew she could not endure another day of silence.

She waited until lunchtime. She made sandwiches and cold cuts. Lucy came to the table to eat, but Wes insisted on remaining in his workshop. He had a set of leather hoof boots to finish making for John Henry, he explained. So the women ate together, and after she had seen Lucy back upstairs, Nell brought Wes's lunch to him on a tray.

A thick frost coated the ground like fur. The forge was cold, the firepot unlit. Wes sat at his worktable, the tools of his craft spread around him. He struggled to bend the leather into shape; the tape binding his broken finger hindered his dexterity. He scarcely looked up as Nell placed the tray next to him.

"You need to eat," Nell reminded him.

"I will. Just not hungry yet."

"One of Grant's boys could make up that boot, you know. Might not be as good as yours, but I reckon it would do."

"Naw. I'd only have to make a better one later on."

Gingerly, she rested her hand on his shoulder. He wore several layers of flannel, but she felt his muscles tense underneath.

"I don't want to find a new job," she said. "I'd like to stay here."

"All right," Wes said. He might as well have been discussing the weather.

She let her hand linger. He shrugged it off.

"God, Nell, what do you want from me?" He shot her an irritated glare over one shoulder. "I'm trying to give you your space. I'm trying to keep my mouth shut. It doesn't help when you're hanging over me like a creeper vine!

"I'm sorry," he said a moment later, recovering himself. "You don't deserve that."

He turned back to his work. He picked up a little pick and began to tool the leather. Nell was torn between flight and fight.

"Aw hell," she muttered. She thrust her hand into her apron pocket and slapped the contents down at Wes's elbow.

Wes stared down at the card for a long moment before he picked it up.

"The Circassian Beauty," he murmured. He looked back at Nell, brow knit in confusion. "You said you lost it."

"I lied."

He didn't know what to say to the revelation. He looked from the card to Nell, then back again.

"I lied about something else," Nell began, hearing the tremor in her voice. "When I said I didn't think about you... about us. I'm always thinking about you. Even with Shiloh..." she saw him flinch at the name, and she rushed onward, "you were the one I wanted. You're the only man I've ever wanted."

He stared at her.

"You know I taught myself never to need anyone, and if I had to, I could go the rest of my life without having you in it. But I won't be happy," she admitted softly. "I... Wes, I don't think I'll ever be happy again if you don't kiss me right now."

He knocked the chair over in his haste to rise. He crossed the floor in two paces and caught her up in his arms, crushing her body against his. His fingers splayed at the back of her head, and his mouth covered hers.

The force of his ardor staggered them. Nell felt the hard edge of the workbench dig into the small of her back. Wes kissed her as if he meant to devour her. As if he meant to condense a lifetime of frustrated love into one heady, brutal embrace. The stubble on his cheeks prickled like nettles, but she didn't care. It was as intoxicating as she'd dared hope in her fantasies... only now she wasn't the swooning girl, helpless in his arms. Now she kissed him back with equal hunger. Her arms wound about his neck; her fingers tangled in his hair. When he broke off abruptly, she heard a pained moan escape her parted lips.

His hand remained at the back of her skull, pressing her forehead to his. His gaze was unfocused, almost wild. "If you're only after the one kiss, you tell me now," he warned, in a voice like a rasp. "'Cause if we keep going, I ain't liable to ever stop."

"You better not stop," Nell growled, as she pulled him back against her.

"Wes?" a man's voice hailed from somewhere outside.

They broke apart, cursing. Wes stumbled back to a respectable distance. They fumbled with their clothes, he trying to smooth out his shirt, she shaking the creases from her dress.

Wes wiped his mouth hurriedly and turned towards the doorway just as the aging stable master shuffled into view.

"In here, Grant," Wes called, his voice cheerful. Nell wondered how he could be so composed, when her legs felt like water and her heart was hammering so hard she was sure her corset strings would snap.

Grant Weatherbee took in the scene without reaction. His gaze swept past Nell as if she didn't exist, but he noticed the tray of food and said, "Oh, you're just setting down to eat. Well, if it'll keep, you mind coming 'round the stables with me? The Cuthberts' mare's come in with a limp. Looks like a sprain to me, but I want a second opinion."

Wes nodded gamely "'Course. Lead the way."

He was the picture of nonchalance as he made to follow. No one would ever guess he'd just had his housekeeper up against his workbench. Deep in the pit of her stomach, Nell felt her excitement sour to shame. Then Wes turned back, and flashed her the lazy smile that had haunted her nights for so many years.

"We'll, uh, finish this up later, Nell," he said, as easily as remarking on the weather. His tone was so light, so dismissive, that old Weatherbee never even looked back, never saw him wink. And just as swiftly as it had faltered, Nell's pulse quickened all over again, until she was burning up with joy.

~ * ~

It was the longest afternoon of Nell's life. She tried to keep her mind occupied. It shouldn't have been hard; there was more than enough to be done in the house. She had fallen well behind on the washing over the last week, and now that both skinwalkers were gone, she had no excuse for leaving the stoves filled with ash. She had always taken solace in the demands of heavy work; the sheer repetition of scrubbing a grate or hemming a sheet could prove hypnotizing. But this time she couldn't lose herself in her labors. Her mind was racing, calculating, predicting. What would happen when Wes returned? Would he sweep her off her feet and continue their fevered embrace right where they had left off? Would she want him to? Her stepfather's caustic words taunted her. *Don't tell me a little tomfoolery is enough for you.*

It wasn't. But what was the alternative? She didn't doubt Wes would stand in the main street and shout his love to the skies if she asked it of him. But why would she? What would that accomplish, beyond making a spectacle of them both?

I want to know I matter.

She thought she heard him come in at one point, while she was on her hands and knees scrubbing the smears of soot and grease from underneath the stove. She could have sworn she heard feet stealing down the hallway. But when she looked up, the back passage was empty. The ceiling creaked over her head and she wondered if he had snuck upstairs to see his mother, but why would he need to hide from her?

She was tossing out the wash water when she spotted him again, cutting through the side yard on his way to the stables. She waved but he did not look up, and she felt too timid to call out.

Lucy came down at teatime, red-eyed and red-nosed, a handkerchief in one hand and a shopping list in the other. "My word. I don't think I've ever seen the kitchen this spotless," she remarked with a nervous smile. "Seems a waste to cook in here and spoil all your hard work."

Nell studied the rag in her hands, feeling awkward. Lucy might not look so favorably on the results if she knew just what thoughts Nell had been trying so desperately to scrub out of her head.

"I reckon—" she sniffed, and dabbed at her nose with her handkerchief, "call me crazy, but I reckon I'm finally getting my appetite back. I've had the queerest craving for some of that chicken pot pie they make over at the Maynard."

"Really? Oh, nothing queer about that." The Maynard House was famous for turning their leftover roasts into the most decadent pies on the Comstock. "Awful rich, though. They do love their lard over there. But if it's chicken you're hankering for, I can cook up a few cuts nice and juicy, and we can try that with some—"

"Do not say toast, and do not say mashed potatoes. I am sick of eating like an infant. And I daresay, you've worked your fingers to the bone already. Now I want you to go put in this order, and you can pick up anything else we need for the pantry while it cooks."

Just looking at the list made Nell's mouth water: pie, cornbread, and three portions of the Maynard's saffron cake for dessert. "Shoot, Mrs. B, if I'd known you wanted cornbread, I could have been baking today—"

"Nell. No offense, honey, and I mean it, but it really is just easier to pay the dime. Now if memory serves me, you used to be quite fond of saffron cakes..."

Especially the ones at the Maynard, which their cook made with oranges and honey and which never sold for less than a quarter a slice.

"...but if you'd rather something else, you just add it on there."

"You sure, Mrs. B?" Lucy's red face suggested she'd spent the whole afternoon wrestling with a phlegm-filled throat. And with her stomach still so tender, she wasn't liable to enjoy more than a few mouthfuls before her digestion protested. Violently.

"Humor an old lady. Now you'd best go before we lose the light."

Nell shook her head inwardly, but she went without further protest. It wasn't her money to waste, after all. And a childish voice inside her head reasoned Lucy's inevitable biliousness would mean more leftovers for herself.

The light was already failing; a heavy cloudbank had settled over the spine of the mountains. She felt the needle-sharpness in the cold air.

Lucy had been thoughtful enough to sign the order in her large, schoolgirl's hand. Nell was grateful for that. It made her feel bold enough to go in the front door of the Maynard to place her order with the bartender.

"Be a while," he told her. "I'll send it 'round back when it's ready."

"I'll be back in a half-hour," Nell countered. "It'll be ready then. Or am I gonna tell Mrs. Benedict you're filling other orders before hers?"

She hiked up to the drug store to replenish their medicine cabinet. On a whim, she also bought a bottle of Wes's favorite birch beer. When she returned to the Maynard twenty-five minutes later, the food was waiting for her, wrapped in brown paper.

"You give Mrs. Benedict my regards, now," the bartender said stiffly.

Though it was scarcely five o'clock, darkness had fallen beyond the reach of the streetlights. Frost crunched underneath her feet. Nell chose her steps carefully, avoiding slick patches. Her worn shoes were meant for walking all day on floorboards, not navigating icy streets. She hugged the steaming-hot parcels to keep warm. Perhaps it was time she bought proper winter boots. She could hardly plead poverty as an excuse anymore.

The parlor of the Benedict house was dark, but she saw a light burning in the dining room. Her arms weighed down with shopping, she fumbled to open the front door.

It swung open before she could find the doorknob. Wes awaited her inside.

"Here, let me help you." He took the parcels of food from her arms before she could protest. She expected to follow him into the kitchen, so she could properly plate the food. But instead he led the way to the dining room, where two places had already been set.

She stared at the table: the lace tablecloth, the fresh beeswax candles in the candelabra, and the filled glasses of wine. She didn't understand at first. She counted the plates and wondered why there wasn't a place for her.

Wes didn't trouble to enlighten her. He had already peeled back the wrapping paper around the pie, and was struggling to shift it onto a serving platter. He swore under his breath as he burned his fingertips on the crust.

"Should... I go get your ma?" Nell asked. "She still upstairs?"

"Oh, she's not joining us."

Nell tsked. "Of course she is. This was all her idea."

Wes grinned boyishly. "Actually, it was mine. Don't worry, I already carried her dinner up to her. Baked potatoes with buttercream fresh from the Capital's kitchens."

"But... I just got dinner at the Maynard," she persisted, stubbornly.

"You're awfully slow tonight, ain't ya?"

Slowly she began to piece together the scheme: Lucy's awkward smile, her firm insistence, the sudden craving that included all of Nell's favorites.

"You set this up," she said at last. "All this... what is this?"

"It's dinner. Our first dinner together. And since I didn't think you'd let me take you up to that fancy restaurant on B Street—"

The laugh erupted from her throat, catching her by surprise. "Wes... are you trying to court me? 'Cause you don't need to bother, you know."

"Of course I do," he said, and the tenderness in his voice made her weak in the knees. When he gestured for her to sit, she did so gratefully. She stared at him across the table, as he continued to clumsily plate their food. Just when she thought she had finally figured him out, he revealed yet another side of himself. Twenty years of loving him and hating him, and she suspected she'd barely scratched the surface. He was like a skinwalker, a different animal under every coat.

"What... what did you tell your ma?" she asked, when she couldn't stand to watch him work in silence any longer.

"Same thing I told you."

"Then she knows? That we're..."

"Courting?" When he lifted his head, she could just make out the playful waggle of his eyebrows under his shaggy bangs.

She blushed. "Don't call it that."

He shrugged. "You brought it up."

"Well, I wish I hadn't." She started to reach for the glass of wine, then checked herself. She placed her napkin in her lap and twisted it in her hands. Suddenly she remembered Lucy's red nose and swollen eyes.

"What did she say when you told her?" she asked. There were so many emotions that could make a person weep.

Now it was his turn to flush. "She told me... how lucky I was to get a second chance with you. No," he corrected. "She said how lucky 'we' were to get a second chance with you. And she's right."

He served her the cornbread and pie, then took his place opposite her and raised his glass in a silent toast. Nell awkwardly mimicked him, then sampled the white wine. She had few points of comparison... the only wine she'd ever had was a vinegary red Shiloh had favored. The white tasted crisp on her tongue and made her throat burn pleasantly at the first sip. But after she'd taken a mouthful of pie, she noticed how well the drink set off the many savoury flavors of the filling.

"I thought we weren't keeping drink in the house," she remarked.

"I picked that up at the Capital, too."

"Should have figured you were up to something. Seems whenever I let you out of my sight nowadays, you're up to no good."

"Guess you'll have to keep a better eye on me."

"I'll keep you on a leash, if you don't watch yourself."

"Reckon I could live with that," he drawled. His smile was easy, but his gaze smoldered.

"We oughta set out some rules," Nell heard herself say, matter-of-factly. She hated herself for it.

"Surely," he said agreeably, but he did not volunteer any himself.

"Like... what this looks like in the house," Nell clarified. "And what it looks like outside. And whether I'm still your housekeeper or your... your sweetheart or whatever you call girls that get courted."

"Sweetheart. I like that."

"Not so sure I do."

"Then I won't call you that."

"You're being awful agreeable."

"You don't approve."

"I ain't used to it, is all. I'm used to a drag-out fight with you. Agreeable gets me worried."

"Don't worry, Nell," he said, and again she was struck by the gentleness in his voice. "And far as I can see, you're still our housekeeper. I mean, if you still want the job. Same work, same pay. Nothing's changed there—the house still needs keeping and Ma still needs to rest more. You have your job and I have mine. And anything we might do outside our jobs... well, that's something else entirely."

It was an eminently sensible proposal. She kept her freedom, to stay or to leave as it suited her. He asked no surrender from her, and she required no concessions from him. Wes knew what she needed to feel safe, and he was prepared to live by her terms.

She ought to be beaming with triumph. Instead she felt oddly sad.

"You do still want the job?" he asked hopefully.

She shrugged. "Girl's gotta do something to feed herself. God knows I ain't letting you keep me."

"Of course not. How's your pie? Not too greasy?"

"Just the way I like it." She took another sip of wine.

"I had another idea," Wes said at length. "If you'll hear me out." She nodded.

"I remember you used to want to run a boarding house."

"Pft. Like I'd ever find the money to buy one."

"I could sell you this one."

"What?"

"I could sell you the house," Wes repeated patiently. "Whatever you could pay for it. A hundred bucks. Fifty bucks. And Ma and I could be your boarders."

Her gaze darted to Wes's wine glass, still more than half full. A tipsy head was the only explanation she could summon for such a nonsensical idea. What would possibly be the point?

"I can't give you my name in Nevada, it's true," Wes went on. "But I can sell you property. Even at a loss."

"But why?" she stammered. "Why would you ever do that?"

"Come on, Nell. Give me some credit. I know what you really want, and it ain't being my housekeeper."

"What?" she prompted. "What do I want?"

"What you've always wanted. To be your own boss. Beholden to no one." Words that once were accusatory now flowed easily from his lips. "I don't want you to be beholden to me. I don't. I don't want you staying under this roof 'cause I'm paying you to. And I don't want you lying awake at night worrying what'll happen to you if I ever decide this—" he gestured to the dinner table—"ain't gonna work."

She winced to hear him voice all her worst fears. She felt ashamed of her doubts, when he seemed to have none. "I always worry," she mumbled lamely. "Shoot, even if I had a ring and your name, I'd still be fretting. I'm always bracing for the worst to happen. I'm always looking for a fight."

"So let me take one worry away," Wes pleaded. "I could sell you the house. Then if the worst does happen…"

"We shouldn't be thinking about that—"

He laughed. "But you will. Whether you should or you shouldn't, you will. I told you, Nell… I know you. As long as I'm your boss I'm sitting up above you."

"You're a man, Wes," she said archly, before she could stop herself. "You'll always be above me."

She wondered if he'd argue the point, if he'd start in on some foolish speech about being the dog at her feet. But to his credit, he only nodded ruefully. "But you'd own the roof over my head. And I'd be beholden to you."

He really meant it, she realized; he was prepared to sign over the deed to his house to buy her peace of mind. She hadn't realized until that moment just how much he was willing to commit to her.

"I don't want you to be. I don't want either of us indebted to the other. If we're gonna be together, I want to be because we both chose it, and we're still choosing it every day."

"Then buy the damn house. We'll call it a business partnership. You hold the house, and I bring in the money to keep it running. And if you disappeared on me or me on you... well, we'd be able to muddle through with the half we got. But we'd never be as happy as when both halves fit together."

She took in his words, savoring them. "'Business partnership' you say. You do know any other girl would say that's a damn feeble proposal." And yet no words could have pleased her more.

He grinned back as if he could read her thoughts. "But you're not any other girl. There ain't another girl on earth like you."

By the time they had cleaned their plates, her head was spinning pleasantly from the wine. The Maynard's saffron cake was as decadent as she remembered. She eyed the remaining slice greedily. "Does your ma even like saffron cake?" she asked.

"It's not her favorite." Wes wrapped it up in the remnants of the brown paper. "Thought we might split it for breakfast."

His smile hinted at all the things that could happen between dinner and breakfast. Nell pressed her lips together tightly to maintain her composure, but she could feel her eyebrows arching wickedly.

"What big eyes you have, Grandma," Wes teased.

He refused her help to clear the table, and insisted on leaving the dishes in the kitchen. "Tonight you're taking the evening off."

He led into the parlor. "What are you doing?" she asked when she saw him open the cabinet for the Gramophone.

"I think we deserve a little music." Wes selected a record from their collection and gingerly placed it on the dish. Nell read the label as he wound up the motor. *A Hot Time in the Old Town.*

"Did your ma tell you that's my favorite?"

He chuckled. "Think I didn't hear you singing that all the time?" When the needle touched the record, the sound of a tinny trumpet filled the parlor. Wes held out his hand with a flamboyant bow. "May I have this dance?"

"I don't dance."

"Then I'll teach you."

"Didn't say I can't. Said I don't." But she took his hand despite herself. When he drew her close and laid his hand high on her back, she swore she could feel the heat of his skin right through dress and underpinnings. He tapped his foot to count off the beats as Dan Quinn began to belt out the lyrics from the Gramophone's horn.

Come along get you ready, wear your bran, bran new gown,
For der's gwine to be a meeting in that good, good old town,
Where you knowed ev'ry body, and they all knowed you,
And you've got a rabbit's foot to keep away the hoodoo.

He tried to lead her in a two-step across the parlor floor. Nell lagged a step behind, awkwardly craning her neck down to keep an eye on their steps. Wes laughed at her studious air.

"You're just gonna get mixed up. Here." He drew her in closer, and his hand slid further down her spine, until it came to rest in the small of her back. "Eyes up. Just follow me."

Where you hear that the preaching does begin,
Bend down low for to drive away your sin
And when you gets religion, you want to shout and sing
There'll be a hot time in the old town tonight!

They tried again, a little slower this time. Pressed tight against him, she couldn't see their feet anymore. She had no choice but to let herself be led. When she caught his toe under her shoe she cursed, but Wes only laughed and kept dancing. Step by step she began to relax. She learned to predict the steps by the shift of his arms, the brush of her skirts between their legs. She felt her smile lose its nervous edge.

When you hear dem a bells go ding, ling ling,
All join 'round and sweetly you must sing
And when the verse am through, in the chorus all join in,
There'll be a hot time in the old town tonight!

They wouldn't win any awards with their shuffling steps. But by the second verse, Nell's arms had lost their steely tension. Her left hand released Wes's shoulder to rest more comfortably against his bicep.

"I'll be damned, I think she's actually enjoying herself," Wes teased.

"You shut your mouth," she mumbled.

"You know, I've been waiting fifteen years to ask you to dance."

"Well, I've been waiting twenty years for you to ask me."

"Think I know why you like this song so much."

"Only an ol' fogey don't like ragtime?"

"No... listen."

The second verse was drawing to a close. Nell's heart beat a little faster as she realized what lines Wes meant for her to hear.

Please, oh please, oh, do not let me fall,
You're all mine and I love you best of all,
And you must be my man, or I'll have no man at all,
There'll be a hot time in the old town tonight!

"I was thinking," he continued. "Come springtime when Ma is better... we might want to go away for a while. The three of us. Go touring or something. I hear the coast is mighty nice. And I would like to see the ocean."

"What? Like Frisco?"

"Was thinking farther north. Maybe Washington state."

She frowned at that. "Washington? Why?" As far as she knew, the state had nothing to recommend it beyond cheap lumber and salmon.

"It's legal there."

For a moment longer she didn't understand his words. Then her throat tightened and she forgot her steps. But Wes's firm hand on her back never faltered.

"You can't… you really mean it?" she asked. She wanted to smack herself; all those years she had reminded herself the law forbade their kind of love, and she had never once bothered to see if the law might be different somewhere else.

"We could walk into any proper courthouse in the state and get a license. We could do it, Nell! We could be married."

A license, with her name and his. She tried to picture it in her hand; more valuable than any bank note. She imagined it framed and hanging in the parlor.

"Now, it wouldn't mean a thing in Nevada," Wes went on. "Not yet. But it would mean the world to me: to know that at least somewhere in the world, you'd be Mrs. Benedict."

She couldn't think, couldn't speak. She could only stare up at him in dazed wonder. The song had finished playing: the only sound in the parlor was the crackling of the low fire, and the tapping of the Gramophone's needle against the record.

"And you must be my wife," Wes murmured. The last word came out in a husky breath, half-pleading, half-commanding. "Or I'll have no wife at all."

"Yes," Nell whispered back. "Yes. To all of it. To the house and Washington and everything. Yes, yes, yes!" Her words ran into a breathless babble, until his mouth descended on hers, and there was nothing left to say.

~ * ~

Lacking a fireplace, Wes's room was frigid in the winter evening. There would be no slow and sensual disrobing straight out of her fantasies; chattering teeth did not make for an erotic atmosphere. Instead, they stripped down to their underclothes with clumsy haste, laughing and shivering at once. As Wes hauled his flannel shirt off over his head, Nell let out a giggle at the sight of his threadbare union suit.

"What?" Wes demanded.

"Goddamn it, how many winters have you been wearing that thing?"

He gestured at her sack-like chemise. "You ain't exactly looking too fancy yourself."

"Tell me you're taking that off!"

"Not before I'm under the blanket, I ain't!"

They stumbled their way to the bed in the darkness. The sheets crackled with cold. Nell seized the heavy buffalo robe and wrapped it tight around her shoulders. "Hey, you gotta share that!" Wes warned as he climbed in after her.

"You still got wool on, you're fine."

"Nell—give it!"

They cursed goodnaturedly as they wrestled over the blanket. By the time they were both covered in buffalo hide, Wes had gotten one arm out of his long underwear, and Nell clung to his shoulder, nearly speechless with laughter.

"What is it?" he asked, sounded slightly wounded. "What?"

"Nothing, nothing. It's only—" she struggled to catch her breath between fits of mirth. "Oh, I must've gone to bed dreaming of this night a thousand times, and I never pictured this!"

"You didn't? Shoot, this is just how I always figured it'd go," he drawled. "Me freezing my ass off, you cackling like some deranged hen…"

"You shut your mouth."

"Make me," he challenged, his voice suddenly husky.

She kissed him.

He pulled her across him so she straddled him, while she fumbled to free his right arm from the confining wool. They kissed with a clumsy abandon, and when they parted they were both grinning like fools.

"Nell…" his hand rose to trace the line of one tightly coiled braid. When he next spoke, his voice turned bashful. "Could I … would you—"

"What?" she asked. At that moment she thought she would do anything for him.

"Take your hair down?" In the darkness it was hard to make out his face, but there was no mistaking the ache in his voice.

She raised her hands to undo a braid. The pins came free in her hands one by one, and she heard them tinkle on the floorboards when she cast them aside. She felt, rather than saw, his eyes hungrily following her every move. As the first braid began to unravel between her fingers, he reached up to help her.

"Careful now, you can't just—ow!—can't brush it like a horse's mane."

"Sorry." His touch returned, more gentle. Instead of trying to run his fingers through her hair, he simply let his fingertips drift over the landscape of her abundant curls. She heard his breath hitch in his throat as she freed the last plait of hair. Gently, Wes weighed a lock in his hand, examining its texture. He fluffed it up to marvel at its volume, its seeming weightlessness.

"Ain't so much taking it down," Nell quipped, as she started to dismantle the second braid.

"Haven't gotten the sight out of my head since that night in the kitchen." His hands fell to her waist so he could pull her flush against him and bury his face in her hair with a sigh of longing. "Haven't gotten the smell out of my head..."

"It's just Golder's pomade."

"Naw, it's honey and flowers and you." He nuzzled her hair eagerly, then gathered it up in a large handful, away from her neck. "I was going mad, having you here, just out of reach."

Nell worked faster to unpin the second braid. She'd spend an hour the next morning hunting for all the hairpins, but she didn't care. Wes kissed her neck, her ear, the line of jaw: a string of fevered kisses. One hand was in her hair, holding her against him, the other working to hitch up her shift. The buffalo robe slipped off her shoulders, but she barely felt the chill. She was burning up inside.

"We—we gotta be careful," she heard herself stammer. "No kids. Not yet."

Wes's hands stilled. "Not yet?" he specified. She heard something like awe in his voice. "You mean... you might..."

She hadn't quite known what she had meant, when the words had fallen from her lips. But now that they were said, she found herself completely without fear. "I mean, lemme get used to one wolf underfoot first, will you?"

He grinned. "Hang on. I got just the thing." He lifted her off him and twisted around to reach the bedside table.

"Ain't you the gentleman," Nell teased, after he'd retrieved the packet from its hiding place.

She could hear the grin in his voice as he caught her up again and rolled her beneath him. "And you say I never think ahead." He nuzzled her neck, whispering her name like a prayer. She shivered at the pleasant rasp of his whiskers against her skin.

"Goddamn," she whispered against his ear. "This is really happening."

She'd be lying if she said it was everything she had always imagined. In all her fantasies, they'd never once had to wrestle with a rubber in the dark, nor break off abruptly when Wes pinned a thick hank of her hair under his elbow, nor curse and laugh when her knee connected with his hip hard enough to bruise. She'd never envisioned his scruffy beard would rub her cheeks raw by the time they had finished, and she'd certainly never thought two practiced adults could be as clumsy as a pair of randy kids.

But she'd never imagined just how right Wes's arms would feel around her, either. Or how tender he would prove to be... the reverence he managed to infuse in every caress. She'd never conceived of a lovemaking punctuated by bursts of infectious laughter and tears of joy. Nor a lover who steadfastly held off his own release until he finally coaxed her to her peak.

"Well," Wes said afterward, breathless but grinning, "I'd say we didn't do half bad for the first try."

Nell's laugh came out as an indecorous snort. She was becoming no better than Charlie.

"Not bad at all," she agreed, as primly as she could manage.

He nuzzled her neck contentedly. "Not saying I ain't willing to try for better, mind," he remarked, and this time Nell laughed heartily.

"Well, thank God for that!"

Wes laughed with her. "And better," he nipped at the underside of her jaw, "and better, and betterrr," he drew out the word in a wolfish growl. The sound sent a frisson down her spine. He breathed her name against her ear and in that moment it seemed to her she couldn't possibly know a greater happiness.

But she was more than willing to be proven wrong.

Eighteen

The full moon hung low in the western sky. In the east, the very first rays of dawn fought their way through a scrim of gray clouds. The wolf padded along the canyon trail, his nose to the frost-covered ground. He smelled the life stories of a dozen different animals that had passed through in the night.

A shrill whistle caught his ear, as distinctive as any wolf's howl. He turned and loped cheerfully back towards his mate. The landscape was broken into a maze of gullies, but he soon caught her distinctive scent of honey and orange blossom, and wool covered with his own shed hairs.

"There you are!" Nell said, as he rounded the corner of the canyon wall. She slapped her knees. "C'mere, you beast."

Wes huffed with delight. He bounded across the last few yards, then leapt up on his hind legs, to better hug her hips with his forepaws. Nell pulled her face out of reach as his muzzle came up, and he could only score a glancing lick to her jaw.

"Not in public," she protested. "Augh, I know I told you to stay where I could see you!"

She had. He could never quite keep track of all her words, but he remembered that warning well enough. He just didn't care to listen.

"He's fine, Nell," Charlie spoke up. "And I'm hardly polite company."

"Still. I know I don't wanna see your man slobbering all over you in front o'me."

Charlie shrugged. "He's just being friendly. You'd give me a big wet kiss to be friendly, wouldn't you, Wes?" she bent her laughing face closer to the red wolf. Wes looked at her skeptically, then glanced back at Nell's disapproving face. This called for a diplomatic touch, and he let his tail drop as he brushed his shoulder against Nell's skirts.

Nell beamed. "Much better mannered than your dog."

"Don't that think was ever in any doubt... where is my dog anyway? Garou? Garou, you big galoot!"

"Sound carries, you know."

"Pft. Not out of these rocks. There's a reason Connor's been bringing Wes out here for years."

"So we're perfectly safe?"

"Perfectly."

"Uh-huh. That's why you brought along your Smith and Wesson."

Charlie looked down at her right hand, currently settled over the handle of her new revolver. "It's my birthday present... I gotta wear it. If Wes bought you... I dunno, some pretty jewelry or something, you'd wear it every chance you got, wouldn't you?"

"I hope Wes would get me something more practical."

Charlie flashed a toothy grin. "This is practical. And pretty." She slid the revolver half out of its holster. The handle caught Wes's gaze. In the pre-dawn light, the polished ivory seemed to glow. The sight ignited a spark of an idea in his wolf's brain. Ivory... hadn't he seen some nice ivory combs in the latest Sears & Roebuck catalogue? If he sent away for one tomorrow morning, would it arrive before Christmas? Would Nell like one? It was surely practical enough, now that she was beginning to experiment with softer pompadours in place of her severe braids. He had to remember to ask his mother for her advice.

Ivory comb... ivory comb... ivory comb... he recited inwardly. He could never predict what he would remember come moonset; like dreams, the memories of his wolf-nights ranged from clear as day to murky fog. But he was close to night's end; he could feel the ache beginning in the bones of his legs, and the vague sense of disquiet that always signalled his transformation back into a man. If he could just keep the thought in his head a little longer, he had a good chance of recalling it later.

Garou appeared at the canyon head, tail held high, shoulder dipped in a play bow. He let out a barking challenge, and Wes promptly forgot all about the concerns of humans.

"Off he goes again," he heard Nell sigh. "Don't go far now! It's nearly time."

He didn't need to be told. His skin felt itchy, like he was infested with fleas. A dull pain pulsed in his legs with each stride. He was running out of time. But he had time enough to show that mangy pup who was the biggest wolf on the Comstock.

Garou ran, inviting him to follow. He chased the wolf-dog up over the rise, then down into another, narrower gully. The broken land south of American Flat was a veritable maze of game trails and coulees, but Wes knew its contours by heart. When Garou tried to veer right into an old blasting crater, Wes took a shortcut over the abandoned tailings pile and caught up with him in a flash.

He threw his forelegs over Garou's rump, easily bringing the wolf-dog down. Garou might stand taller but his legs were thin as twigs compared to Wes's muscled limbs. Within a moment, he had the wolf-dog pinned on his back, and Garou yielded easily, whining and licking Wes's muzzle in abject submission.

All bark and no bite, Wes thought smugly. Though sometimes he wished Garou would put up a little more fight.

Wes let Garou abase himself for a few moments more, then he released him and padded to the other side of the shallow depression.

He could smell the remains of a recent kill: a few droplets of fresh blood and a half-dozen bones, not yet picked clean of meat.

Rabbit, by the smell of it. He wasn't interested in the leftovers, but he felt a passing curiosity about the rabbit's killer.

A shard of metal glinted in the morning light, just beneath his forepaw. His wolf's brain recognized something was amiss, but couldn't make the connection until his paw came down and the steel jaws snapped shut around his leg.

~ * ~

Nell and Charlie heard the high-pitched cry of pain. They raced towards its source, the trouser-clad Charlie quickly outpacing Nell, who struggled to run in the five layers of petticoats and woolen underwear. Her new winter boots had fine soles for trudging along the frost-covered streets, but they weren't meant for mountaineering.

Puffing for breath, she crested the tailing's pile, and found Charlie already at Wes's side. The red wolf lay half on his side, stunned and in pain, his right foreleg caught in the vicious jaws of a leghold trap.

"Wes!" Nell ran down the grade, kicking up pebbles and dust in her wake. She nearly tripped over a divot in the ground—another damned gopher hole!—in her haste to reach him. "How bad, how bad?" she demanded frantically, as she knelt down on the rock-hard ground.

The wound wasn't bleeding much—Wes had kept enough of his wits not to struggle—but the teeth of the trap had sunk deep in his flesh, deep enough to crush the bone, Nell imagined. She groped blindly in the shadows on the ground until she found the trap's chain. Solid metal and less than a foot long, it was connected to a steel spike hammered into the frozen ground. Nell pulled on the stake, but it would not budge.

"The ground's too hard," Charlie said. "We'll never pry it out in time."

Wes whimpered, and tried to lick his injured leg. Nell took his furry head in her hands. "I'm here, I'm here," she murmured. "Just hold still, Wes. You hear me? Whatever you do, don't fuss, and don't pull on that chain! Charlie, what do we do? We gotta get this off him before he changes!"

Charlie drew her revolver, and Nell let out a shriek of horror. "Are you crazy?!" Images of the fool girl trying to shoot the trap chain flashed before her eyes. But instead Charlie swung open the cylinder and let the bullets fall out. Her gun unloaded, she dug the barrel between the trap jaws and tried to lever it open.

"It's no good… I can't get enough pull."

"Lemme try." Nell switched places with Charlie and pulled with all her might. But her sweaty palms kept slipping on the ivory handle.

"I'm going for help," Charlie decided.

Help could only mean one person. Nell looked up at the eastern sky. The gray clouds were painted soft lilac. When they had started their walk in the canyon, Nell had needed to squint to make out the moonlit ground. Now she guessed she could easily read the newspaper unaided.

"It's getting awful light out. Will he still be up?"

"He said he'd wait for me," Charlie said. She handed Nell the revolver. "Here. You keep this. In case you need it."

Nell held up her hands. "I ain't touching that!"

But Charlie slapped the gun into her palm. "Garou!" she commanded. "Stay! Guard!"

Garou moved to Nell's side and sat, ears up, panting heavily. Before Nell could offer another protest, Charlie was off, scrambling over the rocks with the ease of a mountain goat. She soon disappeared behind the hillside; the sound of rattling stones continued to echo for a few heartbeats, before they too faded away, swallowed up by the shadows of the coulees.

Wes began to lick and prod his wound. "No!" Nell warned. She hugged his neck tightly to keep his head immobile. Wes whined. "I know. I know it hurts. Just hold still. Charlie will be back. She'll be back with Connor. He'll know what to do."

Nell waited. The sky grew ever brighter; the shadows around them began to recede. The cold slowly crept up from the ground, through her many layers of flannel, into her skin. She kept Charlie's revolver in the lap of her dress, but she didn't dare try to reload it.

She found the silence the hardest to bear. But for Garou's steady panting and Wes's anguished whimpers, the world was utterly still. Nell didn't understand how it could be so quiet, not a mile away from the ruckus of the stamp mills and mining hoists, and the sounds of the horses and dairy cows, all beginning to stir in the dawning light.

She thought of singing again, to drive away the silence, but her throat was too dry to produce a sound.

Wes shuddered. Nell saw the muscles under his skin contract in a wave that ran from his nose to his tail. Frantically, she looked over her shoulder for the moon, but the mountains blocked her view.

"Please, not yet," she implored. "Try to hold on a little longer."

Garou started to growl. His ears flattened to the back of his skull.

"Garou?" she whispered.

Then she heard the scattering of pebbles, the crunch of frozen dirt under boots.

Wes whimpered. She hugged him tighter. *Mr. Franklin?* she bit her lip to keep the words from escaping. No, it wasn't the deputy. Garou would never growl like that for his master. And Connor would never make so much noise.

The footfalls approached, heavy and purposeful. Nell willed herself into silence, prayed for her companions to be still. Perhaps, if they could only stay quiet enough, this morning hunter would pass them by.

She heard a jaunty whistle float over the rocks. It was "Oh Susanna."

~ * ~

Upon reaching the road, Charlie vaulted astride her paint horse and spurred him into a gallop. "Let's go, let's go dammit!" she urged when Clem took too long to work up to full speed. The marshal's office lay a full mile up the road, and moonset was only minutes away.

Clem showed a caution for running in twilight that another rider might find laudable. But Charlie had to grit her teeth and clench the saddle horn to keep from lashing the horse's flanks with her trailing reins. An eternity had passed for her racing heart before Devil's Gate came into view.

The last minute to the marshal's office proved the longest. She reined up at the hitching post, hard enough to make Clem rear in protest. Stirred from his early morning doze, Washington looked up at her sleepily.

"Connor!" she screamed, in the general direction of the door.

Her husband needed no further explanation. In moments he burst out the door, struggling with his greatcoat, his gun belt in his hands.

"Wes?" he asked, as he made for his own horse.

"Leg-hold trap," she said breathlessly. "Nell's with him. I left Rou behind to guard them."

Connor hitched his belt around his hips and untied Washington's reins. "Can we get to them on horseback?"

She shook her head. "Wouldn't trust it. Not in this light."

Connor swore. "Then lead us as far as you can on the road." He climbed into the saddle and turned Washington downhill. "Let's hope we can get there before the moon gets too low."

Or the sun gets too high, Charlie added silently, glancing eastward. Purple clouds steadily lightened to a dusty rose.

~ * ~

Garou sank into a defensive crouch at the sound of the whistling. The hackles rose on the back of his neck. Nell looked about frantically. What should she do... what could she do? If the trapper found them, she'd never be able to explain.

Her gaze fell on the revolver. In deference to Charlie's smaller hands, Connor had bought her a short-barrelled .22. Compared to the models the lawmen of Gold Hill favored, it looked ridiculously dainty; but in Nell's palm, it felt just as dangerous and unnatural as any gun.

She groped for the discarded bullets. Her hand shook as she tried to slide them into the chambers. *Round end in first*, she told herself. *Round end—come on, Nell! Come on, you stupid—*

John Garrod crested the top of the tailings pile. His face fell as he took in the scene below him. Nell froze, utterly paralysed with fear.

"What the… what are you doing here?" he demanded. "And where'd a wench like you get a fine piece like that?"

Nell looked down at the revolver, half-loaded and hanging useless in her hand. She moved her hand to slide the cylinder closed, and Garrod swiftly drew his own weapon.

"Drop it!" he commanded. "Drop it right now if you know what's good for you."

Reflexively, Nell obeyed. She threw the gun away with a quick snap of her wrist, then held her hands up to show she was unarmed. "Please, Mr. Garrod—lemme explain."

"I knew there was a wolf running loose in these hills! I knew if I set enough traps at the full moon I'd get him."

"He's not dangerous! Please, you can't hurt him!"

"What are you doing out here with Franklin's mongrel? Trying to spring him loose? Was that Injun right about you?" For just an instant, his mask of professional smugness fell away, revealing a flash of fear. "Are you a skinwalker? Is that a skinwalker? Jesus… that's Franklin, isn't it? I knew it! I knew he wasn't human!"

"It's not Mr. Franklin. He's back at the jail on duty, where he's supposed to be. Please—"

"On your feet. Move away from the wolf."

"No. I can't. You can't—just listen to me."

"No backtalk. Now."

Wes twisted away from Nell's side, yowling in fresh pain. Garrod turned his gun on the red wolf. As Nell flung herself over Wes's back to shield him, she saw Garou lunge at the deputy. It was the bravest thing she'd ever seen, and the most foolish. John Garrod calmly shifted his sights and fired. The first shot hit the wolf-dog in the back, the second in the ribs. Garou dropped to the ground like a stone. When he tried to rise, the man fired a third shot into his throat. Garou fell still at last.

Wes bucked underneath Nell's weight. He cried out, in a mournful howl that sounded more human than bestial. The trap's chain pulled taut as he thrashed and clawed at the ground. He threw his head back, and Nell heard the sound of bones snapping.

Garrod raised the gun again. "No, please!" Nell screamed. "Just wait!"

His transformation from man to wolf had been horrible to watch. His transformation back to human was just as nightmarish. Fur retreated into his skin. Flesh rippled as bones broke and reshaped themselves. His frame lengthened, even as his face seemed to collapse in on itself. Ears descended, then disappeared under tousled auburn hair. His muzzle drew back into a nose.

Wes collapsed on the ground, moaning in pain. Fresh blood spilled over the jaws of the trap. The sudden growth of his arm had forced the teeth even deeper into his flesh.

"Benedict?" Garrod scowled. "Wes Benedict?"

Wes hadn't the strength to reply. He shivered violently in the cold. Nell hastened to unwrap her red wool cloak and drape it over his back.

"You're the wolf?" Garrod spat.

"He's a man now," Nell protested. "C'mon Wes, look at me. That's it..."

Slowly, Wes lifted his head. One look in his eyes told her he was nearly insensible with pain.

"He's not a threat," Nell insisted. "Look at him, deputy, he's just a man."

"He's a skinwalker!"

"No..." Wes started to say. He struggled to raise himself up on his one good arm. "Garrod... you gotta calm down."

"I am calm. Considering I just saw a wolf turn into a man right in front of me, I would say I'm exceedingly calm."

"I... ain't... a skinwalker. Skinwalkers choose this. I don't have a choice."

Garrod nodded rapidly. "The moon— I was right, wasn't I? Every time the beast's been spotted, it's been a full moon." He laughed sharply. "I was right."

"You were right," Wes said, grimacing. "And now if you can help me out of this, I can explain everything."

"No… no, I have heard enough. Shut it! Just shut it, both of you! I need to think." His gaze fell on Garou's bloodied corpse and he began to gnaw on his lower lip. "I need to think."

He was half-drunk on fear and worry, Nell realized. She tried to make her voice sound gentle, honey-sweet. "Mr. Garrod… we won't tell no one what happened to the dog," she said.

"The dog? What dog? All I see is a wolf, a wolf that should have been put down years ago! He attacked me. I was utterly justified."

"Sure you were. A-and I'll testify to that." *Keep him talking*, she told herself. *Every minute he's talking, he ain't shooting*. "I'm sure Mr. Franklin will understand you had no choice."

"I'm an officer of the law! My word is more than enough. Certainly more trusted than yours!"

"You're right, sir. You're absolutely right—"

"Shut up!" he thundered. He cocked his revolver, and Nell fell silent.

"For the love of God, Garrod…" Wes stammered. "I'm an unarmed man."

"You're no man. You're an abomination. As bad as those heathen Indians. I should have known there was something bestial about you, Benedict. You always carry yourself like a savage: drinking, whoring, sniffing at your colored girl's skirts!"

"If it's money you want—"

"You can't bribe me… I'm an officer of the law! The only honest officer in all of Storey County. All the sheriff thinks about is his political career… all Crawford thinks about is the end of his shift… and Franklin! Franklin's as much a monster as you! I'm the only one with any integrity, any decency. I'm the only one who actually protects the citizens of this town!"

Wes and Nell could do nothing but nod obediently in the face of his tirade.

"I was doing my job when I shot that skinwalking whore. I was the only one doing his duty. Our fathers came out here to civilize the West... has this whole town forgotten that? Superstition and sorcery... there's no room for that... barbarism in the twentieth century!"

"I'm an honest God-fearing man," Wes insisted. "If... if you've been following me, you know I ain't never killed anyone as a wolf."

"And you never will."

"You can't just shoot him!" Nell shouted. "You'll never get away with it!"

Garrod blinked, momentarily stunned by her outburst. "No... I won't shoot him," he said, something of his unnatural calm returning to his voice. "You will. Yes... the jealous concubine. He was going to turn you out... yes, turn you out, because he couldn't stand the gossip anymore."

"No one will believe you," Wes gasped. "What, hsst, what about this bite your trap took outta me? Folks know what a leg-hold's marks look like."

Again Garrod's face twitched in a moment of fear and uncertainty. Then his mask reasserted itself. "I'll... I'll say I found her trying to dismember the body. I'll say she came at me with a knife—yes, and I was forced to shoot her. And they'll take my word for it. I'm an officer of the law."

"Mr. Franklin won't believe you!" Nell vowed. "And he's already on his way. Charlie went to get him; he'll be here any minute!"

Garrod's jaw tightened. "Then I'd best be quick about this. You first. I am so sick of your mouth."

He took a step forward as he aimed his revolver at Nell's head. His foot came down next to the body of the slain Garou.

The body moved.

The deputy let out a yelp as he tried to sidestep the beast which had suddenly come back to life. Garou sank his teeth into his ankle and held on firmly, even as Garrod fired another shot into his throat. Nell saw her chance and took it.

She scrambled to her feet and ran headlong at John Garrod. Having no weapon, she settled for sheer momentum, leading with her shoulder and crashing into his chest. Garrod lost his footing, and they went down together atop the wolf-dog.

Even stunned and in agony, Garrod held tight to the revolver. He tried to bring it up, and Nell pinned his right hand with both of hers. It took all her strength to hold his arm to the ground. He swore at her and pulled at her hair, but she had him on his back and she sprawled her body atop him, limbs spread wide, a net of flesh.

He spat insults at her; his spittle landed hot on the back of her neck. When he couldn't move her body, he tore free a fistful of curly hair, and Nell screamed at the searing pain in her scalp. She screamed back at him, loud as her lungs could bear, with the most powerful word she could utter.

"NO!"

This would surely prove her final act of defiance, but she meant to die fighting to the last. She shrieked the word, over and over. She kept screaming until Garrod got a better grip on the back of her skull, and beat her forehead to the frozen ground until her nose gushed blood, until she saw stars. As she lay stunned and moaning, she felt him gain the leverage needed to shift her off his chest. Still she clung to his gun with both hands. He would need to pry her fingers loose after he'd shot her.

How many bullets had he discharged into Garou? If she had made him angry enough to waste the last ones on her, might Wes still have a chance of escape?

She heard the gunshot; she braced herself for fresh pain. But the sound of impact came from the hillside above their heads, and she'd felt no jolt under her hands.

The voice of her savior rang out, loud and throaty.

"Hands up or I'll shoot!"

Charlie?

Garrod pulled Nell onto her knees and swung her in front of him as a human shield. His left arm locked tight about her neck while he pressed the revolver against her brow. Nell blinked through the dancing lights in her vision until her eyes focused on Charlie Franklin, standing a half dozen paces away, holding her recovered pistol.

"Let her go!"

Garrod laughed weakly. He staggered to his feet, dragging Nell with him. "Calamity Charlie!" he declared. "Look at you, trying to hold that gun like a real man. But you're just a little girl playing cowboys and Indians. Now put it down."

"Charlie—" Nell began to say, before Garrod's forearm cut off her airway. *Two*, she mouthed desperately. She had only loaded three bullets before Garrod had made her throw away the gun, and Charlie had already wasted one on a warning shot.

"You shot my dog?" Charlie challenged.

"I did. And I still have enough lead in here to finish this."

"You won't get away with this."

"Why? Will you stop me? Look at you... your arms are shaking. You can't even hold that little piece properly. You couldn't even shoot straight at five yards."

"I can."

"Then do it! Show me what a liberated woman can do! Save your two-legged pet's hide."

"I'd love to. But I promised Connor the first crack at you."

Garrod laughed hoarsely. "The illustrious Connor Franklin! The bulletproof deputy! Where is your savior? Where is he?" he roared, when she wouldn't answer. The gun barrel lifted from Nell's forehead to point square at Charlie. "Where is that freak?"

Charlie smiled smugly. "He's right behind you."

Nell felt Garrod's spine stiffen in sudden doubt. She seized on the moment, and swung the heel of her boot into his injured ankle. Garrod bellowed in pain, and his grip on her throat slackened just enough for her to break free.

She fell hard on the ground, caught in a tangle of skirts. She twisted at the waist to look up in his pain-crazed face. She caught sight of a blur of movement behind his shoulder: the flutter of a brown coat, the flash of skin.

Connor Franklin seized Garrod's right arm, and yanked it back so sharply Nell heard the bones snap. The force of the attack lifted Garrod onto his toes, whipped him about in a ghoulish pirouette. His eyes met Connor's just for an instant. Then, still holding Garrod's arm in one hand, Connor balled his other into a fist and threw all his weight behind a right cross to the skull.

His arm moved so fast, Nell could scarcely believe it. The sound of impact reminded her of an eggshell breaking against a mixing bowl.

Then suddenly Garrod's sightless eyes were staring at her, even as his body kept facing Connor. Charlie's hand clapped over Nell's mouth, absorbing her scream.

Garrod's legs gave out. He dropped like a felled tree, his head still twisted backwards on his shattered neck. Connor raised his bloody knuckles to his nose, sniffed once, then scowled and wiped Garrod's blood off on his coat. Nell heard Charlie's hard breathing and knew Connor had managed to surprise even her.

Eyes wide, Nell looked over at Wes. He crouched on the ground, looking as faint as she felt. Nell wriggled and mumbled into Charlie's hand, gesturing towards her trapped lover.

"Don't scream, now," Charlie warned as she released her.

Nell ran to Wes's side and rubbed his shoulders briskly. His skin felt like ice. "You all right? You all right, Wesley? Come on, talk to me." Turning to the Franklins, she barked, "He needs hel—"

Connor was at her side before she could finish. Heedless of the steel barbs, he seized a trap-jaw in either hand and snapped it open as easily as cracking a book. With a hiss, Wes withdrew his hand and clasped it to his chest.

"How's the wrist?" Connor asked.

Wes grimaced. "Feels broken. How's Garou?"

Nell looked up sharply. Charlie knelt at the wolf-dog's side, checking his injuries. Amazingly, Nell saw Garou's hind leg twitch. But surely the only thing Charlie could give him was a clean death.

Connor glanced over his shoulder casually. "He take any in the head?"

"Nope," Charlie said at length.

"Ah, he'll be fine, then. Get up, you malingerer! Take a bite out of our friend there if you need the blood." He looked up at the clouds and scowled. "We gotta hightail it before the sun gets much higher."

Nell stared in disbelief as the wolf-dog slowly rose on shaky legs. Garou whimpered softly, then limped over to investigate the body. At the first sound of feeding, Nell turned her face away.

"You all right, Miss Wallace?" Connor asked gently.

She swung back to face him, incredulous. "What are you?" she demanded, too weary for politeness. She pointed at Garou. "What is he?!"

Connor hesitated a moment. He glanced back at Charlie, who shrugged equably.

"Vampires," both Franklins said in union.

Vampires. After everything that had happened, Nell thought she had lost the ability to be shocked. She'd been wrong. Vampires— *Vampires*?! She stared accusingly at Charlie, silently willing her to say something, anything, to make this moment seem less ludicrous.

Charlie shrugged again. "Don't look at *me*. I'm just his dinner."

Nineteen

The first heavy snowfall of the season coated Gold Hill in white. The playful shrieks of children in sleds echoed up and down Main Street. Nell watched from the parlor window as the Bittner boys chased each other with snowballs. The younger one saw her at the window and stopped to make a face. A snowball hit him square in the head as his brother took advantage of the distraction.

"Pull the drapes, will you?" Wes urged from his armchair. "God, you must be freezing over there."

She'd been colder. The chill seeped in through the windowpane, true, but she had only to turn her cheek to feel the warmth of the crackling fire. Compared to the grim winter nights spent in shoddy lodgings, or the bone-deep cold of that early morning in the gully, the icy draft was nothing but a gentle nip to her fingers. The sort of mild discomfort she needed from time to time, to prove she wasn't dreaming.

She tugged the curtains closed over the frosted glass and turned back to the parlor fire. The flames burned low around the dregs of the log she had placed on the grate hours before. "Want me to put on a fresh log?"

"Naw, I'll settle for body heat." He held out his good hand. "C'mere."

She moved to his side, to adjust the blanket around his shoulders. He caught her elbow and pulled her onto his lap. "Careful!" Nell exclaimed, folding her arms against her chest to keep from jostling his bandaged arm. "Your wrist!"

"It's fine. See?" Wes held up his splinted arm, trying his best not to wince in pain. "Dunno why Connor needed to make it so heavy though!"

"'Cause he knew you'd just go right back to work if he didn't, and you'd be banging that wing into everything."

Wes's broken wrist had posed a bit of challenge. They could hardly let the local doctor see the telltale punctures of a steel trap, and Nell wouldn't hear of simply wrapping it up and hoping for the best. Fortunately Connor Franklin proved himself a skilled bonesetter... no small irony, when Nell considered his talent at breaking them.

She still winced to think of her feeble attempts at conversation, after he'd set Wes's wrist and she'd brewed him a pot of coffee in thanks. "Didn't think vampires drank coffee. You, uh... you don't have to go back to your grave in daylight or anything, do you?"

"Coffin in the cellar does the trick," Connor had said, before his waggling eyebrows told her he was joking. She imagined he could have teased her all morning, but Charlie soon stomped into the kitchen and ordered him to go lie down in Nell's old bed: "Before the sun's too high and you fall asleep on your feet."

Nell had come to regard her friend Charlie in a whole new light. No wonder she had been so blithe about Nell's romantic predicament. She wondered just when Charlie had learned the truth about her husband. She wondered when she would get the courage to ask her.

We can compare notes: dead man against wolf-man. Once the idea might have horrified her, now it only amused her, in a dark sort of way. Sometimes she worried she was growing much too comfortable with insanity.

"I ran into Mac today," Wes said, as he slowly walked his fingers up her arm. "He said the Lyon County sheriff's finally releasing Garrod's body. Just in time for the big freeze-up. Looks like he'll be waiting out the winter in the crypt under the Washoe Club."

Nell shuddered at the thought. "Rather he was six feet under and done with it," she growled.

The memory of Garrod's death and its bloody aftermath was still too fresh in her mind.

Connor had set the body down by the leg-hold trap, then fastened the steel jaws around Garrod's mauled ankle, while his wolf-dog had feasted on the soft flesh of the man's throat. When the Paiute hunters found the body a day later, further scavengers had left their teeth-marks on the body. The cause of death appeared obvious enough. His widow confirmed he had taken to trapping over the past month, encouraged by Adam Blackfell's stories of beast-men.

"Figures a man like Garrod would be fool enough to walk into his own trap," Bill Crawford ruled.

Sheriff Quirk had called for a further investigation, but Bill Crawford quickly pointed out the body had been found across the county line, and typical legal wrangling ensued. Nell was mildly surprised it had taken only a week to wade through the paperwork.

"So the case is closed? Hey, quit it," she squirmed as Wes playfully poked at a puffed sleeve.

"Whacha got in there anyway? Horsehair?"

Nell tsked. "Not since the thirties. It's just cotton. And don't you tease me; I always wanted one of these jackets."

"I like it." Her collar was fastened with a frog-clasp. Wes's wandering fingers fiddled with it until she slapped his hand away lightly.

"Garrod," she reminded him.

Wes grinned wolfishly. "Death by stupidity. The one sin the Comstock won't forgive. Doubt even his widow will shed a tear for him."

"So, we're safe?"

"As safe as we can be."

"What's that supposed to mean?"

His expression turned serious. "Just what it sounds like. Can't say Garrod was the first man who wanted to kill me for being what I am. Can't say he'll be the last. And you're right... there are plenty of folks who don't approve of us." He smiled wanly. "And I can't say Connor will always be around to pull my ass out of the fire."

"I'll always be around," Nell vowed. "I didn't think I could manage it, all of it, all that weight I see you carry around every day. Thought it would break me down if I tried to take it on." She traced a part in his hair, then pushed an errant forelock out of his eyes. "Can't lie, it is mighty heavy. But you know, it's a lot easier to carry when it's the pair of us. And this whole mess with Blackfell and Garrod... strange to say, but I'm grateful for it. Because it showed me I'm a lot tougher than I thought."

Wes grinned boyishly. "I never had any doubt. God, I can still see you wrestling Garrod for that gun... fighting tooth-and-nail like a—"

"A she-wolf?"

"Damned right. My she-wolf." He hugged her close with his good arm.

Nell giggled. "I'll be. He was right all along."

"What?" Wes prompted.

"Blackfell. He said I had a wolf's spirit."

"I'd believe it."

"He said I had a...a mark on me," she continued, more thoughtfully. "Said it would draw a fellow wolf to me. First I thought he was just trying to con me. And when the skinwalker showed up... I spent every night praying he was wrong. Thanked my lucky stars when it looked like he was a fraud all along. Then they found him in wolf skins and I didn't know what to believe!

"But he was right about one thing. 'Cause why else would I have put up with your shenanigans all these years? And why else would you keep pulling me back in, just when you'd finished pushing me away? We had a hundred chances to make a clean break, and we never took them. One way or another, we just kept calling each other back."

"My wolf charmer," Wes breathed, his voice husky, his eyes filled with adoration.

He kissed her, like he never meant to let her go. She kissed him back with a fierceness that told him he'd never have to.

Meet Jane Senese

Jane Senese lives in Victoria, British Columbia. When she is not conjuring imaginary worlds, she teaches French Immersion at her local elementary school. Visit her website at http://www.janesenese .com to learn more about the supernatural in Virginia City and Gold Hill, Nevada's most haunted towns.

Other Works From The Pen Of
Jane Senese

A Ghost Town Vampire - A sworn tomboy finds love and danger when she trades the big city for a mining ghost town, and falls for its undead deputy.

The Ghost in the Machine - A lonely widow is torn between the love of a town marshal and her husband's jealous ghost.

Letter to Our Readers

Enjoy this book?

You can make a difference

As an independent publisher, Wings ePress, Inc. does not have the financial clout of the large New York Publishers. We can't afford large magazine spreads or subway posters to tell people about our quality books.

But, we do have something much more effective and powerful than ads. We have a large base of loyal readers.

Honest Reviews help bring the attention of new readers to our books.

If you enjoyed this book, we would appreciate it if you would spend a few minutes posting a review on the site where you purchased this book or on the Wings ePress, Inc. webpages at: https://wingsepress. com/

Visit Our Website

For The Full Inventory
Of Quality Books:

Wings ePress.Inc
https://wingsepress.com/

Quality trade paperbacks and downloads
in multiple formats,
in genres ranging from light romantic comedy
to general fiction and horror.
Wings has something for every reader's taste.
Visit the website, then bookmark it.
We add new titles each month!

Wings ePress Inc.
3000 N. Rock Road
Newton, KS 67114